SUB ROSA

SUB ROSA

A VALERIUS MYSTERY

JENNIFER BURKE

LEVEL
BEST BOOKS

Historia
ESTABLISHED 2019

First published by Level Best Books/Historia 2023

Copyright © 2023 by Jennifer Burke

This novel is entirely a work of fiction. The names, characters and incidents portrayed in it are the work of the author's imagination. Any resemblance to actual persons, living or dead, events or localities is entirely coincidental.

Jennifer Burke asserts the moral right to be identified as the author of this work.

Author Photo Credit: Donna Larcom, Northern Exposure Photography

First edition

ISBN: 978-1-68512-493-9

Cover art by Level Best Designs

This book was professionally typeset on Reedsy.
Find out more at reedsy.com

To my mum, Glenda, who taught me how to lose myself in books.

— A MAP OF ROME, AD 58 —

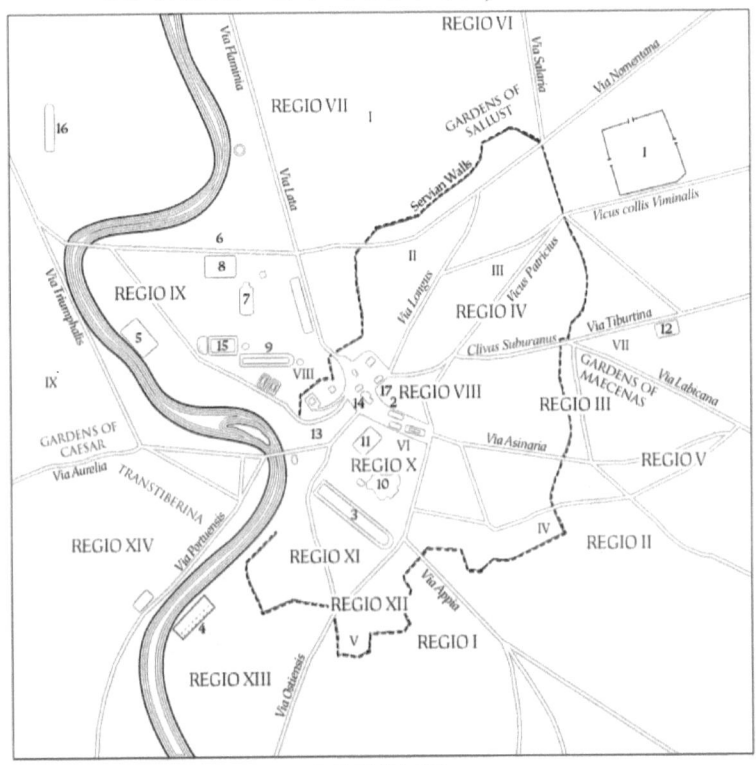

REGIO VI

REGIO VII

GARDENS OF SALLUST

I

Via Flaminia

Via Salaria

Via Nomentana

Servian Walls

Vicus collis Viminalis

16

Via Lata

6

8

REGIO IX

II

Via Langus

III

Vicus Patricius

REGIO IV

Via Tiburtina

12

7

Via Triumphalis

5

15

9

VIII

Clivus Suburanus

VII

GARDENS OF MAECENAS

Via Labicana

IX

17 REGIO VIII

14 2

REGIO III

13

11

VI

Via Asinaria

REGIO V

GARDENS OF CAESAR

Via Aurelia

TRANSTIBERINA

REGIO X

10

3

IV

REGIO II

REGIO XIV

Via Portuensis

REGIO XI

Via Appia

4

REGIO XII

V

REGIO I

REGIO XIII

Via Ostiensis

— LEGEND —

BUILDINGS

1. The Praetorian Guard Camp
2. Forum
3. Circus Maximus
4. Emporium
5. Navilia
6. Campus Martius
7. Baths of Agrippa
8. Baths of Nero
9. Circus Flaminius
10. Domus Augustus
11. Domus Tiberius
12. Praetorian Stables

13. Forum Boarium
14. Mamertine Prison
15. Theatre of Pompey
16. Circus of Nero
17. Basilica Aemilia

HILLS

I. Pincian Hill
II. Quirinal Hill
III. Viminal Hill
IV. Caelian Hill
V. Aventine Hill
VI. Palatine Hill
VII. Esquiline Hill
VIII. Capitoline Hill
IX. Janiculan Hill

Dramatis Personae

The Family Aemilius
Q. Aemilius Valerius; our hero
Fulvia Drusa; his wife
Octavia Junilla; his sister
Julia Drusilla; his stepdaughter; a pain
A. Caldus Ruso aka Mouse; his stepson; a pleasure
G. Aemilius Lucullus Maro; a mad relation
Marcia Laeta; a mad relation by marriage

Patricians, assorted
Gn. Gavius Silanus; Fulvia's ex, Julia's papa; a prick
G. Marcellus Naso; no sense of humour; a pompous prude
G. Marcellus Albanus; no senses; presently posthumous
P. Cornelius Paulinus; nice bloke; a party animal
M. Galerius Nepos; noble; a political animal
Gn. Claudius Rufanus; nobler; a prosperous man
G. Avitus Florian; nothing special; a poor cousin
A. Probus Macrinus; not getting any younger; past it
P. Menenius Carpo; naked; prone to prolonged baths
P. Vibianis Ennius; knob; pasty, podgy and pickled
Gn. Pomptius Voltinian; not home; playing away?
M Antonius Donatus; nonentity, presumably
M. Decius Nasica; no longer with us; parted ways
Gn. Septus Severus; neighbourhood magistrate; past his bedtime

Slaves, assorted
  Juba; a bodyguard
  Cretes; a secretary
  Larius; a waste of space
  Hursa; a waste of money

Miscellaneous Items
  Caraca; an oddball from Gaul
  Alcipides; an honest businessman, honestly
  Philosthones; a bean counter
  L. Junius Atreus; a vigile with a responsibility
  Lucilla; the responsibility
  Leander; a physician or mortician, whatever your need
  Gaius, Vibilus, Brachus, Manius; vigiles, assorted
  Centhus; a barber
  Nicius; a dancer
  Vetus; a plasterer and/or tiler
  Bano; an ugly gangster
  Erastus; a pretty gangster
  Rubio; a waster
  Kaeso; an unsavoury informer
  Colchus; an elusive informer
  Sylvia; an unfortunate bystander
  Eburnus; a pseudonym? Rude of 'im

Historical figures (more or less)
  Nero; the Emperor of Rome
  Agrippina; his mummy dearest
  Seneca; his brains
  Burrus; his brawn
  Anicetus; a shady character; a bit blurry
  Tigellinus; even shadier; Nero's future best buddy
  Corbulo; a general; currently subduing Parthians

Chapter One

If I'd expected the women of my household to greet me at the door with a cup of Falernian, a dish of nuts, and a cloth with which to mop my troubled brow, I was out of luck. As it was, it took an age to rouse the door porter and at least twice as long for Juba and him to pour me out of the litter and drag me inside on my toga. There was an art to it I was mostly unaware of—I was trying to unlace my sandals.

"Hey, Juba!"

"Yes, sir?" Juba was a big, solid lump of Aethiopian with muscles that could crack walnuts and a talent for languages that was wasted on me.

"There's this girl from Campania, and she goes up to her father, and—I can't get this strap undone, you know—and anyway, she goes up to her father and says, 'Papa, I'm pregnant!' Can you just help me get this sandal off, please?"

Hursa, the door porter, knelt down to lend a hand. Hursa was a prime example of why you should never buy sight unseen and, more importantly, why you should never buy off relatives. The word was out that I needed a new door porter. The old one was as deaf as a post, as blind as a bat, and as incontinent as only a blind, deaf old man can be. I'd pensioned him off to my estate in Corduba where I'm sure he had rediscovered the vigour of his youth and would spend his final years impregnating farm girls, brawling with their oily boyfriends, and living it up at my expense.

Ta-da. Mad Uncle Maro to the rescue. As soon as he heard I was after a door porter, he had just the one. An eighteen-year-old German, guaranteed to scare away burglars, door-to-door salesmen, and friends I owed money.

1

Sturdy and strapping? Hardly. Skinny and spotty, and as German as my right foot. His golden locks were less convincing than Aunt Marcia's. Alright, there was German somewhere in his genealogy, but if Hursa so much as glimpsed a bearded barbarian in full-throated war cry, he'd faint like a girl. But he did like a good joke.

"She went to see her father, sir," he reminded me, slipping my sandals off.

"Yes, and she says to her father, 'Papa, I'm pregnant.' Well, the old man is deeply shocked. Deeply!"

Juba hauled me to my bare feet, holding me up by the tunic seams. "I think it's past your bedtime, sir."

"Yes, I was just telling Hursa my new joke," I told him.

Hursa began gathering the heavy folds of my toga into his arms. His watery eyes were bleary with sleep, and his hair was sticking out at odd angles from his head, like uneven bits of straw. It was time he found a good barber. Well, any barber.

"I know a good man in Fish Alley," I confided. "Cheap, but good."

Hursa frowned. "I don't get it," he said unhappily.

"No, that's not the joke." All the wine I'd drunk at dinner was starting to move around in my stomach like it was searching for an exit. I swayed against Juba. "But he is shocked, deeply shocked. Deeply, deeply shocked. Well, you would be, wouldn't you?"

I was losing my audience. Hursa only had two or three brain cells, and my free-ranging conversation had tied them in knots already. And Juba had no discernible sense of humour.

"Bedtime, sir," he said, looking dark and inscrutable. "Mind your step."

"The night is young," I said, but you don't argue too much with someone who could snap your neck between his thumb and forefinger. Juba tucked me under his arm. Squashed by his massive biceps, my toes dragging on the tiles, I was struck by a sudden, strange, and unrelated thought. "Juba, did I really bet Strachus Calpurnius I could make wine come out my nose?"

"So I heard, sir," Juba rumbled and began manoeuvring me towards my bedroom while Hursa fluttered in front with a lamp. "And congratulations on your win."

Bacchus, Bacchus, why? Tonight's meeting of the who's who of the water board was shaping up to be something I'd never hear the end of if any of them ever spoke to me again. As long as I hadn't told the joke about the Vestal and the donkey. A very funny joke, I'm told, in its proper place. If I'd known what its proper place was a month ago at the censor's dinner party, I could have been gainfully employed by now. Still, it was all part of the parry and thrust of job hunting in the big city. My options were currently open, and I still had my head above the poverty line. Way above, if I was honest with myself.

"Thank you, Juba." I was speaking into his ribcage while my legs were trying unsuccessfully to keep pace on the stairs.

There was a comfortable reading couch in my bedroom. Carved legs, polished back, plenty of nicely squashed cushions. A jar of wine hiding in the shadows underneath that I couldn't bear to think about at that moment. Juba piled all of my limbs onto the couch.

"Oooh." The sudden shift to the horizontal unsettled my stomach again. I could feel tonight's stuffed eggs and assorted bits of wildlife bobbing in a sea of exotic sauces and wine. There had been five courses, all punctuated by a different wine. Marcellus Naso had been out to impress. Some senator or another, I think. A short fellow, pasty skin, with a squint, and some type of sexual dysfunction if the graffiti in my gymnasium could be believed. The look on his face when I'd asked if it was true, you'd think I'd suggested he'd murdered his whole family and done unspeakable things with their corpses.

"Are you alright, sir?" Juba asked with a malevolent gleam in his eye.

"Mmm. Get me a jug of water." Not only was Marcellus Naso never going to speak to me again for insulting the senator and blowing wine out of my nose, I'd be lucky if he didn't send some bullyboys after me to break both my legs.

Juba murmured something I didn't catch and made himself scarce.

"And some more cushions!" I yelled after him. I sighed. "You know, Hursa, it took two months to get an invitation to the house of the eminent Marcellus Naso. Pretentious bastard."

3

Hursa was a very sympathetic person—his whole life was such a disaster he related well to failure. He found a sort of solidarity in the misery of others. "I heard Marcellus Naso's wife is screwing a gladiator, sir," he lied winningly.

"Thanks, Hursa," I said with a sigh, "but he's not actually married."

"Possibly because he prefers to sleep with farmyard animals," Hursa said, with more speed than I would have credited his little brain. "How about telling me the rest of your joke, sir?"

Hursa had loved the joke about the Vestal and the donkey. He had been retelling it for days to the rest of the household until Damos, the temperamental cook, hit him over the head with a roasting pan.

"So this girl goes to her father; we did this bit, right?"

Hursa nodded.

"And she says, 'Papa, I'm pregnant', and the old man is shocked!"

"Shocked," Hursa echoed, his eyes as round as saucers.

"And so, he says to her—"

My door swung open, a figure in a diaphanous dressing gown floated through, and a voice finished for me, "'Are you sure it's yours?'"

At last, the womenfolk. One of them, anyway. The most important one. She must have waylaid Juba somewhere downstairs, because she came bearing a jug of water and a cup. No cushions, however.

"Hello," I said. "Did I wake you?"

"Hello, Quintus," she replied, and her gaze travelled the length of my stained and crumpled figure. "You look a bit under the weather. Tell me, are you going to be up bright and early inspecting aqueducts and bossing engineers around?"

"No," I said. "I don't think Naso liked me."

"Oh dear." Fulvia poured me a cup of water. "There you are. Hursa?"

Hursa was still ruminating, as slowly and carefully as a cow chews cud. *Are you sure it's yours,* he mouthed to himself. I could almost see his brain cells buzzing like drowsy wasps inside his empty head. "Ooh!" he whispered at last.

"Hursa!"

4

Hursa blinked owlishly. "Mistress?"

"Back to bed. I can look after the master now."

"Yes, mistress," Hursa said, and trailed away.

"I think he likes my new joke," I said.

"That joke's so old it's found on Etruscan tombs."

"I didn't know you were an expert." I wiped a drop of water from my chin.

"On what? Old jokes or ancient Etruscan tombs?" Fulvia made space for herself on my couch and drew my feet into her lap. She yawned.

"I didn't wake you, did I?" I was tired now, and guilty.

"I'd only just got to sleep," she said. "I was in the middle of a lovely dream when suddenly the swan that had turned into a person, for whatever reason, shouted 'More cushions!' and I woke up." She readjusted my feet.

"Sorry, Fulvia." In just seven months of marriage, I'd said that more times than I cared to remember, but Fulvia was always good enough not to keep count.

She acknowledged the apology by patting my feet. "Do you want to tell me about your dinner?"

"Not really," I said, but I told her what I could remember anyway. She was silent for a little while after I explained how I'd asked about the senator and the goats.

"Well," she said at last, "you weren't too keen on the aqueducts, were you?"

"Or public works," I added.

"Or the honorary priesthood," she said.

"I'd forgotten about that."

"It's your career," Fulvia told me. "You needn't feel despondent because you're not rushing into the Senate. You're still young."

I grunted.

"Actually, I have some news for you." She was wearing a careful frown.

"What?" I was suspicious now.

Fulvia plucked at the sleeve of her gown. It was a nervous habit she wasn't aware of, but I'd already learned to expect trouble whenever I saw it. "Julia's had a fight with her father—don't scowl, Quintus—and she's here."

"No," I groaned, pressing a cushion over my head. "She hates me!"

Fulvia put on her sensible and determined face. "I've already said you don't mind. Really, what a fuss you can make!"

"I hate her too."

Fulvia did not hear that. Like all reasonable wives, she was deaf to what she decided was unimportant or disagreeable. She had once told me that she believed it was the duty of a good wife to avoid conflict with her husband and master. In her case, this meant ignoring me. This was not explained to me before I signed the marriage contract. Nor were nasty adolescent stepdaughters like Julia, who could land on my doorstep whenever they fancied and then have the gall to complain about the size of their bedrooms.

I could be reasonable as well. "Fulvia, I've had a terrible night. I don't really want to talk about this now, alright?"

The woman was a virago. "It has to be discussed now."

"Well, can I go and stay with Uncle Maro while she's here?"

"You're being silly, Quintus," Fulvia answered. "And besides, you should be at least a little bit sympathetic."

A cryptic remark if I'd ever heard one. "Why?"

Like all cryptic remarks, it was destined to be understood only by my wife and possibly a few of her friends. "Don't be obtuse, Quintus."

I shoved the cushion back behind my head. "How am I being obtuse?"

Fulvia sighed. "Quintus, can she stay or not?"

"Alright!" I couldn't argue with Fulvia anymore. It's not that she was right, it's just that I was very drunk, very tired, and she'd completely worn me out.

"Good," she said. "Thank you, Quintus."

"How long is she going to stay?" I asked wearily.

"She didn't say."

Oh, Jupiter. It was too awful to contemplate. Julia had a fight with her precious papa and threatened to leave the house forever. And while her precious papa tried to tempt her back with jewellery and cash in hand, I got to play the wicked stepfather who wouldn't let her entertain her little girly friends in his house and who didn't pay as much pocket money as papa.

Fulvia noticed my despair. She slipped out from under my feet. "Quintus?"

"What?"

"Really, thank you." She leaned over and brushed my forehead with a kiss. "Shall I ask Juba to bring you some more cushions if you're going to sleep there?"

"Yes, please."

My better half frowned at me gently, decided to save a scolding for the morning, and closed the door quietly as she left. I didn't know if she managed to track Juba down or not, because I was asleep as soon as the bedroom was empty. I dreamed about the look I'd see on Marcellus Naso's face the day I got to cold shoulder him inside the Curia and wonder loudly to my illustrious friends and many admirers why the old has-been hadn't been forced to retire to the coast.

* * *

Breakfast was a hit-and-miss affair: I'd hit the piss the night before, so I missed it. I was still snoring gently on my reading couch while the womenfolk were stuffing themselves silly on something delicious my cook had made. I staggered downstairs, hoping there was more than a cold pastry and half an apple left and knowing, even if there wasn't, that those paltry offerings would still be more appetising than the company awaiting me.

Julia Drusilla had the fortune to have inherited her mother's looks and the misfortune to have inherited her father's personality. I would have liked her more the other way around, plain and sweet like honey on bread. As I arrived in the doorway of the sitting room, I almost choked on her perfume. Sixteen and sloe-eyed, she was always surrounded by clouds of the stuff that stole around corners before her like some advance scout party that went straight for the throat. Fulvia seemed to have developed an immunity—she was seated across from her poisonous daughter, looking firm but fair.

From my vantage point in the doorway, I could only see the back of Julia's head. Her hair was red this time, and little twists and ringlets slipped artfully out of her combs to rest against the back of her slender neck. I could see a pink indentation on her skin where the clasp of a necklace heavier than the one she was wearing now had marked her. Gold drop earrings swayed underneath her earlobes.

Fulvia glanced up at my arrival. Julia twisted her neck and stared.

"Good morning, Julia," I said nicely and walked forward to greet her. She stood up with a rattle of jewellery and scowled when I kissed her dutifully on the cheek.

"Good morning," she murmured in that sulky tone her father seemed to find enchanting. The poor fool beamed every time she snapped, like a man proud of a pet crocodile.

"How long will you be staying?" It was like watching a nymph transform into one of the less attractive furies.

Julia screwed up her pretty face. "See!" she petitioned her mother tearfully. "See!" She dropped back into her seat and started weeping.

"Julia!" Fulvia said in her I-can-feel-a-headache-coming-on voice. "Julia!" When there was no response, she rounded on me. "Oh, Quintus!"

A few slaves peered fearfully around the doorway. Seeing it was the old story of the joys of putting Julia Drusilla and Aemilius Valerius in the same room, they backed off again.

"What?" I demanded. "What did *I* do? Oh, shut up, Julia!"

This seemed to have the opposite effect. Julia was working up to a crescendo.

Fulvia scowled at me, and I knew what Julia would look like when she had a few more years behind her. "Quintus, *please!*" She pressed her fingertips to her temples. "Shut *up*, Julia!"

Coming from her, it worked. Julia, blotchy and tear-streaked, blubbered quietly to herself.

"Let's start again, shall we?" Fulvia said sternly to the pair of us. "Sit down, Quintus."

I sat beside Fulvia and stared at the floor for a while. It needed sweeping, if the slaves were ever brave enough to come in here again. This was not my favourite room. It was not my room at all, really. This was where Fulvia and my sister Octavia whiled away their hours. Besides the reading couches, there was a small trunk full of whatever it was they needed to do all the weaving that good Roman women were supposed to be able to do, and in the far corner, a suspiciously dusty loom.

Fulvia elbowed me discreetly.

I cleared my throat. "Julia, you must stay as long as you like."

She sniffled.

"You're always welcome in this house." Did I really say that?

I felt Fulvia relax. Until then, I hadn't noticed how rigid her posture had been. She settled back and exhaled heavily. "Julia?" she prompted.

Julia peered at me from under her coppery ringlets. "Thank you for letting me stay, Valerius." She would hate herself later for that one.

"Good," said Fulvia. "Now I'm sure we can all be civil to one another."

Apparently it was up to me to make conversation. "Is your father well?"

Julia's mouth hardened, and then her lip trembled dangerously.

"What?" I mouthed to Fulvia as she rolled her eyes at some new stupidity she had discovered in me.

I tried another tack. "I like your new hair colour." Next I'd be discussing manicurists and the latest sandal styles.

"My friend Portia has a new hairdresser who used to be owned by Sabina Mettia," said Julia.

"Sabina Mettia? Really?" I had no idea who that was. I looked at Fulvia for help, and she looked as blank as me.

"Oh, yes," said Julia.

Fulvia leaned forward. "Julia, have I met Portia? You must invite her around once you've settled in."

"I will," said the darling, with a quick malicious glance in my direction.

Octavia's entrance saved me from having to think up anything else to say. My sister looked cool and demure. Her perfume was soft and light and crept up on Julia's heavy-handed scent like a few silent Persian archers sneaking around a phalanx of Greek bullyboys.

"Hello, Julia Drusilla. How nice to see you again."

"Thank you, Octavia Junilla. I'm glad to be here." Julia was so polite it didn't ring true.

I stretched out in my seat and smiled broadly at my extended family.

Fulvia twiddled her thumbs. "Perhaps you'd like a rest before lunch, Julia?"

"No, thank you," Julia replied. The colour was starting to come back into her face now, and she would be able to pretend the whole slanging match had never happened. That was always the way with Julia. She was like her indulgent Papa: she overlooked her own faults.

Octavia took a seat and arranged the fall of her stola over her knees. She leaned forward slightly. "Julia, your hair looks lovely."

This seemed to be the only safe topic of conversation, and Octavia had sniffed it out at once. It was all those mornings women spend in the company of one another. They were finely tuned to nuances a man wouldn't notice if they struck him sharply over the head. I remember Numerius, a friend from my misspent youth, commenting on his aunt's divorce. *She said she knew he had a mistress,* he had said in a wondering tone, *because he started chewing mint leaves after breakfast!* A sudden craving for mint, and the man was an adulterer. It was true—he had a dainty thing stashed away in an apartment where she spent her days appreciating the expensive gifts he gave her and wondering if they were worth the price of his bad breath.

"My friend Portia has a hairdresser who used to belong to Sabina Mettia," Julia answered earnestly.

"Really?" Octavia said in a tone that might have convinced Julia she was fascinated but didn't work on me. "She is certainly very stylish."

"Who are we talking about?" I muttered in Fulvia's ear.

Fulvia jabbed a finger in my ribs.

"Yes, but she's not that *naturally* beautiful," Julia said. "It's all about hair and cosmetics, isn't it, Mother?"

"Possibly, dear," Fulvia answered.

"Well, it is." Julia sighed at the naïveté of parents who just didn't understand how the world worked. She had found her stride. "After all, it's what men notice first, isn't it, Valerius? How beautiful a woman is?"

Was she asking me personally—because I wasn't sure she knew how uniquely unqualified I was to answer that question—or was I expected to be the spokesman for all men? I felt a sudden rush of male bravado. I *could* defend the indefensible. "To be fair, Julia, I don't think—"

"Well, of course, you won't admit it now," she shot back. "But it's most certainly true!"

Fine then. I sat back in my seat.

"I don't think I see your point, dear," Fulvia murmured, patting my arm gently in consolation. She'd made the mistake of assuming Julia had one.

"Isn't it obvious?" Julia stared around at us incredulously. "Beauty transcends social boundaries!"

"*What?*" I might have stood a better chance in the argument if I'd known who we were talking about to begin with.

"You must tell me all about it, Julia," Fulvia said firmly, "when we are free to speak alone."

Poor Fulvia. Always the peacemaker when Julia and I clashed. I reached for her hand and curled my fingers around hers. Julia looked faintly disgusted at this show of affection that had come without warning. She glanced around the room, pretending not to notice. She twirled one of her earrings.

Octavia looked amused, but I could tell she was starting to soften towards Julia. Maybe it was because she was slightly older than her last visit and maybe even slightly less silly, and Octavia had always been more sympathetic to Julia than necessary. I often told myself that Octavia never went through this stage, but I didn't know that for sure. I was away playing armies when she would have been throwing Julia's sort of screaming tantrums, and she would have been throwing them under her husband's roof anyway. Somehow, though, I couldn't see it in Octavia.

Xanthus, the indoor slave, who must have figured we'd struck some sort of truce, tiptoed in with a jug of wine, a jug of water, and a dish of figs. I took my wine watered down like the ladies took theirs. After last night I wasn't even sure I could face the stuff again. I still had the aching reminder of a headache and an urge to hibernate.

I sipped my wine carefully and let Fulvia pick over the figs for me. Julia didn't feel as scary anymore, and I finally realised why. She didn't have backup. "Julia, why haven't you got your maid with you?"

Julia looked almost defiant. "She's at my father's house, Aemilius Valerius."

"I gathered that. Is she sick or something?" Choked on her own gall, no doubt.

Julia crossed her slender ankles and inspected her hemline carefully. "If you must know, Valerius, I have left home."

"*What?*"

Julia drew a deep breath. "And naturally, I had to leave my maid at home, because my father said neither of us was to leave the house." She looked proud of her own courage, but it was easier for her to disobey her doting father than it ever would be for her slave to disobey an angry master.

"Why wasn't I told?" I asked around a mouthful of fig. I looked at Fulvia. I looked at Octavia. They were in the know, that was certain.

Fulvia didn't even have the grace to look guilty. "I was going to tell you last night, Quintus, but you were in no condition for a conversation."

So it was my fault. I closed my eyes briefly and thought longingly of my bachelor days. I rubbed my temples. "Why have you left home, Julia?"

Something traumatic, no doubt. Papa didn't like the new hairstyle? No, it was nothing as simple as that. Julia's bottom lip started quavering again. The hand holding her glass shook, and wine slopped over the edge onto her pretty dress. When she spoke, she sounded for all the world like a child. "Because Papa went and got me engaged."

So, this was the source of Fulvia's concern and Octavia's sympathy. In one horrible moment, Julia had gone from the little mistress of her papa's household to one of his chattels to be sold to the highest bidder. Probably nothing in her pampered past had prepared her for the shock.

"What do you expect me to do about it?" It sounded harsh even to my ears.

Julia looked as shocked as if I'd slapped her.

"I'm sorry, Julia," I said, trying to find a tone that walked a fine line between reason and sympathy. "But I don't know how we can help. Your mother's got no say in things. What can you expect us to do?"

12

"Well, how would you like it if your father told you that you had to get married to someone you didn't even know!" Tears were welling now.

"He *did*, Julia."

For once in her life, she didn't have a smart answer.

"I've told Julia she can stay," said Fulvia firmly, "until we work something out with Silanus."

"Like what?" I asked.

"We'll work something out," Fulvia said between clenched teeth. She stopped just short of a snarl.

Working something out with Julia's unreasonable papa didn't sound like much fun, but I found myself agreeing anyway. Self-preservation was a deciding factor.

"Alright," I said, "we'll work something out. Until then, I have some things to catch up on."

I think they all knew I was going back to bed. Julia gave me a pretty smile I could have done without, and I downed the rest of my wine. I could have shouted a few choice words at Fulvia at this point, but instead, I headed straight for my bedroom. I tucked my head under the blankets and wished the world away.

* * *

The world was back within the hour, uninvited. It came in the massive form of Juba, who leaned over my bed and shook me by the shoulder. I felt like I was waking up to an earthquake. I gripped the pillows for fear of falling.

"Your accountant is here to see you, sir," he said in his thick accent.

"Can't I get a moment's peace?"

Juba's brow creased. "Sir, today you woke up, had breakfast, and went back to bed."

"Sarcasm does not become you, Juba," I said sternly and swung my legs over the edge of the bed.

"No, sir," Juba agreed, barefaced.

13

"Just tell me," I said as I strapped on my sandals, "did I make this appointment, or have I suddenly gone bankrupt?"

"You made this appointment," Juba replied. "Hursa wrote it down so he didn't forget. As for going bankrupt, I can't say. Maybe."

I eyed him suspiciously. "You're getting very impertinent, Juba."

He bared his teeth in a grin as I headed downstairs.

Aulus, Fulvia's son from her second marriage, was playing with a wooden centurion and a bronze horse in the atrium.

"Good morning, Mouse."

He waved at me. "Hello! Do you want to play soldiers with me?"

Mouse was eleven, a skinny little boy with a mop of dark curls, and he wouldn't say boo to a goose—hence the nickname.

"I wish I could, but my accountant is here."

Philosthones was already ensconced in the tablinum, arranging his scrolls and wax tablets around him like careful temple offerings. A little oil lamp spluttered by his elbow, despite the afternoon light that washed in from the atrium. The old man was rolling the beads of his abacus along their tracks with his knobbly fingers.

"Hello, Philosthones," I said, tipping a few loose papers and a couple of pens off a chair. I lounged, and my feet searched around for a footstool. I hooked one with my toes and drew it closer.

"Hmmm," he said, with the air of a grave physician about to give a sad diagnosis. "I wonder why you ask for my advice, Quintus."

A freedman of my father, Philosthones's familiarity was matched only by his disapproval. He'd been calling me by my praenomen since I was a boy, and he'd taught me to count on that same old abacus he still carried around.

"Because I feel obliged to keep you gainfully employed."

His raised eyebrow told me that obligation was all on his side.

"I saw my banker last week," I said. "He told me you've got a gambling problem."

Philosthones curled his lip.

"Have you been going through the figures?" I asked.

14

"Hmmm." That same doleful note.

"Well, am I still rich?" Accountants hated that sort of flippancy about the things they took so seriously. Philosthones would consider dropping a quadrans in the street an act of sheer recklessness.

Philosthones cleared his throat and laced his long, knobbly fingers together. "The price of olive oil is up. Your estate in Corduba has made a killing. I would tell you down to the last *as*, but I know you don't care to hear it. Rest assured that if you ever visit, you will appear as a Croesus to your neighbours."

"A Croesus?" I liked the sound of that.

"You are in an enviable position," he continued. "You have no significant debts, and your earnings would cover your expenses ten times over." It would have been a good moment to grin, except the canny old man narrowed his eyes quickly and snapped out: "However!"

I tried to look meek.

"However," Philosthones said again, in a less severe tone, "your farm in Calabria is barely turning a profit."

I was genuinely puzzled. "I can't understand why. Marius Palentius has made so much from his Calabrian farm that he can afford to keep his new girlfriend in a place on the Viminal. *And* his wife on the Esquiline."

Philosthones looked less than impressed with my financial acumen. "Well, I can tell you why. The farm overseer is cheating you."

"Oh, that's no good."

"I'm glad we're in agreement," Philosthones said dryly. "Now, I intend to pay your farm a little visit. My expenses, I promise, are considerably less than what you are losing at the moment."

"Sure, Philosthones. I'll sack the overseer then, shall I?"

He looked at me and sighed. Maybe he was wondering why he had taught me to count in the first place, but I'd never pretended to have a head for figures. Both he and my banker could testify to that.

"I shall go next month," he said. He glanced down at the scroll that lay weighted on the desk. "I shall leave the figures here with you to peruse. I hope that on my return, you will have gone through them all."

"Consider it done."

"Good," he said. "I can't stop long today. I have an appointment elsewhere."

His tone implied my little business affairs were trifling in the larger scheme, and I'm sure they were. Philosthones was a great accountant, and I knew my father had been sorry to see him go, but with his head for figures, he'd saved up the money for his manumission within a few years. He might not have had a gambling problem like Oufentius, my banker wanted me to believe, but I bet he'd spent a bit of time at the races turning his copper into silver in those days.

"Just one last thing," he said, catching my attention again.

"What?"

"Sell Felix."

I groaned. "Come on, that's just a harmless hobby. Besides, Felix is worth what I paid for him." I couldn't name the amount because I'd been slightly intoxicated at the time of purchase. "He'll come good."

Philosthones frowned. "Quintus, all it does is eat its own weight in feed every day. It's had six starts and comes last every time. My advice to you is to sell your share in the syndicate to someone from out of town."

"That's brutal, Philosthones."

"That's business, my boy," he said smugly and turned his attention to packing up his pens, his scrolls, and penknives and inks, and styluses and tablets.

"Accountants are no fun."

Philosthones's nose twitched as he reached the door. "That'll be your lunch cooking, Quintus. I think I'll just pop into the kitchen and say hello."

My household slaves might have been jealous of Philosthones and his freedom and his modest apartment, but in the end, they would all be sitting around in the kitchen guzzling leftovers and swapping dirty jokes, and Philosthones would be heading home, where he got to play master to his own slaves and never went into the kitchen. A while in the countryside of Calabria might loosen him up. It was about time Philosthones got some fresh air and a new audit scroll—he loved both of those things. I seemed to remember there was a woman there who was once on close terms with Philosthones when my father dragged the household out into the countryside on his annual pilgrimages—when he tucked his toga up under his arms and waded around in the mud trying to feel like a farmer. I preferred to leave farming to the farmers, which probably explained how my overseer was robbing me blind.

From the tablinum, I listened to Philosthones holding forth in the kitchen about the responsibilities of running a household. He was probably counting the candle stubs.

But now it was time for my lunch.

* * *

Gavius Silanus drifted into my house like an unwelcome smell. Hursa obviously thought Silanus had proprietary rights on the place by virtue of his being the first in the modest line of Fulvia's husbands. He made it all the way to the informal triclinium without anyone querying him, which made me wonder about the appalling lack of curiosity the slaves in my household had developed.

"Hello, Valerius," he sneered. Silanus had never made any secret of the fact he disliked me. I was younger, wealthier, and a damned sight handsomer.

I lounged in an aggravating manner while he stood there stiff-necked like he was modelling for a particularly pompous bust. A nondescript slave hovered behind him. *Ah, Gavius Silanus, his descendants will whisper reverently as they draw the children in around the household shrine, a man of great honour and morality, ever conscious of his duty, a man who always wore a toga in public. A man who died horribly, face down in a ditch, an inexplicable vegetable inserted into his body.*

"Good day, Silanus." I had a vivid mental picture and an idiotic smile plastered over my face.

"I hope you're well."

"Do you? Thanks." Silanus thought I was mentally challenged. He couldn't understand how Fulvia put up with me when she'd been the one to

17

initiate their divorce. I could see it written all over his face as he watched me let Mouse use my forearm as a battlement for his centurion. And Julia was sitting beside me and not looking like she hated it. My sloppy charm was stealing all the women in his life.

"We need to talk, Julia," he said sternly, and she ignored him.

I sucked garum sauce off my finger and watched him.

"I could drag you out of here now!"

Julia scowled. "You wouldn't dare!"

The wooden centurion beat a hasty retreat, and Mouse shrank in beside me and tried to disappear.

Fulvia cleared her throat. "Let's not have any unpleasantness. Octavia, if you could please take the children to their rooms, there are some things Quintus and I need to discuss with Gavius Silanus."

They made a good team, my womenfolk. Octavia swept Mouse and Julia away with military efficiency.

We all watched each other for a long moment in the sudden silence. I could hear the swish of a broom from the atrium. A moment later, I heard the sound of Mouse's sandals slapping out towards the peristyle where I knew he'd left his bronze horse. Perella, the daughter of Fulvia's maid, skipped heedlessly past the doorway in pursuit of him.

Silanus glared at me.

Like always, Fulvia got straight to the point. "Gnaeus, sit down, can't you?"

Silanus strode forward, huffed and puffed, and plonked himself down on the edge of a couch that creaked under his weight. He sat there breathing like an angry bull. His hair was tufted in strange directions, and his face was red and shiny. For a man as tense as Silanus even the short walk from the litter in the street could bring on a stroke.

"Julia tells me you've got her engaged," Fulvia said.

"She's of an age," Silanus replied defensively.

"Yes, she is," Fulvia said, and her eyes flashed. I bet Medusa's had done that. "And did you speak to her first, or did you just surprise her?"

"She's of an age," he muttered.

18

"Oh, Gnaeus," Fulvia said with an impatient sigh. "How could you be so stupid?"

He had to have a bit of a think about that.

It had always been a surprise to me that Fulvia managed to produce a beauty like Julia using Silanus as a starting point. He was florid and porcine. At that, it had always been a surprise to me that she'd slept with him in the first place.

I tried to look responsible so he wouldn't just snort at me like usual. "Who have you got lined up as a son-in-law, Silanus?"

"Marcellus Albanus," he said. "Young fellow. Wealthy. Right connections."

"Is he a relative of Marcellus Naso?" My favourite senator in the whole world.

"Nephew." Silanus was incapable of speaking in complete sentences to me. Perhaps he just thought I was a waste of good grammar.

"Has Julia met him?" Fulvia asked.

"Once or twice. I've had him around to dinner a few times, and she's been introduced. I'm sure she'd remember him."

I doubted that. Silanus was the sort of senator who always had a flock of young hopefuls hanging around on his doorstep, trying to climb the greasy pole. If I'd been more career-conscious, I might have been there myself, elbowing my way to the front of the crowd. And it would be no exaggeration to call it a crowd. Julia had probably been woken by their bleating every day of her life. If Marcellus Albanus was anything like his uncle, I could just imagine the sort of inbred, pretentious idiot my stepdaughter was about to be hooked up with. The city was full of them, and most of them found their way to positions of responsibility eventually. Sometimes, I found myself wishing I'd stayed in the army, but then I remembered there were plenty of idiots there as well, and day and night, you were stuck with them. Mouse had left his little centurion on the table. I picked it up and fiddled with it and thought for a moment about the frontiers.

Fulvia had been quiet for a long time. When she spoke, her tone was thoughtful. "Obviously, Julia knew she'd have to get married one day, but it's just as obvious to me, Gnaeus, that you have entirely mishandled the situation."

He gaped like a fish.

Fulvia displayed her palms. "I can talk her around, don't worry about that. But I'll only talk her around once I'm satisfied that this Albanus character is right for her."

"But, but," Silanus stammered, as though it had just occurred to him that Fulvia's selection criteria might be tougher than his own, "but I've promised him!"

I could picture that as well: A drunken senator spotted a similarly drunken young fool, weighed down dangerously by his purse. *What a charming fellow, how witty and urbane*, thought the drunken senator. *If only I had a son just like him. Oh, hang on, that gives me an idea...*I think the term was 'mutually beneficial.' Except silly little Julia couldn't see why she should be sold just so Papa could afford to have the *Rape of the Sabines* painted in the formal triclinium.

"Promising him was probably your first mistake," Fulvia said. "I won't help you, Gnaeus, unless I'm completely satisfied."

He nodded slowly, like he wasn't sure.

The slave Calliope, who had been fidgeting in the shadows, came forward and started to clear the dishes away. Silanus didn't even notice her, which made me think of how little went on in a household, even in supposed privacy, that the slaves didn't know about.

"Are we agreed?" Fulvia asked.

"Yes," Silanus said at last, and the breath escaped his body like squeaky bellows. "I'm sure you'll find the fellow quite suitable. Jupiter knows he's absolutely loaded, and that should keep any girl happy."

Fulvia smiled thinly. "When can I meet him?"

"Meet him?" His broad face fell before he could stop it. I knew then, and so did Fulvia, that there was something about Marcellus Albanus that Fulvia would not approve of. Maybe he wasn't Bachelor of the Year after all.

"Strange as it may seem to you, I do actually want to meet him," Fulvia replied. Twice as much, now Silanus had tried to throw her off.

"Well, he's a busy man," Silanus puffed. "I know for a fact he's got engagements all this week. There's a party at his house tonight, and there will be some extremely important people there. I shall be attending myself."

"Perhaps Marcellus Albanus would like to invite his future bride's mother," Fulvia suggested evilly. I could see where this was going, even if Silanus couldn't.

"I don't think it's that sort of party," Silanus huffed.

"Men only, I suppose."

"Oh, yes," Silanus answered gratefully.

"You can take Quintus then," Fulvia said with a smile.

"I don't *think* so," Silanus said, as if she had suggested he eat dung. His respect for me was boundless.

Fulvia narrowed her eyes at him. "I only want what's best for Julia. I had always assumed you agreed with me on that."

That settled it, then. He'd be an absolute bastard if he dug his heels in now. She had him cornered, and he knew it. Maybe that was why he had agreed to their divorce. Maybe he'd got sick and tired of coming off second-best in their battles.

"Fine," he snapped and rose to his feet. For a moment, I thought the pulsing vein in his left temple was going to burst like a badly constructed aqueduct, but the human body was a remarkable thing. It held. "Fine! Valerius can come as long as he brings some wine." He glowered and huffed some more.

I grinned at him like the drunkard he thought I was. "Do you know, I think I can just about manage that?"

Chapter Two

An invitation to dinner meant a trip to Fish Alley.

"Are you *sure*, sir?" Hursa asked, looking me up and down.

A man of my rank should have thought about wearing a toga in public, especially when he was trying to land just the right sort of high-return, low-stress vocation. It was important to make the right impression—well bred, well dressed, *welcome aboard, son!* Today I was wearing a tunic and a pair of comfortable sandals.

"It's *clean*, Hursa!"

Hursa wrinkled his nose, and Juba and I set off from the house.

From my house on the Caelian Hill, the road sloped downwards towards the Forum on a gentle incline, dipped sharply where the Caelian met the Esquiline, and flattened out at a busy intersection where crowded apartment buildings suddenly blocked out the sunlight and balconies blossomed from faded facades and overhung the street. This neighbourhood was full of tradesmen and artisans who were on the way up, and the middle rankers who despised them but couldn't afford to move. This was where the bustle of the city really began, and from here, it was only a short hop to the Forum.

Like most of the people in the big city, we were headed to the Forum. If you stood in the Forum on a busy day, sooner or later, all the people you needed to see (and a couple you needed to avoid) would cross your path.

The Forum was busy, awash with the usual crowd. The posers in clean tunics *and* togas making the right impression and drifting towards the Curia like flies on the trail of something, particularly rancid; the wheelers and dealers who ran the currency through their fingers like sand; the lawyers and clerks touting for business and pretending not to be, and the mob of tourists and wastrels with nowhere else to be.

We cut through the Forum and headed for my barber, who kept a few stools under a chalked sign in Fish Alley. The streets were narrower further away from the Forum and more crowded with artisans and their associated smells. My father had kept a barber at the house, but for all that, my banker Oufentius said that I was irresponsible, I knew an unnecessary expense when I saw one.

"Morning, Centhus, what's the news in Fish Alley?" I asked when I sat myself down in front of my barber's chalked sign. Juba took the stool next to me and watched as Centhus wielded his collection of razors deftly and tucked the spares into his low-slung apron with the recklessness of a man who placed no value on his testicles.

"The news in Fish Alley, Aemilius Valerius, is that Masso has sold his bakery to cover his gambling debts, and his wife is going to throttle him for it." His eyes twinkled as he sharpened his razor. "Pollia Marca is pregnant again, this time to the sandal maker's younger son. The boy's been sent to visit relatives somewhere, so Pollia's on her own still."

"At least she'll have plenty of children to provide for her in her old age."

Centhus laughed and pulled a few of my stray curls over the razor. "Oh! And old Xeno finally paid the ferryman."

Xeno was the senile old fishmonger who used to natter on in about twelve different languages, none of them intelligible, and force people to buy fish against their will. Many a time, I'd presented a massive, smelly specimen to my cook, only to have him feed it to the cat because it was no longer fit for human consumption. Fish Alley had lost its last fishmonger. It was the end of an era in this neighbourhood.

"That's a shame." I found it easy to feel real affection for people when they were no longer around to torment me.

"We're running a collection for his wife and children," Centhus added pointedly. "Lean your head back for me, sir."

"I didn't know he had any family."

"Oh, yes," said Centhus, shearing off another patch of wild curls. "Com-

23

pletely destitute now. Mind you, they always were. I suppose you could say now they're completely destitute without the consolation of the old lunatic's company."

"Very charitable of you," I commented, feeling in my purse for a few coins to salve my conscience.

Fish Alley was as crowded and as busy as always. The bakery smelled of smoke and fresh bread and was a hive of activity. People haggled, pushed and shoved, and hit each other with their baskets. A couple of likely lads leaned against the fountain at the entrance to the alley, doing their best to look muscular and dangerous. Up and down the alley, children played recklessly, screaming and yelling and ignoring their mothers. A group of muscular-armed harpies cackled outside a laundry and emptied their washing tubs out into the street. People hung out of windows and over balconies, calling to one another. Most of it was unfit for my ears. Clusters of baskets, gourds, and sandals hung under shop awnings, smacking unwary pedestrians in the head. An old woman was beating a swinging gourd with her walking stick and swearing. She turned her stick on the stall owner when he tried to stop her. A pair from the Urban Cohorts glanced into the alley from near the fountain, had a quiet word to the likely lads, roughed them up a bit, and told them to move on about their business. The real criminals slipped back out of the shadows they had popped into the moment the law appeared.

There were one or two faces I recognised. Masso, the baker, escaped the heat of his ovens and caught some fresh air out the front of his shop. He eyed the street warily and then slipped into the wineshop next door. The sandal maker, whose name I could never remember, sat under his awning, cutting strips of leather. Lacus, the beggar, meandered along the alley. A skinny little girl, her tunic hitched up indecently, sat at the counter of Fish Alley's one and only thermopolium and leered at the skinny little boys. The waiter leaned over the counter and shoved her off the stool. He was pelted with bits of rubbish by her tribe of little boyfriends. Lacus, the beggar, sympathised hopefully with the waiter.

Centhus brushed the hair from my shoulders, whipped me around on

24

the stool, and gave me a snappy shave. I closed my eyes rather than watch the razor flitting about in my line of vision.

I counted out my money to Centhus, with a bit of extra for the gossip. "See you next time, Centhus."

"A pleasure as always, Valerius." Centhus grinned. A pleasure because he overcharged me. I only let him because he was still cheap by comparison. My revenge was recommending him to Hursa.

Then, to punish Juba for getting more dimpled smiles from all the girls in Fish Alley than I did, I bought a box of scrolls just to make him carry it, and then made him wait outside on the street outside my baths while I splashed around annoying everyone else. A particularly cantankerous old senator called me a lowly bastard son of a bitch. It was mad Uncle Maro.

"How's the job hunting going?" he asked after his initial pleasantries.

"Same as always," I answered, floating away from him lazily.

"It's been months, Quintus." He waggled his finger at me like a stern tutor. "You need to pull yourself together. Your father's reputation won't keep yours afloat forever."

"Well, not every generation can be greater than the last."

"You shouldn't be so determined to prove that." Maro plucked at some of the strange hair that grew out of his ears and fixed me with a hard stare. "At your age, I was up at dawn waiting inside my patron's house every day until I landed a position."

"At my age, Maro," I told him, "you were still sitting in a fort in Helvetica, freezing your backside off. When you came back to Rome, you didn't have seven years to kill before you were the right age to stand for an election! Besides, I don't have a patron."

"You've got me," he said smugly and wiggled his fingers across the surface of the water.

I moved out of the way of the swell he was creating and rolled my eyes. "Yes, but I don't need to be at your house every day at dawn since you always invite me in anyway. Anyway, I heard somewhere that it was out of fashion to get up that early."

"Ah!" my mad relation replied. "That's what you young idiots think, but

I'll tell you something, Quintus. Fashion is nothing against tradition. The old men who pull the strings like to see their atriums full of hopefuls when they wander out from bed. You should be concentrating now on making the sort of connections that will be useful to you when you do reach thirty. By the way, are you free for dinner tonight?"

I told him about my invitation to attend dinner with Silanus. He was suitably sympathetic, so I stopped splashing him and let him tell me stories about the old days (this meant any time before I was born when, apparently, Maro was like a god among men) until we were both standing outside again, pink and clean. I loaded Uncle Maro into his litter, and Juba and I turned for home.

* * *

As the afternoon drew slowly towards evening, I sat on my favourite garden bench and began to sort through my new collection of scrolls. Memoirs of the illustrious Julius Caesar: a few pages only with none of the battles and skirmishes in Gaul, or run-ins with spooky druids and their bloody human sacrifices. A dull tract by Cicero rambling on about Duty, a couple of verses from an anonymous and asinine poet, some surprising pornography with instructional diagrams, and a few useful recipes I would pass on to my cook—fish garnished with eggs and a garum and vinegar dressing. The scroll box wasn't a total loss then.

"Is that all men think about, Quintus?" My sister Octavia was wearing her disapproving face.

I tucked the pornography back into the box. "I was actually thinking about dinner."

She sat down beside me and snatched the page back out of the scroll box. She scrutinised it from all angles.

In theory, I was responsible for Octavia Junilla, since she didn't have a husband or father left to lecture her. Some people might have suggested my responsibilities went as far as keeping dirty pictures out of my little sister's hands, but anyone who suggested it didn't have a sister like mine. We were never close as children. Boys who have three years over their sisters develop a superior sneer whenever they catch a glimpse of braids, bracelets, and corn dollies. We rubbed along well enough throughout our respective childhoods until our father obviously decided we cramped his style. In the same week I got the news that I was being packed out to the provinces to learn how to become a junior tribune, our father brought home Marcus Decius Nasica. *What a find!* It was written all over the old man's face. A high-flyer, bound straight for the broad stripes of senator. Wealthy, ambitious, popular, and generous beyond our father's wildest dreams, Nasica was also young and handsome enough for Octavia to convince herself the old man hadn't entirely overlooked her priorities.

He treated me like a brother. He threw me a farewell party; fifty close friends, the run of his house, a lot of dancing girls, and amphorae as far as the eye could see. He even gave me the earnest drunken talk about how much he respected my family and would always treat my little sister well. I had *liked* him, and it had all ended so badly.

I stole a quick look at Octavia while she was preoccupied. Her forehead was creased with amusement, and she was smiling. I liked to see her smiling again, which was probably why I let her look at dirty pictures against all better judgement.

Octavia was still mulling over the diagrams. "Now, surely *that* one," she said, "is impossible!"

"I think you're holding it the wrong way up."

"Oh, yes, that makes more sense." She squinted. "Oh, I see. It doesn't look like much fun though, does it? Frankly, it's about as appealing as Greek wrestling. Grease me up. I'm going in!"

"Octavia!" I plucked the page away from her.

Octavia smiled again. She had a smile that could light up dark rooms, my sister, when she used it. Since her divorce, I'd been beating suitors away from the front door with a stick. That wasn't entirely true, of course—that would be Hursa's job. But I had received a few enquiries, ranging from the reasonably subtle "You and Fulvia must come for dinner soon, Valerius. Oh, and bring your sister!" to the downright blatant "What's your sister's dowry worth these days?" I had a feeling that most of them would be surprised by her Greek wrestling fixation.

Octavia leaned forward, and her earrings jangled. One thing I'd say for Nasica, he'd left Octavia in a good position after the divorce. She kept her dowry, her wedding gifts, and all the jewellery Nasica had managed to shower on her before their irreconcilable differences. She wasn't relying on my charity yet.

She glanced at me sideways. "You're hiding out here from Julia, aren't you?"

"Aren't you?"

"No," Octavia replied, rifling through my busted scroll box. "Is that Cicero? Why do you never think to buy me anything when you're throwing your money around at the Emporium?"

I had missed this Octavia. The last few months had tested our friendship, but it felt like we were slowly rebuilding our bridges. I hoped we were.

"The Saepta Julia," I corrected her. "Anyway, why do you never think to buy *me* anything when you and Fulvia are throwing my money around at the Emporium?"

Octavia unrolled Cicero across her knees and chose to ignore me. "'It is the duty of a magistrate to understand that he represents the whole citizen body and that he must therefore uphold the dignity and honour of the state...' You were ripped off, Quintus."

"I know."

The slave Larius brought out a tray of fruit. Larius technically belonged to Octavia, but on the fair and just grounds that I was paying for his upkeep, I used him as an extra indoor slave. Why Octavia bought him, I didn't know. He was young and handsome, and I was suspicious of her motives. If Larius himself hadn't been so thoroughly terrified of me, I would have made Octavia pack him off to one of the family estates long ago to avoid complications on that front.

I glared at him unhappily as he set the tray down.

He stepped back again, his gaze on the ground. I would never have the same relationship with him that I did with Juba. When I bullied Juba, it

28

was funny, the same as when Juba bullied me. Neither of us took it too seriously.

Octavia hummed as she perused Cicero.

The garden was pleasant at this hour. Afternoon shadows were just starting to creep in at the edges, and they brought with them a cooling breeze that let me forget about the heat of the day outside. The fountain behind me was babbling to itself in that mesmerising way that fountains have, and I had to think hard about whether it was telling me I needed to sleep or I needed to piss. I quietly regretted having to leave the house for the party tonight. While usually, the prospect of free food and wine and entertainment was one that delighted me, being stuck with Silanus for hours would no doubt suck all the fun out of it. The man was a leech. I would have preferred to stay home with my family. Even Julia.

Later, while everyone else was getting ready for an informal meal, Juba was helping me into a toga. Hursa brought me a clean napkin and found me a large jar of Falernian of a good vintage. If Marcellus Albanus was a half-decent host, some of it would find its way back into my cup at dinner. If he was a lousy host, he would hoard it away for later and serve his guests vinegar from the Vatican Hill.

After dressing, I wandered about in my study, not wanting to sit down and ruin the fall of my toga. I hoped Silanus would not be tardy.

Gavius Silanus was always as good as his word and never any better. He turned up at the house just as dusk was starting to steal the afternoon light and sent a slave in to announce he was waiting.

I sailed out the front door. It was all for Silanus's effect, to let him know how well I could scrub up, but the curtains of his litter were closed. Muttering at him under my breath, I climbed into my own waiting litter and nursed my jar of Falernian. Our little procession set off awkwardly; my litter bearers took a while to match their steps. Juba was walking beside me. He was carrying a torch. He needn't have bothered.

* * *

Marcellus Albanus lived only a short distance away from my house on the Caelian Hill. The litters climbed up the gentle slope easily, and I watched the fronts of the large houses go by. There were very few shops at this end of the hill; we patricians didn't like artisans cluttering up our entrances. To buy a pie in this area, a man had to be lucky enough to have a stall set up each morning at the end of his street, or he had to send a slave down the hill to where the residents were happy to rent their frontage to bakers and butchers, wine sellers and candle makers, and to have their homes smelling of burnt sausage, lamp oil, bleach vats, and new leather. On this side of the hill, the streets were wide and free of clutter, all bare walls and porticoes. The houses and gardens behind the walls were large and comfortable; some were downright lavish, but the streets presented a closed face.

A few more litters had joined us now from the narrow streets that fed onto this one. Their sweaty bearers might have run all the way from the other side of the city.

I guessed Marcellus Albanus lived in one of the most luxurious houses along this road if the initial spectacle was anything to go by. It was as light as day. Along the entire length of the street leading to the house stood a veritable army of slaves, each holding a torch to guide their master's guests. In the river of flickering light, musicians played and sang, and a troupe of dancers did their thing. I even caught a glimpse of a water organ, a monstrous contraption that was mercifully suffering from some mechanical fault as we passed. A trio of girls got up as the Graces were flinging flowers in front of the litters. Marcellus Albanus was having a party, and he wanted the whole world to know. I could only imagine what his neighbours thought.

At the front of the house (candles floating in a trough that lined the entry, more flowers, more dancers) there was a short queue. I knew then what sort of host Marcellus Albanus was: the sort who invited more than he could feed and relegated the less important guests to standing room only. As someone who'd often been among that number, I was already annoyed.

To my surprise Silanus and I were ushered to the front of the queue. A girl with soft hands and a softer smile removed our sandals and washed our feet.

The water that trickled over our toes was cloudy with rose perfume. She passed us deftly into the hands of a well-groomed slave who asked for my name in an undertone and showed us into the triclinium. The household already knew Silanus.

I pressed my jar of Falernian into the hands of a slave who didn't look too busy.

The triclinium was larger than my own formal dining room. The fresco that covered the four walls depicted a lot of girls reclining, surrounded by fruit and docile-looking wildlife. It was a common enough theme for a dining room, except the girls were all stark naked and in positions that were either artistic or pornographic. The fruit theme continued on the floor; small circular mosaics depicted bunches of grapes spilling from cornucopias. Similarly designed bronze cornucopias protruded from the walls. The lamps were set into these. The triclinium was spacious but garish, with four large tables each with couches arranged around them. These seemed already full, but the slave led us through to the main table and announced us by our formal names:

"Gnaeus Gavius and Quintus Aemilius, master."

A pasty-faced young man rose to his feet and trotted around the couch. He pressed Silanus's hand and smiled broadly. He was older than me, maybe close to thirty, of average height, and had unremarkable features. He was no Adonis, but Julia couldn't have everything. He appeared neither serious nor silly, neither learned nor stupid; he was just one of hundreds you could find on any given day hanging about the Forum.

"Welcome," he said with due respect to his potential father-in-law and his potential father-in-law's hanger-on. "Please, make yourselves comfortable." He was polite, but not warm. I wasn't impressed, but Silanus looked like every word that fell from the young man's lips was divinely inspired. Money could turn men like Silanus into sycophants.

Space had miraculously appeared at the main table. The previous occupants were being resettled elsewhere by the same efficient slave who had shown us in. They had the grace not to look too put out.

"Aemilius Valerius," I heard the man next to Albanus saying in an undertone as I was arranging my toga after reclining. This man obviously knew me from somewhere. "Decius Nasica's wife's brother."

Ex-wife's brother, I wanted to say out of habit, but it was easier to pretend I hadn't heard.

Silanus had the place of honour on the main couch. I was squeezed in on the next couch, between a bearded fellow wearing the broad senatorial stripe on his toga, and a small dark fellow whose fresh toga smelled faintly of bleach. We smiled warily at one another like people who knew they were going to have to make small talk sooner or later.

There was very little conversation at first. The whole room was busy scoffing itself silly. The eggs came first, arranged like bunches of grapes on vine leaf beds, then loaves of fine white bread, followed by sausages on a silver grill. The musicians that had trailed in from the street began to play, and the obligatory dancers from Hispania began to gyrate. The musicians were squashed up against one of the walls, the standing guests made the best of things down in their crammed third of the room, and the dancers had to twirl right in front of the main table. That was fine. I had my first cup of honeyed wine, and then my second.

A pair of slaves appeared with the shellfish. The shellfish was arranged on a massive bronze dish, stacked cunningly in the shape of a trireme, with oars made of lobster claws and a sail of some translucent fabric. The trireme sailed in an ocean of dark wine that splashed up against its hull of shells. The detail was intricate, and the whole room cried out in amazement, which had a lot to do with the fact that everyone was knocking back mulsum as fast as the slaves could pour it.

The bearded senator whose toga I was leaning on reached for his ivory shellfish knife with the *humph* of a man who was determined not to be impressed.

My eye was caught by one of the dancers—a dark-skinned, bold-eyed beauty who was doing some interesting things with his veils. The light caught in his bracelet of glass beads, and it seemed as though his wrist was ringed with blue fire.

The senator had noticed the direction of my stare. He picked some stray food from his beard. "Now *that's* worth looking at." He seemed friendlier at once. "Cornelius Paulinus. Let's make it Paulinus, shall we?"

"Fine by me, Paulinus," I said. "Aemilius Valerius."

"Oh yes?" He eyed me curiously; everybody loves a scandal. "Nasica's brother-in-law."

"Ex," I said shortly. I did not discuss Octavia's ex-husband in public, and I didn't want Nasica's cloud hanging over me tonight. I had no idea he knew this crowd. I didn't remember having met any of them before, and there had been a time when I'd thought all Nasica's friends were mine. Then again, there had been a time when I'd thought he was a brother to me, a part of my family, which only goes to show how wrong I was.

"Unfortunate," said Paulinus vaguely.

"Mmm." In case my monosyllabic reply didn't give him the hint, I changed the subject. "And how do you know our host?"

Paulinus snorted. "I know almost everyone in the city, Valerius." His tone implied he thought he would be better off if he didn't. "I knew your father, for example—he was a good man—and I knew your name although I hadn't put a face to it. I remember when he decided to marry that Nasica spoke highly of your family."

Back to him again.

"I'd appreciate it if we didn't talk about him here, Paulinus," I said, wondering if I could concentrate on who was on my other side. The small dark man was silent, though, and had spent the dinner smiling benignly at everyone through half-closed eyes.

"Of course," Paulinus said. He tugged his beard. "I'm sorry. It was impolite." He looked into his cup of wine accusingly.

I ate my shellfish and watched Albanus. He was flanked by Silanus on one side, and a man I didn't recognise on the other. I didn't know him, but he was the one who had placed me immediately as Nasica's wife's brother. Ex. Both he and Silanus were whispering jokes into Albanus's ear, and Albanus was laughing like an idiot. They looked as cosy as three peas in a pod.

"Who's that?" I pointed out Albanus's other mate to Paulinus.

"Claudius Rufanus. Of *the* Claudians, you know."

Albanus was moving in high circles. That might please Fulvia. It might not. It wouldn't be a favourable report from my point of view, even if I had made it onto the main table. I didn't like a man who made some of his guests stand, and I didn't like the sort of flashy displays of vanity I had seen here. The frescoes on the wall were new and had too much gold in them. They made my eyes burn. The couches were polished, the cushions fresh and firm. All the marble tabletops gleamed, and all the plates and utensils were uniformly matched. Even the slaves were decked out in nearly as much finery as their master. I could almost see the tidemark where Albanus had pissed his money up against the wall.

I leaned towards Paulinus. "Who's this next to me?"

Paulinus grinned. "Some provincial. Rich as a fart but can hardly speak the language. He'll probably enjoy himself more than the rest of us combined."

"How's that?"

"He doesn't need to listen to Albanus prattle on!" Paulinus laughed loudly.

I didn't look at Albanus in case he'd heard. Our provincial friend smiled happily at us and slurped his wine.

Paulinus went through the remaining couch at our table for me. "Avitus Florian, soon to depart on a glorious military career!" He sniggered. I could appreciate his cynicism. I'd been where Florian was.

He continued. "Galerius Nepos, odds on favourite for consul next year. And good old Marcellus Naso, Albanus's uncle. I believe you know him."

My heart sank. I hadn't recognised Marcellus Naso with a smile on his face and a laurel wreath slipping over his forehead. Paulinus was grinning to himself.

"You heard about that?"

"Who hasn't ended up face-down in an impluvium at least once in their life?" Paulinus asked.

I snorted, warming to him, and raised my glass at him.

The dishes were cleared away to make room for more. Roast beef, boiled calf, lamprey, mullet, capon and goose liver. Platters of vegetables: asparagus, mushrooms, cabbage, lentils, beans, radishes, turnips, lettuce

34

and gourds. This time, it was served with Setinum instead of mulsum; the drinking was getting serious.

"Fuck," Paulinus said suddenly.

It took me a while to follow his gaze. My vision was blurred. I saw a man of average height, slightly fleshy and in his middle years, standing in polite conversation with an elderly man at the end of the triclinium.

"Who's that?" I asked.

"Anicetus," Paulinus murmured, dropping his tone. "Head of the fleet at Misenum."

I didn't get it.

"Ex-slave," said Paulinus gruffly.

"Ah," I said and concentrated on my Setinum. "Is that Macrinus he's talking to?"

I hadn't noticed the old man before and wondered what he was doing at this kind of party. Probus Macrinus was a family friend, I supposed, but I was not very fond of him. He was perpetually at death's door and tended to capitalise on the fact that no one liked to say no to a frail, doddering old man. He'd wrangled dinner invitations off more important men than me. He had officially retired from his distinguished public life at least twenty years ago, but he still hung around the city like a bad smell. My mad Uncle Maro told me he was venerable. I leaned more towards viral. I hoped I could avoid him for the rest of the night.

The Hispanian dancer moved in my direction again.

I was drunk already, and getting drunker by the moment. The room was noisy now, with dozens of different conversations competing to be heard. Paulinus proved to be a good companion—he knew more smutty jokes than I did. With a few gestures and the use of some crude props, we soon had our provincial friend hugging his stomach in hysterics. He took to us like family. If we were ever in Gaul...

Dessert was fruit and confectionaries, and the immortal Falernian. I could have gone to sleep where I lay, watching the Hispanian dancer with the glass bracelet gyrating just out of reach and wearing less and less every time I raised my spinning head to gaze at him. By the time Albanus announced I was invited to the commissatio, I was almost unconscious.

* * *

The commissatio was the last thing I needed. I was pleased Albanus had invited me because it would give me the opportunity to gather intelligence for Fulvia, but the last thing my stomach and my head needed was a drinking match. It was for younger men only, which was another point in its favour. It meant that Marcellus Naso, uptight old bastard, and Gavius Silanus, general bastard, were obliged to say their farewells and head off. Paulinus was borderline, but he had dogged determination on his side. He and I, and young Avitus Florian, were the only guests from the main table that made it in.

The commissatio was in a second, smaller dining room. The couches were arranged around the walls. On the low marble table in the centre of the room was a cratera for mixing the wine and a large jug for being sick into. Albanus had thought of everything. I needed a breath of fresh air before getting in there.

I slunk off to the peristyle and supported myself with the intricate columns that bordered it. I was in comfortable shadow now and fighting the desire to be sick. I could make that fountain in time, but that was possibly something Albanus would hold against me—clogging up his water supply with a second look at his expensive feast.

And now, here was the man himself, looking as proud as a peacock strutting through his domain. And why wouldn't he be? Young, wealthy, and with a pretty fiancée lined up to add to his luxurious possessions. I was about to call out to him—I was here to make his acquaintance, after all—but I saw that he was flanked by Paulinus and that neither of them looked happy. I didn't intend to eavesdrop. Anything that passed between them remained between them as far as I was concerned, but they were loud.

"I didn't invite him!" said Albanus. "He just turned up!"

"Well, get him out of here!" Paulinus returned angrily.

They both stalked away. Then I noticed someone else had been watching them from the shadows of the colonnaded peristyle: Claudius Rufanus, of *the* Claudians, whose age had precluded him from the drinking match and who should have already gone home.

I gave everyone a few moments to clear out, and then wandered back to join the commissatio. I was let in by a worried slave who was explaining to Anicetus, former slave and head of the fleet at Misenum, that there was no room for him at the commissatio. Anicetus smiled politely, like a man who'd heard that line his entire life, and left.

Everyone was there now, and everyone was friends. I had missed the beginning—there was already someone lying on the floor, assuring everyone loudly that he wasn't going to throw up. I pushed my way through the crowd (this is what all those who'd had to stand up at dinner had come for) and found myself leaning against the wall beside one of my fellows from the main table, Avitus Florian. He watched the progression of the jugs of wine being passed around and looked worried.

"About to go into the army, are you?" I asked to make conversation. "You should enjoy all of this while you can. There's not much debauchery on the frontiers, you know."

He gave me a distracted smile. "So they tell me. I'm Florian."

"Yep, Paulinus told me your name." I snorted. "I think he picked up what an antisocial bastard I've become. I don't know anyone in the city anymore."

"Paulinus?" Florian blinked. He looked around and sighed. "I don't know anyone either, really. These are my cousin's friends." The jug had arrived in his hands, and he passed it on to me without drinking.

Funny. Just that afternoon, I was telling myself I needed to find some drunken young idiots to be friends with. Now, I was standing in the middle of a group that fulfilled all three criteria, and I couldn't be bothered with them. Albanus was holding forth in the middle of the room, singling out the weak to drink first. That was his prerogative in what could be a cruel game. I already knew who he would pick.

"Paulinus!" he cried, spinning in a drunken circle.

Paulinus, who'd had the gall to demand Albanus throw out the ex-slave Anicetus. Albanus didn't strike me as the sort of person who liked being told what to do. He was punishing Paulinus, and I wondered how he would punish a wife for a similar trifling offence.

Florian and I watched Paulinus take up the challenge with a grim smile. He raised the jug, growled at the room, and tipped his head back. The room stamped their feet in time as he drank. Paulinus slammed the jug back down on the table, wiped his beard, and grinned broadly. He threw out his chest and raised his arms: "I salute the sun!"

A few of the other drunken idiots in the room did the same, roaring in unison. The rest of us wondered what was going on.

Florian glanced at me. "They were in the Third Gallica. That's where I'm going."

He looked uncomfortable at the idea of forsaking his hometown gods. He was in for a rough time in that case. Every legion had its strange habits, and some were stranger than others. I could still remember how to pray to Mithras if I'd drunk just the right amount to become maudlin. It explained a lot, too. My ex-brother-in-law Nasica had been in the Third Gallica, which was why his name had been cropping up and why I was being placed in relation to him.

Paulinus gave another drunken roar. He looked in my direction, and my stomach lurched. "I pick Florian!"

The look on Florian's face said he knew he'd been chosen because he was going to lose. A mock cheer washed around the room. I don't know who started it, but I was embarrassed for him.

Florian managed to drink most of it before he disgraced himself by being the first one to vomit. I was glad it wasn't me. I told myself that I mightn't be as young as most of the drunken idiots in this room, but I could still outdrink every one of them. I'd show Marcellus Albanus what sort of family he was marrying into.

I lasted less than an hour before I was carried out calling for the Hispanian dancer.

* * *

I woke in a strange bed, on a mattress with the lumps in all the wrong places and blankets that smelt like they hadn't seen fresh air since the days of the great Augustus. I had apparently used these to mop up some of my more interesting bodily fluids in my sleep—they were damp with Falernian-scented sweat and dribble.

Someone had glued my eyelids together.

Someone else was running their fingers along my unsettled stomach.

My eyelids ripped open.

It took a moment to get my bearings: strange bed, strange room, strange partner. Those were the only bearings I could wrap my head around at that moment.

"You're awake then?" Was this the same sublime creature who had teased me with his flimsy veils? Even in the meagre light of a single lamp, this fellow was scrawny and harsh and wearing too much kohl around his sagging eyelids. The sinewy hand tracing up towards my chest was wearing a bracelet of cool glass beads. He'd either stolen it off his younger, prettier brother, or once again, I was the victim of unlimited free wine.

Bacchus, Bacchus, what did I ever do to you?

I grunted in reply. I had a feeling that his little hand, probably with a grip as deadly as the clenched talons of an eagle, was searching for any spare cash I might have secreted about my person.

"Listen…what's your name?" I had found my voice at last, hidden at the bottom of my throat under a pile of gravel.

"Nicius," he muttered, eyeing me suspiciously. "I suppose you want to try again then?"

"Oh yes." I closed my eyes. "You just go on whispering sweet nothings."

I had confused him. I heard the rattle of his bracelet as he pulled his hand away. "Well, do you?"

"No, Nicius, thank you." When I ended up so drunk, I found myself in bed with a cheap dancer and so drunk I couldn't even take advantage of that—sober me would have known better than to bother—I knew it was time to go home.

He didn't look very sorry to see me go and didn't even offer to help me with my toga, which suddenly seemed to have at least a dozen different sides and be the wrong shape altogether. I would need Juba for this.

I took the lamp with me.

The house seemed to be all in darkness now. There wasn't even a sound from the kitchens. It must have been hours. I slunk around, trailing my toga and trying not to sound like a burglar.

The formal triclinium was empty. In the smaller dining room, the scene of my shame, the evidence of the commissatio remained. An upended couch, a bit of smashed glassware, a river of spilled wine, and quite a few patches of drying vomit. I doubted Albanus would care so long as he'd had his fun.

The next room looked to be a sitting room. It was small and intimate, with a single table only and some chairs. This was probably as informal as things got around here. My lamp showed me a wall covered in rose-garlanded nymphs, but with surprisingly little gold detailing. The nymphs were cavorting around a bull. By the look of the bull's exaggerated anatomy, he was enjoying himself as much as the nymphs. One of the plumper nymphs seemed to be about to lose the impractical scrap of drapery she was only just wearing. I moved forward into the room, holding up my lamp to cast more light on the intriguing scene that spread up towards the ceiling.

I slipped, landed on my arse, and my lamp smashed. The oil spilled, flared, and in the instant before it all went dark, I saw Marcellus Albanus lying on the floor with someone kneeling over him.

I had slipped in his blood.

Chapter Three

The ancients taught us that each person had a star in the heavens that shone bright in their ascendancy and dimmed in times of personal and public decline. The great Julius Caesar's, for that man who had since taken his place as a god, was the first star that rose in the evening and the last that faded at dawn. The divine Augustus Caesar could claim a comet that tore a fiery path through the heavens and was visible even in the brightest hour of the day. Not all of us made such an impression on the cosmos. I had often pondered the spread of stars across the sky and wondered which modest glow belonged to me. Mine must have been brighter than some; the river boatmen ferrying down the Tiber each night would not be able to pick their single star from the multitude that join to spread a hazy light across the glowing sky. Mine must have also been more constant than some; Marcellus Albanus's star had burned bright for an instant and was gone. I doubted that it would even be remembered.

My bare feet and one leg were sticky with his blood. My eyes had squeezed shut as I hit the floor, but the flare of the lamp was burned in my vision, and in that, I could still see him lying there, one leg bent up under him as he had fallen, his mouth agape, his eyes stuck wide open, and the blood-soaked tunic and toga. And he hadn't been alone. There had been someone kneeling beside him.

"*Valerius?*"

I didn't recognise the voice, and I hadn't seen the face. I had sudden, horrible visions of a knife in the dark. "Who's that?"

"It's Florian," the shaky voice returned. "He's dead, Valerius!"

I blinked in the darkness and saw Albanus all over again. They say Caesar pulled his toga over his face as he was stabbed. No such luck for Marcellus Albanus.

"What happened?" I croaked.

"I don't know!"

I climbed to my feet with some difficulty. My toga was tangled around my legs. I backed away towards the door.

I could hear a commotion in the household now. My smashed lamp had woken someone, and I could see the shadows their lamps threw up against the walls before they found us. After the first slave shrieked, the rest came running. I picked one of them from the crowd, a bleary-eyed fellow who had announced my name at dinner.

"What's your name?"

"Helios, sir," he stammered, wide-eyed at finding himself singled out.

"Send your fastest runner to fetch a magistrate."

He nodded. "Yes, sir, and a physician, sir?"

I glanced down at Albanus. There was something obscene about the fact he lay twisted and uncovered. Something barbarous. "I think it's a bit late for that, Helios."

Helios chewed his knuckles to prevent a cry escaping his pale face.

I took charge. They had no one else to do it. "Everyone out." It was like herding geese. The ones at the front kept trying to escape around me and go back for a decent look. "Out, come on!"

I went back and stood behind Florian. There was blood on his toga, but no more than was on mine. His hands, I noted, were clean.

"Florian," I said. "Come on."

With his help, I laid Albanus straight while I tried to think about what I was going to tell Fulvia. *Well, I didn't like him very much, his place was too showy, and his friends were too stupid and drunk, but never mind because he's dead anyway.*

I would have to have a rethink before I got home.

Julia, good news!

I hoped Fulvia wasn't waiting up for my return. Our few months of marriage should have taught her that to wait up for Aemilius Valerius on a night out was folly. I had no idea of the time by now. It felt way past midnight, and for all I knew, dawn was already creeping in. Explaining this to Fulvia would be worse than explaining the dinner at which I'd disgraced myself in front of Marcellus Naso. I could even feel a bit of sympathy for that old sod tonight.

I closed Albanus's eyes. It was the least I could do to show him some respect in his ignoble death. I covered his face with his toga.

Florian and I stood in silence for a moment. I had no appropriate things to say. I didn't know his family. I didn't know what his friends and loved ones would remember him for. I didn't know his history at all. *Marcellus Albanus, hail and farewell.*

I stepped outside and sent Helios to fetch me a jug of water. I drank a few mouthfuls and used the rest to wash the blood away. There was a dark patch of it on my toga, but the night felt colder now, so I kept it on. The slaves were milling around aimlessly. They were in shock, and most of them were drunk from Albanus's leftovers. It would start to sink in soon, and there would be a panic.

"What's going on?" a drunk slurred. One of Albanus's idiot friends.

I broke the news to him. He didn't believe me and went to look for himself. Moments later, he stumbled back outside with tears streaming down his cheeks, gulping and gasping. He pushed past me, and I lost him to the darkness.

I moved into the peristyle and looked up at the stars. I could only see a few— the torches being lit all around me were dimming the night sky up above. There was a haze of cloud moving across the sky slowly. It felt curiously apt. I remember the night sky seemed low and brilliant in those wastelands at the eastern edges of the empire. Maybe that was how heroism snagged me—my star zoomed down and clipped me around the ear. Rome was a world away from that wilderness where the cold nights blew down on our camp. It was just us against the world, and that was probably why the stars shone so bright out there.

Helios came to stand beside me as I leaned on the fountain. I think he was too frightened to stand alone.

"What will I do? What will I do?" He was starting to panic. Once the others caught on, I wasn't sure what might happen. Nothing spread faster than panic.

There was a clamour at the door and then the clatter of hobnailed boots across the intricate mosaics that Albanus had spent a fortune on. My job was over. The law was here.

* * *

The first thing the law did was plant a pair of beefy vigiles on the front door and start rounding up the slaves for a headcount. The slaves were marched to the huge triclinium and assembled in straight lines. After them went the dancers and musicians, some of whom had stuck around for the leftover food and wine and curled up in shadowed corners to sleep it off. Nicius, the Hispanian dancer, was with them.

The vigiles hunted up a few more sleeping guests from the other bedrooms and spared them the indignity of waiting with the slaves. They were settled in a small room just off the atrium. I recognised a few of them from the commissatio. None of them were in my league; they started mentioning their fathers' names because they thought they were in trouble. When I got into trouble, I had to get myself out of it.

The leader of this small party of the law was only a young man, but tall. He was probably tougher for it—the tall one always gets singled out by brawlers who think they can take him.

"Good evening, sir," he said to me after he slipped through the shadowed colonnades to join me by the fountain. His accent was pure plebeian, but there was nothing common about his manner. He looked more bookish than thuggish, which had to be something of a rarity in the vigiles. In one swift glance, he took in my toga with its narrow purple stripe and bloodstain. "My name is Junius Atreus. I'm in charge until the magistrate arrives. What happened here tonight?"

"Your guess is as good as mine," I said. "My name is Aemilius Valerius.

44

I was a guest at the party here tonight. I was sleeping off a bit too much wine, got up for a wander, and tripped over Albanus. Our host."

He was silent for a long moment. His shadowed face gave nothing away. "That would be Marcellus Albanus."

"That's right."

He was silent again. I wondered if it was a tactic, or if it was really taking that long for my responses to sink into his skull. The suddenness of his next question convinced me it was a tactic: "Let's go and have a look at him, shall we?"

We returned to the smallest dining room. Things were pretty much as Helios and I had left them, except now there were lamps placed on the couches and a thin, sallow man crouching beside the body as though he was praying over it. Florian was lingering anxiously by the door.

"This is our physician," Atreus said, nodding at the sallow man.

Free from the darkness of the colonnades, I took the opportunity to get a better look at the vigile. Atreus was about my age, maybe a few years older, and tall. He was well-built, supple, and lean, but with broad shoulders that hinted at underlying strength. His hair was brownish-gold, and he had a few freckles hiding under his sun-browned skin. His eyes were green. All small things, but I wondered if his mother had once been on friendly terms with a lonely barbarian. If my scrutiny made him uneasy, he gave no sign of it.

At long length the physician sighed. He leaned back and rested his weight on his heels. "Can you describe how you found him, sir?"

I moved forward for a better look. "His left leg was bent up under him like he'd fallen. His hands were by his sides, just so. The only thing we did was straighten his leg, close his eyes, and cover his face."

I looked towards Florian for confirmation, but he had his eyes closed and was fiddling with something in his hands. He looked like he was about to pass out. He wouldn't last a week in the legions.

"Like he'd fallen, you say?" the physician asked.

"Yes."

The physician nodded to himself for a moment, probably a tactic he had stolen from his boss and adapted for his own use, and then peeled the edge of the toga back. Albanus was white; all the blood had drained away from his face. There was nothing frightening in it, this unanimated flesh devoid of any expression. His mouth remained open, frozen in surprise. His lips were bloodless blue.

Atreus looked appropriately sombre.

The physician continued his examination. He drew the folds of the toga away from Albanus's body, dropping the fabric into the crusted pool of blood that still carried my footprints and the long, wide streak where I had slipped. The physician shuffled closer on his knees, oblivious to the mess. His probing fingers found a tear in Albanus's rich orange tunic. He reminded me of scouts who trace a river to its source.

He had found it. His fingers widened the tear in the fabric and exposed the gaping flesh underneath. "There you are," he said. "Stabbed between the ribs and up into the heart."

Florian turned away. The vigile and I both crouched down on the cleaner side of Albanus.

"A lucky stroke?" Atreus peered at the wound.

"Doubt it." The physician wiped his hands on Albanus's tunic. "Looks quick and hard to me."

I looked down at the body of the man who might have been my stepdaughter's husband. The things Julia wanted to know about her betrothed probably didn't include the quickest way to his heart.

The Greek tapped his fingers against the curve of Albanus's jaw. "See that bruising there?"

It was bright as day now he had pointed it out. A puffy ridge of purplish discolouration stood out against the bloodless flesh.

"Someone grabbed his jaw, like so." The physician reached out over the corpse to grasp Atreus's chin and manoeuvred his fingers into position. "See, thumb on this side, and fingers there."

Atreus twisted free and bent closer to Albanus's slack face. "What does that mean?" he asked, massaging his jaw.

The physician smiled at him. "If you will help me with his toga…"

46

The physician and the vigile began to unwrap Albanus's sticky toga from his body. The physician laid the folds above Albanus's shoulder and then regarded the corpse thoughtfully. Albanus was wearing a long-sleeved tunic with fine embroidery along the sleeves and hem. The physician lifted one of his arms and pushed the sleeve up. Just like the purplish discolouration on his jaw, Albanus was bruised on his upper arms. This time I could make out the marks of the fingers before the physician pointed them out.

"His arms were held behind his back," said the physician. "A second man held his jaw."

"Someone gave him a proper talking to," said Atreus sombrely.

"And then stabbed him," the physician agreed.

Atreus looked over to Florian. "And you were asleep, sir, next door and didn't hear a thing?"

Florian didn't answer.

"Sir?" the vigile asked, narrowing his eyes. He stood up. "Sir? What's that you have there, sir?"

Florian started and looked down into his hand in surprise. He was holding an amulet of some sort. "I-I don't know," he stammered. "It was on the floor."

Atreus reached out for the object and studied it for a moment before holding it out towards me. "Do you know what this is, sir?"

It was a round medallion made of bronze with a fish on it. The fish had the letters *XP* underneath it, overlaid in a monogram: *chi rho*. The medallion had a hole punched through with a leather thong threaded through it.

"A gift from the guild of Greek fishmongers?" I suggested.

The vigile's brows drew together, and he stared at me as though he was wondering if I was an idiot.

"I've heard about these," I said, finding my solemnity again. "I haven't seen one, no, but if you're asking me what I think that is, I think it's a Christian talisman."

I was no shy flower. I'd been around and seen a few strange things in my time, and I'd come across a few strange cults as well. In the Tenth Legion, it was Mithras, an eastern cult popular with the legionaries. Mithras was like

47

a forgotten acquaintance now I was back in the civilised world, but that didn't mean I'd never heard of him or seen his name scratched into helmets for luck. I wasn't blameless. Everyone in the Tenth sacrificed to Mithras. We said our prayers to the gods, to the lares, to the great Caesar and his descendants, but out there, it was Mithras who protected us. Back from the Tenth, I locked Mithras away with my helmet and armour and skipped merrily off to the hometown temples again. Hadn't I seen the same thing here tonight? Drunken former military tribunes, saluting the sun. I could defend my time praying to Mithras by saying it was harmless. Not all cults were. I shook away thoughts of Mithras and tried to remember what I'd heard about these Christians.

"It's a Jewish sect," I said. "I don't know much about it, but their god was crucified." Which wasn't much of an end for any kind of god. "And something about fish, obviously."

"And what could Albanus have to do with that?" Atreus asked, regarding the dead man thoughtfully.

"I don't know," I said. "Tonight was the first time I ever met him. I certainly didn't know him well enough to ask if he had more than a passing interest in strange cults."

"Sir?" the vigile asked Florian.

"No," said Florian, his eyes wide. "No, I don't think so."

Atreus was silent again.

"I think that's everything," said the physician, at last, patting Albanus's forearm absently.

"Thanks, Leander." Atreus flipped the amulet over in his palm, inspecting both sides carefully, and then reached under his cloak to loop the little artefact onto his belt. He looked at Florian for a moment and then turned his gaze back to me. "I think you can help me, sir, by telling me who was at this dinner."

"Of course."

Atreus and I moved into the triclinium where the commissatio had taken place. I took a couch, and he took one opposite. Atreus played the silent game again and waited for me to tell him something while his gaze slid over

48

the room. The upturned couch, the smashed glassware, the spilled wine, and the vomit. Drunkenness and debauchery, the twin staples of bachelors' parties since time immemorial. It took me back to my own misspent youth. And to a few hours ago, obviously. I was still misspending it.

Finally, his gaze slipped back to me again.

I sighed. "I already told you I didn't know anyone here. I came with Gavius Silanus, who was trying to hitch his daughter up with Albanus."

"Are you a friend of his?"

"No, I'm his ex-wife's current husband," I said and gave him a moment to work through that. "My wife asked me to come and check out Albanus, so I came."

If he thought I was henpecked, he didn't say. He reached under his cloak and produced a wax tablet and a stylus. "Who else was here tonight?"

"Jupiter," I said, trying to cast my mind back. "Everyone. Even old Macrinus turned up. It was standing room only. I was surprised I made it to the main table. You'd have to ask the slaves."

Atreus nodded, but he didn't give up. "What about the others at your table?"

I thought back. "Albanus. Silanus, obviously. Um, Marcellus Naso, who is Albanus's uncle. Some senator called Nepos, who is a dead certain for consul next year, and Claudius Rufanus of *the* Claudians. And Florian, of course."

Atreus raised his eyebrows. "Yes, sir, the man who *found* the body."

I waved the insinuation away. "Look, Florian probably never made it out of the commissatio. He was a mess. He probably came to and stumbled over Albanus, just like I did. There was no knife in that room, his hands were clean, and the body was already cold."

The vigile nodded. "Yes, there was no knife. Who else was at your table, sir?"

"A senator called Paulinus, and some provincial called Caraca who didn't understand a word all night." The mention of Paulinus had made me think of the argument I had witnessed in the peristyle.

Atreus was observant. "What is it?"

"I did see Paulinus and Albanus arguing."

"What about?"

"A freedman called Anicetus turned up uninvited," I said. "He's the head of the fleet at Misenum, but he still wasn't welcome here. Paulinus told Albanus to get rid of him. Albanus did, and they were friends again."

"I'm sure this is very helpful," the vigile said in a doubtful tone. He frowned. "Who do you think killed him?"

I was surprised at the suddenness of the question. "I really have no idea. Frankly, Albanus seemed an idiot. Whether he was an idiot who made enemies or not, I don't know."

I could tell he didn't like my answer. He wanted to narrow the field. "How close are you to your wife's daughter?"

"I'd love it if Julia got married and got out of my hair for good, except if she was miserable, then her mother would be miserable. And then I would be miserable. So while I might want her tucked up with a husband somewhere, I don't wish a bad husband on her." I narrowed my eyes. "And I wouldn't kill a husband I didn't approve of either."

I would leave that to Fulvia, obviously.

Atreus took another tack. "Did you hear anything in the night?"

"No," I said. "I was holed up in a bedroom with one of the dancers, and I was unconscious the moment I hit the mattress."

He looked slightly concerned, as if he thought I should have tried to keep that to myself. "I see."

I didn't need to justify myself to a moralistic plebeian vigile who had apparently forgotten the word *sir*. I was getting tired of all this. I felt queasy. I wanted my own bed and someone to mop my troubled brow. I wanted to have a whinge to Fulvia about how I was mistreated by the vigiles.

I exhaled heavily. "We're done."

He looked surprised at finding out I had a backbone after all.

"Thank you for your time, sir," he said, remembering his manners too late.

I wasn't completely unsympathetic. I could imagine the solid walls men like Atreus came up against whenever they dealt with patricians, but if they

50

forgot their place as often as he managed, I wasn't surprised. He had no authority over me. The man who did, but who would be far too socially conscious to exert it, was just arriving. He barged in looking important, freshly shaved, and wearing an immaculate toga. No wonder the vigiles had beaten him—they hadn't stopped for manicures.

It was a face I recognised from Uncle Maro's. Septus Severus must have been the closest magistrate, a praetor who strutted about proudly showing off his influence. Severus was a portly man with a face flushed with good health. Rumour had it that was because his third wife was twenty years younger than him and athletic in ways he'd never imagined.

Atreus rose to his feet.

"Ah, Valerius!" Severus exclaimed, ignoring the vigile completely. "How are you?" Then he remembered. "It's a terrible business, just terrible. Have you seen the body?"

"I'm afraid so, Severus," I said solemnly. I would teach Atreus a thing or two about manners. "I hope you are well. How is Lucia Balbia? And your children?"

He looked pleased at the remembrances in these difficult circumstances. "Very well, thank you. I shall pass your good wishes on. I hope your household is also well. Is Fulvia Drusa in good health?"

"She is, thank you." I noticed that Atreus was fidgeting. "I saw my Uncle Maro this morning. He holds you in the highest regard." That wasn't true, but who would care? Who would even know? Maro was mad, but not crazy enough to run down a praetor in public.

"That regard is mutual, Valerius," Severus said. "Your family is always in our prayers."

"You honour us," I replied. "And likewise."

Our unnecessary pleasantries over, Severus turned to the fidgeting vigile. "Where's your centurion, whatsit?"

"Atticus is visiting his family outside the city, sir."

"Who are you then?"

"Junius Atreus, sir." A resentful tone that Severus was too self-important to notice.

"Well, I hope you haven't kept Quintus Aemilius too long!" Severus exclaimed. He shot me a concerned look.

I shrugged and smiled, like a man who had been hassled unbearably but was too polite to say so.

"Well, get out, get out!" Severus chided.

"Sir?" Atreus asked.

Severus scowled at him. "Go and take the slaves away. Make yourself useful, can't you?"

Atreus snapped his wax tablet shut and strode outside.

Severus lowered himself onto a couch. "Honestly, Valerius, I can't do a thing with them! Such insolence!"

"Public duty can take a heavy toll," I sympathised.

"Certainly, certainly," Severus sighed. He gave me a worried glance. "Any luck on a position for yourself yet?"

* * *

The slaves were herded away. Some shouted, some begged, and some wept. It was a long procession, and I turned slightly in my seat so I wouldn't have to watch it pass. They would all be questioned, under torture as the law dictated, and probably executed unless it could be proved beyond doubt that none of them had killed their master. And even if the murderer cowered somewhere in those wailing ranks, what a waste it was.

"Wine, Valerius?" Severus asked in a friendly tone. He had uncovered an unopened jar from under his couch.

"Yes, thank you."

"The cratera has been broken," he said fretfully.

"We'll have to drink it straight then."

"Oh, yes," said Severus with a smile. Outside, a child was crying.

I understood the law as follows: the slave who killed his master was executed for murder, and his fellows for keeping their silence and making it a conspiracy. How unfair for them if the killer had plotted alone as he went about his duties, or if he spilled blood in a moment of great passion without

52

any thought for the consequences. This was why we Romans encouraged our slaves to intermingle and produce families within our households. It was a civilised form of hostage-taking that safeguarded us.

"This is a fine vintage," Severus said, raising his voice to be heard over the wailing outside.

"I think I brought that," I agreed. "I think it's left over from my wedding feast." I leaned forward to check the label. "Yes, that's the one."

"Excellent taste," Severus said approvingly. I wondered if he meant the Falernian or me.

We sat for a moment, savouring our lucky find.

"Listen, Severus," I said when I couldn't keep my thoughts off matters any longer. "The strangest thing turned up in that room."

"Really?"

"A Christian talisman, of all things," I said. I lowered my voice to a conspiring tone, hoping to draw him in. "What would Albanus have to do with that?"

"I can't imagine!" Severus looked appropriately shocked.

"It's an intriguing thought, this link to a strange cult."

Severus's unhappy face told him I was breaching the protocol of such things. "Please, Valerius," he said firmly. "This is neither the time nor the place. Whatever the facts, I'll pass them on as soon as I'm fully appraised."

"Of course, I apologise."

I paddled my bare feet on the floor. The one concession we were making to the circumstances was remaining seated upright and not reclining as we drank our very fine wine and ignored the fact there was a corpse lying in the next room.

"Master! Master!"

For a moment, I thought one of the slaves was crying out for Albanus. It took my addled brain a little while to recognise that voice.

"Wait!" To the surprise of Severus, I flew outside and grabbed the nearest vigile. It wasn't Atreus. "Wait! That one's mine!"

Juba's dark face flooded with relief. His massive shoulders sagged. He stepped gladly away from the custody of the vigiles.

"I told them I didn't live here," he muttered to me.

I gave Juba a reassuring smile and then waved my hand at the vigile in that lazy patrician manner that most plebeians didn't like much. "Where are my litter bearers?"

"All the litter bearers are outside in the street still, sir," growled the burly vigile.

Thank Jupiter for that. I would have hated to walk home.

"Perhaps you should tell your acting centurion that he would do well not to deprive tonight's guests of their property," I said. Rounding up Albanus's slaves was bad enough. Rounding up everyone else's would be a travesty.

"Yes, sir," the vigile grumbled.

I looked around the atrium. The musicians were collecting their instruments, and the dancers were searching for their discarded scarves. They were about to slink off without pay; a sad day was breaking for them. Not as sad as the one about to break for Albanus's slaves, but at least they wouldn't have long to wallow in self-pity. In hindsight, that probably wasn't much consolation at all.

I wandered back to Severus, accompanied by Juba, who was sticking to me like a limpet. "I think I'll head home, Severus. If you need to talk to me, you know where to find me."

He waved me away. "I doubt I'll have to bother you with this again, Valerius!"

How he possibly thought a small conversation about the health of our families and the vintage of a jar of Falernian constituted an investigation, I would never know. He might have been a competent jurist and prosecutor, but the truth struck me that Severus couldn't find an elephant with a nosebleed in the snow.

"Goodnight, Severus." I moved towards the atrium. "Juba, see if you can find my sandals. I'll be outside. If you have any problems, just yell."

Juba padded off warily, but the vigiles knew his face now. He would be fine. I had to find the front door and get home and into bed before my family started asking awkward questions like *What do you mean he's dead?*

The vigile Junius Atreus was standing by the door. I ignored him and

54

swept past. I could feel his gaze on me as I stood out in the street, waiting for my sandals and my litter. I needed at least one of them to get home. While I waited on the impressive portico that still smelled of rosewater, I saw Ledo, one of my litter bearers, heading down the street towards me.

"What's happened, sir?" he asked.

I spoke in an undertone so the vigile couldn't hear me. "Did the vigiles give you any grief, Ledo?"

"No, sir," said Ledo. "They took our names and our masters' names."

"Good," I said. "Go and fetch the litter."

He headed off again.

Juba met me at the portico shortly afterward. He still looked shaken.

"Juba, did the vigiles do a headcount of the slaves?"

"They're doing it now," Juba said.

"Well?"

Juba nodded, collecting his thoughts. "It looks like they're weeding out all the guests' slaves now. Most of the boys from the commissatio are still here. There are no slaves missing, though."

"How do you know that?"

Juba shrugged. "I was in line next to Albanus's secretary. He told me so."

I sighed and looked down the street. I could see my litter bearers approaching.

"A moment, sir!" Atreus was stubborn.

"What is it?"

The vigile moved to get between me and my approaching litter. "I wanted to apologise, sir. I was rude, and I'm sorry."

I was suspicious. Rude, certainly, but apologetic? I doubted that. "There's no need to apologise."

"I want to make it up to you, sir," he said doggedly.

"How's that?"

He gave me a smile that was calculated to be charming. I had my own charming smile, so I wasn't fooled.

"Allow me to escort you home," he said.

"That's not necessary."

"I insist, sir."

Great. Now he knew where I lived.

* * *

I felt sober by the time we had shuffled to a stop outside my house; all that wine I had guzzled had worn off rapidly since Marcellus Albanus, and I had our final fateful meeting. Sober, but I wouldn't have trusted myself to start juggling Samian dinnerware. It was easy to feel wrung out once the party was over and the wine had worked its way out of your body one way or another, but with a corpse thrown in as well, it was no wonder I sat in my litter looking pensive. I was the picture of sombre Roman nobility. I was showing the world my profile, resting my chin against my knuckles in brooding thought. The world was asleep and didn't give a fuck.

All the way home Juba's torch had been throwing back strange shadows that played across the street and the closed walls we passed. Once I glimpsed the vigile mooching along in the shadows, looking even more dark and brooding than I did, but he must have slipped away by the time Juba helped me out of the litter at home, and I found my feet again. I had never been so glad to see my familiar portico.

"Goodnight, sir," a voice called. The vigile was hanging about still, and he had the satisfaction of seeing my startled face before he loped off into the darkness. Hopefully, he would get mugged on his way to whatever Transtiberina rat-infested diseased bolthole he called home.

Juba pounded against the door until Hursa, bleary-eyed and unkempt, opened it and peered at us warily as though he thought burglars might knock.

"Did you hear any good jokes tonight, sir?" he asked as he ushered us in.

"Not really." It seemed like an age since Paulinus had entertained the Gaul and me with his smutty jokes.

Hursa's face fell.

"Go and wake the mistress," I told him.

"At this hour, sir?"

"Go on." I wanted Fulvia to know before the whole city did, and that wouldn't take long. If dawn was already as close as I suspected, respectable men would be getting out of bed already and preparing to head to the Forum to conduct their daily business of schmoozing and gossiping.

Fulvia met me in my bedroom, where I spilled the whole sorry tale. Apart, of course, from the bit about the Hispanian dancer. I wasn't a total idiot.

"Oh, Quintus, you poor thing," she said and held me while I felt miserable. There was nothing sweeter than Fulvia's sympathy.

Chapter Four

Mad Uncle Maro was the first to turn up on my doorstep the next morning to congratulate me on attending the most talked about banquet in months. Not since Justus Lupercius had destroyed his career, reputation, and family name by being discovered behind a curtain taking it up the arse from a gladiator had patricians the length of the city wished they got out more. The Forum was buzzing with the news, the bathhouses were awash with it, and my name was already being mentioned as the man who was in the know when it came to the gory details. It had been a party to remember, and not in the way Marcellus Albanus had intended. No one cared how many slaves held up how many torches, or how many musicians played for how many dancers. No one even cared if the shellfish was done up as a trireme or an anatomically correct sculpture of Venus and Mars with mechanical moving parts. All anyone wanted to know was exactly what Maro asked me as he kicked me out of bed.

"Who did the poor idiot in?" He leered at me suspiciously and tugged at the hair that grew out of his ears.

"How should I know?" I ached all over. My eyeballs hurt. I needed to sleep for another few days, at least.

"Come off it, Quintus! What happened?" His balding crown gleamed in the morning light. He reminded me of a manic stork—long legs, flapping arms, and a pointed beak. I felt like a frog under attack.

I struggled out of bed, picked myself up off the floor, and staggered over to my washbasin. I splashed myself for a little while, wiped myself on last night's sweaty tunic, and hunted for something clean to wear. Maro watched me, squint-eyed.

I was looking forward to a leisurely breakfast followed by a lengthy nap on my reading couch, then maybe a little snack, a trip to the baths, and home again for dinner and a good night's sleep. Whatever happened last night to Marcellus Albanus was no business of mine. I had done my bit—like a community-spirited patrician, I had given my testament to the representatives of the law. It wasn't my problem that one of them (the vigile) was a suspicious-minded plebeian with an inferiority complex, and the other (Septus Severus) could only be the result of generations of reckless inbreeding. I had my own business to worry about.

Maro, reading my expression, growled and scrubbed his stubby fingers over the remains of his hair. He regarded me unhappily, like something that had crawled out of a bog onto his favourite couch. "You're a disgrace."

I shrugged, knowing there was no real insult in his words.

Despite all his moralising of late, there wasn't a single other person in the city whose couches I could lounge on, whose wine I could drink, and whose daily business I could interrupt as freely as Uncle Maro's. I needed to cultivate a circle of friends. Before I was sent away to play soldier, I had a whole tribe of drunken young idiots I called friends. Our fathers must have got together and hatched a conspiracy to free us from their purse strings. More or less, we were all shipped off to the army at the same time in our spanking new uniforms, creaking leather, and polished greaves, hoping our helmets would hide our pale homesickness. Most of those drunken young idiots were now still serving in legions sitting on the edges of the empire. Stuck in windy forts, thinking about their careers, the ineptitude of their superiors, the attitude of their subordinates, that girl at the taberna with the big breasts, and probably wishing they were back in Rome like me. I didn't know any drunken young idiots anymore. I only knew a few dull middle-aged senators, a few pretentious old senators, and at least one quaestor who was working on becoming both dull and pretentious as he got older.

My father had been embarrassingly proud of me when I'd been recalled to Rome. I was mentioned in the Curia, and I met the emperor. I think I realised before my father did that the job offers weren't going to come flooding in. I had saved the life of the celebrated general Domitius Corbulo, and Corbulo had sent me back to Rome in the expectation that it would make my career. It hadn't. There were politics at work that neither of us had anticipated. Rome was ruled by a young emperor who had never led an army and who possibly feared that those armies were more loyal to their generals than to him. Nero was wary of Corbulo's success and maybe even jealous of his popularity. Thus, I was publicly feted by the emperor, but not privately rewarded. My father didn't understand it, and the disappointment had worn him down almost overnight. He had been disappointed with Nero for not promising me a plum position, disappointed with his friends for following the emperor's lead, disappointed with Corbulo for sending me home for nothing, and ultimately disappointed with me for having failed to live up to his expectations. He had died disappointed. I regretted that.

"Come on, get moving!"

Uncle Maro, with no consideration for my aching head, called for Juba to wrap me in a toga, and then I was bundled out of my own front door with an apple in my cupped palms and into Maro's palatial litter. His squad of bearers hoisted us up into the air, and we moved with the speed of a furious tempest. My eyes told me I was in the litter, my brain told me I was still in bed, and my stomach told me I was going to be sick. I stuck my head out and twisted my neck to get a look at my receding front portico. Juba was walking behind the litter with the resigned look of someone who didn't know where he was being led but was obliged to follow all the same. I knew how he felt, but at least I wasn't walking. Uncle Maro tried to cross-examine me. I closed my eyes and tried not to hear him.

The city was already awake and noisy, two things I held against it. The tradesmen at the bottom of the hill had been at work for hours; they were clattering and hammering away at whatever it was they did to pay the rent. We turned towards the low-lying Forum, nestled between the serpentine river and the encircling hills, and joined the traffic heading that way. At the intersection of two main roads, we met a crowd. Maro's litter bearers took the opportunity for a breather, and I tossed my apple core outside.

Maro was seated opposite me; our knees rubbed together every jolt of the journey. Maro was not a traveller. He disliked even small journeys. When he went to Baiae for the summer, he took almost his whole household, including most of the strange furniture he and Aunt Marcia couldn't bear to be without. He would take the whole neighbourhood if there were any way of packing it. Even in his litter, for the short trips across Rome, he kept close to hand the comforts of home—scrolls he felt the need to peruse every few moments, letters he could answer between his house on the Esquiline and the Curia, a jar of wine, a small box of dried fruit pieces, and enough cushions to fill the Circus Maximus. He was wedged comfortably among all these items, as snug as a bug in a rug.

"So, what happened?" he said, in a serious tone this time.

I told him everything. Well, apart from Nicius, the Hispanian dancer. I named all of the guests I could remember, I repeated those parts of conversations that were still with me this morning, and I even mentioned what I thought of Severus and his total lack of investigative skills.

"Sounds like Albanus had friends in high places," my mad relation pondered. He knew the who's who of the city backwards. "Nepos is bound to make consul next year, Macrinus is very distinguished, and Claudius Rufanus is one of *the* Claudians, you know."

"So I've heard."

My mad relation sucked his teeth for a moment. "And, invited or not, Anicetus is Anicetus."

"What does that mean?" The man who had been identified to me as the head of the fleet at Misenum and an ex-slave, had seemed bland and inoffensive. He had looked more like a nondescript little bureaucrat than a naval commander.

Maro looked wary. "If you are friends with Anicetus, you are friends with the palace."

"Strange that they chucked him out then," I said. "So, who is this Anicetus?"

"He should be a nobody. He's an ex-slave who has wormed his way upwards. Rumour has it that if you cross the palace, it's Anicetus you'll meet in a dark alley."

I was intrigued by Maro's guarded tone. "Do you fear Anicetus?"

"Loyal subjects of the emperor have no need to fear Anicetus." Maro was tricky. He would never answer a question like that directly.

"The emperor's just a boy," I said dismissively. "Since when did he start ruling the empire anyway?"

The litter bearers moved forward again, taking us into the stream of pedestrian traffic that headed towards the Forum. I suspected that I knew our destination. If I was right, we would branch off before reaching that great buzzing hive of activity.

Maro raised his eyebrows. "About the same time you started marching up and down the frontiers yelling at legionaries and picking lice out of your blankets, my boy. The triumvirate isn't what it was."

Not since the late great J.C. came up with the idea had a more effective triumvirate ruled Rome. The triumvirates of Caesar and Octavian were notoriously unbalanced (who remembers Lepidus these days?) and created to crumble so that those two great men could shrug their shoulders and pretend they'd had a real go at sharing the reins of power, and it was unfortunate in the end they'd had to kill the other guys. Ever since Octavian got rid of that pesky Antony, Rome had been ruled by one man alone, for better or for worse. That's the road that J.C. paved with his dictatorship, that Octavian trod carefully in his years as Augustus, and their successors had either trudged along miserably complaining about the blisters (Tiberius), skipped along like a loon giggling madly (good old Caligula), and finally limped along cautiously waiting for an ambush (Claudius). Bets were still on for how Nero would travel, although most would agree he'd started well enough. Not that he had walked, of course—he had been carried. Which brought me to the triumvirate.

First there was Burrus, prefect of the Praetorian Guard. A big man with an impressive pedigree and an unswerving devotion to Nero. Next, there was Seneca, ex-tutor and chief advisor to the young emperor. He was learned, disciplined, and had a large enough collection of moral essays to justify nasty political decisions from which less well-read men would quail. Finally, there was Agrippina, Nero's doting mother. Beautiful, charming, and plotting away for years to get herself back into the family's favour. She married her uncle Claudius and made him adopt Nero as his heir. She was the ambition, and at one time, she was rapacious. Between the three of them, they had ruled the emperor and the world. Maro was right, though. While I'd been struggling to liberate Armenia from the Parthians, Nero had been struggling to liberate himself from the triumvirate. Accusations of conspiracy and embezzlement were enough for Burrus and Seneca to pull their heads in and let the emperor make his own decisions, but Agrippina was made of sterner stuff. Nero owed her his empire, and they both knew it.

I learned all my politics from Uncle Maro. He was always far more open than my father, who wore himself ragged trying to stay on the right side of powerful men. Maro detested the machinations of politics. Never a friend, never an enemy, Maro had generally kept his head down his whole career. He was known for it. The divine Claudius had even laughed when he'd found out Maro had been the only man who hadn't added his support to a motion by the senate to give Claudius some new title because he had been distracted designing his new peristyle. Corinthian or Doric—Maro's dilemmas were so much simpler than politics.

My father had been the exact opposite. He had courted important men, he had voted the right way, and he had loved Britannicus. Britannicus, he had lectured me, was sensible, intelligent, and modest, the flower of a family that had managed to all but wipe itself out in a few generations of power lust. Despite his mother's immodest temperament, and despite his father's physical infirmities, Britannicus was the model of young Roman manhood. He was all of those things, and he was Claudius's natural son. He had been a risk the triumvirate couldn't allow. His poisoning had been purely political, but my father had taken it personally. At the time, I had selfishly wondered if my father would have regretted my passing so bitterly.

My knees knocked against Maro's as we traversed the city.

"I wonder if Anicetus works for the emperor or his mother," Maro mused. "It used to be the same thing."

Mari shrugged. "Not anymore."

Agrippina had tried to keep Nero in line, like any mother. She tolerated his drunkenness, his fits of pique, his poetry, and his music. The one thing she had never tolerated was his public infidelity with the freedwoman Acte and Nero's desire to divorce his wife to marry her. Her recent withdrawal from public life reflected her disapproval. Agrippina was ambitious, and she had even been cruel to satisfy that ambition, but that was the worst anyone could say of her.

We turned off the main road. Uncle Maro was still deep in thought.

"Where are we going exactly?" I asked him at last, although I already knew. I was thinking longingly of my reading couch and wondering if I had the energy today to attend to my household responsibilities.

Mad Uncle Maro drew a deep breath. "We are going to visit Marcellus Naso." He gave me a moment to groan, which he would have pounced on like a cat on a mouse, and when I didn't whinge, he looked miffed.

"Yes, I should pay my respects."

"Yes, you should," he said suspiciously, searching for sarcasm. "I expect he'll have some questions for you as well. If you play it right, Quintus, you could come out of this with Naso's respect."

"Hmm." I doubted there was anything I could do to win Naso's respect. I could only try to be courteous and sincere and not think about the last time I was at Naso's house when I made an idiot of myself and lost the chance of a good job.

Marcellus Naso kept a house on the other side of the Campus Martius, nestled in a sinuous bend of the Tiber. From his back garden, a series of paved terraces looked out over the river. Naso's section of the river was restful and exclusive, but not too far along, the drowsy flowing water turned into a jammed highway of river traffic. Barges, skiffs, flotillas of abusive boatmen, people spitting from bridges, and the refuse of the whole city washing up in the Transtiberina.

I knew the house well enough, although my memories were blurred at the edges. I had reclined in his airy dining room, paced admiringly over his sloping terraces, leaned against his elegant colonnades, toured his private library, thrown up in his potted palms, and collapsed into his impluvium. Naso was on the water board. Thanks to the embarrassment I'd caused him as a guest only two nights ago, I never would be.

Marcellus Naso's house was a house of mourning. There was no outward sign of it, but a tradesman was being turned away from the front door as we arrived at the spacious portico. A small group of idle sightseers had gathered on the road. A pie cart had been trundled along to cater for them. I could hear bets being laid as to whether or not Maro and I would make it inside. We walked to the portico slowly.

"Know this," said Maro in an undertone as we approached the door. "Every new scandal wipes our slate clean, just a little bit. Act well."

If Naso had banned me from ever crossing his threshold again, it was already forgotten. A subdued door porter admitted us without fuss. The house felt empty. All daily activity had been suspended out of respect for the grieving master. As we gazed at the tastefully expensive mosaics, the only noise we heard was the door porter treading quietly back to fetch us.

Marcellus Naso met Uncle Maro and me in his library. An entire wall was given over to a row of narrow shelves containing scrolls, all tagged and pigeonholed and the envy of a modest collector like myself. This library was large and airy. It was furnished with several reading couches, the busts of a few illustrious Marcellii, what looked like a collection of Etruscan sculptures, and a large rosewood table with scalloped edges and curved legs inlaid with enough mother-of-pearl to feed a family of twelve for a month. Despite the opulence, the library had a comfortable, lived-in feel. I could imagine myself with a library like this. In a riverside property like this. With polite slaves like the one who now offered up a platter of perfect breakfast pastries and pretended he didn't remember fishing me out of the impluvium two nights ago.

Naso was seated on a stool at the far end of the library. There was a young man seated on the floor at his feet. From his position, I initially thought it must have been a slave, offering his master some silent comfort, but I saw that it was a familiar face from last night: young Avitus Florian. When he saw us, he climbed to his feet and lent Marcellus Naso his arm.

Naso rose slowly. His eyes were red and rimmed with shadows. He was unshaven and looked like he had aged a decade overnight. He was wearing a long tunic and had bare feet. I had never seen him without a toga before.

Uncle Maro furrowed his brow. "My condolences, Naso. How are you keeping?"

"Ah, Maro!" Naso looked distraught suddenly. Maybe every new face intruding on his privacy would witness his grief freshly. Then, abruptly, he sighed. "Oh, I am well, I am well."

My uncle had no answer for such a blatant lie, so he reached out and embraced Naso. I had forgotten what close friends they had been in their youth and had hardly believed it when I'd first been told. Maro was a mad old lunatic, and Naso was a pretentious old git. What could they ever have had in common?

Naso stepped away from the embrace finally and seemed to recover himself. His eyes glinted with some of their customary ferocity, but then softened when they fell on me. Perhaps he was thinking of irresponsible nephews all over the world.

"Valerius, when I left before the commissatio I had no thought as to how tragedy would strike my poor boy down. What happened?"

I felt like a prisoner under excruciating torture. I told him about the commissatio, looking to Avitus Florian for his unhappy nods of confirmation. I told him about drinking too much wine. I told him about stumbling over Albanus. I told him about the blood because he didn't want to be spared the details, and the wound, and the way the upstart of a vigile seemed at least competent. And following the golden rule about never running down those men who were more socially and politically important than yourself, I finished by stating that the magistrate Severus had everything under control. I kept something back: the little bronze amulet that Florian had discovered. I weighed up my omission with sophistry. I mentioned how much I had liked Albanus, what a tragic loss he was, and how I knew he would have made Julia a fine husband.

"I appreciate your coming here to tell me all of this," said Naso at length. He looked bitter. "None of his other *friends* have done so, except for Florian." His face screwed up again, and he looked to my uncle for support. Uncle Maro drew Naso aside, leaving me to make awkward conversation with Avitus Florian.

I glanced at Florian. His face was pale. "It was good of you to come," I said.

"Albanus was my cousin," the young man said, and I felt a rush of sympathy for him. No wonder he had been such a mess last night.

"I didn't know, I'm sorry. Your uncle must be comforted by your presence." I hunted for a few more platitudes.

"He's not my uncle." Florian motioned the slave with the pastries back over and gave us both the chance to feed our hangovers. "Albanus and I were cousins on our mothers' side. Naso was his paternal uncle."

"Then it was good of you to come," I said, meaning it this time. He only looked about nineteen or twenty, wasn't even related by blood to the old man, and here he was making an effort to pay his respects when he could have been at home receiving condolences from his own friends.

Florian lowered his voice and nodded in Naso's direction. "Marcellus Naso has always been kind to me. I couldn't let him spend today alone."

"And how are *you* holding up?" I helped myself to a pastry.

Florian managed a slight smile. "I don't know. Ask me again in a month."

He looked lost. I put my hand on his shoulder like we were old friends. I'd felt sorry for Florian last night at the commissatio because he'd been forced to drink, and I had thought he was weak. His actions today convinced me that he had a reserve of strength that most of those other fools at the commissatio would have envied had they understood it. None of them were here.

"Thank you," said Florian at last.

I helped myself to another pastry. It was delicious—savoury and hot—and I no longer regretted being dragged here by Uncle Maro. The pastries were just what I needed to rediscover my vitality. Uncle Maro, who must have guessed this was not the time for me to rediscover it, announced that he would remain with Naso for a while, and I was welcome to take his litter home.

Naso thanked me again. I murmured something about my great sympathy to both Naso and Florian, and left Uncle Maro to take care of them. On the way out, I asked the door porter if there were any more pastries left. He snarled at me, and I guessed who had to clean up the potted palms on my last visit.

I met Juba outside and let him clear a way through the questioning sightseers to the pie cart.

I bought a pie each for Juba and myself and then lounged comfortably in Uncle Maro's litter and waited to be carried aloft.

Juba's pie was a bribe. By the disgusted look on his face, not a very good one. I motioned him to the side of the litter and had him commit to memory a message I needed delivered. He set off in a direction away from home.

If the death of Marcellus Albanus had taught me anything, it was that life was fleeting. I had wasted too many months wallowing in regret. Today I was going to get sorted out, get organised, and become the young Roman patrician I should have been by now. Today I would sort out my accounts, buy some new slaves, plot selling a quarter of a racehorse to someone stupid enough to buy it, and then I would go home and be learned and strict, and disciplined and sober, and before you knew it the old Aemilius Valerius would be, but a shadow, and in his place would stand the new, improved paterfamilias.

* * *

Alcipides was an Alexandrian Greek with a dark, pointed beard and slicked back hair. He wore a dark crown of oiled curls plastered to his forehead, a slathering of perfume, and enough heavy jewellery that if he ever slid underwater in the baths, he'd be in serious trouble. He'd leave nothing behind but a surprised masseuse and an oil slick.

His warehouse was behind the Emporium, beside a rundown temple to some has-been cult. The ragged priest sat on the steps, chopping beans on a board that rested across his knees. He didn't even glance up as Maro's impressive litter was carried past. I left Maro's litter bearers at the door, where they briefly renewed their acquaintance with Juba. Having trotted here briskly, Juba was shiny with sweat, and he didn't look happy. I nodded at him that he should follow me in.

I'd only been here once before, a greasy little sprog at my father's side. Alcipides didn't remember me, and I didn't expect him to, but he knew to expect me thanks to the message Juba had delivered a little while earlier. By the time I reached him he had already placed me in his mental ledger according to my wealth and reputation. Way below Caesar and, if my accountant Philosthones was right, somewhere very close to Croesus.

"Quintus Aemilius," he said, annunciating my formal name in a smooth and deferential tone that made me worry about my personal safety. "Your father was a valued client of mine, and I was honoured to also consider him a friend."

My smile felt as insincere as his toadying. I addressed him in that special tone Roman patricians kept for foreigners. The one that was slightly too loud and slow, as though all foreigners were deaf. "I hope you can assist me in locating what I need."

"Of course!" Alcipides smiled and nodded. "Please, sit down."

I sat, and Juba stood behind me. I could feel his agitation. He had been here before and under very different circumstances. Alcipides waved a slave over, and the child set wine down before us. Setinum. Good quality.

Alcipides consulted a little wax tablet that lay in front of him. "I don't have much on the premises at the moment, Quintus Aemilius. What were you after?"

I wasn't going to give this man the impression my house was understaffed. "I am in the process of expanding one of my villas, and I have need of a small complement. I need litter bearers, an outdoor slave, and a secretary."

He consulted the list, and, like a true salesman, ignored what I'd just told him. "I have a good cook I came by through the estate of Fulvius Lanius."

"I have no need of a cook."

Alcipides smiled. "Of course. Litter bearers, I can supply immediately.

How many do you require?"

"Four should be sufficient at this time."

"Are you sure?" Alcipides obviously thought I was stinting myself.

"Quite."

"I have several suitable outdoor slaves. Male or female?"

"Either. What about a secretary?"

Alcipides showed me his palms. "That may be more difficult, Quintus Aemilius. I'm not sure I have anything suitable."

"The estate of Fulvius Lanius did not offer up anything at all?"

Alcipides gave me a pained look. "Perhaps there is something I can do."

This would cost me.

"I was keeping a secretary aside for another client."

Oh yes, this would cost me a lot.

"My client will be disappointed, naturally."

I could see my bank box in the Basilica Julia start to haemorrhage money.

"I'm afraid I couldn't let this slave go cheaply."

Visions of my entire family begging in an Aventine alleyway.

"He is highly educated."

My end in a mass grave, so tragically young.

"You understand, of course."

"Of course." Why was he wearing an unhappy look like I was forcing him to try to bankrupt me? I drank my wine and tried not to look ripped off. *What is mere money to me? Son of a senator, descendant of Marcus Aemilius Scaurus etcetera.* "When can I have a look at them?"

Alcipides consulted his list. "I have most of them out the back at the moment. One of the litter bearers will need to come from my place in Ostia."

"What about the secretary?" I wasn't going to order sight unseen for a secretary. I wanted to be absolutely sure about the high levels of education I was mortgaging my future for.

"He is here now. I was going to send him to his new household this afternoon." Alcipides gave me a friendly wink. "Unfortunately, he has been taken badly with a fever and will probably die."

I couldn't help but be impressed by his underhanded tactics. "Can I see him?"

"Please, come this way."

Juba and I fell in behind him.

The bulk of the warehouse was in stark contrast to the office. It was largely bare, with row upon row of hard benches upon which were seated row upon row of slaves. I didn't like to think about how many slaves passed through here in any given week, either sent out to the markets with Alcipides's agents or kept for private sale. The men sat on one side, the women on the other. Like the artefacts in Alcipides's office, they could be read as a guide to the empire. Tall hulking Africans, pale blonde Germans, dark little Britons, bronze-skinned Syrians, bearded Judaeans, and narrow-faced Egyptians. Men, women, children, something for everyone. They were guarded by burly men carrying sticks. It was probably an unnecessary precaution. Most of these slaves would have had the fight beaten out of them a long time ago. Those that hadn't would be served up in the arena. I found myself thinking about Marcellus Albanus's slaves and wondering if any of them would survive to find their way back into bare barracks like these.

Alcipides went over his list with the overseer. A few slaves were being picked out by the numerical tags they wore around their necks. Alcipides would have no time for names. He saw hundreds of slaves a year.

I was shown one of my new litter bearers. He looked young enough and big enough to lift and carry for years to come. I queried his background. Originally a prisoner of war, he had since had two masters and come back to Alcipides after their respective exile and death highly recommended. Not highly enough, but litter bearers were always at the bottom of the list when it came to granting manumissions. My new outdoor slave looked competent enough to carry a platter without dropping it and capable of keeping the garden neat and tidy. My new expensive secretary was Greek, always a good sign. He wasn't exactly elderly, but neither was he in his prime.

"What's your name?"

"Cretes, sir," he answered, bobbing his balding head respectfully. He cleared his throat like an actor about to deliver a monologue. "I am fully skilled in all the aspects of account keeping, of running a domestic household, and of all fiscal responsibilities attached. I am fluent in speaking, writing, and reading both Latin and Greek, and also have some knowledge of conversational Egyptian."

I could tell he would be a barrel of laughs.

"I trust everything is to your liking," Alcipides smarmed.

"They all seem good quality." I glanced quickly at Juba, and he nodded imperceptibly. I trusted his judgment. He could read these people better than I could. He had the experience. "Send your account to my household."

That would show Alcipides what real wealth meant. Real wealth meant living on credit as far as possible and never carrying around enough cash to buy anything except for a bit of lunch.

I was about to leave when my gaze caught on a golden-haired girl seated on one of the benches. Her skin was as pale as ivory, and even in the gloom of the warehouse, her eyes were a striking blue.

"Ah!" Alcipides followed my gaze. "She would make an excellent pleasure slave, sir."

"No."

Alcipides raised his perfectly sculpted eyebrows and smiled. "Perhaps a boy, sir? I have a lovely youth, as pretty as Narcissus and—"

"No." My stomach twisted. "That will be all."

I declined his offer of another drink in his opulent office and escaped back outside into the sunny street. I sent Maro's litter bearers back to wait for him, and then Juba and I walked briskly towards the shade of the rundown temple. I divested myself of my toga and gave it to Juba to carry. I'd had enough of standing with my arms at odd angles to keep the folds in place. The temple priest, who had looked up hopefully when we wandered towards his sacred shrine, went back to his beans.

There was a greasy caupona on the street corner, and I made a beeline for it, hoping I could outpace the knowing smirk Alcipides had given me when he'd assumed my tastes ran to pretty boys. I secured us a stained table away from the door and ordered bread and stew from the surly waiter.

"It was Alcipides you came from, wasn't it, Juba?" I asked when the food arrived. Making conversation seemed like a safer option than eating. There were some unidentifiable lumps of meat and pale vegetables swirling in the depths of the thin stew and spots of oil floating on top. I felt the pie I had eaten in the litter turn over in my stomach.

Juba nodded. "Yes."

"And?"

"And he's a bastard." There wasn't any rancour in his tone.

Juba had been bought when I was away in the army. I hadn't wondered about his origins further than his being Aethiopian. It had never occurred to ask how he had come to Rome. And glancing at him now, looking all inscrutable, I wondered if I really wanted to know or not.

Juba shot me a wry look.

Sipping my sour wine, I turned my thoughts back to Marcellus Albanus, and I wondered, not for the first time since seeing it, what that strange little amulet had signified. And, of course, I had just walked out of a place where the odds were fair someone might have been able to tell me. Somehow, though, I doubted they would have.

"Did you ever meet any Christians, Juba?" I asked him. "In a place like that, you must talk, yes?"

"In a place like that," he said frankly, "you keep your head down and your mouth shut."

I tipped some of the stew onto the table and traced my finger through it. "Do you know what that is?"

It was the Greek letters *XP*, overlaid, so that the letters formed the same cross I had seen on the amulet that had been discovered with Marcellus Albanus's corpse.

"*Chi rho*," said my astute bodyguard. "Is it Christian?"

"Apparently." I sighed.

"In a place like that, sir," Juba said, "I met a lot of men who prayed to a lot of different gods, but I don't know the difference between a Christian and a Jew."

Neither did I. The Christians might have been a subversive lot, but so were the Jews. They were still known to make a fuss when the legions wanted to have a look in their temples. The difference was that the Jews would behave themselves as long as we Romans gave nominal deference to their traditions and didn't hang legionary standards from their sacred places. From what I'd heard, and it was all rumour, the Christians were a lot more sinister. They wanted to upset the balance.

I wondered what Marcellus Albanus could have had to do with a cult that didn't believe in the supremacy of Rome, that didn't honour the emperor as pontifex maximus, and if that was what had killed him. It was none of my business, but I wanted to know.

"I was in a Mithraic cult when I was in the army."

"That's not illegal, sir."

"It's none of my business what happened to Albanus." I stirred my spoon around in the stew. "I've got enough problems of my own."

I earned another wry look.

"What?"

Juba shrugged. "You have a cook at home, sir, and every day, you go out and buy lunch from a place like this."

I knew what he was getting at. I had neglected my responsibilities for too long, and my problems were my own fault. I'd come home from the army with Corbulo's praise ringing in my ears. It had led nowhere, and my pride was stung. The cynic in me had pretended not to care, had pretended that politics was for hypocrites, and that a father's disappointment was the natural order of things. Politics had snubbed me, so I had snubbed a political career. I got my hair cut in Fish Alley. I played dice in dodgy wine bars and, as Juba had pointed out, I bought food in places that even the rats avoided. I should have redeemed myself before now, but my father's death had shaken me. My father's death, my sister's divorce, Maro's support for an unpopular vote in the senate, and my own drunken behaviour—my family's reputation had taken a battering this year. Fortune turned quickly, and I knew it wouldn't turn back again without a concerted push on my behalf.

I looked sideways at Juba. "You're wasted as a bodyguard."

"I know, sir."

We ate our lunch, and I ordered more wine. The surly waiter grumbled about having to open a new amphora, but it turned out to be worth it. The second batch was better than the first. It was still as thin as vinegar but had less of the sting. It was almost palatable. I might have ordered another cup if the waiter hadn't vanished.

"Look," said Juba, drawing my attention to the shutters that opened out onto the street.

Standing on the footpath, trying to look inconspicuous, was a tall young man who would have looked more familiar to me standing over a corpse. It was Junius Atreus, my friendly neighbourhood vigile.

* * *

I was being plagued by people I would have preferred not to see. When I got home, I found another one talking to Octavia in the garden. It was doddering old Probus Macrinus, a man I had done my best to avoid for months. His presence only ever served to upset Octavia. Macrinus was a reminder of the unhappy end to her marriage. The old man was a relative of Octavia's ex, and had been his patron, and had tried to remain on friendly terms with Octavia. Macrinus was speaking earnestly with her in the shade of the colonnades when I wandered outside.

"Good afternoon, Valerius."

"Good afternoon." I wasn't happy about his being here, but I hoped it didn't show. Macrinus was elderly and esteemed, and a much more important man than I was. "I saw you last night at Albanus's party."

"Oh, yes," said Macrinus in his tremulous old man's voice. "A terrible thing. Terrible."

I nodded gravely. "Yes."

"I wonder what the world is coming to," he said, shaking his head. "It seems like one thing after another lately."

He was right about that.

Macrinus blinked his rheumy eyes. "It does me good to see you're well, though. I wonder if I could ask a favour?"

"Of course." I didn't like Macrinus much, but I knew better than to offend a man of his standing. And I needed to redeem myself for my recent history of stupid drunken behaviour. Macrinus was the one asking me for a favour, but we both knew the obligation was on my side.

The old man shook his head and wheezed a sigh. "The house, Valerius. I must rent it out. It does no good just sitting there."

"No," I agreed, glancing at Octavia. My sister's composure didn't slip.

"If you know of someone looking, do let me know," Macrinus said.

"I will, of course."

"It would be a weight off my mind." Macrinus patted me on the arm with a trembling hand. "I'll be on my way."

He tottered out on a pair of fragile skinny legs that looked like they should have snapped off years ago. One big muscular slave supported him. The other, a dusky-skinned youth with a lazy eye, followed them out.

Octavia watched them go. "You ought to be nicer to him."

"I don't like him coming here. The gall of it! Talking about the house!"

"Quintus," Octavia said, "Macrinus feels that he doesn't have much time left—"

"He's been saying that for years."

She ignored that. "He's an old man, Quintus. Show some pity."

"What did he bring you this time?" I asked. "Money? Jewellery? More fripperies and finery?"

"A necklace," said Octavia. "A necklace that belonged to his wife."

I bristled. "I don't like him coming here! I wish you wouldn't see him!"

I should have said: *He upsets you. I don't like it when you're upset.* Instead, I went and upset her further.

Octavia stood up, hands on hips. "He's an old man, Quintus. He likes to visit me! Where have you been anyway? Leaving me to guess what in Tartarus happened last night from the drunken, garbled report you gave to Fulvia? Where have you even *been*?"

I frowned. "Listen, Octavia, I went to pay my respects to Marcellus Naso, which I think you'll agree was the right thing to do. After that, because I remembered how much you had been whinging about not having enough slaves to curl your hair or pluck your eyebrows, or whatever it is you spend your days doing, I went and bought some!"

It was an unfair blow. Octavia drew herself up to her full height, but since she was shorter than me anyway, it didn't have much effect. "I have never complained about the lack of slaves in this house, as well you know! If you must attack me, Quintus, I know you can do better than some *imagined* slight!"

Five words, uttered in the heat of the moment months before, and I wished I'd taken them back the moment I'd said them: *"Octavia, what did you do?"* Because when I'd found out that Nasica was divorcing my sister, I shouldn't have said that. He might have been my friend, but she was my sister.

"Octavia, I didn't mean it." I reached for her hand, but she pulled back.

"It's fine," she said stonily. "It's fine."

She swept away.

I sat down and knocked my knuckles against my forehead. *Idiot. Idiot. Idiot.* I wanted some peace and quiet, but I didn't get any.

"It's all your fault!" Another female attacking me, for the second time in moments. This histrionic wail had come from another direction though, unless Octavia could throw her voice, and I turned around to look for its charming source. "I *know* it must be your fault!"

Julia was weaving towards me, looking blotchy and tear-stained. I looked around for help. I was alone.

"Good afternoon, Julia," I said cheerfully. I hoped to put her off. A legion of battle-hardened mercenaries couldn't put her off.

"What happened?" she wailed, twisting her hands together. "Everyone's talking about it! No one will want to marry me now! I'll be a bad omen! How could you let this happen to me?"

As she began to recite her increasingly irrational litany of woes, I smiled benignly at her and waited for Fulvia to come and rescue me.

Chapter Five

I spent the next few days playing social butterfly. I went to the baths, and instead of slinking by men I knew and hiding in clouds of steam, I strutted around renewing my acquaintance with a few familiar faces and used the publicity of Albanus's death to make myself known to the men who wielded influence in the city. Vague offers of hospitality were bandied about in the gymnasium, on the massage benches, and afterwards as we undid all our good work with a jug of wine and a platter of sweet pastries. I used those baths like a miser, determined to get my money's worth each day.

Initially, I wasn't hopeful. I'd had experience with currying favour in these circles. Too often, the invitation you were promised was not forthcoming, and the influential men who treated you like a brother yesterday suddenly couldn't remember your name. All at once, you were further down the scale than where you started, and you didn't really know how it had happened. This time, things were different. Each morning Hursa opened the door to the self-important slaves of self-important men, bearing formal invitations. My new secretary Cretes dusted off the family calendar, told me where I would be dining that evening, and reminded me of my host's name.

I didn't dine at home once in days. I dined on the Esquiline, on the Palatine, on the Viminal, and closer to home on the Caelian. I had to send out for several new togas because the laundry couldn't keep up with me. The nasty murder of Marcellus Albanus had been good to me and in more ways than one. Gavius Silanus and I were no longer on speaking terms (the loss of a rich potential son-in-law had hurt him deeply), the eminent

Marcellus Naso no longer hated me, and Julia was so upset with me, she was seriously thinking of going home. If I'd known all this would be the result of a gruesome murder, I might have been sharpening my knives a long time ago.

Five days after the death of Marcellus Albanus, Uncle Maro and I had joined his funeral procession as it wound its way out of the city from the Forum to his family tomb on the Via Appia. There, surrounded by the tombs of all the great families, Naso gave his nephew's eulogy. The old man was composed and dignified. I hoped the mask wouldn't slip until he was in private again.

I saw several familiar faces from Albanus's party and couldn't help but wonder if any of them knew the real reason we were all standing there watching his body burn on its pyre. Florian was there to honour his cousin. He looked hollow-eyed as he watched the smoke billow from the pyre. I saw Claudius Rufanus, of *the* Claudians, and also Galerius Nepos. I saw Paulinus as well, but he was stuck on the other side of the crowd, and doddering old Macrinus. Silanus was there, looking the most mournful of all of them. Who was he going to hitch Julia to now?

Anyone who was anyone was at Marcellus Albanus's funeral. Those who hadn't been at the dinner party didn't dare miss the funeral. Marcellus Albanus was *somebody* now, thanks to the way he'd died. Something more than the acrid smoke left a bitter taste in my mouth. Was it my own hypocrisy? I was relieved when the funeral was over.

After the funeral, there were still the mundane matters to attend. There were the new slaves, although they fell to Juba to supervise. Juba was sulky. He knew he was good enough to be my secretary, and the only reason he was my bodyguard instead was because he was so big. I just didn't appreciate him for his mind.

My new secretary Cretes was competent and judicious. Within the week, he had introduced a filing system that actually worked and an accounting system that Philosthones grudgingly approved when he next visited. Cretes had even started to chase up the missing shipment of glassware my father had purchased, which had never been delivered, without so far offending the old man's business partner, who had more senatorial connections than I did. Daddy was a senator, mummy was Agrippa's great-niece, uncle was governor of Dalmatia, and his two brothers were serving as tribunes in the legions—junior himself had a longer pedigree than the emperor's favourite hunting dog and he also had the same business acumen. For Cretes to tell a family of that standing that one of them owed me money and not get his head kicked in, he was both clever and discreet. I ruminated on that while I sat in the tablinum going through the morning's pile of invitations, given verbally at the front door and written down in Hursa's painful chicken-scratch handwriting. At that moment, Cretes glanced up and said in his educated accent, "Sir, there is still the problem of your racehorse."

I sighed. "What do you suggest?"

He looked at the wax tablet in his hand. "I have gone over the figures Philosthones left, and even if you sold your share to your partners, you would be substantially out of pocket."

"You think I should just cut my losses?"

He gave a cautious smile. "I am told, sir, that at the house of Marcellus Albanus on the night he was killed, you were seated next to a man from Gaul."

Gossip in my household moved faster than any living creature could hope to equal. Particularly Felix. "So?"

"Well, sir, I am aware that in parts of Gaul, the horse is a highly prized animal in terms of social standing." Was it my imagination, or was Cretes starting to look smug? "If this man is in the city to better his social status, then I'm certain he would look favourably on an offer to buy your share of Felix."

"He'd be an idiot."

Cretes still didn't know me well enough to know if he should laugh or not. "I am sorry, sir, but that's not the point. Romans wear togas instead of trousers, drink wine instead of mead, and live in villas instead of huts. A lot of wealthy Romans own racehorses. If this man wants to seem more Roman, he will jump at the idea. It doesn't matter that it doesn't win. It will only matter that he owns it."

He had a point. The Gaul probably had money to burn in Rome, and who was I to stand in the way of that?

"Except I don't know how to track him down." Oh, here was an invitation from Frontus Terentianus, whom I had recently offended by asking if it was really true if he felt that way about livestock. No chance!

Cretes cleared his throat and looked carefully proud. "I think, sir, in that stack of invitations, you will find several from men who were at the house of Marcellus Albanus the night he died. One of them would surely know how to find the man from Gaul, if he was important enough to be at the main table."

"That's good thinking," I told him, and he beamed.

I began to look through the invitations, properly this time. There was one from Paulinus. It was either in Paulinus's typically abrupt style, or Hursa was cutting corners when he wrote stuff down: *Valerius, come around for dinner. Just a few friends, no toga. Paulinus.* It looked the most appealing so far.

"Send Juba with an answer to Paulinus. I'll go around tonight. Ignore all the others for a while."

"Yes, sir."

I had a nap before lunch, which was just what I needed. I bounced out of bed feeling bright and sparkling and ready to face the afternoon. I lunched with the ladies. Julia was more talkative than she had been in days, and for once, it wasn't about cosmetics.

"Aemilius Valerius," she said as she helped herself to the boiled eggs, "who do you think killed Marcellus Albanus?"

"I don't know, Julia."

"I'm sorry for yelling at you after it happened," she said, looking shifty. "I didn't mean to imply you were responsible in any way."

If I remembered rightly, wailing *'It's all your fault!'* actually did imply that, but I let it go for the sake of peace and concentrated on filling up on bread. "Of course, I wasn't responsible."

Fulvia sighed. "Are we really going to talk about this while we're eating?"

"Apparently," murmured Octavia with a small smile.

I shot Octavia a careful look and saw that we were friends again. We had been awkward around one another since our last slanging match, but Octavia could never hold a grudge.

"Well, obviously," Julia said, pressing on regardless. She tilted her head, and her little ringlets bounced, and her earrings jangled. "I mean, you don't have a reason, do you? You'd never met him before, and for all you know, he might have been very marriageable."

"No offence, Julia, but even if he wasn't, I wouldn't have killed him."

Julia and I shared a quick grin, probably our first and last. When she smiled, she looked like her mother.

Outside, I could hear the sounds of mad chattering echoing in the atrium and heading closer. Hursa stuck his head around the door to announce them pointlessly: "Aemilius Lucullus Maro, and Marcia Laeta."

Aunt Marcia almost knocked Hursa down in her rush to get inside. Marcia was a small, rotund woman, she bustled more than she walked, and she tried to pinch the cheeks of unsuspecting children. She headed straight for Julia and squeezed herself down on the couch beside her. She fussed over her as though she was a baby. Mad Uncle Maro brought up the rear.

"You should have sent word you were coming," I said to Maro. "We've just finished eating."

"Oh, this is just a quick visit," said Maro cheerfully. He rocked back and forth on his heels and hummed for a moment. He looked suspiciously pleased with himself.

"What's the news, Maro?"

Maro smiled broadly. "I've been pulling some strings for you, my boy!"

I glanced at Fulvia warily. Last time mad Uncle Maro had pulled strings for me, I'd just escaped being initiated into the priesthood of the arvales by the skin of my teeth. Maro maintained it would have been a good career move. I maintained I didn't like silly hats.

"What sort of strings, Maro?"

My mad uncle plonked himself down on an empty couch. "Remember how I said you could win Marcellus Naso's respect over this Albanus business?"

"I remember you said I should *pay* my respects."

Uncle Maro waved his hand. "Never mind that, Quintus, I've done one better! I've been speaking to Severus, and he wants you on board!"

"What do you mean?"

"He wants you to help with the investigation," said Maro proudly.

I was intrigued.

I knew I needed to apply myself to a career, and I had considered most of the options. I could stab Parthians, but to be honest, I wanted to leave the frontiers in the past. That was when I was younger, single, my father's heir, and Corbulo's golden boy. Looking at it like that, heroism was inevitable. Now, I was a husband, a stepfather, a guardian, and a paterfamilias. I had more responsibilities now and a strong feeling that soldiering wouldn't suit them. There was a plethora of civil duties I was qualified to undertake, in that the only qualifications necessary were a pedigree and some cash. I had already failed to secure some of these: aqueducts, roads, monuments, and public buildings. Not my style anyway. However much I wanted, I just couldn't get interested in bricks. There were religious duties as well, but knowing my luck, I would end up with the short straw and find myself an advocate of abstention from all my favourite things. There was one area that had always piqued my interest: the law. I could be a magistrate when I reached the right age. I might have been of the senatorial class, but at twenty-three, I was still too young to be considered. I could get there, though, if I applied myself. And working with Severus would be a good start. Given that my military career had been curtailed by my own heroism and I was still seven years short of being able to stand for election as a quaestor, it would make for a very long apprenticeship. But it had to be more interesting than aqueducts.

"What would it involve?"

Maro was delighted at my receptiveness. "Severus hates dealing with the vigiles, his own people are tied up with some big prosecution or another, and he's happy to take you on as his intermediary in the investigation. It's as simple as that!"

I wondered what the vigiles would think of that. They would probably be glad to have Severus remove himself, but not too happy about his replacement: another rich idiot with friends in the right places. That was how the system worked. Remove nepotism, and there was nothing left. I could handle them, though. I had dealt with subordinates who hated me in the past. Really hated me.

The Tenth Legion had been something different to what I had expected. It was the legion formed by the great Julius Caesar himself, and it had a distinguished history. It had served in Gaul, Spain, Pharsalus, and Thapsus. Disbanded after Caesar's death, it had been reformed by Lepidus and passed to Mark Antony. It fought with Antony at Philippi, and at Actium, after which it passed to the command of the great Augustus. When I joined, I'd expected it to have retained something of its former glory.

It hadn't.

The legionaries were mostly older men, lazy and out of shape, and they ignored us or spat at our feet. They'd been in one place for too long, and they didn't want to move. They didn't like authority. One of my fellow junior tribunes was sent to the surgeon on a stretcher after being discovered unconscious one morning behind the Questorian. He had been unable to identify his attackers, and the legionaries weren't talking. The new general had stewed for a while, and the Tenth thought it had him where it wanted him. But Corbulo was a soldier. He knew the guilty men wouldn't come forward while the legion was united against authority, so he sowed dissent. One in every ten men had been flogged. I could still remember the stench of the blood, running in rivulets over the dusty ground while I watched, pale-faced and nauseous under my helmet like every other junior tribune there. The general had walked a fine line that day and took us with him. The Tenth was like a wild animal. It could have turned at any time. For weeks, there had been whispers of mutiny. But for all that the men of the Tenth thought they could do it, they knew there were other legions in the area that would be brought in to take them out if they hanged Corbulo and his officers from the Praetorian Gate. Those first few weeks with the Tenth had been terrifying. The Parthians had been the least of our worries. We thought we were going to be killed in our own beds, by our own men. That was intimidation. If I could stand that, I could stand anything a cohort of dissatisfied vigiles could throw at me.

I was cautiously optimistic. "And when would I start?"

Maro beamed. "Good for you, Quintus! Good for you! Naso and I thought you'd jump at it!"

"Naso?" I asked, surprised.

Maro clapped his hand on my shoulder. "He told me Albanus had always been good to his slaves, and I said it wasn't one of his slaves, that *you'd* already figured that out. He took that to mean you'll ask the right questions, and we approached Severus."

"Oh." Without knowing it, without trying to, I'd impressed an important man and got myself a job.

"I'll tell Severus to send his man around," said Uncle Maro. He rubbed his hands together, and his eyes gleamed. "Now, what are the chances of some of those sausages in pastry your cook makes?"

* * *

I had an afternoon nap, sprawled out on my reading couch with my arms dangling over the sides. Juba woke me before dusk and helped me get ready for dinner with Paulinus. I intended to start my investigation into Albanus's death by removing Cornelius Paulinus from the picture, and I had a vague idea how to go about it. Also, I wanted to sell my racehorse.

Paulinus met me at his front door himself, looking as cheerful and friendly as I remembered. He greeted me like a long-lost friend: "Valerius! Glad you could fit me in! You're quite the man about town now, eh?" He gave me a theatrical wink.

I passed my cloak to a waiting slave. "What can I say? A free meal is a free meal, and, truth be told, I could do a lot worse than ingratiate myself with the rich and powerful."

We both laughed at how poor I was pretending to be.

A simple meal was laid out in an informal triclinium. The couches were comfortable and knocked about a bit. The walls were free of pornographic frescoes and painted instead with rustic scenes. People squashing grapes into wine, picking apples, herding cattle, feeding chickens. I liked it. It was unpretentious.

"It's not the Imperial Palace," Paulinus said, completely unashamed, "but it suits me fine."

There were only five of us, so I had a couch to myself. If I had been more socially conscious, I would have been secretly fretting about how I got the lowest position, but frankly, I knew that none of that counted in this unfussy triclinium. I was introduced to Nonius, Paulinus's brother-in-law visiting from his retirement in Paestum, and also to Plotius and Strabo, a couple of friends who treated Paulinus's place like a second home. They were both senators, but neither of them was wearing a toga, and neither of them had done anything politically significant in their careers. I liked them as well.

The food was excellent, not too rich, and not too much. Nonius, the brother-in-law, looked a bit disappointed to learn there were only two courses, but maybe Paulinus had promised him wild revelry. This dinner reminded me more of the sort of meals that families across the city, well, the richer parts of the city, would be eating right now. It said a lot more to me than a shellfish trireme.

Paulinus began to quarter an apple with his fruit knife. "That wife of yours, Valerius, what's her name? The one that was married to Gavius Silanus?"

"I've only got the one." I grinned. Plotius and Strabo thought I was the funniest man in the world, but they had been quietly hitting the wine. "Fulvia Drusa."

"Oh yes!" Paulinus said. "I knew her second husband, Fimbria." This confirmed what he had told me at Albanus's place—he did know everyone in the city. "I haven't seen Fulvia Drusa for years. She'd be a lot older than you, I imagine."

"Twelve years," I told him. "You know how it is. I needed a wife with a good family name, and she wanted to be free of Fimbria's relatives."

"You get along then?"

"We muddle through." But my smile implied more than that.

"Lucky you! My wife's an absolute cow!" Paulinus laughed at his brother-in-law's scowl. "Calm down, Nonius. You've got no sense of humour! Have some more wine!"

Ah, the wine. It was good, and there was a lot of it. We drank it with a nominal splash of water, but that amount got smaller and smaller with every cratera that Paulinus mixed. Sooner or later, we were drinking it straight from the jar. I splashed some onto the table and traced my finger through it. I had come to get answers, or at least to allay my worst suspicions.

The slave who had been serving had wandered off with our empty dishes, so Paulinus weaved his way over to my couch. He blinked at the little *XP* I had drawn in the wine with my finger, but he neither jumped with shock nor pretended he hadn't seen it. He only blinked at it and poured my wine.

"There you are, Valerius."

It meant nothing to him. My drunken little trap had failed. I was pleased.

The wine was good, very good. It had definitely impaired my investigative abilities, which were questionable in the first place. Satisfied that Paulinus wouldn't know a Christian from a Cretan, I went straight for the obvious question: "Hey, Paulinus, who do you reckon did Albanus in?"

A shadow passed over Paulinus's friendly face, and he sighed. "I don't know."

"Sorry," I said. "Were you close friends?"

Paulinus considered the question for a moment. "Not close, no. Personally, I didn't much care for him, but you know how these things are, Valerius. You meet some fellow who's been in your old legion, and you're obligated to drink together. Sometimes you get into the habit. I didn't really know Albanus that well at all, but we had become part of the same group."

It was a reasonable answer, but something itched at the back of my wine-addled brain. I wasn't sure such a casual relationship reflected Paulinus's position of honour on the main table at Albanus's party. There were nuances involved that were beyond my grasp at that moment.

Paulinus shook off his gravity. "More wine?"

I held out my glass. "Why not?"

The wine was starting to taste less good. The quality hadn't declined, but my stomach was rebelling. Plotius was the first to leave. "Shorry, yes, sh-shorry. I'm exshpected elsewhere. Thank you, and g'night...where's Shtrabo?"

Strabo was unconscious under his couch.

"He can stay! Thanks for coming, Plotius!" Paulinus gave him a cheery wave.

Plotius swayed in the doorway until his slaves came and escorted him gently away. "Yes, bye."

Paulinus called for his own slaves to remove Strabo to a bedroom. "I like the pair of them, but they can't hold their wine!"

I just smiled, because I had a fair suspicion I was at the slurring stage myself. The slaves brought in some sweet asparagus, which revived me enough to trust myself. "Listen, Paulinus, I've got an ulterior motive in coming here tonight."

"Oh, yes? What's that?" He didn't look at all concerned.

"That Gaul who was sitting next to us at Albanus's house, d'you reckon he'd buy a share in a useless racehorse?"

Paulinus stroked his beard and then burst out laughing. "I believe he would!"

"Do you remember his name? I can't, for the life of me."

Paulinus furrowed his brow. "Caraca, from some little shithole town in Lugdunensis that now has a forum and thinks it's Roman. He's rich, though. I think he's staying on the Viminal, with half his tribe and a fair few wives!"

We both had a bit of a drunken ponder about the logistics of managing a fair few wives.

"If you like, I can bring him around to your house for lunch tomorrow and tell him to bring his banker."

I liked Paulinus! We drank another jar of wine to my health, a contradiction in terms by that stage. Afterwards I mumbled something vague and polite to Nonius, and regretfully farewelled Paulinus. Juba reappeared clutching an amphora that was almost as tall as he was.

"A gift to your household from mine," Paulinus smiled. "It's excellent quality, much too good for everyday use. Put it away for a special occasion, will you? One day we'll drink to lost friends." He gave a bit of a cryptic wink.

"Oh, thank you." By that stage, I was swaying on my feet, and that small part of my brain that wasn't concentrating on how to stay perpendicular was marvelling at the man's staying power.

"There you are then!" Paulinus said, slapping me on the back. "I'll see you tomorrow, Valerius!"

Juba manhandled the amphora into the litter, jammed me in afterwards, and we all set off for home. I felt like a contortionist, and when I spoke, I was talking to the roof of the litter. "Juba, I'm having lunch with some important men at the house tomorrow, can you tell Damos?"

"Yes, sir."

"And can you get someone to scrub the floor of the main triclinium?"

"Yes, sir."

"And take Hursa for a haircut or something? First impressions count, even to barbarians."

Juba sighed deeply. "If I must, sir."

Things were looking up. I was going to sell my racehorse to a provincial who didn't know any better. I had met some senators I didn't actively dislike, and I was pretty sure that Paulinus hadn't killed Albanus. It was a good night's work.

* * *

I woke to the sound of heavy rain on the roof tiles and torrents of it being channelled down into the impluvium. My house had its own private waterfall, and I could hear Mouse and Perella slapping through it in wet sandals, shrieking and laughing. I crawled out of bed and washed my face. I doubted I would have time to get to the baths and back before lunch. Did I even have any fresh clothes on hand? Should I wear a toga to impress a provincial from Lugdunensis?

"Perella! Get out of the wet at once!" Thetis, Perella's mother, had a voice that commanded respect, and she wasn't afraid to use it on Mouse either. "And you, Aulus! You're soaking wet! I've got a good mind to throttle the pair of you!"

By this time, I'd pulled on a clean tunic and trailed out to watch the drama unfolding below. Thetis, hands on hips, was berating the children from under cover. "I said get out of the rain, *now!*"

The children ran like startled deer, and Thetis pursued them with blankets and dry tunics.

"Some days, it's like a madhouse." I hadn't noticed Octavia coming to stand beside me. "We've all had our breakfast, but I suppose you had a late night again?"

"But the good news is, I found a buyer for Felix."

"Well done, Quintus. What next? The Labours of Hercules?"

"Why do you mock me?"

"It's a hobby of mine." She smiled warmly. "I hear we're having guests for lunch. Men only?"

I shrugged. "You can come."

Octavia raised her eyebrows. "Oh, *thank you*, Quintus. How magnanimous!"

"You're doing it again," I said.

"It's second nature to me now."

Juba interrupted our friendly little chat. "Sir, Centhus is here."

"My barber?"

"Yes, sir."

"Did I ask you to send for him?"

"No, sir," replied Juba. "I used my initiative."

"Oh, well, good work then!"

Centhus was waiting for me in my study. "Nice place you have here, Aemilius Valerius. You know, I don't usually do house calls."

"I know," I said, settling down on my stool. "I'm sure I'll recompense you handsomely for all your trouble."

Centhus chuckled as he selected his razors. "Handsomely, hmm? I like

90

the sound of that."

"So what's the gossip in Fish Alley?"

"Well, the big news, Aemilius Valerius, is that the sandal maker's son has proposed marriage to Pollia Marca."

"Really?"

Centhus laughed. "His father won't allow it, of course."

"That's a shame. I'd like to see someone try and make Pollia a respectable woman."

"Yes, that'd be a battle of the Titans indeed," Centhus said, tipping my head back. "But from what I hear, it's me who should be asking you for the gossip. I hear you were on the spot when some high-ranker got disembowelled with a cargo hook. Is it true they left his organs laid out beside him?"

Gossip travelled fast, but never accurately. By the time Centhus finished, I'd filled him in on the basic facts. I think he gave me a discount because of it. He was certainly smiling as he left.

Paulinus arrived early. He would have been earlier, but Hursa had somehow side-tracked him into conversation. I had no idea how long Paulinus stood at my front door, but he didn't seem at all put out. I made a mental note to have a word with Hursa about his manners and apologised to Paulinus.

Paulinus waved it off cheerfully. "Don't let it trouble you, Valerius. I like a porter with a bit of character."

I looked back at Hursa, who was shifting from foot to foot and inspecting his grubby fingernails. Bags of character.

I was prepared to forgo the standard tour of the house and gardens, but Paulinus seemed interested, so we wandered through.

Caraca the Gaul turned up at lunchtime, just as the rain was picking up again. He brought with him a couple of slaves, and also a few brothers or cousins, or honoured kinsmen of some sort that was lost in translation. They were all wearing togas and torques, an odd mix. Caraca was very impressed with my big house, thought that my wife was beautiful, that Julia would carry strong babies, and that my son would make a fine warrior, according to the translator. The translator only had marginally better Latin than Caraca.

Octavia, despite her earlier teasing, did not come down to lunch after all.

Mouse, who had never met anyone from Gaul before, was on his best behaviour. He was seated beside one of Caraca's honoured kinsmen, who kept baring his teeth in a beardy grin and showing off the tattoos that climbed up his arms.

Calliope and Xanthus were busy flitting back and forth from the kitchen. Thetis was helping them.

"Where's Larius?" I asked Xanthus in an undertone as he came back bearing a cratera of wine.

"Sick, sir," Xanthus murmured in reply, raising his eyebrows.

Paulinus sat on the couch next to mine. Together, we had the dubious honour of watching men who had never handled cutlery in their lives trying to eat shellfish. Julia looked faintly disgusted at the proceedings, but I think Fulvia enjoyed the show.

Caraca had brought two of his women with him, and even the translator couldn't make me understand which was his wife, or if both were his wives, or what their relationship might be to the man himself. After we ate, Fulvia and Julia took his womenfolk away to compare their jewellery and clothing and men in private. Mouse took his new bearded friend away to show him off to Perella. My new secretary, Cretes, entered after the dishes had been cleared away, ready for business.

The translator, who had a name entirely unpronounceable to civilised people, glared. This was not as hostile as I thought. "Caraca wants to buy horse."

"Excellent. I have the documents here."

"Good. We buy. How much?"

"You do understand that this is only a share in the horse, not a complete horse?"

"Yes, horse stays in Rome with brother owners."

That was more or less correct. "Well, how much is Caraca willing to pay?"

"Not sestertius or denarius, have none of them," said the translator after a quick guttural exchange with Caraca.

I exchanged a puzzled look with Paulinus. He shrugged.

"Well, I paid for it originally in sestertius and denarius." I was falling into the trap of talking on the translator's level while trying to be proud and Roman.

"Yes! No!" the translator said, smiling and nodding.

"Excuse me?"

"Yes, we pay you now!"

A few of the Gauls, looking uncomfortable and itchy in their togas, moved forward. One of them was carrying a small wooden box. He placed it down on the table in front of me and opened it. A gold torque stared up at me, blinking in the light. Its pure radiant glow was interrupted rudely by small pieces of polished onyx and teensy little gemstones. It wasn't lonely in its box either—it had a couple of chunky bracelets to keep it company.

"Great Jupiter!" breathed Paulinus into his beard.

"This is from big mine in Gaul," said the translator proudly, nodding in response to something Caraca said. "This was made a long time before now, when mine was not Roman. All mines in Gaul are now Roman. In old times we made fortune digging from mine. Now we make fortune from selling things to important Romans who watch the slaves do digging!" He laughed at what might have been an attempt at irony.

I laughed as well, and the translator and Caraca beamed at one another. I tried to collect my thoughts. "You want to pay for a share of a horse, with what's in this box?"

"Yes, yes, you keep box. Is good box! Nice wood."

"I can see that. And also, what's in the box?"

"Yes, yes, you keep adornments. Catch on box in design of god in Gaul, see?" the translator said winningly.

I pretended to look at the catch. "Well, isn't that nice?"

"We buy now?"

I tried not to sound eager. "Yes."

Caraca solemnly shook my hand and took possession of Felix's papers. Then, unable to contain his delight at what he thought was the coup of the century, he gave me a big hug and slapped me on the back several times. We drank to the success of Felix, to the friendship between Lugdunensis and Rome, to the friendship between Caraca and me. When I swore I would come and visit him in Gaul, I actually meant it. It was with real regret that I farewelled Caraca and his honoured kinsmen, all of them still grinning and whooping because they owned a real Roman racehorse.

Paulinus left soon after, both of us delighted at my windfall. "You owe me, Valerius!" he laughed as he was loaded into his litter.

"Thanks, Paulinus!" I gave him a cheery wave and then headed back into the triclinium to gaze at my treasures.

"Jupiter!" said Fulvia, when my family had reappeared. "Jupiter, it's all real!"

Octavia might have missed lunch, but she had turned up afterwards to try to take the moral high ground. "Quintus, you're a scoundrel for taking this much for a useless racehorse!"

I could tell she was having difficulty trying to keep the admiration out of her tone.

"He practically forced me to, isn't that right, Cretes?"

Even Cretes was smiling. "Yes, sir!"

"Let's drink a toast to Caraca and his tribe!"

We sat down to the remains of the shellfish. We had our wine watered down, but our spirits were high. Even Julia had recovered enough from the horror of the Gauls' table manners to appreciate my astonishing good fortune. She sat beside Mouse, who chattered on and on about his new hairy friend Boudanas and got so excited he spilled his water all over the floor. The ladies were trying on the torque and bracelets when Hursa appeared.

"Sir, there's someone here to see you."

"If it's Caraca, he's not getting his stuff back." I grinned.

It's not him," Hursa said, combing his sticky-out hair back with his fingers. "It's someone called Junius Atreus, says he's a vigile."

Chapter Six

I met the vigile Junius Atreus in my study, leaving my family to finish up the lunch scraps and marvel at my windfall. I'd forgotten how tall Atreus was and found it unsettling to have to look up at him when he stepped forward to greet me. Patrician noses were made to look down, not the other way around.

"Aemilius Valerius, good afternoon." He was polite and respectful; someone had adjusted his attitude since we last met. I wondered if it was Severus, my new patron.

"Atreus, isn't it?" I pretended not to remember.

"Yes, sir."

I took a seat and then realised I now had even further to look up at him. "Sit down."

"Thank you." Atreus sat, looking troubled. This was probably less to do with his investigation into a terrible murder and more to do with his new working arrangements. "Aemilius Valerius, I have spoken to the magistrate Septus Severus. He informs me that you are to act on his behalf."

"That's right."

Atreus clenched his jaw for a moment as though he was fighting with what he *really* wanted to say and then said at last, prudently, "How do you wish to proceed, sir?"

I shrugged lazily. "I don't know. Read your reports, I suppose, or your notes, or whatever. Do you have any?"

"Not with me."

"Well, what does Severus normally do?"

"Septus Severus normally does nothing," said Atreus frankly. That explained why he hadn't brought his notes.

"Oh," I said. I was good at doing nothing, an expert, but for once in my life, it wasn't the approach I'd been intending. "In that case, Atreus, I mean to be more involved."

Atreus regarded me carefully. After a moment, he said, "Very well, sir."

Ours would be a rocky relationship, I could tell. We had an uneven association. He had the knowledge and experience to run a murder investigation, I hoped, while I just had friends in high places. What really rankled, though, what had to, was the fact that I would always come out on top. Men like Atreus would always be subordinate to men like me, and it didn't matter how intelligent, resourceful, or deserving they were. That was just the way things were.

Atreus didn't look happy. He shifted in his seat restlessly. "While I am here, sir, could I speak to the litter bearers who took you to Albanus's house? Since I saw you last there—"

"You saw me last at the slave trader's warehouse," I reminded him helpfully.

The vigile had the grace to look slightly put out. "Yes, sir."

I gave him a moment longer to look uncomfortable. "You were saying?"

"Yes, sir." He glanced down briefly. "I need to speak to your litter bearers, sir. I need them to corroborate a version of events."

Movement caught my eye. Larius was hovering by the door. I waved at him to enter, and he did so, looking customarily timid. I wasn't very impressed. "Xanthus said you were sick."

"I am well now, master," he mumbled.

"Ah, a miraculous recovery, right after all the work's been done," I said. There was no safe answer for that, so he kept his mouth shut. "Make yourself useful and go and fetch some wine. And tell Casso, Ledo, Spirus, and Macius they are wanted."

"Yes, master." He disappeared.

I turned my attention back to Atreus. I couldn't imagine how my litter bearers could be useful to him. "What have you found out?"

"Very little, I'm afraid, sir." He looked honestly disappointed, and for the first time, I noticed that his handsome face had the drawn look of someone who hadn't been sleeping. Mine had the same look, but for a different, more entertainment-related reason. "While we're waiting, sir, I understand that you had dinner last night with Cornelius Paulinus."

"How long *have* you been following me?" I asked, startled.

Atreus met my eyes with a gaze so direct it would have frozen Medusa in her tracks. "I was not following you, sir. On this occasion, I was following Cornelius Paulinus."

"And why is that?"

"He's on my list, sir," replied Atreus. Before I could ask what list, he'd thrown in another question. "Will you tell me what was discussed?"

Atreus wasn't sharing information. He wasn't keeping me abreast. He was trying to pretend he was, but he was actually interrogating me. Maybe he really did think I was as stupid as Severus.

Larius came back with a jug of wine already mixed with water in an acceptable daylight ratio. He had located some green glassware that was expensive enough to intimidate a working-class boy from the Transtiberina, but Atreus took the glass without even blinking and pretended he didn't notice how rich I was.

"You can't expect me to tell you what was discussed at a private dinner," I said to remind him who was in charge. I was the son of a senator and the descendant of Marcus Aemilius Scaurus, *princeps senatus*. My ancestors were building the great Roman Republic while his were still figuring out how to build a fire.

Atreus held my gaze for a moment and then shrugged. "No, I can't expect you to, sir. Why would you? I've spent the last week trying to get patrician delinquents to speak to me without reporting me to the prefect, the magistrate, or their fathers. I've had my men track down every one of the dancers and musicians that night, and most of them wanted hard cash before they'd open their mouths to tell me nothing. I've heard the testimony of Albanus's slaves, and *that* was not pleasant." His tone grew harder, and I found I didn't want to think about why. "I've got subordinates who don't care, a magistrate who just wants the whole thing to go away, and now I'm expected to report to you. If you're a part of this investigation, sir, you can at least do me the favour of telling me what was discussed with Paulinus. I haven't got time to play this game with you, sir. I just want to know what happened to Marcellus Albanus."

As speeches went, he was no orator. It did the trick, though.

I held out my glass for Larius to refill, then settled back into my seat. "Yes, I had dinner last night with Paulinus. He invited me, so I went. We didn't talk much about Albanus at all."

"Really?"

I thought back. "No, not much at all. I had a horse I needed to sell, and Paulinus set it up. I asked Paulinus if he knew who had killed Albanus, but that was the extent of it. He said he didn't know. He said they weren't close." I shrugged. "And I happen to know that Paulinus is no Christian."

Atreus leaned forward. "How can you know that, sir?"

"Like this." I stood and crossed to my desk, tipped some wine on the surface, and traced *XP* through it. "Paulinus didn't recognise it."

Atreus spent a long moment weighing me up, and then shook his head briefly. "So Paulinus isn't a Christian. I can't say that surprises me."

"Why's that?" I asked.

"According to his slaves, Paulinus hasn't been to a temple in months, and most of the time, he forgets to pray to his lares."

I was confused. "Well, if he's neglected his devotions…"

Atreus shook his head. "If you were part of a secret, illegal sect, more radical than even the Pharisees, that does not recognise the emperor as pontifex maximus, nor any form of Roman authority, would you neglect your public displays of devotion? Wouldn't you instead make a great show of your piety to remain above suspicion?"

"I don't think Paulinus is that devious," I mused. I still wanted to know more about these Christians, and Atreus knew more than I did. What was a Pharisee? You didn't go flinging around words like that unless you knew a thing or two about foreign religions. Atreus probably even knew where the fish fitted in. Then it occurred to me that I didn't want my slaves listening to what was secret, illegal, and radical. "Larius, go and find something else to do, can't you?"

"Yes, master," he replied and slipped away.

"So, Atreus, what have you found out about these Christians?"

He didn't get the chance to answer. At that moment, Octavia interrupted in the way that only Octavia could. She wavered on the threshold, looking tentative about intruding, and then came in anyway. "I'm sorry, Quintus, but this bracelet is stuck."

Of course. And there was nobody else in the entire household more qualified than myself in undoing tricky clasps. She was as transparent as an exotic dancer's underwear.

"Is it?" I asked and raised my eyebrows at her.

"Yes," she said, looking flustered and feminine. She held her shapely arm out in my direction, but she was smiling at the vigile.

It was one of the bracelets from Caraca, a heavy gold-plated monstrosity with a scrolling circular pattern. It was so heavy it needed two clasps, and one of these was actually stuck fast. The bracelet had left Octavia's forearm red and angry-looking where she had scraped it around, trying to get a better grip on the clasp.

"Junius Atreus, this is my sister, Octavia Junilla," I said.

Octavia smiled demurely and managed to stand upright while I wrestled with the damn bracelet, wrenching her arm back and forth. Her smile got less demure the longer I took. When one wrench finally caused an earring to go flying, Atreus intervened.

"Please, allow me!" The vigile looked aghast, like I was a barbarian, Octavia was a Vestal, and he had seen something no good Roman should ever have to witness.

Atreus stood and gave Octavia his seat. He knelt on the floor in front of her and took her gently by the wrist to examine the clasp. His back was to me, but I didn't like the idea that his gaze might have strayed from the bracelet and moved further up my sister's arm into forbidden territory. Maybe it was the tell-tale blush on Octavia's face. Not even my sister could fake a blush.

"What have you found out about these Christians?" I asked loudly.

Atreus glanced back towards me. "Are you sure, sir?"

"I'm sure."

Atreus cleared his throat. "From what I can gather, the Christians are a Jewish sect that came about initially in Judaea. You told me as much yourself the night we met. They believe in a kingdom in the afterlife, ruled over by their god, and reject all earthly kingdoms. This includes their rejection of the Roman state."

"Anarchy," Octavia murmured.

Atreus nodded. "More than that, perhaps. I don't think it is unrealistic to presume attacks of violence against Rome, and Romans, may result."

"So Albanus was Christian?" I asked, surprised that any well-bred Roman would go down that strange path.

"I don't know," said Atreus. "It's possible the amulet was placed there after his death, maybe even to mark a sacrifice. Perhaps we have witnessed the first Christian attack against Rome."

"Albanus was the best representation of Roman authority they could find?" I asked, deeply amused by that.

Atreus looked over his shoulder at me. "Perhaps he wasn't even the target. It was dark."

"So now you're saying Albanus wasn't even the intended victim?"

"No, sir, I'm saying that we can assume nothing."

"Over a week, and you're still assuming nothing? I can see why Severus doesn't want to know!" I poured myself another wine.

"That's not what I meant, sir," Atreus protested. He fiddled a little bit longer with the clasp of Octavia's bracelet. At last, it got the better of him, and he rose to his feet and turned back to face me. "I mean that the longer I look at things, the more imprecise they become. If I had to pick someone to arrest that night, I probably would have picked you!" He waited a moment to see if I would be offended enough to have him thrown out of the house. I wasn't, and his face cracked with a crooked smile. "The point is, there were over a hundred and fifty people who were at that party, counting the guests, slaves, and entertainers, and I don't have a single clear suspect."

We sat in silence for a moment, and then—*clatter!* Octavia's heavy-plated bracelet dropped to the tiles.

"Well," she said unconvincingly, "look at that. It fell off."

"You'll have to excuse my sister," I said to the vigile. "She has this insatiable curiosity about things that are none of her business."

Atreus looked hesitantly at Octavia.

"Oh, really, Quintus," said Octavia and blushed again. Great Jupiter! She *could* fake a blush!

The vigile leaned his lanky frame against my desk and said politely, "Curiosity is no fault in my line of work."

Octavia wasn't a woman scorned. She was woman miffed, and she shrugged it off stoically. She'd wormed her way into our conversation, which had been her objective all along. She looked at Atreus expectantly, waiting for some more interesting details.

He said, finally, "Do you know, sir, where the Third Gallica calls home?"

"Damascus," I said, glancing at Octavia. I could see what Atreus was getting at. It was an interesting connection and one I hadn't made. It might be possible, geographically, but it didn't ring true to me. I countered: "Except everyone in the Third Gallica salutes the sun, and while the legions might be a good breeding place for strange cults, I think we can make an exception for one that vilifies Rome."

Atreus was silent again. He bent down and picked up the gold-drop earring that had been dislodged during my earlier wrestling match with the bracelet. He passed it back to Octavia.

"Thank you." She bent her head and hooked the earring back through her lobe.

Atreus stared at the pattern of tiles on the floor for a moment. "I keep coming back to the argument you witnessed, sir," he mused at last.

"Do you really think that's significant? A fight over a gate crasher?"

Atreus nodded. "Perhaps. Why would Anicetus turn up uninvited, and why would it bother Paulinus so much?"

"I'm told that Anicetus is a powerful man with imperial connections," I said. "But maybe it was as simple as the fact that Paulinus thought there

101

was no place there for an ex-slave."

I didn't have to tell Atreus about snobbery, I was sure. No doubt he'd encountered it before. A plebeian with his attitude? Doors were probably slammed shut in his face every day.

Atreus pondered things silently.

"Sir?" Casso, the litter bearer stuck his head around the door. "You wanted us, sir?"

"Come in," I said to him. "Junius Atreus has some questions for you."

Casso and Ledo entered. They were both big and hulking, but they looked worried.

"Where are the others?" I asked.

Ledo looked relieved to be asked a question he could answer. "Gone shopping with Damos, sir, to carry for him."

"Fine." I leaned back in my chair.

Ledo and Casso regarded the vigile warily.

"Just a few questions," said Atreus, to put them at their ease. As long as he wasn't asking for official testimony, they were safe from torture. "On the night of Albanus's death, did you see anything strange?"

My litter bearers looked puzzled. Litter bearers were not known for creative thought.

"I'm sorry," said Atreus. "I should be more specific. At any time, did you see any other litter bearers enter Albanus's house?"

"Oh, yes," said Ledo immediately. "Two of them. It was after the commissatio. Everything was quiet."

This was all news to me.

Casso was nodding. "Yes. Macius said at the time they'd be in for it, but the porter mustn't have seen them. Probably drunk. They were inside for a little while, then they came out again, and the other two fetched their litter up to the portico. They walked right past us when they left, but the curtains were drawn."

I saw how this fitted in. Two men had held Albanus, one by the arms and the other around the jaw. Then the man holding him by the jaw had stabbed him. A quick, strong stroke. A stroke with a lot of strength behind

102

it. The same strength, probably, that it took to carry a man in a litter.

"Did you recognise these men?" Atreus asked. "Would you know them again?"

My litter bearers shook their heads.

"Did you recognise the litter?" Atreus asked.

"It was dark by then," said Ledo. "All of the torches had burned out. It was just a normal litter, as far as I could see."

Casso nodded in agreement.

"Thank you," said Atreus, and they left. Atreus took his seat again and sighed. "I've heard the same testimony from others. I just wanted to confirm it."

"It's a shame it doesn't tell us much," I said.

"It tells you a lot," said Octavia, who had always had a quick mind. "For a start, everyone who was at the house when Junius Atreus arrived is innocent. Good news for you, Quintus!"

I smiled wanly at her, annoyed I hadn't picked up on that.

Octavia was on a roll. "And it tells you it was probably someone who stayed for the commissatio."

"Not all the dinner guests went home," I told her. "Claudius Rufanus was still hanging around for one. Jupiter knows who else was. I'm sure a few of them got drunk enough at dinner that they crashed in the guest rooms, or just took a while to get going. And the slaves were all drunk as well. They wouldn't remember who was where."

Octavia nodded. "True."

Atreus had taken in our exchange with interest. "I have a list of the dinner guests," he said. "I have removed the names of those who definitely left while the slaves were sober enough to remember and those who were there when I arrived. There are ten names on it, ten men who I cannot confirm left after dinner when the porter was still at his post but who were not at the house when I arrived. It's still a lot."

Having nothing to add to that, I nodded sagely.

Atreus sighed and ran a hand through his hair. He looked weary. "It's a lot," he repeated.

I had overestimated him. Atreus was out of his depth as well. I felt sorry for him. I felt sorrier for my career. It was still in its infancy, and its chances for survival were bleak.

"Atreus," I asked, "you have investigated murders before, haven't you?"

"Not like this one," he said. He didn't elaborate. That made me feel worse.

"I'll need to look at your list," I told him. "I can open some doors for you, and I can ask the questions you can't, if you tell me what they are." I had to get something straight with Atreus. He probably thought I was cut from the same cloth as Severus: let the plebs do all the work and then sweep in and take the credit. "Day or night," I said. "Any time. If you find anything new, I want to know about it. If you need any doors opened, come to me. I'm probably not much of an investigator, Atreus, but I mean to be more of a help than a hindrance."

The look on Atreus's face told me he'd never heard those words from a patrician before, but my tone must have convinced him that I was sincere. He reached over my desk and helped himself to a blank wax tablet and a stylus. A few scratches and flourishes later, and he handed the tablet to me.

"That's the list, sir," he said.

"Thank you."

Octavia had the decency not to try to wrestle the list off me until Atreus had left. She made sure the front door was well and truly closed behind him before she made her move, but I was ready for her.

"No," I said.

"Why not?"

I should have tried to reassert myself as paterfamilias and gently reminded my little sister that some things really weren't suitable for a woman to get involved with and, despite her cleverness, a murder investigation was one of them. I didn't say it quite like that, however. Instead of the moral lecture, I reverted to sarcasm.

"Go and play with Caraca's bracelets like a good girl, Octavia."

Her glare would have made a gorgon think twice, but I was made of tougher stuff. Holding the wax tablet out of her reach, I swept past her into the atrium and headed for the stairs. I took the steps two at a time and retreated to my bedroom. I closed the curtains behind me and retreated to my comfortable old reading couch.

Atreus's list was a revelation. Not only did I recognise many of the names, but to my surprise, most of them were men who'd been at the main table. My new friend Paulinus was one of them, and I hoped that Atreus would reconsider and cross him off now he knew he was not a Christian. Claudius Rufanus was next on the list. I knew nothing about him, except he was one of *the* Claudians. His pedigree didn't intimidate me too much. I had one of my own, though not as shiny. Galerius Nepos was on the list as well. Odds on to be a consul, Paulinus had told me. Nepos had not been at the commissatio, so why hadn't he left after dinner? That was a question I would have to ask him, I reminded myself. I would have to ask every single man on this list why he had not left Albanus's house as soon as the party was over but had somehow disappeared before the law arrived.

Avitus Florian, the reluctant drinker from the commissatio, was also on the list. I wasn't sure why, since he didn't fulfill any of Atreus's criteria. He had not been unaccounted for. He had been right there. Doddering old Macrinus had made the list by being unnoticed by the household slaves as he'd tottered away. How unlike him not to be tucked up in bed by dusk!

The next few names I recognised, but couldn't put faces to: Menenius Carpo, Pomptius Voltinian, Vibianus Ennius, and Antonius Donatus. I recognised their names because their families were as old as mine, but if I had met these men at Albanus's house, none of them had made an impression on me. I couldn't guess if they were just drunks with bad timing, or if any of them could have had a more sinister reason for staying after the party was over but clearing out before the vigiles turned up.

The last name on the list stood out, partly for its discrepancy and partly for its brevity: Anicetus. The ex-slave didn't belong on that list alongside Roman patricians any more than he had belonged at the party. That had been made abundantly clear on the night. Was it enough to make him plot his revenge? But of course, Anicetus was more than just an ex-slave made good. I remembered what Uncle Maro had told me. Was Anicetus really the palace's man? If that was true, was it relevant?

I paced the floor while I pondered and wondered whether my father would have approved of my accidental career choice. I couldn't even hazard a guess. My father and I had rarely seen eye to eye, and it was a good indicator that if I liked something, he wouldn't. And vice versa. I regretted that. My father had never *got* me. He hadn't really got Octavia either, the difference being that because she was a girl, he had never felt the need. Me, on the other hand, he'd wanted to train up, and I was a great disappointment to him. My brief and glorious military career, which must have seemed like a turning point for the old man after my lazy adolescence, hadn't translated into success. I was a hero, quite beyond my father's wildest hopes and all my own expectations, but nothing had come of it.

These same feet that now paced my bedroom tiles had once carried me deep inside Parthian territory. The Parthians had prowled around us like wolves, howling out war cries that turned my blood to ice, and somehow, I had lived to tell the tale. What was it about being back in Rome that had made me go soft? Could I really investigate this murder? Was I clever enough? Was I tough enough? I was worried that I didn't know.

Fulvia found me a few hours later with all my military equipment strewn out over my floor, cleaning it up and reminiscing.

* * *

Mad Uncle Maro dropped in after dinner, totally uninvited. He brought a large jar of oysters, as though this would make up for it. It did. We sat together in the outdoor triclinium, on the hard stone benches that had been gradually worn down by generations of our illustrious family's backsides, and enjoyed the smell of the damp earth after the rain. I had always enjoyed that sort of weather, at that time of evening. Even on the outer edges of the empire, where the rain felt like it was hard enough to dent helmets, I could always savour the sense of the earth being replenished and the seasons falling into place. I should have been a poet and written tedious pastorals.

Uncle Maro sucked on an oyster thoughtfully, as though he had discovered a vaguely unpleasant aftertaste. "I heard you had your first visit from

106

the vigiles today."

"Just the one," I told him, "and how did you know anyway?"

My mad relation tapped the side of his nose.

"Oh, don't even pretend you have a spy network! Did Hursa tell you when you arrived?"

Maro shrugged, nodded, and popped another oyster in his mouth. "Is it all going well?"

"It seems to be," I said and then had a rethink. "I don't really know. I think all we can do at the moment is try and get the testimony of some of the guests and see where that takes us."

Maro sighed suddenly. "Poor Marcellus Albanus."

"Poor Albanus," I agreed dryly. "Do you know, Maro, he was a spoilt idiot with far too much money who covered his house in pornography."

"That's not the point," Maro said huffily, and I realised too late that Maro was overly sensitive when it came to interior decorating. His never-ending home renovations were of questionable taste. Everyone he had ever met questioned them, but it never put him off. "The point is that he's dead, and it's not right to speak ill of him. You should know better, Quintus."

A lecture on etiquette from a crazy person, but I relented. He was mostly right about everything. "I only said it because it was you, Maro. I wouldn't say it to anyone else."

"What about the vigile?"

I frowned. "Is there a problem telling the vigile what I thought of the man? Atreus is investigating a murder, Maro. He's not some informer or spy sneaking around after gossip."

"You must decide that for yourself."

"I've decided."

"Fine." Maro showed me his palms in a conciliatory way. "I just want you to be sure you aren't shovelling your stupid opinions and baseless prejudices into the ears of a man who will take them as the truth."

"He won't."

"Fine."

We ate some more oysters and didn't talk for what felt like a long time.

When Maro finally rose, much earlier than he was accustomed to leaving, our goodnights sounded hollow and insincere. The old relation huffed to himself, pulled his cloak up around his ears, and tottered off without a backward glance.

I didn't like fighting with Uncle Maro. We were two of a kind, Maro and me. He was old and crazy, and I was young and irresponsible, but generally, that worked out just fine between us. We both knew, secretly, that we were better than our reputations. All throughout my life, Uncle Maro had supported me against my father. Maybe it was because he had no surviving children of his own, or maybe it was because he had just enjoyed annoying my father.

When I'd left for the army, my father had given me some speech on duty and honour and loyalty, probably the very same speech he had received from his own father. Maro, on the other hand, had given me tips on how to handle incompetent superiors, how to pick the cleanest whore in the brothel, how to recognise a swindle, how to get involved in the business end of a swindle, and how to keep my head when the enemy came swarming. *The thing about heroes, Quintus,* he'd said, *is you'll notice most of them are dead.* And, when I came home after my own encounter with heroism: *Didn't you listen to a thing I told you? Idiot!* We rarely fell out, and I hated it when we did.

Fulvia, having picked everything up from the few curt words Maro had exchanged with her as he was leaving, came out to see me. "Are you alright, Quintus?"

I could pretend to be angry now. "That old fool Maro thinks I should be keeping some things back from the vigile, like what an idiot Albanus was!"

"Well," said Fulvia, sitting down beside me, "he may be right."

"Fulvia!" I was surprised at her.

"Hear me out, Quintus," my wife answered. "I'm not saying that you should hold back any facts, but how is it going to help anyone if you vent your spleen by rambling on about what you thought of Albanus? How will it help your career when Marcellus Naso finds out what you really thought of his nephew? 'Well, I thought he was a showy bastard who probably deserved everything he got!'"

She did a good impression of me, stupid and blustering.

"You know that's not what I really think."

Fulvia sighed and held my hand gently. "Just be discreet, Quintus. You don't want every ill-considered opinion ending up in a report."

I felt miserable now. "How come you're so sensible?"

"It's my job." She smiled and curled her fingers through mine. We sat in silence for a while, but I could feel Fulvia drawing up for another attack. "Quintus," she said at last, "are you happy?"

"What sort of question is that?"

"Quite a simple one," she said. "Are you?"

"I don't know," I answered, unwilling to commit myself before I knew where all this was leading. I felt suddenly suspicious. "Are you?"

She squeezed my hand reassuringly. "Yes, I am."

"I thought for a moment I was about to become the latest on your list of ex-husbands," I mumbled.

"Oh, you can't get rid of me that easily," Fulvia said airily. "I like our marriage, and I think you do too."

We were mismatched in so many ways, Fulvia and I, but somehow it worked. I was twenty-three, and she was thirty-five. It was not entirely uncommon for marriages to be made on such uneven terms when it was beneficial for both families. Fulvia came from a good family and had been married twice already to prominent men. Silanus had been her first husband, and things had ended badly. She got Julia and a divorce. Caldus Fimbria had been her second husband, and she was just as unlucky there. She got Mouse, which was a step up, but she also discovered widowhood and was stuck with Fimbria's awful relations. When my father had mentioned to her that he had a son who needed a wife to further his career, she had been glad to be shot of Fimbria's appalling family. I had married her to improve my name, and she had married me to escape her overbearing in-laws, but it worked.

I sighed. "You know I do."

She pressed on. "But you don't seem very happy. Do you know what your problem is, Quintus?"

"No, but you're going to tell me, aren't you?"

Fulvia laughed. "I'm afraid so." She reached out with her free hand and stroked my hair. "I hope that working for Severus will suit you. I've been quite worried about you."

"How do you mean?"

"This afternoon, I found you staring at your military kit. That's the sort of thing old men do when they know their glory days are over."

"You think I should rejoin?"

Fulvia tapped me lightly on the temple. "Is any of this getting through? Quintus, find something you want to do—I don't care what—and then do it. If that happens to be investigating the death of Marcellus Albanus, so be it. But whatever you do, do it wholeheartedly."

I felt more depressed now than ever.

Fulvia sighed and then leaned in and pressed a kiss to my cheek. "Be happy, Quintus. You're too young to be melancholy."

* * *

I napped again in the afternoon, woke up when it was already dark, and then wandered downstairs in search of something to eat.

"Good evening, sir." Juba appeared out of nowhere.

I thought back to my household responsibilities. "I need to talk to Hursa and Larius."

Juba knew why. "In your study, sir?"

"The kitchen," I said. "I'm also hungry."

Juba peeled away from my side.

The kitchen was deserted at this hour. The ovens were still warm, but the dishes had been washed and stacked, and the kitchen slaves had retired to their beds. There was a single oil lamp left burning on the table.

I slid into the bench at the kitchen table and watched the play of shadows on the wall. The kitchen smelled of warm bread and olive oil. There was a bowl of nuts on the table. I helped myself to a handful.

CHAPTER SIX

Hursa was the first to appear, tugging his hair nervously. "You wanted to see me, sir?"

I sighed. It felt like I was always lecturing Hursa on something, and we were both getting sick of it. Hursa's problem was there was no simple duty that he couldn't make a dog's breakfast out of in a heartbeat.

"Hursa," I said sternly, "you're a door porter. I expect you to admit guests and announce them, not engage them in conversation."

Hursa opened and closed his mouth like a landed fish. He found his voice at last. It was squeaky with indignation. "Do you mean Cornelius Paulinus at lunch, sir?"

I nodded sternly.

Hursa looked pained. "Sir, Cornelius Paulinus was talking to me, not the other way around!"

"Come on, Hursa! Why would Paulinus talk to you?"

I'd hurt his feelings. He hugged his arms to his narrow chest. "Sir, Paulinus was asking about the house. How long it had been in the family, how many slaves you had, and whether or not you had a good secretary!"

So Paulinus was trying to poach my new secretary, was he? Good secretaries were hard to find, and worth their weight in gold. I already owed Paulinus a favour. I would have to repay it before he asked to buy Cretes.

"And what did you tell Paulinus?"

"I told him Cretes wasn't for sale. I said you'd only just got him, and he wasn't for sale! Paulinus said he was looking for a new secretary, someone good, and young. I told him Cretes was old, and he's probably only got another few years in him anyway, and he would do better to look elsewhere!" Hursa screwed up his face unhappily.

He'd been looking out for my interests, after all. "Alright, Hursa, that's fine. In future though, just send my guests straight through."

"Yes, sir," said Hursa. He relaxed his crumpled face. "Can I go now?"

I nodded, and he trotted off.

Larius was next in line, and Juba accompanied him. Larius stood anxiously on the other side of the kitchen table, and Juba stood behind

111

him, looking large and intimidating. Larius's handsome face was pale, and he kept his gaze downcast. I could see that he was doing his best to look composed, but his hands, clasped in front of him, were white-knuckled.

I let him stew for a moment.

Larius swallowed, still avoiding my gaze.

"Larius," I said, and his head snapped up. "Why weren't you serving lunch today?"

"I was sick, master," he answered in a miserable whisper.

"And then you got better," I said. "Just like that."

He looked down again.

"Take off your tunic and turn around," I said.

Larius stood frozen to the spot for a moment until Juba made a move towards him. Then he hurriedly pulled his tunic over his head. He held it in front of himself while he turned around to show me his back. His flesh was unscarred, unblemished. I could see that he was visibly shaking now, and his breathing was fast. Possibly, he thought he was going to be beaten. Possibly, he thought it was something else altogether.

"That's fine, Larius. Get dressed again."

He quickly pulled his tunic back on. When he turned back to me, his face was red, and he couldn't raise his gaze to meet mine.

"I won't have laziness in this household," I told him. "Look at me! Next time you get sick, you report it to Juba. Think about that tomorrow when you're working on an empty stomach."

"Yes, master," he whispered.

"And if it happens again, I will make certain your back wears its first scars." It was not an empty threat, and he knew it.

"Yes, master," he whispered.

"Go back to bed." I frowned, and he slipped away. I said to Juba: "Make sure he doesn't eat tomorrow and get him to scrub all the floors. Let Xanthus and Calliope have a day out. He can do their work."

Juba nodded.

I regarded Juba thoughtfully. "So why isn't he fitting in?"

Juba smiled. "He's unhappy."

"You don't sound very sympathetic," I commented. "I assume he hasn't endeared himself to the household?"

Juba nodded. "He's unhappy because he thinks he's too good to fetch and carry. He's clever enough to try to hide it, but we're not stupid. We can tell."

"He's offended you," I said, liking Larius even less.

Juba shrugged. "Some indulgent master spoilt him until he was rotten, sir, and now we're stuck with him. He got the better end of the deal."

I made a face. "You saw how frightened he was."

Juba snorted. "Only because you caught him out, sir."

"What do you think I should do with him?" I would always trust Juba's opinions on the rest of the slaves.

"I think you should tell Octavia Junilla to sell him on," said Juba, "or send him to one of the estates."

I trusted Juba on a lot more than the running of the household as well.

"And what do you think of this Albanus business?" I asked, finishing my handful of nuts.

Juba tilted his head thoughtfully. "I don't know what happened to Marcellus Albanus," he decided at last, "but if you must get involved in finding out, sir, I think there are worse men to work with than Junius Atreus."

He was probably right.

Chapter Seven

The vigile Atreus turned up again the next morning as I was enjoying breakfast with my family, although enjoying may not have been the most accurate description. Julia had slapped Mouse when he'd helped himself to one of her eggs, Fulvia had shouted at her for it, Julia had shouted back, things had degenerated from there, and when Atreus walked into the triclinium my wife was scowling, and both of my stepchildren were sobbing. Mouse because he'd been hit and didn't like it, and Julia because she'd been put in her place and liked it even less. A cloud of ill-will hung over the triclinium.

"Junius Atreus, sir," Hursa announced.

Julia stopped blubbing immediately and tried to look fragile and victimised.

"Atreus," I said, "my wife Fulvia Drusa, her daughter Julia Drusilla, her son Aulus, and you've met my sister Octavia Junilla."

Atreus nodded around the room apprehensively.

"Sit down and have some breakfast," I offered through a mouthful of porridge and honey.

"No, thank you, sir. I've already eaten." Atreus took a seat, though, on the only unoccupied couch.

Octavia immediately started up an inappropriate conversation, as was her wont. I used to ask teasingly how her husband put up with it. We no longer joked about him. We no longer even spoke his name.

"Junius Atreus," my sister began brazenly, "have you discovered any further information about Albanus's murder?"

114

Atreus glanced at me for permission before answering. Or perhaps the glance was censorious. I was willing to bet that Atreus's womenfolk were cut from a different cloth than mine if he really believed all that paterfamilias guff. My womenfolk had never deferred to me on anything. Certainly not on anything they felt was important. If I was honest with myself, they didn't even defer to me on matters they felt were just vaguely interesting.

"Not at this stage, Octavia Junilla," he said politely.

I thought he was holding something back, but I didn't know him well enough to be sure. Octavia raised her eyebrows. She obviously thought the same thing.

I finished my porridge. "I suppose we should visit Severus today."

"Yes, sir," said Atreus. "Septus Severus is requesting daily reports in relation to Albanus's death."

Probably only so he could sound off importantly at his bathhouse about how well-informed he was. But whatever I thought of him personally, I was obligated. Nepotism was a double-edged sword. I got this job in order to increase my social standing and theoretical political career. I had to repay Severus by showing him a due amount of honour. That would mean a lot of visits to his house.

I pushed the remains of my breakfast aside. "We should get started."

Octavia rose with us and walked us to the atrium. Xanthus and Calliope were waiting there. They were watching Larius, who was on his hands and knees on the tiles, working away with a scrubbing brush. He looked as miserable as always. He would be more miserable by nightfall after working all day on an empty stomach, but it would give him a chance to adjust his attitude.

"Are you going out?" I asked Octavia.

"I'm going shopping," she said, adjusting her stola.

"Take Juba."

Octavia smiled at me. "Jupiter, Quintus, I'm only going to the Emporium, and it's broad daylight!"

"Fine," I said. "Be careful."

Atreus and I walked with Octavia's litter as far as the intersection just down the hill, and there we parted ways in the bustle of early morning pedestrian traffic. Xanthus and Calliope were delighted to be out for the day. They walked behind Octavia's litter, chattering happily.

The city in the morning was a wonderful thing, full of promise and activity. No wonder Octavia had laughed off my concerns. The day was bright and cheerful after yesterday's rain and felt about as dangerous as a newborn kitten.

Severus lived a few blocks away from me on the Caelian Hill in a spacious house surrounded by what must have been extensive gardens. Tree branches overhung his garden walls into the road, waving gently in the breeze and ushering us up towards the wide portico of the house.

The door slave was well-groomed and efficient. He took our names and allowed us into the atrium to wait. There were already a few men standing around, trying not to look too bored as they waited to see if Severus would fulfill his obligations as a patron and make time to see them. They looked at us curiously.

The atrium was full of light. It washed over the walls and danced in the waters of the impluvium. It sparkled. The whole place looked freshly tiled and painted. It was welcoming. Slaves hurried back and forth through the atrium, carrying scrolls and papers and wax tablets and all the tools of their master's trade. He must have had an army of secretaries, scribes, and clerks.

The door slave returned moments later and gestured for us to follow him. That earned us a few jealous glances from the other hopefuls.

Septus Severus met us in his outdoor triclinium. He was seated on a shaded couch, reading from a scroll. He rose to his feet to meet us. He grasped my arm warmly and gestured to a couch across from his own. I sat down and adjusted the cushions more comfortably. Atreus was not offered a seat.

Severus put his scroll aside carefully. "How are you finding it, Valerius?"

"Interesting," I replied truthfully.

"Aha!" said Severus in a delighted tone. "Good! Good! And are there any developments?"

"I'm afraid not, Severus."

Severus's friendly round face fell.

I leaned forward, summoning up an encouraging tone. "There is some good news, Severus. We have a list of only ten suspects. I'm sure it will be only a matter of time before the culprit becomes known."

A slave brought out a platter of fruit and placed it on the low stone table between Severus and me. I helped myself to a few grapes, but breakfast was still sitting heavily in my stomach, and I didn't want to overdo it.

"It was Junius Atreus who compiled the list from over a hundred and fifty names initially," I said, unsuccessfully trying to give credit where credit was due.

Severus didn't even turn his head to acknowledge Atreus. "Is there any name you favour?"

"Not yet." I resisted the urge to look at Atreus for guidance. We hadn't had a chance yet to broach the subject. "We're still looking into it."

"I don't investigate, Valerius," Severus said. "I'm a jurist, not an informer! But for a matter as important as this, I'm not going to trust it to the vigiles. I need you to bring me someone I can prosecute."

"I'll do my best."

"Good," said Severus, popping a grape into his mouth. "Keep me updated."

I had expected that Severus would want to know a little more than that. The names of our suspects, for example, or our next move. Instead, I found myself back out on the street again in moments, kind remembrances to my wife and family ringing in my ears.

"Is he always like that?" I asked Atreus.

Atreus considered my question for a moment and then smiled slightly. "No, sir. Most of the time, he is less interested."

"Really?" I tried to picture that. "Why?"

"Because his brother-in-law is an equite and is aspiring to become Praetorian Prefect," Atreus said frankly. "Severus hoped that an association with the Urban Cohorts would help him pave his brother-in-law's way into the Praetorians, but instead he got us vigiles. He thinks we are all ex-slaves and foreigners."

I had also been labouring under that misapprehension.

I almost felt sorry for Severus. I would be bitter as well if I'd been hoping for a plum magisterial position with the Urban Cohorts or their big brothers the Praetorians. Any way you looked at it, the vigiles were the black sheep of the family. They were the night watchmen of the city and made up mostly of ex-slaves wishing for a decent wage, foreigners wishing for citizenship, and presumably freeborn citizens wishing they'd done better at school. I wondered which category Atreus belonged in.

I shook it off. "Well, what's next?"

"I'll show you, sir."

When the divine Augustus had divided the city into administrative districts, he had given each district large barracks that were shared, grudgingly, between the vigiles and the Urban Cohorts. In addition to those barracks, there was an ever-expanding network of excubitoria, smaller satellite stations. The excubitorium of the first century of the Fifth Cohort of Vigiles was located at the bottom of the Caelian Hill. Entry was via an archway in the wall into a cobbled yard with a small shrine to Neptune on one side (for the vigiles), and Mercury on the other (for the Urban Cohort).

The excubitorium itself was a two-storey brick building with a peeling plaster veneer. The building had a central courtyard that served as a training ground. As we walked through, I saw a couple of vigiles half-heartedly going through their paces in the drowsy sunlight, one attacking with a short sword and the other defending with only a cudgel. Ironically, there was an unattended torch smouldering in the courtyard that had been allowed to burn overnight.

The main duty of the vigiles was not policing their districts and putting an end to criminal activity, it was firefighting. This was reflected in their high mortality rate. In Rome, the insulae were built very close together, and not all of them were structurally sound. When fires started, whole neighbourhoods blazed and crumbled. It was up to Atreus and his men to keep that from happening in their regions—the Porta Capena and the Caelian Hill. Most of the Caelian was a good area with generally affluent residents who lived in one or two storeys, and whose houses were spaced well apart by gardens. The Porta Capena, where it touched on the Aventine district, was filled with artisans' workshops, bakeries, laundries, olive oil shops, hot food stalls, and streets of crowded insulae.

We passed through the dusty courtyard and into the shade of the southern side of the building. The sound of our footsteps brought a vigile lumbering out of an interior room. His attitude relaxed when he saw us. "Morning, boss."

"What's happening, Gaius?" Atreus asked.

"Not much, boss," the vigile replied. "Vibilus got done over last night. He's down the hall now."

Atreus led me down the passage towards a closed door. He knocked, and we were admitted by the Greek physician Leander. It was only a small room, but it gave itself away immediately. In the middle of the room there was a large, scarred table that held all the old stains of the physician's trade. There was a vigile sitting on it at present, looking bruised and angry.

"Morning, boss," said the man and winced when the physician returned to his side and applied pressure to his ribs.

"What happened to you, Vibilus?" Atreus asked.

The vigile scowled. "I met up with some of Bano's men behind Actia's laundry last night."

"I hope you gave as good as you got."

The vigile grimaced, showing broken teeth. "One got away, but the other one's recovering in a cell."

"Good," said Atreus. "Where was your partner?"

"Chasing the other two."

Atreus nodded. "Head out there again this evening and take a few more men with you. I want to know if they're putting pressure on the shop owners. Ask Actia. She knows everything that goes on."

"Yeah, she knows, boss, but she's not talking," the vigile said, lifting his arms while Leander strapped his ribs. Then he stood carefully, touched his ribs experimentally, and limped outside.

"Is he alright?" Atreus asked the physician.

Leander nodded, rolling up the unused portion of bandage. "He'll be fine."

We headed back out into the corridor. Atreus led me up the steps to another office, and we stepped through the doorway. I took a seat and looked around. The office was larger than I'd expected. It was sparsely furnished, with only the desk and a few stools. There was a scroll box on the desk and a stack of wax tablets. There was also a jar of what I hoped was wine on the desk and a couple of cups.

Atreus crossed to the window and pushed the shutters open, letting the daylight flood inside. "Would you like a drink, sir?"

"Thanks," I said. I took the wine he offered me and had another look around the office. "You know, I hadn't expected you to have an office."

"It's not mine," Atreus said, sitting down. "I just borrow it."

He'd mentioned something to Severus about a boss that night of Albanus's party, but so far, I'd seen no evidence that Atreus was getting his orders from anyone higher up the pole. In fact, he seemed to be the one giving all the orders. "So, you're not in charge?"

Atreus shook his head. "Only while our centurion Atticus is away. And we always have the tribunes and the prefect to answer to, of course, sir, but with seven centuries in the cohort, we're given free rein."

"What's Atticus like then?"

"He's an ex-legionary centurion. He served his twenty years in Baetica and now runs our century," Atreus said. It wasn't really an answer, but I thought I could guess the rest by Atreus's omissions.

Atreus leaned down under the desk, and I heard a scraping sound. He hauled a small wooden box onto the desk. It was full of scrolls, tablets, scraps of paper, and other bits of detritus best summed up as a pile of rubbish.

"What's all that?" I asked.

"This is everything I could get out of Albanus's tablinum."

I looked at him in astonishment. "Are you *allowed* to do that?"

"Jupiter, no," he said with a crooked grin I immediately warmed to. "I took it all on that first night. The house is locked up tighter than a tomb now."

"You've checked?"

Atreus nodded. "They've even cut back the branches overhanging the garden wall. It's to keep sightseers away, I suppose, but I'm not welcome there either."

I gestured to the box. "So why did you help yourself that night?"

"Motive," said Atreus simply. "The ten men on that list are all going to claim they did nothing, just like everyone else. Nine of them are probably telling the truth, but we might not know which one is lying. And unless we can establish a motive, we'll never know."

That made sense.

"Stealing off the dead seems a bit extreme," I commented, leaning forward to rifle through the crate. I trusted to Fortuna that the first piece of detritus I grabbed would be useful.

Atreus shrugged. "Sir, in my experience, there are very few motives for murder. Greed, jealousy, love and hate. I'd hoped something here might be useful."

"You told me that you've never investigated a murder like this before," I reminded him as I studied the thin wax tablet I'd liberated from the pile. Fortuna was a bitch. It wasn't useful at all. It was the dinner menu from the party. Reading over it I could taste the feast all over again: the beef, the boiled calf, the goose liver, the vegetables, the shellfish trireme, and the wine. The wine I remembered with mixed emotions. Sweet, heady, intoxicating, but Jupiter, it packed a punch.

Atreus looked at me ruefully. "I haven't. The last murder I investigated was a horse trainer. He'd been hacked to pieces in his stables. His money was missing, so was his wife, and everyone in the neighbourhood knew she'd been screwing around on him with a butcher. We found the pair of them trying to get on a boat at Ostia."

"Gruesome."

"But straightforward." Atreus sighed. "With Albanus, I can't see a motive yet. There's not much there."

I looked at the crate with interest. "What else is in there?"

Atreus leaned back again. "Some papers relating to household purchases.

A couple of outstanding bills, but not for very large amounts. There are some accounts, I think, but I can't make sense of them. Albanus's secretary had no knowledge of them. He says Albanus must have done them himself. Does that seem strange to you, sir?"

"To me, sure," I said, "but I can barely count. Maybe Albanus liked to keep an eye on his finances. My Uncle Maro does all his own accounts for that reason. I don't. I use an accountant."

Atreus nodded slowly. "There's also a draft of his will."

That caught my attention. Albanus was a rich man. He must have had some relatives wishing he'd topple off his perch and spread the family money around. "What does it say?"

"He left almost everything to Marcellus Naso," Atreus replied. "If his will was unchanged, of course. The official will won't be read for another two weeks."

"I doubt it will have changed," I commented. "Naso was his patron and his closest relative. If he didn't have any heirs of his own, it would make sense to leave everything to Naso. Before I was married, not that I had much, my will left everything to my father."

"Before you were married," mused Atreus. He frowned slightly and tapped his fingers on the desk for a moment. "So after Albanus was married, presumably, he would have changed his will?"

"Maybe," I said, although it was by no means a certainty. "He would have if he'd had children."

Atreus liked the idea. "And the night of the party, Gavius Silanus was trying to get his daughter married to Albanus. Perhaps Marcellus Naso didn't want that to happen."

I shook my head. "No. Marcellus Naso is already rich. He owns half of Samnium. To hear you suggesting that he killed Albanus for money, I'm assuming you've never seen inside his house. If Naso has benefited from Albanus's will, it's coincidental, I'm sure of it. If you're looking for a motive, you'll need to look further than that."

"Alright," said Atreus. He leaned back in his seat and crossed his arms. "So, who else benefited from Albanus's death? His cousin Avitus Florian?"

"I can't see how if Albanus left everything to Naso."

"*Almost* everything. Apparently, Avitus Florian gets the house." Atreus drummed his fingers on the desk pensively. "And it's a big house."

"A house like that might be a drop in the ocean to Florian."

"I appreciate that." Atreus nodded, but I could see that he couldn't let the thought go. He frowned slightly and said at last, "I wonder why he didn't speak at the funeral."

"You were there?" I asked, astonished. "Jupiter! You've been following everyone! No wonder Bano and his protection racket are running rings around your men—half the cohort's sneaking around after Albanus's guests!"

"I've got a lid on Bano, sir," Atreus replied, not looking offended. "Does it seem strange to you that Avitus Florian did not speak?"

I saw his point, and I understood it to a certain extent. In my experience, there was nothing like a death in the family to make you run off to all the temples you had previously neglected. It wasn't enough to offer the dinner scraps to the lares and penates when a beloved relative was sailing on the Styx. It was fatted calves, gluttonous goats, and shiny pink piglets as far as the eye could see for those first few weeks until the gods had scoffed themselves silly on your barbeque and had reserved a nice shady corner of Elysium for your dearly departed. I sounded cynical, and that's the face I showed to the world, but when my father died, I would have mortgaged my entire future for his funeral. I gave the eulogy then, trying too late to show him the respect I hadn't during his life. But I had believed that Florian's grief was sincere when I'd seen him sitting at Marcellus Naso's feet and then when I saw him hollow-eyed at the funeral, and I still believed it now.

"It's not so strange," I said. "Florian wasn't Albanus's main heir, so there was no obligation for him to do a eulogy. I thought he looked grief-stricken at the funeral. He didn't look like he was capable of speaking, even if he'd wanted to."

Atreus reached into the pouch around his belt and drew out the small bronze amulet that Florian had discovered on the floor beside his cousin's corpse. "But what about this?"

I stared at the amulet on the desk for a moment. "What's your point?" Atreus didn't say anything.

"What are you suggesting?" I asked. "That Florian didn't speak because he is a Christian? That doesn't make much sense. You said yourself that you believed Paulinus was not a Christian because he'd neglected his devotions and that anyone involved in such a cult would not risk being seen to do that. You can't condemn Florian now for the same offence."

That was logical and judicial, surely worthy of Cicero himself, or Cato, or any one of the stern orators of the old republic that still cast their long shadows over the judicial system.

"I know." Atreus sighed.

"I think you should look elsewhere for the killer," I said firmly.

I took a handful of papers off the top of the crate and settled down in my seat to have a look at them. They made as much sense to me as my own household accounts. That is, none at all. Except where at least mine were decipherable, Albanus seemed to have written his almost entirely in abbreviations. The particular page I was looking at seemed to be a list of figures, whether incoming or outgoing cash, I couldn't tell, with the letters *D, B,* or *A* beside them, or any combination of them all. Whether the *D* stood for *donum, dedit* or even *dies,* I couldn't tell. Likewise, the *A* was probably either for *aurum,* or *annus,* but it could have been for *amicus,* for all I could tell. *B* might have stood for *beneficiarius,* or *bonus,* or possibly even *bona fortuna* if the cash had been an unexpected windfall. It might have been a list of money he had been doling out to his clients. It might have been the list of amounts he had received from his own patron. Jupiter, it might have been a list of his winnings at the races for all I knew. But it also might have been a motive.

I looked at Atreus. "This is impossible."

"I know," Atreus replied. "I've spent the last few days going over those pages, and they still don't make any sense."

I was struck by a sudden idea. "They make no sense to us, Atreus, but I think I know someone who might be able to help."

While we waited for my good idea to materialise, Atreus showed me around the half of the excubitorium occupied by the vigiles. We ended up watching the men go through their paces in the training yard. I recognised something in Atreus's stance that was familiar from my days as a junior tribune. It manifested itself as a grave sort of paternalism as you watched your men train. In my case, it had taken a while. When your subordinates wanted to kill you, it was hard not to wish the same on them. But it did manifest itself eventually, after the Tenth got a batch of new recruits who weren't old, jaded, and mutinous. I had watched those recruits train with the same serious look on my face that I saw on Atreus's now. It crept up on you, the responsibility. It started out as your job and became second nature.

A dozen of them fought in the training yard, going at one another fiercely with staffs and clubs. I was used to more orthodox weapons, but I didn't suppose the criminal element of the city kitted up with swords and shields. The vigiles of the first century of the Fifth Cohort didn't have to know how to break a tortoise formation; they needed to know how to break kneecaps. And, watching them from the shade of a stringy tree that grew at the edge of the training ground, I decided I didn't ever want to cross them. Even the youngest, who must have been about fifteen at the most, was swinging his staff with a single-minded intensity that scared the shit out of me. Vibilus, the vigile whose injured ribs precluded him from taking part in the morning training session, was stacking fire mats.

I found myself wondering where they put this training to use. Shouldn't they have been learning how to bring down burning roofs with grappling hooks or walls with battering rams? The fire mats that Vibilus was stacking were blackened, showing they had regular use, but that morning in the training yard, I only saw the vigiles practicing how to fight.

I watched Atreus while he watched his vigiles. I watched the way the sun illuminated the planes of his face and the fine hair on his arms. I watched the way his muscles corded in his forearms when he grabbed one of his men by the tunic to adjust his stance and how easily that long, lean body of his moved in the sunlight. I glanced away again before he caught me staring.

At last, the lumbering vigile who'd earlier scowled at me from the front entrance of the station house poked his head outside. "Boss!" he called. "Hey, boss!"

"What is it, Gaius?" Atreus asked.

"Someone here to see you," Gaius replied. "Some accountant."

Atreus and I headed back inside.

When Philosthones met us in the passageway, he arched a single thin eyebrow.

"Jupiter, Quintus, have you been arrested?" he asked dryly.

I made a face at him. "Actually, Philosthones, I'm helping the vigiles with their enquiries, but not in the way you're assuming."

The old man looked at me curiously as we began to climb the stairs towards Atreus's office.

"I'm looking into the murder of Marcellus Albanus."

Philosthones looked at me more keenly. "Really? *You* are?"

His respect for me was awesome.

"This is Junius Atreus," I said, waving vaguely at Atreus. "Atreus, this is Philosthones, my accountant. If you want someone to make any sense of all that rubbish, he's the man to ask."

"Please, sit down," said Atreus.

Atreus and I took our previous positions around the desk, and Philosthones pulled up another chair to the desk. He gestured to the little crate. "Is this it, then?"

"Yes, sir," Atreus said.

Philosthones liked the vigile's respectful tone. His eyes gleamed happily as he reached into the crate and gently lifted out the first sheet. He perused it quietly for a moment and then sat it down carefully on the table and blinked at us like an owl.

"Oh, my," he said. He looked down at the page again. I could hear him muttering to himself: *"Donum? Dedit? Dono donavit?"*

Atreus looked at me worriedly.

126

I helped myself to Philosthones's old abacus and clicked the beads along. "Don't worry, Atreus," I said. "Philosthones is a genius."

"My," said Philosthones again. He frowned at the page. "This *is* interesting. It's indecipherable!"

"Yes, that's why we sent for you." I leaned back in my chair and stretched. "What can you tell us?"

Philosthones reclaimed his abacus. "Well, Quintus, when you do your accounts, don't you try and make them legible?"

"*You* do my accounts."

Philosthones sighed and fixed me with a stare. "Quintus, my boy, it's the Socratic method. Try and keep up."

I looked at Atreus. He ducked his head.

Philosthones tried again. "What is the purpose of keeping accounts?"

I had been asking myself the same question for a long time. To me, account-keeping had always seemed just like something that got in the way of enjoying life. Like having a tooth pulled or sitting through anything by Sophocles.

Philosthones looked to Atreus. "Perhaps you can answer me?"

"Ah, to make sure you're not overspending the rent money," Atreus suggested.

Philosthones made a *tut-tut* noise and shook his head. "The purpose of keeping accounts is to keep control of your assets, down to the last *quadrans*. Most patrician families have one ambitious objective in mind, and that is to make all of their sons senators. To become a senator, how much does a man need to have invested in land?" He looked at me sharply.

"A million sesterces," I said, feeling like I was eight years old again and Philosthones was about to rap me over the knuckles if I got the answer wrong.

Philosthones nodded. "That's right, a million for each son. Over the generations, important families develop investment portfolios complicated enough to rival their genealogies. And since they're passed along just like the family pedigree, they are *never* unintelligible. They simply can't afford to be." He shot me a sideways glance. "Which is what I have been trying to get through your head for years, by the way."

I ignored that as well.

"I don't follow," said Atreus guardedly.

Philosthones regrouped. "Well, put simply, to keep the family fortune on track, the family finances have to be well kept. You might understand your shorthand, but you can be sure your great-grandson won't." He gestured to the page in front of him. "I am quite certain that these figures do not relate to the Marcellus family assets. These, I suspect, are account records that were intentionally made indecipherable in case of discovery. I would stake my reputation on the fact that Marcellus Albanus had something to hide."

"I thought it might be gambling," I said helpfully.

"Really?" Philosthones asked me. He tapped the page. "And how do you suppose this payment of fifty *aurei* relates to the racetrack?"

I ignored his sarcasm and whistled lowly. "That's a lot of money."

Atreus shook his head slowly. If it was a lot of money for me, it was a lot more money for Atreus. For me, it was a huge chunk of cash. For Atreus, I suspected it was a completely abstract concept. For Philosthones, it was just another figure, and he loved figures. His eyes lit up as he had a look at the next page. He was in his element.

"*Aurum,* or *aurei,*" murmured Atreus to himself. "Or possibly *Avitus.*"

He wasn't going to let it go. Atreus didn't like Avitus Florian. From what I'd seen of Atreus in action, he probably managed to alienate everyone he spoke to. Maybe Florian had put him in his place, and it rankled. Whatever the case, it was apparent to me that when we each thought of young Florian, Atreus and I might as well have been thinking of different people. I thought of the young man I'd seen sitting at Marcellus Naso's feet the day after Albanus was killed. Jupiter only knows what Atreus thought.

"I want to talk to Avitus Florian," said Atreus suddenly. "He benefited from his cousin's death. I want to know by how much."

I couldn't argue with that, however much I thought Atreus was still barking up the wrong tree. I could only be on hand to bring him to heel if he needed it.

Atreus rose to his feet and said to Philosthones, "Gaius will take this back to your house, sir. You will be recompensed for your time."

Philosthones looked up from the accounts and smiled vaguely. "Yes, of course, Junius Atreus, thank you."

Atreus didn't realise that Philosthones would probably do it just for the love of it, for the challenge, and for our friendship. I kept my mouth shut. Why shouldn't the old man benefit?

Atreus and I headed back outside again in the hope that we would learn something useful from young Avitus Florian.

* * *

Florian lived in a modestly affluent neighbourhood on the other side of the Caelian Hill. I hadn't known we were neighbours until we were approaching the portico. The portico was wide and inviting, but, like the rest of the neighbourhood, it was nothing flash. As we approached, I couldn't help wondering how much Florian's circumstances had been improved by Marcellus Albanus's sudden death. He certainly now had a much nicer, much larger house to move into.

A well-mannered young slave opened the door to us.

Florian met us in the atrium. "Valerius. How nice to see you again."

So he remembered me, possibly from those few exchanged words at the commissatio, but more likely from our awkward conversation at Marcellus Naso's house. But why shouldn't he remember me, regardless of the circumstances? I was a few rungs further up the social ladder than him.

Florian had an earnest face. "Come through, please."

Florian was not my ideal murderer. He looked more like the kind of young man who would rescue birds from cats, orphans from the street, and women of all ages from distress. He showed us into a pleasant sitting room.

Atreus spoke. "I am Junius Atreus. I spoke to you the night Marcellus Albanus died."

"Yes, of course," said Florian politely.

I looked around the room. Florian was unmarried, but the place had a woman's touch and a palla discarded on one of the cushioned seats.

Florian noticed my gaze. "I live with my aunt. She's not here today."

"We need to talk," I said, sitting down without a proper invitation. Atreus took my cue and sat down as well.

Florian sat cautiously on the other side of a low table. He looked wary. His puppy-dog eyes were wide with apprehension. "Do we?"

"I think you know what it's about," I said. By prearrangement with Atreus, I was to begin questioning him. He was less likely to take offence and refuse to answer if the questions started coming from one of his social peers.

"Would you like a drink?" Florian asked us, trying to play the good host. He was too nervous to pull it off, and I wondered why.

"No, thank you," I said. I jumped right in. "Florian, I'm acting on behalf of the magistrate Septus Severus. I'm investigating the murder of your cousin Marcellus Albanus."

"I see."

I went on the attack. "The amulet, Florian. The one you found. It's very strange, isn't it?"

"Is it?" Florian asked. He cleared his throat.

Atreus reached into the pouch around his belt and pulled out the little trinket on its leather strap. He placed it on the table. "This amulet. You found it with your cousin's body."

"Yes," said Florian, eyeing the thing uneasily.

Atreus nodded to himself for a moment and then smiled slightly. "I'm surprised by your answer, sir."

"Surprised?" Florian asked worriedly.

"Very surprised," agreed Atreus and then changed subjects completely. "Why didn't you leave the party earlier, sir?"

"I was asleep," Florian floundered. "I drank too much and—"

"And what time did you leave?" asked Atreus, reclaiming the strange little amulet. "Did you stay until the morning?"

"No, I left after I talked to you," said Florian. "Is that important?"

"And will your litter bearers confirm that, sir?" asked Atreus.

"I walked," said Florian.

I wouldn't have been more surprised if he'd said he'd flown. "You *walked*?"

Florian flushed. "Yes. I enjoy walking."

Translation: money was tight. I took another look around the sitting room and noticed where the furniture had been moved to hide the peeling plaster. Admitting financial difficulties was like admitting to a hideous deformity, strange sexual proclivities, or descent from freedmen.

"It was a pleasant evening, so I decided to walk."

"You mean you don't have a litter?" I clarified.

Florian went red. "My aunt was using it."

I gave him a moment to recover from his shame and then got straight to the point. "Is there any reason, Florian, that you didn't give a eulogy at your cousin's funeral?" I felt like a bastard even asking, because I'd read his face that day, but Atreus wanted it asked. "You were closely related. You were on the main table at his dinner party. I'm sure you were great friends."

"I couldn't talk," said Florian. It sounded like it was an effort for him even now. He leaned back in his seat and sighed suddenly. "And yes, we were friends when I was growing up. He was like an older brother to me."

Atreus's face was unreadable. "What happened?"

Florian looked at him guardedly for a moment but continued. "We were very close, but when he joined the army, we lost touch. When he came home, we had very little in common anymore. He had new friends and a lifestyle I couldn't afford to match. He did me a favour by putting my name up for the Third Gallica, but I wasn't keen to go. I probably won't now."

"Why not?" I asked, curious as to why he was going to throw a conventional career away. Almost everyone started out as a junior tribune. It was the first rung on the very rickety ladder of political success. There were ways around it, but they took longer.

"I didn't like his friends," said Florian. He saw our blank faces and explained. "There's a whole group of them, and they're always getting together for parties. I'm not a drinker, Valerius. You saw that at the commissatio. Albanus wanted me to join the Third Gallica just so I could be in his stupid drinking club." He sighed again. "Albanus loved the military life. He spent five years with the Third, when he could have come home earlier."

For a murder suspect, he was offering up a lot of things freely, just not the things we wanted to hear. I tried to steer him back towards Albanus's legacy, but Atreus chimed in suddenly.

"The guests at Albanus's party," the vigile asked. "Were any of them in the drinking club?"

Florian shrugged. "I don't know. I think so. Albanus tried to make out it was a real club, with a secretary and everything, but as far as I know, it was just an excuse to get together for parties."

I was familiar with the scenario myself. I might have been the paterfamilias, but in reality, I was ruled by my womenfolk. So were most men I knew. Sometimes, we'd use any excuse to get together with a group of likeminded fellows and act like boys again. That old military chestnut was perfect. I remembered what Paulinus had told me at his house: *"You know how it is, Valerius. You meet some fellow who's been in the same legion, and you're obligated to drink together."* Paulinus might have called it an obligation, but I suspected it was a happy duty.

"Who else was in this group?" Atreus asked.

Florian looked baffled. "I don't really know." He shrugged. "I never wanted to be involved. I think that Nepos was in it, and maybe Rufanus."

"And Paulinus?" I asked.

Florian shrugged again. "I think so. I presume most of them were at the party. I mean, a lot of men saluted the sun at the commissatio."

Atreus cleared his throat. "Avitus Florian, where did they meet?

Florian shook his head. "I don't know, I never went. Albanus was going to be my patron and introduce me, but it never happened." He looked shamefaced. "On the day of the party, we had a falling out."

That caught my attention. "What about?"

Florian sighed, and then looked at me apologetically, and said something so unexpected that it almost floored me then and there: "It was about Julia Drusilla."

"Julia Drusilla?" I asked, reeling. *"My* Julia Drusilla?"

I'd never called her that before, but I was shocked to hear her name mentioned, and some hitherto undiscovered protectiveness suddenly asserted itself. Florian had the decency to look ashamed. I looked around at Atreus, stunned, and I could see exactly what he was thinking, because I was suddenly thinking it myself: *There's his motive.*

I tried not to get angry, but I could feel rage rising up in me. "How long, Florian, have you been pursuing my stepdaughter behind her parents' backs?"

Florian looked stung. "It's not what you think!"

"What is it then?" I demanded. "Little notes, love tokens? What is she to you? Is she some naïve little rich girl just begging to be seduced, or is it true love?" I sounded even more sarcastic than I had intended.

Florian shook his head, mute for a moment. The words, when they came, were small. "I love Julia."

He sounded as though he actually meant it.

Atreus leaned forward again. "I expect it must have come as something of a relief when your rival Albanus was murdered."

"No!" Florian objected, seeing exactly where Atreus was leading him. Our sceptical faces caused him to have a rethink. "Well, *yes,* in the sense that I knew he wouldn't treat her well, but I didn't do it. He was my *cousin.*"

"I think I liked you more when you killed him for his house," Atreus said to Florian.

"What?" Florian managed. He struggled to compose himself. "It was a joke. He was like that."

"What do you mean?" Atreus asked.

"It was a joke," Florian repeated. "Before he joined the legion, he decided to make a will. He told me he'd leave me the house, because he said that otherwise I'd be stuck with Aunt Sempronia forever. But I didn't want it. It was his joke."

Atreus and I exchanged a dubious look.

Florian flushed. "It's stupid. Look, I might have the house, but I've got nothing else. I don't have any money. I don't even own any slaves. I can't afford to live there. That's what made it *funny,* because I'd still be stuck with my aunt anyway. And that's why I never approached Gavius Silanus about Julia Drusilla. I wasn't going behind his back, because I've never approached *her* either. We spoke several times, that's all, but I made no declarations of my feelings." He shrugged helplessly. "I couldn't. I'm not rich. I've got nothing."

It explained to me why we'd never met on the social circuit before. He couldn't afford to play. It also explained why he no longer wanted to join the Third Gallica. Without Albanus behind him, he probably couldn't pay for his kit.

Atreus was wearing a thoughtful frown. "If you never approached Julia Drusilla, and you never approached her father, why were you arguing with Albanus about her?"

Florian slumped back in his seat, looking defeated. "Because he knew, and he teased me about it. So I told him I was fed up with him, and fed up with his friends, and that I'd manage on my own from now on." He smiled slightly. "Stupid."

"How can you say you love Julia if you've never approached her?" I asked. I really wanted to ask: *How can you say you love Julia? Were you dropped on your head as an infant?*

"I've met her," Florian clarified. "I've met her a few times, mostly at her father's house when I went there with Albanus. We spoke on several occasions, once, um, once alone, but you must believe me, Valerius, when I swear to you that nothing happened!"

"I'm reserving judgement."

"Nothing happened," Florian repeated. "We only talked. She knew I was Albanus's cousin, but I don't think she realised until it was already agreed upon that her father was thinking of marrying her to Albanus. She told me I betrayed her by not telling her." He looked miserable. "I didn't understand until then that she returned my feelings."

I thought back to Julia's histrionics the day she'd turned up at my house. It wasn't just the fact that her father had gone and got her engaged. It was because she'd had someone else in mind, without knowing he was below consideration.

"If what you're saying is true," said Atreus finally, "then because of your financial situation, you actually gained nothing from Marcellus Albanus's death. I need you to be absolutely clear. Is that what you're telling us?"

"Yes," said Florian candidly and then paused. A shadow crossed his face, and he frowned. "Well, it *was* true."

"What do you mean?" Atreus asked.

"But isn't that why you're here?" Florian asked. He looked miserable again. "Of course, you don't know."

"Don't know what?" Atreus asked.

Florian sighed. "I've got the best motive in the world, I'm afraid." He looked tired. "How do I put it? Well then, finding himself with no other heir, and despite our not being blood relations, the eminent Marcellus Naso has decided to do me the honour of adopting me."

* * *

Outside in the street, Atreus and I stood in the shade of a large fig tree and tried to make up our minds about Florian. We had both walked into his house with certain preconceptions. I'd thought he was innocent. Atreus had thought he was guilty. Now neither of us was sure. Florian's revelation, just as I was starting to believe him innocent of murder, did actually give him a motive for killing Albanus, but only if he could have known that Marcellus Naso would adopt him as his heir afterwards. If he had done it, he had taken a big gamble.

"He was lying about the amulet," Atreus said firmly.

"Who cares about that?" I asked. "Jupiter, Atreus, he just came out and admitted that Albanus's death is the best thing that's ever happened to him."

Except for his grief.

Atreus kicked the dust and sighed. "Yes, he has the best motive in the world, but he *walked*. He had no litter bearers with him."

I looked at him sideways. "I thought you'd be happier about it."

Atreus didn't look happy. He looked annoyed. "The problem is, sir, I think I believe him. He didn't have to admit that he and Albanus had fought on the day he died, he didn't have to admit he was in love with Albanus's fiancée, and he certainly didn't have to admit he is now Marcellus Naso's

135

heir!"

Three motives in a matter of moments, but Atreus just wasn't happy. I glanced at his frowning face and knew the reason. Atreus wasn't happy because although all of those motives were good, and put together they were great, none of them suited Florian. He had offered them all up too freely for any one of them to fit.

"After all," said Atreus, catching up to me, "you wouldn't kill a man on the slim chance his patron would adopt you instead, would you?"

"Probably not."

"But he was lying about the amulet," Atreus maintained.

I grunted noncommittally, and Atreus and I stood in the street and pondered matters for a little while longer. Having an attention span only slightly longer than the much-maligned Hursa's, I got bored first.

"So, Atreus, what's for lunch?"

Chapter Eight

Atreus and I went to the nearest caupona for lunch. Neither of us was familiar with the place. We'd never been there before and, considering what passed for service, we weren't likely to go there again. We should have guessed by the fact it was almost deserted. Our wine was served by a skinny waiter with an interesting skin condition. We watched him scratching himself while he stood over our cups at the counter. The food wasn't much better, but at least the cook who brought it out wasn't scabby and flaking.

The house specialty was mushroom soup. Carefully working my way through it, I couldn't help thinking of how Sulla got rid of the troublesome women in his life. As a bonus, their wealthy legacies had kick-started his political career. He'd started his life hanging around with comics, lute-players, and prostitutes and ended up dictator of Rome. Not bad for the cost of a few mushrooms.

The soup was barely palatable. Whether it was actually poisonous, only time would tell. Feeling slightly replenished, we headed back outside again. Menenius Carpo was next on the list. The choice was purely geographical. Carpo lived on the Caelian Hill, not too far away from Florian. Atreus filled me in while we trudged up the hill.

"Menenius Carpo is the son of Menenius Carpo Dalmatius," Atreus said. "Do you know the father?"

"No, but I'm guessing he did something heroic in Dalmatia in his glory days."

"He was a general, sir," Atreus confirmed, "and very hard-headed. He won't let me near junior, and I'm not sure whether it's because he thinks the boy's got something to hide or if he's just being obstinate."

"He doesn't like you?" I asked, trying to sound surprised.

"He called me an intrusive upstart son of a bitch."

As it happened, neither Menenius Carpo nor his charming father were at home when we called. The suspicious door slave, who recognised Atreus, wasn't forthcoming at all.

"My master and his son are out," he said primly and tried to shut the door.

Atreus held it open. "Where are they?" he asked.

The door slave gave up the battle with the door and glared at us. "Menenius Carpo Dalmatius is at the Curia," he said huffily. "I cannot disclose the whereabouts of young Menenius Carpo."

"Are you sure about that?" Atreus flicked a coin at him, and the door slave caught it deftly.

The slave inspected the coin and found it too small for his liking. "Yes, sir," he replied archly, tucking the coin into his yellow tunic, "I am quite sure."

Atreus looked annoyed, but I couldn't help snorting with laughter.

"You'll have to forgive the vigile," I told the slave. "Over in the Transtiberina, a quadrans is a fortune!"

The slave smirked slightly, warming to me.

I had dealt with snobbish slaves before. They liked to feel just as important as their patrician masters. In many households, they were. Just because the door slave wasn't a free man didn't mean he couldn't lord it over plebeians like Atreus. He was more sophisticated, more educated, and possibly even richer than the vigile. Atreus's coin wouldn't be the last he got his sticky little hands on. Anyone who wanted to see Menenius Carpo Dalmatius, whether to inveigle a social invitation or be hired to plaster the walls, had to pass the door slave. A clever door slave could make that worth his while, and I could see that this one was clever.

I reached into the purse around my belt and found a brass dupondius. I held it up so it caught the light. "Of course, this is not the Transtiberina."

"No, sir," the slave agreed happily.

"I wonder where I might happen to cross paths with young Menenius Carpo," I mused, extending my hand.

The door slave plucked the dupondius from my fingers. It disappeared the way of the first coin into the folds of his tunic. He inclined his head respectfully in my direction. "If sir happens to find himself in the bathhouse of the Three Dolphins presently, he may find that question answered to his satisfaction."

"By fortunate coincidence, I was just heading that way," I said. "Would that be the Three Dolphins near the Porta Capena?"

"Yes, sir," said the door slave, still smirking a little at Atreus.

Atreus looked back at him with a face like thunder. The slave wasn't bothered. He huffed to himself one last time, and then, finding our business at an end, he closed the door on us.

Atreus looked annoyed as we headed back down the hill towards the Porta Capena, smarting at being put in his place by a door slave. I found him surprisingly thin-skinned for a vigile. Mad Uncle Maro and Marcellus Naso had been right to push Severus into making me his representative. Atreus had no idea how to deal with the wealthy and powerful, or their slaves. I reflected on that as we walked. Perhaps that was unjust. Perhaps Atreus did have the *idea*—he had tried to bribe the slave after all—but it had been poorly executed. I couldn't imagine being in a financial position where a slave looked down on me. It must have rankled.

"I don't live in the Transtiberina, sir," he said out of nowhere as we headed towards the Porta Capena.

"I had to say something to get the door slave on our side," I said, wondering if I'd actually offended him.

The more I thought about that, the more I could see why Atreus was still wearing his scowl. It had mostly worn off by the time we reached the vicinity of Porta Capena, but the shadow of it remained cast over his serious face.

The Three Dolphins bathhouse, creatively named for the fountain out the front, was situated a block away from the Porta Capena, the massive gate in the Servian Wall where the Via Appia began. I felt like we were crisscrossing the Caelian Hill like ants on a mound, and my feet were starting to ache. The Three Dolphins was not a public bathhouse. Like my own, it was for private members only, meaning that you didn't need to run into plasterers and bricklayers in the changing room. The Three Dolphins was only a small facility, but it gave the impression of exclusivity. Most of that was down to the marble floor tiles, the gleaming bronze fixtures, and the well-bred slave in the atrium who recognised me immediately as worthy of his attention and talked me through the features of the place in a friendly and professional manner.

The door slave was small and spry and shiny with sweat, a workplace hazard of his. The heat from the caldarium was apparent even from the atrium. It seeped up through the tiles from the underbelly of the bathhouse, where a small army of unseen slaves crawled around under the floor to keep the furnaces burning.

The amicable little slave was trying to sell me on the merits of the place. Maybe he earned a commission from a generous master. "We have both a sudatorium, *and* a laconium. We also have a gymnasium, sir, both indoor and outdoor, and our masseuses are first-rate."

The way he told it, the Three Dolphins had everything. It had the usual three pools, the aforementioned steam rooms, and all the small luxuries that weren't available at most of the public baths, like free house wine, food, and musicians. Like my own bathhouse, it even had a library. Then, the slave ushered us through to the changing rooms, and I got an eyeful of at least one major difference.

Most public baths in the city were open in the mornings for women and the afternoons for men. This was the main reason I preferred a private bathhouse—it didn't allow women, so the men could bathe at any time of day. Management of the Three Dolphins had taken a different approach to the constraints of conventional morality by disregarding them altogether. It was unisex. There was a naked woman in the changing room, inspecting herself in the hazy reflection of a brass mirror tacked up on the wall. She turned around when she heard us and planted her hands on her hips. I got an eyeful of the naked woman, and she got an eyeful of me. She got the better deal. Yeah, that was one thing my bathhouse didn't have: prostitutes.

"This is Scylla," said the door slave.

"Are these new clients?" the woman asked, still not moving to cover up at all.

"Actually, we're just here to meet a friend," I said, disappointing the pair of them, who both thought they were in the money. "Young Menenius Carpo, have you seen him?"

"He's in the tepidarium," said the prostitute, reaching for her tunic at last.

Atreus and I swept through the changing rooms into the caldarium. The place was blanketed in clouds of steam. My tunic had stuck to my skin by the time we'd traversed the length of the pool and moved on into the tepidarium. It wasn't quite as hot in the tepidarium, but it was still clammy. Atreus and I crossed to the pool and scanned the occupants. There were seven bodies in the pool: four men and three women. Only one of the men was unencumbered by a playmate and too old to be Menenius Carpo. I had the creepy feeling that he just liked to watch.

The tepidarium smelled of incense and perfumed oils. The water was cloudy with oil and other fluids I didn't want to think about.

I crouched down on the side of the pool. "Hey, Carpo!"

A naked, sodden youth disentangled himself from his naked, sodden companion. He frowned when he spotted me. "Do I know you?"

I gave a broad smile. "Sure, don't you remember?"

Young Menenius Carpo had never been troubled by debt collectors if he fell for that old trick. He swam over to the side of the pool towards us, lazily showing off a body that had spent more time at the table than in the gymnasium. He was soft around the edges.

"The name's Aemilius Valerius," I told him. "We met at Albanus's place the night of his party."

That wasn't true as far as I knew, but it might have been. If Carpo had been even half as drunk as me that night, we might have sworn lifelong brotherhood for all I remembered. I'd done stupider things while drunk. Jupiter Optimus Maximus, I'd done stupider things that night. Nicius the Hispanian dancer still haunted me.

"Oh," he said and wiped his dripping hair out of his eyes. He had a round face that gleamed wetly in the confines of the bathhouse. He looked doughy and unfinished and damp, like clay before firing.

"Actually, I'm investigating Albanus's death," I said.

"Oh," Carpo said again, and his eyebrows shot up. "Really?"

I gestured to Atreus. "This is Junius Atreus, a vigile. We're working under the magistrate Septus Severus."

Carpo rested his arms over the edge of the pool. He shrugged his round shoulders. "Alright."

I caught a glimpse of silver around Carpo's neck and leaned closer to the tepid waters of the pool. "That's a nice amulet," I said, hoping for a closer look.

Carpo had nothing to hide. He hooked his thumb around the leather thong and held the amulet out for me. It was a little silver figure with a pointy hat and winged sandals.

"It's Mercury," Carpo said. "My mother bought it for me."

The little silver figure gleamed damply: Mercury, messenger of the gods, patron god of travellers and smooth-talkers, and about as Roman as it was possible to get. Meaning essentially that we'd nicked it off the Greeks, changed its name, and made it better. It was a far cry from Albanus's little Christian amulet.

Atreus crouched down beside the pool as well. "Menenius Carpo, we found an amulet beside Marcellus Albanus's body. Have you ever seen one of these before?"

He dangled the Christian amulet in front of Carpo's round face.

"Is that bronze?" Carpo blinked damply at the amulet. This boy wouldn't be seen dead in bronze. "Is it meant to be a fish?"

Atreus tucked the amulet away again. "Menenius Carpo, when did you leave the party on the night Albanus died?"

"I don't remember," said Carpo frankly, readjusting his Mercury. "I was so drunk I was throwing up all the next day."

"Would your litter bearers know?" Atreus asked.

"Maybe," Carpo said and shrugged lazily again. "Why are you asking?"

142

I wondered if he'd steamed his brains out in the bath.

"Well, sir," said Atreus patiently, "I need to know who killed him, and you have been unable to provide an alibi. In fact, up until now, you've refused to speak with me at all."

"*I* haven't," corrected Carpo. "It's my father that's refused to let the vigiles see me."

"Why would he do that?" asked Atreus.

Carpo rolled his eyes. "He's worried there's a scandal, and I'm somehow involved. He's *always* worried that I'm involved." He wrinkled his nose as a drop of water chased down his round face. "I'm not, though. I hardly knew Albanus. Why would I want to kill him?"

"Why were you at his party if you didn't know him well?" Atreus asked. He really had no idea.

"Because it was free, and I got an invitation," Carpo said. "I didn't have a couch or anything, but I was there for the entertainment." He looked at me wide-eyed. "How amazing was that trireme?"

"Very," I agreed dryly.

"Amazing!" Carpo whistled lowly. He ducked back into the water briefly and then popped out again like a well-greased seal. He rested his weight on his elbows. "My father was horrified when he found out what had happened, even though it's like the best scandal *ever*. He's so old-fashioned. He thinks that it's bad to be associated with anything shocking and that I'll never be a consul if I keep on the way I am."

I imagined echoes of my own father in Menenius Carpo Dalmatius.

Carpo grinned. "Lucky he doesn't know about this place."

So young Menenius Carpo was misspending his youth in a bathhouse that doubled as a brothel and probably in a hundred other ways of which his father disapproved. I was no stranger to that scenario myself, but I'd always preferred to spend my money at the racetrack, where I still believed you got more value for your money than in a brothel. A good time at the races could last all day. At a brothel, you were bound to run out of stamina in an hour or two, although young Menenius Carpo looked like he knew how to pace himself. Maybe the buoyancy helped.

Still, it was the oldest tale in the book. An ambitious father, a lazy son, and it was difficult to see eye to eye on anything. The old man was obviously trying to keep his son's reputation intact. His son didn't give a damn about his reputation. Old men like Carpo's father, and Marcellus Naso, and even my mad Uncle Maro thought that respectability still counted for something in public life. Young cynics, like myself and Carpo, knew that wasn't true. We'd seen too many flashy scandal-makers and dodgy operators make good to believe that hard work and clean living had anything to do with political success. Whether they liked it or not, the days of Cicero, the Republic's last true friend, were long gone. He was a great man, Cicero, upright and moralistic, and look at how he ended up. With his head and his hands nailed to the Rostra.

A splash caught my attention. Carpo's swimming companion was doing a languid backstroke on the other side of the pool. She looked like a goddess kidnapped by Neptune and ensnared in his watery kingdom, and she gave me a smile that suggested she was up for anything, at the right price.

I cleared my throat. "So you don't remember anything about when you left?"

Carpo wrinkled his damp forehead in thought. "Actually, I think I left before the commissatio had even ended." He grinned at me. "I saw *you* get carried out calling for that dancer. Was he any good?"

I felt Atreus's gaze burning into me. "I'm afraid I was too drunk to remember."

And too drunk to get it up, though that was no surprise.

Carpo hummed sympathetically. "Anyway, Albanus had laid on a lot of wine for the commissatio, and I thought all the drinking was over when a couple of slaves brought in another amphora. I figured at that time that I was already as drunk as ten men, and I'd only throw up if I stayed there, so I went and found the front door."

"And none of the household slaves saw you?" asked Atreus.

"I don't know," Carpo answered. "I don't remember seeing any of them. I don't remember seeing *anything*." He laughed. "I do remember lying on the road looking at the sky while a bunch of litter bearers tried to figure out who I belonged to. They must have found my bearers in the end, because I got home alright."

The gods protected the drunk and the stupid, thankfully for all of us who'd ever been in that position. Carpo had staggered unseen out onto the street, collapsed onto the road in a drunken stupor, and woken up in his own bed the next day with no idea of how he'd got there. It wasn't exactly an alibi, but it was plausible. I thought Carpo was exactly what he appeared: a shiftless but guileless youth, like a thousand others in the city, who would probably surprise everyone who knew him by being consul one day and shutting down bathhouses like this one to protect public morality.

"Thank you for your time, sir," said Atreus.

"No problem," said Carpo in a friendly tone, and splashed his way back over towards his waiting playmate.

"Well," I said to Atreus as we headed back towards the entrance, "I don't think I'll be seeking membership to this place."

Atreus nodded. "Though Carpo certainly seems to like spending time with Amatheia of the lovely locks."

I hadn't expected a plebeian vigile to make such an obscure reference to *The Illiad*. Strange that he saw her as a nereid, rather than just as a water-logged prostitute. I would have expected someone in his line of work to be more pragmatic.

"I don't think it's her locks he's interested in."

"No, sir," Atreus agreed.

"Besides," I said as we sailed past the door slave and back outside into the sunlight, "I make it a policy to never trust a place where the prostitutes use the same changing room as the patrons. Do you really think your purse would be there when you got back?"

"Probably not," said Atreus as we stood for a moment by the fountain and steamed slightly. "The dancer..."

I met his gaze unflinchingly. "What about him?"

Atreus looked away. "Nothing. Sorry."

I perched on the edge of the fountain, just out of range of the water-spouting dolphins, and squinted in the sunlight. There was a laundry across the street from the bathhouse that seemed to be doing a brisk trade and a potter's shop right next door. An old man sat on a stool outside the potter's shop, his hands clasping his kneecaps, staring fixedly at a pigeon that bobbed along the street just out of kicking range. I dabbled my fingers in the fountain for a moment and then turned my attention back to Atreus.

"Do we believe Carpo?"

Atreus nodded slightly. "I think so, sir. At this stage, it would certainly be impractical to chase up every litter bearer who was waiting out in the street just to ask if they remembered him."

"Right," I agreed. We already had enough people to chase up.

Atreus leaned up against the fountain beside me. "And, of course," he said thoughtfully, "at least two of those litter bearers might lie anyway."

Ledo and Casso had seen two litter bearers entering the house, presumably at the behest of their master, who didn't want to face Marcellus Albanus in a fair fight. Menenius Carpo didn't seem the sort of fellow who planned ahead at all. And we had found no motive. If it was true that Carpo hardly knew Albanus, I couldn't imagine that he had any reason to plot his murder.

"So, can we cross Carpo off the list?" I asked.

Atreus crossed his arms over his chest. "I think so. He's either a very good liar, or he's exactly what meets the eye."

We sat for a moment longer in silence, and then Atreus exhaled slowly, wearily, like a man with the weight of the world on his shoulders. The afternoon was stretching on. I wanted nothing more than to head home, put my feet up, and relax with a cup of wine. I was kidding myself, though. We weren't finished yet.

* * *

For the rest of the afternoon, we had mixed success, and my feet started to hurt like they hadn't since my army days. We attended the home of Pomptius Voltinian on the Palatine Hill and found that the man himself was currently relaxing in his villa at Baiae. It seemed like a good place for a murderer to hide out after the fact, but Pomptius Voltinian had extremely talkative slaves who soon removed any suspicions we might have been formulating. The door slave fetched the litter bearers, and the whole lot of us had a conference outside the front portico in the shade of a sweet-smelling laurel tree. I doubted that any litter bearers who had helped their master commit a murder would volunteer for a friendly chat with a vigile and a magistrate's assistant. Not only that, but the door slave even produced a dish of olives to tide us over while we talked. Atreus's money was welcome at this house, and I didn't have to resort to opening my own purse this time.

The breeze rustled through the laurel leaves, wafting their scent through the air and making me think of ceremonial wreaths and farm kitchens and soup in winter.

"Do you remember what time your master left the party?" Atreus asked the litter bearers.

The first litter bearer was a big, hulking African who spoke very little Latin but thought he made up for it by nodding a lot. It was up to his compatriot to translate for him. They chattered amongst themselves for a little while before they reached a consensus. The third and fourth litter bearers were both tall and blonde, with massive shoulders and arms as thick as tree trunks. They had less Latin than the Africans. I wondered how the four of them ever got into step.

"They are Helvetii," said the door slave helpfully, catching my gaze.

"Ah," I said. I helped myself to another olive while I waited and hoped all our future interviewees would be as hospitable as this lot.

"It was before the torches burned down," said the second African finally. "After the drinking match, a whole lot of men came out at once, but our master didn't. It was a long time before he came out."

The first litter bearer said something, gesturing at his companion.

The second one grimaced. "Yes, the master had lost his silk napkin and wanted us to find it. I tried to raise the door porter to go and look for it, but he wasn't at his post. So I told the master we would come back for it in the morning, and he fell asleep in the litter."

The first litter bearer said something else in a despondent tone.

"No, we never did get it back," the second agreed.

Atreus nodded thoughtfully. "And did you see any litter bearers enter the house?"

"No, sir," said the second litter bearer. "I went to the entrance only to see if the porter was there. I never went inside, and I didn't see anyone else either."

Pomptius Voltinian's door slave chimed in, eager to earn his quadrans. "I helped the master to bed when he got home. He didn't have any blood on him."

"Did you look?" Atreus asked, surprised. It had caught my attention as well. What sort of man was Pomptius Voltinian that his slaves checked him out for signs of bloodshed after a dinner party?

"Not that night, sir, no!" the door porter exclaimed. "But the next morning, we sent a boy to fetch the master's napkin and found out what had happened. When I went to wake the master and tell him, I saw then that his toga and tunic were clean."

"Did you have any reason to be suspicious?" Atreus asked him.

"No, sir," replied the door slave, turning red. "It was just something that I saw. I thought how awful it would be to walk into my master's bedroom and see blood on his clothes and realise he was a murderer! I didn't *believe* it, sir, but once the thought was in my head, I had to check!"

Atreus gave him an encouraging smile. "You were reassuring yourself?"

"Yes, sir," agreed the embarrassed slave.

I had another olive.

"Was your master close to Marcellus Albanus?" Atreus asked the door slave.

"They were good friends at one time," the slave replied. "Years ago, they were both investing capital in the Greens racing team and went to the Circus Maximus almost every week together, but that was before Albanus went away with the legions. As far as I know, they remained friends after Albanus returned, but they were no longer so close."

"How long have you been in your master's service?" Atreus asked.

"Um," said the door slave and paused to think. "Nine, no, *ten* years. I have found him to be a very good master." He looked at Atreus worriedly,

148

as though he thought the vigile was going to force him to re-evaluate his judgement.

Atreus gave him another encouraging smile.

My opinions of people were often influenced by what their slaves thought about them. In households like this one, where the slaves were well-fed and chatty, it was a fair bet the master was a decent man. In households where the slaves were obviously mistreated or strangely silent, I distrusted the temperament of the master. It was easy for a man to show a respectable face to the world, but it was behind closed doors where the truth came out. Because his slaves liked him, I decided that Pomptius Voltinian was no murderer.

"Thanks for your help," said Atreus to the slaves and looked at me pointedly.

I sighed and reached into my purse. I didn't see the point of a reward as well as a bribe, but I suppose they had deserved it. Well, the Africans and the door slave had. The two Helvetii had been no use at all.

Five beaming smiles of gratitude almost made up for the fact that we hadn't been able to speak to Pomptius Voltinian directly.

Atreus and I wandered back down the street. My feet were still hurting, and now I had pains shooting through my shins, but I wasn't prepared to admit defeat just yet. I only hoped that our next customer didn't live too far away from Voltinian.

He didn't.

It was Manius Galerius Nepos, and he also resided in a large house on the exclusive Palatine Hill. Like Pomptius Voltinian, he wasn't home. Unlike Voltinian, his slaves were nowhere near as forthcoming. This door slave proved unbribable. I was prepared to go as high as a sestertius, but he was having none of that. Nepos was odds-on to be a consul next time around; the slave was used to getting rid of visitors, both more important and more annoying than me.

"Sir, I will advise my master of your visit when he returns," the door slave informed me and closed the door very firmly in our faces.

There was a wineshop a little way down the hill that was calling us. It was nicer than the one we'd tried earlier. As befitted the neighbourhood, the waiter was cleaner, the shop was busier, and the wine was sweeter.

It was good to get out of the sun for a while. I stretched out my legs under the table and wondered if we'd actually accomplished anything so far. At this rate, it would take the better part of a week to interview everyone on Atreus's list, and that was presupposing everything went smoothly. I wasn't sure what to expect from a murder investigation. Would one man on the list give himself away easily? It hadn't happened yet. Worse still, what if we made it to the end of the list and still couldn't identify our killer?

I glanced at Atreus surreptitiously and wondered if he was as worried as I was. He didn't look it. He looked relaxed and thoughtful as he leaned back on his stool and rested against the wall.

"So," I said airily as I nursed my cup of wine, "how do you feel it's going?"

"It's too early to tell, sir. Things will become clearer as we progress, I'm sure." Atreus rolled his shoulders and drew a deep breath. "It's getting late. Shall we see who's coming out of the Curia?"

* * *

It was late afternoon by the time Atreus and I arrived at the Curia. For a long while, we watched the who's who of the city drifting down the steps into their waiting litters or gathering together in little groups to continue the day's debate in the golden afternoon sunlight. It was hard to pick one from the other. I saw Marcellus Naso, looking older and frailer than I had known him, leaning on the arm of a younger senator as he descended the broad marble steps. I even saw my mad Uncle Maro, busily inspecting a scroll and almost tripping down the steps. His litter bearers, who knew to watch out for that, met him on the steps before he did himself any serious damage and escorted him the rest of the way. They eased him into his litter where he could read his scroll without risking further injury. Knowing Maro it was the plans for his latest home renovation.

"If I can just remove a wall or two here," he'd exclaimed to me enthusiastically a week or two before, *"think how much it will open up the space!"*

"It will open up the space because the roof will collapse."

Atreus and I stood like sightseers at the bottom of the Curia steps, waiting for a familiar face. At last, we saw one: Claudius Rufanus, of *the* Claudians. I remembered his face from the main table on the night of the party. He had been seated right beside Albanus, and he had known my name before I knew his. He had placed me as Decius Nasica's brother-in-law.

Claudius Rufanus was standing on the steps of the Curia, looking every inch the important senator and discussing the taxation of the senatorial provinces with a group of equally important-looking senators. Their bored litter bearers and attendants were playing knucklebones at the bottom of the steps, each one of them glancing up every now and then to see if their masters were coming yet or if they had finally taken root.

The afternoon shadows were lengthening, and the activity in the buzzing Forum was starting to slow down. Soon, everyone would be heading off to their homes for dinner, giving the city streets a brief respite before the evening kicked in and the social rounds began. Dinner, the theatre, and parties for the rich. For the poor, I didn't know. I knew that a lot of them clogged up the streets after dark with wagons and carts and all the associated detritus of their particular industries, but I was sketchy on the details.

"Claudius Rufanus," I called, climbing the steps and insinuating myself into the group. "Salve!"

I looked out of place with my tunic, my cloak, and my shadowing vigile. Every single one of them was wearing a toga, vigileless, and standing like rigid statues to hold the folds in place. Rufanus looked down his patrician nose at me. He was not a physically impressive man, being middle-aged and fleshy, but he had presence. I could tell just by looking at him that his birthright was bigger than mine.

"Aemilius Valerius," he acknowledged.

I nodded deferentially. "You may have heard, Rufanus, that the magistrate Septus Severus has asked me to assist him in investigating the murder of Marcellus Albanus."

Rufanus gestured politely to his cronies, took me by the elbow, and drew me down the steps out of earshot. Atreus followed us.

"I had heard, yes," Rufanus said, releasing my elbow and rocking back on his heels. "I'd be interested to know what it has to do with me, Valerius."

Rufanus was a career politician with a sharp mind. His greying eyebrows drew together keenly as he waited for my answer. Whether by accident or design, he had me standing so I was staring into the sun. I was reminded of those potentates and kings who built low doorways, so their subjects had to bow as they entered a room. It put adversaries on the back foot immediately. I wondered if Rufanus considered me an adversary, or if he tried this trick on everyone he met.

I shaded my eyes with my hand and squinted unattractively in Rufanus's direction. I tried to sound both professional and humble as I spoke. "Simply put, Rufanus, you are one of very few men who cannot provide an alibi," I said.

"I don't recall being asked to provide one."

"Actually, sir," interjected Atreus unhelpfully, "I spoke to your secretary two days ago asking to see you."

"Did you?" Rufanus looked him up and down. "Perhaps you forgot to leave your name."

"Well," I said, still squinting, "if you were unable to make time for Atreus, would you mind speaking to me instead?"

The sun hurt my eyes, so I had to move down a step closer to the street. Now he could really look down on me.

Rufanus arched his brows. "I can spare you a few moments, Valerius, nothing more. What is it you need to know?"

I resisted the urge to turn around to Atreus for guidance. Rufanus wouldn't respect me at all if I had to get prompted by a plebeian vigile. I wouldn't respect myself much, either. "Were you good friends with Albanus?"

"We were acquaintances," Rufanus replied. "We met through mutual friends."

We'd yet to meet anyone who actually described Marcellus Albanus as a friend. Even Florian, who loved his cousin, had said they were no longer close. I wondered if anyone at that party had even liked our host.

"You had a position on the main couch," I reminded him. "That implies more than a casual acquaintance."

Rufanus snorted with amusement. "It can imply whatever you wish it to imply, Valerius, I'm not the arbiter of any conclusions you might draw."

"Yes, of course."

Rufanus gave me a moment to remember how much he outranked me before he took pity on me. "I was on the main couch because I was an honoured guest. My family is very well connected. I am accustomed to being on the main couch in most of the houses I visit."

He had more front than the Temple of Jupiter, but it was true. There would have been very few social gatherings where Rufanus didn't find himself at the top of the heap.

"And do you recall when you left the house?"

"Yes, it was after the commissatio."

"You were not invited into the commissatio if my memory serves me."

Rufanus arched his brows again. "Considering the state you were in, Valerius, I would be distrustful indeed of your memory." Having got that dig in, he smiled at me tightly. "As it happens, I had some business to discuss with young Albanus, but after the commissatio he was in no condition to speak, and I departed."

"What sort of business did you have?"

"It was a private matter that I assure you is of no consequence to your investigation," said Rufanus firmly. I'd pushed my luck as far as it would go, and it was clear he wouldn't elaborate.

Private usually translated as *financial*. We patricians didn't discuss our financial matters with third parties. We were either wealthy beyond all comprehension or staying afloat only because of a complicated system of loans. Sometimes, thanks to the perversity of accountancy, it was both. Perhaps Rufanus was asset-rich and capital-poor, a common condition, and Albanus had been lending him some cash. Perhaps it was the other way around.

"Thank you for your time, Claudius Rufanus," I said. There was no point hanging around for a dinner invitation.

Atreus and I headed back down the stairs onto the street. When I looked back at Rufanus he had rejoined his fellow senators and was immersed in conversation.

"You didn't ask him about the amulet," Atreus pointed out as we headed east towards the Caelian Hill again.

"There was no point," I said. "Rufanus isn't going to be any more forthcoming than that, and, unlike the usual methods employed by the vigiles, we can't beat him up until he changes his mind, or get a torturer involved."

Atreus looked like he was considering it.

"And for all we know, he's telling the truth," I said. "He hasn't said anything to implicate himself."

I remembered what Atreus had told me in the wineshop earlier and hoped he was right. The sooner things got clearer, the better, but it was difficult to shake the feeling that we'd wasted our day completely. We'd spoken to Florian, who had a motive for every eventuality, but who didn't feel like a murderer. We'd spoken to young Carpo, who had no motive that he admitted to, but also didn't feel like a murderer. We had failed to manage an interview with Pomptius Voltinian, but his slaves had done a good job clearing him. We had also failed to speak to Galerius Nepos and failed to glean any information whatsoever at his address. Claudius Rufanus had graciously made himself available to speak with us for several moments out of his busy day, for what little it was worth. If things didn't get clearer soon, my fledgling career would implode. It was only my first full day working under Severus, and I wasn't optimistic. I was tired. The late afternoon shadows were darkening, and the sunlight was beginning to fade. The day was dying.

"At what point in the day, Atreus, is it acceptable to pack it in and go home?"

Atreus drew a deep breath and let it out again slowly. He looked over his shoulder at the Forum, now bathed in golden light. "I think, sir, that it's any time now."

I couldn't have agreed more.

* * *

It was growing dark by the time Atreus and I found ourselves treading back up the gentle incline of the Caelian Hill. As we approached my familiar portico, I thought I should offer Atreus some hospitality.

"Would you like to stay for dinner, Atreus?" It seemed ungracious to make him walk all the way up the hill without even offering.

Atreus shook his head. "No, thank you, sir. I like to eat with Lucilla."

I felt an unwelcome pang of disappointment in my chest, and I was glad the growing gloom hid whatever expression crossed my face at the revelation that he had a wife or a girlfriend waiting for him in whatever place he called home—a wife or a girlfriend he cared enough about to go home to every evening, however many nereids he'd gazed at. I'd hoped that he would accept my invitation as a friend, but perhaps underneath that had lain a different, secret hope, as foolish and hollow and reckless as ever.

As impossible as ever.

"I'll see you tomorrow then," I said.

"Yes, sir." He turned away.

"Hey, Atreus?" I asked, realising suddenly that I didn't know the first thing about him and wondering if I should try and remedy that since we were working together.

"Sir?"

I leaned on one of the columns of my portico. "Where *do* you live?"

"The Aventine, sir," he said, and he smiled slightly as if he knew exactly what I was thinking—not *quite* the slum I'd imagined for him. "Goodnight."

"Goodnight."

He walked off into the gathering darkness.

Chapter Nine

I woke up the next morning with sore feet. Elevating them for bed the night before had only delayed the inevitable. As soon as they touched the floor, the blood pooled back into them, and they started to hurt. I promised myself that if I ever became a magistrate, I would be just like Severus and get someone else to do all the legwork. I wondered how many of the seven hills I would have to climb today and how many times.

I dressed slowly. Most of my muscles hurt, even the ones I wasn't aware I had needed for walking. It was a depressing reminder that in the months since my return to Rome, I'd become lazy and undisciplined.

I stepped outside my bedroom door and gazed down into the atrium. My usually peaceful house was full of people. As I watched, a quartet of strangers manhandled a large couch towards the front of the house. They were followed by Thetis, who was haranguing them about the dirt they'd tracked through from the yard. Little Perella brought up the rear with her broom. From the opposite direction came a small army of my household slaves, armed with scrubbing brushes and buckets. The two groups met at the impluvium and jostled around one another.

I slunk down the stairs once the atrium had cleared. I made it as far as the large triclinium, normally as quiet and shadowed as a crypt, and discovered that it was full to the brim with household slaves. Fulvia was standing in the midst of the chaos, looking serene and determined at the same time, issuing orders and marshalling the troops. I bet Julius Caesar had the same imperious look in his eye when he was in the process of dividing and conquering the Gauls.

156

"Fulvia," I called out from the doorway. Then, when I got no response, I bellowed: *"Fulvia!"*

The slaves froze.

My wife turned her head, saw it was me, and narrowed her eyes like she'd discovered a dissenter in her ranks and was wondering if crucifixion was too good for him. Then she put on her most reasonable smile and crossed over to me.

"Fulvia," I said, more calmly this time, "what's going on?"

"Keep working," she told the worried slaves. She took me by the arm and drew me out of the doorway. "Come with me, dear. We're having breakfast in the garden."

The garden was pleasant at this hour. It was still in shade, and cool. A light breeze ruffled the leaves in the trees and carried the faint scent of laurel throughout the garden. Breakfast had been laid out on the table beside my favourite bench. Larius was standing behind the bench holding a jug of water, and he looked suitably chastened after yesterday's punishment. He glanced up as Fulvia and I walked towards the bench, saw that it was me, and dropped his gaze again immediately. Respectful or resentful, I couldn't tell. I didn't even much care. It was too early in the morning, the house was in an uproar, and I ached in odd places.

It was breakfast with the three womenfolk only. Mouse was already being force-fed Greek verbs in the house, making the meal an affair for the adults. The adults and Julia Drusilla. When she mumbled her salutations, I thought of Florian.

Octavia was more cheerful. "Good morning, Quintus!"

I curled my lips in an approximation of a smile and waited for my womenfolk to tell me what in Tartarus was going in.

As always, Fulvia got straight to the point. She sat down beside me and folded her hands in her lap. "About the triclinium. You have the patronage of a magistrate now, Quintus. It is only right that you entertain Severus in your home, so Octavia and I are getting the place up to scratch."

"Are you doing the whole house?" I asked, not looking forward to spending the rest of my natural life avoiding pushy tradesmen.

"We're just doing the formal triclinium," Fulvia assured me. "It looks far worse than it is."

"I'm glad to hear it," I said, greatly relieved. I didn't want to end up like mad Uncle Maro and mad Aunt Marcia, dodging scaffolding every day. There was a reason they were both mad.

"We're just replacing the couches for now and giving it a good clean," Fulvia said. "You know, I don't think anyone's used that triclinium for years. We didn't even use it for our wedding feast."

She was probably right, but the only thing I really remembered from our wedding was an oppressive sense of impending doom. Fulvia, who always knew what I was thinking, gave me a wry look.

Fulvia liked to organise things. I liked to let her. And it was right of her and Octavia to prepare the house for my fledgling political career. My name was already becoming known in important circles. Sooner or later, I would have to show my face as well, and if I was going to invite important men to my house, I had to do better than sit them in a dusty old room with faded frescoes and rundown furniture.

I thought of Marcellus Albanus and his gaudy, over-decorated house and prayed that Jupiter would strike me down with a thunderbolt if I ever thought that lewd nymphs were a suitable theme for a dining room. Had Albanus lived to marry, I wondered what Julia Drusilla would have made of them. I wondered what she made of the whole business, actually. I watched her a little more than usual as the four of us ate and talked, letting most threads of conversation pass me by. The women chattered on happily without me. Julia commented on what Octavia had bought at the Emporium yesterday (her friend Portia had a scarf like that, but not as nice). She seemed impressed at her mother's idea of checking the warehouses by the Saepta Julia for new furnishings for the triclinium ("We should!") and even agreed with Octavia when she said it might pay to get the frescoes redone (an emphatic nod). I couldn't tell if she was being artful or not. I didn't know her well enough.

I ruminated on it while I picked over a dish of fruit. It was the first time I had seen Julia since Florian's startling declaration of love for her. Had I

158

really expected her to look different somehow? She was pretty, certainly, but nowhere near as striking as her mother. Perhaps that would come with maturity. She looked vaguely unfinished, like young Carpo. Her father had brought her up in a cosy cocoon, safely cushioned from any life experience that didn't involve cosmetics and fashion. I tried, but I couldn't see her through fresh eyes. What most clouded any impartial judgement was my unfortunate knowledge of her personality. I knew she had a nasty streak. Perhaps maturity would change that as well.

I wondered how to broach things with her.

A piece of good luck came my way after breakfast. Octavia and Fulvia left the garden, discussing the best plan of attack for the cobwebs in the triclinium. This did not excite Julia. She was dragging her feet, literally, and one of her sandal laces snapped. It slowed her down enough that Octavia and Fulvia were out of earshot by the time she'd pulled off the offending footwear.

"Can I have a word, Julia?" We only had a few moments before Larius returned to clear away the dishes.

Julia was inspecting her sandal. "About what?" she asked, distracted.

"About Avitus Florian."

Julia looked up sharply and quickly hobbled towards the house to make sure her mother was long gone. She glared at me urgently and then hobbled back over. She sat down on the couch beside me and shot me a narrow look. "What did he say?" she hissed.

"He said he loves you."

A change came over her. First, she went deathly pale, and then she flushed all the way to the roots of her fake copper-coloured curls. "Did he?" she asked primly.

I leaned forward so I could speak without being overheard if anyone passed by. "Julia, has Florian approached you since Albanus was killed?"

"No."

I considered that for a moment and then asked the burning question: "Do you think he did it?"

"No!" Julia exclaimed. She looked suddenly awkward and embarrassed.

"He's a *good* man, I'm sure of it, but there was nothing between us."

I wasn't sure that was true. I believed Julia, certainly, but just because she said it, and even if she meant it, it didn't mean it was true. Wasn't it just last night I'd secretly hoped for something more than friendship with Atreus? Just because your head knew better didn't mean your heart listened.

"Are you going to tell Mother about this?" Julia looked worried. Her lower lip trembled.

"Not unless I have to."

Julia closed her eyes and inhaled sharply as the implications of that hit her. "We didn't *do* anything," she murmured, and her eyes snapped open. "Well, you know, not anything *bad*. I met him alone in the garden once, and I know that was wrong, but we just talked. We didn't do anything else! Nothing, *you know!*"

How sweet of her to try to protect me from the facts of life. I felt as old as she thought I was.

"Julia," I said, feeling like the world's biggest hypocrite, "didn't you think of your reputation?"

"He seemed so *nice*," Julia said sadly.

I didn't know whether to console her or not. Ours was not that sort of relationship. I squirmed uncomfortably instead. I would die a happy man if I crossed the Styx in total ignorance of Julia's love life. We sat quietly together for a moment, both of us concentrating on not making eye contact and both of us acutely aware that we didn't want to take this conversation any further. Then Julia stood up in a rustle of fabric.

"I will thank you, Valerius, not to mention this to my parents," she said primly. Then the mask slipped, and she looked younger than her sixteen years. "Please, if you don't have to."

"You have my word."

I was rewarded with a tiny smile.

Holding her broken sandal in one hand, Julia walked unevenly away, leaving me sitting alone in the garden, wondering if I'd somehow managed to misjudge her all along.

CHAPTER NINE

* * *

Atreus hadn't turned up by the time I'd finished breakfast, so I shut myself in my tablinum and played paterfamilias. I glanced at some of the household accounts and calculated a few sums on a wax tablet to make sure that my womenfolk's home improvements weren't going to bankrupt me. They weren't. With the money coming in from the properties and farms, I could afford a more luxurious lifestyle than the one I currently enjoyed. While my father would have been proud of my quasi-spartan frugality, it was as a result of laziness rather than discipline that I lived the way I did. I just couldn't be bothered to change anything. If I'd wanted, I could have hosted wild revelries every night and woken each morning to the murmur of a crowd of clients in my atrium. As it was, I hated hosting parties, and I could count my clients on one hand. They were the freedmen of my father, and they knew better than to wait for me to get out of bed in the morning. They had their own lives to lead.

In the days of the Republic, when a man needed to cultivate voters, the patron-client system between patricians and plebeians had been a valuable one. Now, it was a relic of another era. The tradition persevered, but it was hollow. The freedmen who'd adopted the family name kept us in their prayers and were given the occasional gratuity, but that was as far as it went. I didn't need the entire Aemilius tribe, in all their glory, to turn out on the Field of Mars and vote for me to become an aedile or a quaestor. I just needed a few patrician senators like Septus Severus, mad Uncle Maro, and old Marcellus Naso to drop my name in high places. In theory, anyway. I had upset the process, without even realising it, when I saved Corbulo's life. No good deed ever went unpunished.

I growled to myself and put my feet up on my desk. I wondered whether or not investigating the murder of Marcellus Albanus was the best way to go about establishing my political reputation. It might have been smarter to have accepted that honorary priesthood, stupid hat or not.

Leaning back with my feet up on the desk was not the most comfortable position in the world, but it worked. I don't know how long I dozed for, but I was jolted awake by the sound of Hursa's sandals slapping on the tiles.

"What is it, Hursa?" I asked crossly, putting my feet back on the floor and trying to look busy. One of my wax tablets had a heel print in it. "Is Atreus here?"

"Yes, sir," Hursa said and then lowered his voice. "He looks awful!"

"Just show him in."

Hursa was right. When Atreus crossed my threshold, it was obvious by his haggard face that he hadn't slept a wink all night. He looked terrible. Also, he smelled funny. Hursa buzzed around him like a fly.

"What happened to you, Atreus?" I asked curiously, tamping down the rush of concern that rose in my chest. "And what's that smell?"

Atreus cleared his throat a couple of times before he could speak. "There was a fire last night in the oil shop behind Actia's laundry," he rasped eventually. "It spread to the butcher's next door and the apartments above it before we could contain it. It took us five hours to get it out. I'm sorry, sir, but I've come straight from there."

No wonder he smelled like a burnt omelette.

"Take a seat," I said, gesturing. "Hursa, go and fetch Atreus a jug of wine."

"Just water, sir, if I may," Atreus croaked, sitting heavily.

I nodded at Hursa, and he trotted away unwillingly. "Was anyone hurt?" I asked Atreus.

Atreus cleared his throat again. "An old woman in the apartment block died. She wasn't burned. I think it was the smoke that got to her. But it wasn't as bad as it could have been. The whole neighbourhood could have gone up."

"Do you know what started it?" There was a heavy penalty for leaving torches unattended at night, with good reason.

Atreus scrubbed his tired face with his hands. "I know exactly what started it," he said, his voice hardening. "The oil shop owner wouldn't pay Bano any protection money."

I remembered the name from the station house. The standover man.

"Can you prove it? Can you arrest him?"

Atreus looked drained, his eyes bloodshot. "Sir, we've had enough

162

evidence to arrest Bano for the past eight months. We just can't find the bastard. He's holed up somewhere in our district, but we don't know where. And for every man of his we arrest, he recruits another two, like that thing, you know, sir, with all the heads. The, um, the hydra."

Yesterday in the bathhouse, Atreus had remembered the name of an obscure nereid. Today, he had stumbled over the hydra. He must have been beyond tired.

"Did you get any sleep at all last night?"

"I'm fine, sir," Atreus said, rallying. He drew a deep breath and shook his head as though shaking himself awake. "Actually, sir, this will interest you. An informer of mine swears he knows where a group of Christians were gathering before they skipped out on the rent. It's in the Aventine. I was going to have a look last night before the fire. Would you like to come with me now?"

A chance to get a firsthand look at an illegal cult's temple in the heart of Rome? I couldn't get my sandals on quickly enough.

* * *

Atreus, Juba, and I set off down the slope of the Caelian Hill. We fell into a steady pace. The sunlight had revived Atreus somewhat. As we walked, he drew his wax tablet out of his belt and flipped open the cover.

"Avitus Florian," he said suddenly.

"What about him?" I asked, sidestepping a slave who was staggering up the hill with baskets too heavy for her.

Atreus frowned. "For all that he talked, sir, he's holding something back."

"Maybe," I said. "I spoke to Julia. Her story matches."

"I don't know," Atreus said. He led us off into a side street I was not familiar with and down a set of uneven steps that surprised me by depositing us very close to the Porta Capena. "I have no doubt that what he told us was the truth, sir. I just feel like he was keeping something back."

"So you're not ready to cross him off the list just yet?"

Atreus smiled wearily. "No, sir, not just yet."

163

Our next shortcut took us southwest towards the Aventine. From the narrow, twisting streets, the southern end of the Circus Maximus kept appearing and disappearing and then appearing again from unexpected directions as we descended into the bustling city.

"What about Carpo?" I asked, thinking of the candid youth in his pool of harmless debauchery.

"I think we can cross him off," Atreus said. "As well as Pomptius Voltinian, since his litter bearers vouched for him, and his slave very helpfully checked him for bloodstains. Also, I don't imagine you send your slaves back the next day to collect the napkin you left behind if you've killed your host."

"There's no accounting for some people," I said, and Juba grinned at me.

"Claudius Rufanus, however, remains on the list," Atreus said. He bridled. Claudius Rufanus had rubbed Atreus the wrong way. He'd done the same with me, but I didn't take it personally. Rufanus outranked me and most of the other patricians in the city. Pomposity was second nature to him.

"Fine," I said, "but I'm not sure he'll be any more forthcoming than he was yesterday."

"Probably not, sir," Atreus said gloomily. "Speaking of which, we should try and see Galerius Nepos again today, if his door slave will admit us."

I didn't like our chances, but I nodded. I was picturing a day just like yesterday. It was going to kill my already tender feet, however many shortcuts Atreus knew. I took the opportunity to stop at an unfamiliar thermopolium.

Atreus consulted his list. "That leaves us Vibianus Ennius, Antonius Donatus, Probus Macrinus, and, ah, Anicetus."

Anicetus: the only man on the list without a full complement of names and with a background just as vague. It wasn't *his* name I'd curled my lip at, however.

"Sir?" Atreus asked.

"Probus Macrinus," I told him as I counted out coins.

"You don't like him, sir?"

"It's complicated," I said, the thought of doddering old Macrinus souring my mood. "He's a relative of Octavia's ex, and he's constantly finding

164

excuses to see her. His visits only serve to remind her of the unhappy end to her marriage."

"I see." Atreus looked meditative.

"It's not that I don't like him," I clarified, "it's just an awkward situation. The old man's always been nice to me. He still is, in fact. He's always finding little jobs for me to do like a patron, even though he's under no obligation. I have to find tenants for a property of his, for instance. He's been good to me. And I hardly think he's a killer."

The thought actually made me smile. Old Macrinus, with his tremulous voice and his skinny old man's legs, couldn't go ten rounds with a toddler.

I picked at my stuffed vine leaf as we walked towards the Aventine. The Aventine was full of weird temples and shrines, but we headed for a rundown insula instead. The rooms, situated above an olive oil shop, were sparsely furnished, dingy, and there was no longer anyone living there. I had hoped for something that might indicate we were in the shadow of a strange foreign god, but there was nothing here. The landlord who had shown us to the room hung around long enough for a tip and then lumbered back down the steps before we could demand our money back.

"Are you sure this is the right place, Atreus?" I asked him as I pulled back a stained curtain to reveal a bedroom.

"I believe so, sir," Atreus said, but he sounded as dubious as me.

There wasn't a god in the place, not a single effigy.

I looked around the bedroom. It was devoid of everything except the bed. The bed was large and cumbersome. It must have taken a team of men to get it up the stairs. It looked old enough to have been in the place since the days of the divine Augustus, and it wasn't going anywhere now. It must have slept countless tenants over the years and was probably teeming with lice. My skin crawled just looking at it.

There was no window in the bedroom. Even in the middle of the day, it was dark. It was a miserable bedroom in a dingy apartment, and the whole place stank of olive oil. I tugged the curtain back into place and happened to glance up at the wall as I did. There, just above the ratty curtain, I saw a symbol scrawled on the wall. It was only faint, as though someone had attempted to scrub it off before leaving, but the shadow of it remained: it was an enclosed circle crossed through several times, like an eight-spoked wheel. I wasn't familiar with it, but something about its untidiness intrigued me.

Atreus saw that I had found something and came to stand beside me. "What is it?"

"It's not a fish," I said thoughtfully.

"I'm sorry, sir," he said. "I've wasted your time."

I studied the strange symbol a moment longer, and then it occurred to me. The symbol hadn't been scrawled untidily; it had been *overwritten*. I was reminded of old wax tablets, scored by styluses. Sometimes, the bare bones of letters and words remained on the board after the wax was removed, waiting for the right pair of eyes to rediscover them. As children, Octavia and I had pored over the backing boards of old tablets, trying to spot accidental obscenities.

"It is Christian," I said as it fell into place.

"How do you know that, sir?" Atreus asked.

"I was mistaken," I said, gesturing to the symbol. "It *is* a fish."

Atreus didn't follow. How could he? He was a plebeian vigile from the Aventine who'd grown up mudlarking instead of having his knuckles cracked by a sadistic Greek tutor for every tiny mistake.

"The fish," I said, tapping the wall with my fingers. "These Christians use Greek, do you remember? The *chi rho* on the amulet, for example. And it obviously has something to do with fish. With *this* fish."

"But that's a wheel," Atreus said.

"It is," I said. I crouched down, beckoning Atreus to follow. The floor was covered in a thin layer of greasy dust, courtesy of the shop downstairs. It made the perfect tablet. "What's Greek for fish?"

Atreus shook his head.

"Ichthys," I said. I began to trace the Greek letters over one another: "Iota, chi, theta, upsilon, sigma. And there it is."

Atreus frowned at the eight-spoked wheel I had created on the floor. He studied it for a moment and then looked back at me with something that was almost like admiration. "I wouldn't have spotted that, sir."

I stood up and wiped my finger on my tunic. "I was in a Mithraic cult in the army. I suppose I've developed an eye for this sort of thing."

The cult of Mithras was full of symbols and codes that only the initiated could read. An uninitiated man could step into a mithraeum and leave none the wiser when everything he needed to know was right in front of him. I suspected the same was true of any cult, especially the illegal ones. And in any place of worship, whether an elaborately constructed underground mithraeum or just a dodgy flat in the Transtiberina, the placement of the symbols was not without purpose.

I looked at the symbol above the bedroom curtain again. "It would have been visible from the front door. Open it, look over your host's shoulder, and if you are a Christian, you would immediately know that you are among your fellows. It is spelled out for you, literally, but the uninitiated man sees nothing of interest."

Atreus shook his head, but the look he gave me was one that warmed me. I had surprised him, and in a good way. I liked that feeling more than I should have. More than was prudent.

I turned away from his gaze, my heart beating faster.

There were no other mysteries to discover in the place. We poked around for a while longer, disturbing the dust and a nest of spiders, but there was nothing else to be found in the room. No symbols, no cryptograms, nothing. The Christians had long gone, taking most of their secrets with them.

* * *

Coming down the stairs, Atreus stumbled. Juba caught him by the arm before he landed face-first in the street, but it was a near thing.

"What with your fire, did you get any sleep last night?" I asked him.

Atreus had to think about that for a moment, which made me suspect he was lying anyway when he answered: "Some, yes."

I regarded him carefully. "Then there's no point in running around half the city today chasing up names on our list."

167

"Sir?"

"I'll go and see Severus and fill him in on how we spent yesterday," I said. "Why don't you go and get some rest, and we'll pick it up again tomorrow?"

Atreus looked torn. I could see that he didn't want to chuck it in for the day, but I could also see he was dog-tired. He fought a hard battle with himself.

"I don't know, sir," he said slowly, unwillingly.

"Go on, Atreus," I said, dismissing his concerns with a lazy wave of my hand. I could see he was wavering. "If I need you, I'll send for you. I'm only going to see Severus. You won't miss anything."

Atreus exhaled heavily, and I knew I'd won. "If you're sure, sir."

"I'm sure," I said. "Go and have a bath, and then go home and get some sleep. I'll see you tomorrow morning."

"Can you find your way from here?"

"Atreus," I said, "we can see the river from here."

After Atreus left us, Juba and I headed back towards the Caelian Hill. Presently, we found ourselves in the wide, familiar streets of my neighbourhood, and we slowed to a leisurely pace. It was too nice a day to rush around, working up a sweat. This unofficial time off from investigation gave me the chance to recuperate and to leave all the problems of Albanus's murder on a slow boil at the back of my mind. I would revisit them at my leisure to see what had developed.

Juba was in a good mood. He whistled to himself as we walked along. I shot him a sidelong glance, wondering why his world was so rosy. His whistle transformed into a maddeningly cheerful hum. By the time we reached Severus's house, I was sorry I'd brought him, bodyguard or not.

My second visit to Severus went much better than my first. It was much later in the day than my previous visit, and so all of Severus's hopeful clients had long ago been seen or dismissed. The door slave was competent enough not to have to take my name a second time and offered me a drink while I waited.

Severus met me in a large reception room, dismissed his small army of scribes and secretaries, and we both reclined on comfortable couches and enjoyed sweet mulsum wine. The sunlight was shining into the atrium outside, and the house was bathed in light. Severus's slaves, well-dressed and efficient, went quietly about their household duties. From somewhere in the house, I could hear the sounds of children playing. It reminded me of home. The comparison, in turn, reminded me that if things went well, I might one day be in Severus's position: a magistrate, a senator, and a man of importance. Who would have ever guessed that underneath my attractive, boyish exterior, there lurked such calculating ambition?

I opened with a dinner invitation, which was received well by Severus and led us into a sociable discussion. We spoke of mutual friends and acquaintances. Severus knew my old general, Corbulo, and counted him a family friend. We spoke of Corbulo's command of the legions in the east, including the Tenth. We spoke of his ongoing mission to deliver Armenia from the Parthians and the problems not only with the Parthians but also with the Armenians, many of whom did not want to be delivered. I told Severus of my very high regard for Corbulo, and we drank to his continuing success.

Severus also knew my mad Uncle Maro and spoke of him very highly, which only confirmed my suspicions that mad Uncle Maro was generally viewed as charmingly eccentric in public and saved his true madness to inflict on his family alone.

"Aemilius Lucullus Maro is a dear friend," Severus said earnestly. "Tell me, does he still have the villa at Capua?"

"I think so," I replied, stretching, "although it's been years since he's used it."

"He held a party down there once that—" Severus caught himself and chuckled. "Well, I'm sure I don't need to tell *you*, Valerius, what happens when young men have parties!"

I smiled at his good humour, but part of me thought: *When young men have parties, they are murdered for their trouble.*

Severus's smile faded. He'd obviously had the same thought. He stared off into space for a while and then leaned forward and adjusted the fall of his voluminous tunic. "And has there been any progress on the investigation?"

I nodded. "Some, yes. You'll remember I spoke of a list of men who could not account for their movements after the party? I have managed to eliminate some names from the list."

I took out my wax tablet, and together, we went through the list. Being a magistrate, Severus knew more important people in the city than I did, and he raised his eyebrows as he came across a few familiar names.

"Who has been eliminated so far?" he asked, concerned.

"Young Menenius Carpo has been eliminated," I said, "and also Pomptius Voltinian." I hesitated. "And Avitus Florian was very forthcoming."

Severus didn't pick up on the implication.

I was still in two minds about Florian. I thought he was innocent, but I also trusted that Atreus's suspicion of him was reasonable.

"Are you certain, Valerius, that it wasn't a slave or intruder?" Severus asked hopefully as he looked at the remaining names.

"It seems quite certain that it was a guest," I said. "Most likely, it was a guest who was assisted in the act by his litter bearers, who would certainly have had no other reason to enter the house."

"And what of the amulet?"

"Ah, the amulet," I sighed. I took a sip of wine and continued. "I have to admit, Severus, I'm at a loss there. How does one go about tracking down an illegal cult, let alone in identifying the individual members in the hope that we can connect one with Albanus?"

Severus frowned. "Do you think it was Christians?"

"There is obviously a connection," I replied. "I even saw a Christian meeting place this morning, but they were long gone."

Severus looked down at the list worriedly. "It bothers me to see names that I know here. You are aware, I presume, that Claudius Rufanus is of *the* Claudians, that Galerius Nepos will probably be our next consul, that Vibianus Ennius's father is governor of an imperial province, and that Probus Macrinus is venerated throughout the city?"

"I am aware that there are some very important names on that list."

"To say nothing of Anicetus," Severus added.

"What do you know about Anicetus?" I asked, wondering if he could help me pin down that elusive name.

"Not much," Severus admitted. "I know his name, certainly. I know he's an ex-slave and currently head of the fleet at Misenum, although he spends most of his time in the city. He is *very* close to the palace."

Not for the first time, I wondered whose man Anicetus was. Was it enough to say that he was close to the palace? The palace was no longer a united front. Nero's mother, Agrippina, had been pushed to withdraw from public life. Seneca was attempting to retire gracefully, while the old soldier Burrus was ridden with health problems and not the man he was. And, of course, there was also Nero's wife, his ex-mistress, and his current mistress. All of those closest to the young emperor had different agendas, so whose man was Anicetus? Was his star on the rise or the wane? I didn't even know if it mattered for my purposes. It was quite possible that Anicetus hadn't had anything to do with Albanus's death.

"Uncle Maro says that if you cross the palace, it's Anicetus you will meet in a dark alley," I mused.

Severus didn't answer that, meaning it was probably true. He inhaled deeply. "I don't know which is worse," he said at last. "The idea that one of these men is a murderer, or the idea that one of them is a Christian!"

"It's the murderer we're hunting, Severus," I said. "What difference does the motive make?"

Severus shook his head. "Don't you understand, Valerius? I don't want to have to tell the palace that Rome is under attack from within by cult members!"

"I don't know, Severus," I mused. "Uncover a conspiracy like that, and it might make your career."

"Are you joking?" Severus asked, and his face fell. "If you want to tell the imperial spies that they've missed the boat on these Christians, you can be my guest! I don't need to make enemies in those sorts of circles!"

The thought hadn't even occurred to me before now. I tried to laugh it off. "Don't worry about it, Severus," I said. "We're all on the same side, aren't we?"

Severus looked at me worriedly for a moment and then drained his cup of wine. "I hope so, Valerius, I hope so."

* * *

Later that day, with nothing to do, I began to regret sending Atreus home to sleep. Like a child deprived of a playmate, I wandered around the house, annoying everyone else. I started in the kitchen, where I sat at the table and gave Damos some helpful hints I'd read on how to cook shellfish until he said, finally, through grated teeth: "Sir, *must* you?" Making it a policy never to outstay my welcome with a man brandishing a knife in one hand and a roasting pan in the other, I grabbed an apple and headed outside again.

My next stop was the formal triclinium, where most of the work had been done. A few of the slaves were still working in the triclinium, giggling as they jumped up and down with their brooms to get the last few cobwebs hanging in the corners. I looked around the room with interest. Fulvia was right: the place hadn't been touched in months. It was amazing the difference a few brooms and scrubbing brushes made, and a few extra hands to wield them. I could actually see the frescoes, if not in all their former glory, then at least no longer hidden by a coat of dust. My father had commissioned the frescoes. He had always favoured pastoral scenes, and the formal triclinium was full of them. Each wall showed scenes of farm life, and wildlife and birdlife, and of simple pleasures. My father believed that a pastoral life was, by extension, a virtuous life, which was a leap of faith for a man who had lived most of his life inside the Servian Walls.

I looked up at the ceiling. The slaves' brooms had uncovered the old painted rose in the centre of the ceiling that dated back to my great-grandfather's day. It was faded now, but still discernible. Dinners in the formal triclinium were held sub rosa. As children, Octavia and I had sometimes speculated about what conspiracies were hatched under the implicit secrecy of that rose, but the rose was probably just the traditional reminder of good manners—what was said under the influence of wine should not be repeated.

The marble tabletops in the formal triclinium gleamed. The new couches looked wide and comfortable. There was scented oil burning in the small brazier in the middle of the room. The place looked good. I could almost see it with lamps and torches lighted and filled with music and guests. I could almost imagine myself playing host here, conversing with important men as I inched my way up the ladder of political success and finally became the man my father had always hoped I would become.

Having anticipated a busy day and been let down, I found it difficult to settle in the evening. I thought fleetingly of heading to the theatre. Even if I couldn't get a seat, there was always some action down that way at night. Sometimes, that meant pulling up a stool at a wineshop and watching the prostitutes tout aggressively for clients. It was usually funnier than anything by Plautus.

I decided against it in the end. The theatre was a sure-fire way to run into old acquaintances, and I didn't need to do that at the moment. I could just imagine it: *So, Valerius, I hear you're investigating Albanus's death? Who do you reckon did it? Don't keep it to yourself, man!* At this stage in the investigation, that was not an option. I promised myself a big night out when Albanus's murderer was put up in front of the judges. On the other side of the coin, if Albanus's murderer was never found, I would suffer the painful death of my fledgling public career.

I went to bed early and read a few tracts of Cicero by the flickering light of my bedroom brazier. There was nothing like a solemn reminder about Morals and Duty to really put me to sleep, and Cicero worked like a charm every time. In the back of my mind, the whole Albanus puzzle was bubbling away where I'd left it.

It gave me strange dreams the whole night.

Chapter Ten

A day later, and Atreus and I were getting nowhere. I wasn't surprised. I was worried, but not surprised. My fledgling career hinged on this investigation, and I'd jumped in headfirst without much regard for the consequences if I were to fail. I was starting to feel some empathy for Damocles, when he'd looked up at the end of the feast and seen the sword hanging over him. I was expecting a similar moment of sick realisation any day now.

We had made some progress earlier that morning. We had interviewed Vibianus Ennius at his home on the Viminal Hill and discovered that he was either a consummate liar, or a habitual drunk with no brain function left at all. He had been at Albanus's party; he remembered that, but everything else was a blank. He gave the impression that everything had very much been a blank since he'd discovered the fruits of Bacchus in his teens. He had not only been drunk the night of the party, he was drunk when we spoke to him over his breakfast. Ennius was a worthless specimen, even by my low standards. He was more useless than young Menenius Carpo and had none of Carpo's friendly charm. Ennius was a podgy, pasty youth with a receding hairline, bad pores, and no discernible chin. He made up for it with an excess of nose. He had narrow-set eyes the colour of dried dung and, despite his youth, a deep line across his forehead that indicated he was more of a frowner than a giggler. He was not my idea of friendship material. He was rich, though, which accounted for his acquaintance with Marcellus Albanus. They were in the same spoilt, feckless circle of friends. Idiots like Vibianus Ennius were the reason for half the satirical graffiti in the city. It was wasted on him, though. He didn't get that he was the joke. Meeting Ennius put me in a bad mood, and our next destination did nothing to cheer me up.

Old Macrinus lived in a fine house on the southern edge of the Palatine Hill. It was an exclusive neighbourhood in that it was owned almost exclusively by the Julio-Claudians. It was close to the imperial palace and just a stone's throw from the grand Temple of Apollo. The gardens overlooked the Circus Maximus, and since Macrinus's so-called retirement from public life, he'd had the luxury of watching the races from his back gardens without having to totter down the hill. So-called retirement, because he still managed to pop up and insinuate himself into the social and political scene whenever he fancied.

I had seen Macrinus at Albanus's party, but we had not spoken. We had last spoken the day after when he'd turned up uninvited to my house. I was perversely pleased to be able to return the imposition.

The door slave ushered us through to a large sitting room. There we sat and waited until the old man finally appeared.

Macrinus was old and thin and looked closer to death's door every time I saw him. He was old enough to remember the great Augustus—their few brief conversations featured heavily in all of his anecdotes. Macrinus looked pleased to see me. I was a tenuous link, I supposed, to a happier time in his life.

He shuffled over to the couch, a slave under each elbow, wheezing. After sitting down, it took him a while to get his breath back, so he continued to wheeze while he smiled at me and owlishly blinked his watery eyes.

"Hello, Valerius," he said in his reed-thin old man's voice. "How nice of you to come."

"I hope you are keeping well, Macrinus."

"Oh, yes, quite well," he wheezed. If I lived to be six hundred years old, I'd consider barely breathing the epitome of health as well. "Have you found me a tenant for the house?"

"Not yet, I'm afraid," I said. "This is Junius Atreus. He's a vigile. He and I are investigating the murder of Marcellus Albanus, under the magistrate

Septus Severus."

"You what?" Macrinus cupped a hand behind one of his large ears.

I repeated it all for him, and he nodded at last.

"I see," he said at last. "Under Severus, you say? I am pleased for you, Valerius. Well, what do you want to know from me?"

He could have been difficult. He had every right. Retired or not, his name still carried weight in the city. But Macrinus liked me.

Atreus cleared his throat. "Sir, it appears that you left the party some time after the commissatio, to which you were not invited, but before the vigiles arrived. Can you explain that at all?"

"Oh, yes," said Macrinus. "I was chatting with some young fellow about the problems with the Parthian campaign—I was quite a tactician in my day, you know—and we ended up in one of the sitting rooms. He left when the commissatio was called, and I must have dozed off on the couch."

"Do you remember the young man's name?" I asked him.

Macrinus sucked his gums for a moment. "Was it Urbanus? Suburanus? No, no, it will come to me though."

Atreus frowned. "Sir, what were you doing at the party? Most of the guests were, well, younger."

Macrinus took no insult. "Why did I go? Well, I was invited first of all. And I might be retired, but I like to keep my finger on the pulse. As young Valerius here can attest, hmm, Valerius?" The old man gave a wheezy laugh. "If I restricted myself to dining with my peers, I'd have starved by now."

Atreus smiled at the morbid joke. "So, sir, when you woke up it was late?"

"Quite late, yes," Macrinus agreed. He folded his thin hands together in his lap and looked at Atreus as keenly as he could through his bleary eyes. "I can't be sure of the hour, but certainly, the commissatio was finished. The house was quiet. I passed the door porter on the way out, drunk and asleep."

"Thank you, sir, for your time," said Atreus.

Macrinus looked at me expectantly, but I had nothing else either.

"How is your sister?" the old man asked me.

"She is well."

Macrinus smiled. "Yes, she is always in my prayers. She is a dear, sweet girl."

"Yes."

"Oh!" said Macrinus suddenly, rubbing his papery old hands together. "I almost forgot! I have a necklace for her." He smiled again. "When you reach my age, young man, it is important to get your affairs into order."

"Of course," I said, wishing I could refuse instead.

Macrinus summoned a slave, the same dark youth with the lazy eye who had accompanied him on his last visit to my house, and sent him off to fetch the necklace. When the youth returned, Macrinus gestured that he hand it to me. The gold felt cool in the palm of my hand. It was an impressive piece. From the look on Atreus's face, I could guess it was worth more than he made in a year and maybe more than he could hope to earn in a lifetime. The necklace was quite heavy. It was like thin rope. There was a blue lapis pendant hanging off it. It wouldn't have looked out of place resting on Cleopatra's cleavage.

"It was my mother's," said Macrinus proudly.

"Thank you, Macrinus," I said with all the hollow sincerity I could manage. The old man looked pleased.

We escaped shortly afterwards. Macrinus did try to inveigle an invitation to dinner, but I sidestepped it in the full knowledge he'd turn up whenever he wanted anyway. He didn't press me. He knew he would as well.

Afterwards, standing in the street and gazing at the facades of the grand houses, Atreus said in a casual tone, "So that is the man you dislike for bothering Octavia Junilla."

"That's him," I replied grimly, shoving the necklace down the front of my tunic for safekeeping. "I know he looks like he wouldn't trouble a fly, but he somehow finds a way to insinuate himself into things." I caught myself before I went too far and looked sidelong at the vigile. "And now you're thinking I'm a bastard for not inviting a lonely old man to my dinner party."

"Not at all, sir," said Atreus.

I admired his ability to lie.

* * *

By that evening, just in time for my dinner party, the house had been transformed. The strategic placement of torches and braziers hid the fact that the frescoes had seen better days. The nicest and newest pieces of furniture had been brought into the large triclinium, and a small army of statues had been procured from Jupiter knows where. Mad Uncle Maro's place, probably. Nymphs and nereids stood coyly in the corners, guarding their modesty with marble draperies. A tall bronze brazier I had never seen before gleamed at the entry to the formal triclinium. Tiny plumes of sweet-scented smoke curled out of the brazier and wafted through the house.

The slaves were decked out in matching blue tunics: Juba looked magnificent, and Hursa looked human. Even his raggedy straw-coloured hair had been tamed into neatness. From the moment he opened the door to me, I felt like I was in someone else's house.

My womenfolk were also decked out in all of their finery. Fulvia wore a simple white tunic covered with a shimmering cerulean stola. I don't know what the fabric was, but it looked like it had cost a fortune, and I hoped one of her ex-husbands had bankrolled it. Octavia wore green. She always did, because she knew it suited her, and the look in her eye dared me to tell her otherwise. Julia had gone to town, literally. She must have spent the entire afternoon at the Emporium. She was wearing enough jewellery to sink a trireme. Even her sandals sparkled. She had tried to look sophisticated, but she had tried too hard. She looked younger than her sixteen years.

Aulus had been scrubbed until his face glowed.

"Do we pass inspection?" Fulvia asked.

"Of course," I said. "May I kiss you, or will it wreck your makeup?"

"It will wreck my makeup," my wife replied, but allowed me to peck her cheek in any case. "Now go and get dressed."

When I came back down, trying not to sweep the stairs with my toga, my family was already in the dining room. I had only just joined them when the first guests arrived. It was Severus and his wife and children. They were followed almost immediately by mad Uncle Maro and mad Aunt Marcia and then finally by Marcellus Naso, sad and solitary.

Unlike Marcellus Albanus, I didn't expect the slaves of the guests I'd invited to clog up the street with their litters while their masters partied the night away. My dinner party was smaller, so there was enough room for all of the litter bearers and their litters in the stable yard. The stable yard was a relic of another age. It belonged to the era when men kept their horses in the city and grazed sheep on the Campus Martius. Using it for the litter bearers saved my guests the indignity of a drunken exit through my front door.

I couldn't help noticing that the slave Larius was absent from yet another gathering where he should have been making himself useful.

"Is that lazy wretch pretending to be sick again?" I murmured when Xanthus came to fill my cup.

"No, sir," he whispered back. "He dropped one of Octavia Junilla's glass perfume bottles earlier, and she ordered him punished. He is shackled in our room with no food until the day after tomorrow."

I raised my eyebrows at that. I wasn't happy that Larius was a clumsy oaf, but at least Octavia had taken him in hand at last.

My dinner party was a success, despite the lack of musicians and indecent dancers. Calliope and Xanthus served us the finest Falernian my house had to offer. Even Naso was brought around by the taste of it. He managed a smile at one of mad Uncle Maro's off-colour jokes. Our talk, inevitably, came back to Marcellus Albanus and the investigation.

"Naso, you've made Florian your heir, he tells me." I had meant to frame it as a question, but the Falernian was working its magic already.

"He's a good boy," Naso replied thickly. Clearly, I wasn't the only one feeling the effects of the wine. "And someday, he'll be a great man."

"He tells me," I said, "that he isn't keen about joining the legions."

Naso shrugged his shoulders. "Some are suited for it, Valerius, and some aren't. Do you know who was never cut out for the military? Cicero, that's who."

"True," I managed, and it seemed ungracious to point out that at least

Cicero had tried. In the end, Cicero had chosen to fight his battles in a different arena—the senate. Much bloodier.

"And the legions, pah!" Naso continued. "What can the legions teach a boy except how to spend his money on wine and whores?"

There were a few other things, I was sure, but couldn't think of them off the top of my head. I nodded wisely instead.

"So how are things going, anyway, Quintus?" mad Uncle Maro asked me.

"Good," I said, with more confidence than I could justify. "We are definitely making progress." Then, worried in case they asked for details, I looked at Severus. "Isn't that right, Severus?"

"Oh, yes," the magistrate replied emphatically. He'd have to agree, or we'd both look like fools. "I have all the confidence in the world in Valerius. He's making excellent progress. Excellent!"

Mad Uncle Maro beamed at me, Naso looked at me gratefully, and I drowned my doubts in another glass of wine. I glanced over at the women, and Fulvia caught my eye. She gave me a smile of encouragement before returning to her conversation.

"Yes," I lied confidently, "things are progressing well."

I called for more wine.

The night progressed. Severus's children and Mouse trailed back in from hide and seek one by one, with dirty feet and faces full of yawns. By midnight, the whole thing was winding down. I saw my guests out towards the stable yards and waited while they were loaded into their litters. Severus and his wife were the last to leave; there was some awkward juggling with sleeping children involved. After the wide doors to the street had been closed and barred again, I struggled free of my toga and headed upstairs.

I was pleased with myself. I had the patronage of Severus, the approval of Marcellus Naso, and the grudging respect of mad Uncle Maro and my womenfolk. Everything had gone right. I had talked myself up so much throughout the evening that I'd started to believe my own hype. Discovering the murderer of Marcellus Albanus was as good as done. Some of my attitude was inherent patrician arrogance, most was the wine. I went to bed feeling like a king. And then, to punish me for my pride, the gods struck down Claudius Rufanus.

(Of *the* Claudians.)

* * *

It was my third night as a magistrate's assistant, or a vigile's supervisor, or whatever in Tartarus my ill-defined career could actually be called, and it wasn't going very well. It was chilly, and it was dark. The wind picked up the edges of my cloak and tried to dislodge it. I was still half asleep, still half drunk, and I really wasn't enjoying myself as Atreus, Juba, and I headed up the darkened street. I was uneasy out at this time of night, even with Juba and his cudgel. There was nothing like being out at this hour to really make you think hard about the laws that forbade you from carrying a sword in public, and just how much you suddenly didn't agree with them. The streets could get very mean very quickly after dark, even in a familiar neighbourhood, and from the few words Atreus had spoken when I met him at the door, I knew we were not going to a familiar neighbourhood.

The Transtiberina. *The* neighbourhood your parents warned you to stay away from. The home of every cutthroat, thug, murderer, and rapist in the city. If they weren't born there, they gravitated there, like flies to shit.

Was I safer with or without Atreus? He was probably good in a fight, but how many fights did he attract just because the local roughs knew he was a vigile? And while Atreus might have been able to defend himself in a fight, could I? The last time I was in any real danger, I'd faced it with a sword, armour, and five hundred legionaries. The sword and the armour were nice, but it was the five hundred legionaries that had really given my self-confidence a boost.

All things considered, I would have preferred to stay in bed. So would Claudius Rufanus, no doubt, given the choice.

I thought of Claudius Rufanus, of *the* Claudians, and his monumental self-importance. I hoped to be that pompous myself someday. It had grated with Atreus, though, like most things. He had a chip on his shoulder the size of the Tarpeian Rock.

"You didn't like Rufanus, did you?" I asked as we passed a portico with lighted torches that threw our menacing shadows up against a wall.

"I like him now," said Atreus.

I couldn't tell if it was a joke or not.

* * *

Had Claudius Rufanus had more socially acceptable peccadilloes or a more flexible sense of personal morality, he might have lived a longer life. As it was, he was too ashamed of his vices to embrace them openly and indulged them far from home on the third storey of a Transtiberina insula that overlooked the muddy banks of the river. In the daylight, the aspect might have almost been pleasant, affording as it did a view from the balcony across the water towards the Emporium. At night, it was bleak, and the cold wind blew straight in off the river.

Rufanus had brought his bodyguard with him, our inquiries revealed, but he couldn't bear the thought of the slave telling tales, because the bodyguard had been left to bide his time at the end of the street and had fallen asleep in the doorway of a potter's workshop. He was only woken again when the first vigiles arrived and was still looking distraught when we arrived on scene sometime after that.

I had last seen Rufanus standing proudly on the steps of the Curia, looking noble and important. Now, I had the unpleasant task of seeing him again, under very different circumstances.

I followed Atreus up the uneven insula steps. They were interior steps, dark and narrow. A rough attempt had been made to plaster over the brickwork, but it hadn't helped much. The whole place was depressing. It reeked of poverty, misfortune, and other less conceptual odours. I almost gagged when the smell first hit me.

Juba rumbled to himself from the darkness behind me and followed us stoically up the steps.

We found the apartment we were looking for on the third floor. We followed the sound of curious neighbours and sightseers towards the door we wanted. It was quite a social get-together in the hallway. Everyone had turned up, from aged grandmothers to squealing toddlers, and they were swapping gossip and chatting like it was a day at the races. Everyone was interested in the room at the far end of the hallway, but it was apparent from their loud speculation that none of them had been admitted inside for a decent look. The pair of vigiles stationed at the end of the passage had something to do with that.

The Transtiberina did not fall within the jurisdiction of the Fifth Cohort of Vigiles, but Atreus had spread the word throughout his circles, and the men from the Seventh had sent for him. This pair was cut from the same cloth. They were both big and beefy, built like barbarians, and looked like they shared less than a brain cell between them.

"Where's your boss?" Atreus asked.

"Gone to wake the centurion," said the first of them. He nodded at the broken door. "Do you want to take a look?"

There had been a struggle. Atreus and I stepped over a broken footstool to enter the single-room apartment. It was a complete mess inside. A chair had been broken against a wall. There was a smashed cratera at the end of the narrow bed and a pool of wine spread across the floor that sparkled with shards of broken glass. The whole place glimmered and shone eerily in the light of the lamp.

"Jupiter," said Juba to himself, leaning in the doorway but not coming any further.

"He was on the bed when we got here," the first vigile said through missing teeth. "He was already cold."

Claudius Rufanus was lying on the narrow bed. He was naked and undignified. His tunic lay on the bed beside him, stained with wine and blood. The wound was fresh and clean; the knife had made a path straight through his sagging middle-aged breast and into his heart. It looked quick.

"So, who put up the fight?" Atreus asked curiously.

I edged my way around the gruesome bed towards the balcony, hoping for some fresh air, or at least whatever passed for fresh air this close to the stinking river. Suddenly, the answer to Atreus's question stared me right in the face.

"Sylvia did," said the first vigile.

A slender young thing in a yellow robe was lying on the floor beside the bed. She was lying on her side, with one arm stretched out. Her face was framed by a mass of curls, and even in the gloom I could see that she was wearing too much makeup. Less is more, Ovid liked to tell the ladies, but I didn't imagine many of the girls in the Transtiberina read Ovid. I couldn't see any blood. From the awkward angle of her head, however, I guessed that they had just snapped her neck.

I sighed and turned towards the balcony. It was either too late at night or too early in the morning for this, and all the wine I'd drunk at dinner had worn off on the walk to the Transtiberina. I had the beginnings of a headache.

Atreus craned his head to look at Sylvia and then turned his attention back to Claudius Rufanus. He regarded Rufanus in silence for a moment and said to the vigiles, "How did you know who he was?"

The second vigile managed to unpeel himself from the wall. "The neighbours told us. Sylvia liked to brag. The bodyguard confirmed it." He looked pensive, and it didn't sit easily across his thuggish features. "One of *the* Claudians, ay?"

"Who raised the alarm?" Atreus asked. He lifted his lantern and began to inspect the room more carefully.

"The old man next door," said the first vigile. "He's gone back to bed now."

Obviously, it would take more than the gruesome murder of a senator and his mistress to keep the neighbour interested. And since that hadn't, I had to wonder what would. Probably just bread and circuses.

"I don't get it," I mused. "Why would somebody like Claudius Rufanus come all the way into the Transtiberina for the sake of a mistress? Why not put her up somewhere closer to home?"

The vigiles all looked at me strangely.

"Poor girl," I said.

"Sir," said the second vigile patiently, "Sylvia's not a girl."

"Oh," I said, startled. I took another look. It explained why Claudius

Rufanus kept her in the Transtiberina, at least.

The two beefy vigiles sniggered. Even Atreus hid a smile.

They thought I was naïve.

I slipped onto the balcony, trusting it to hold my weight, and adjusted my cloak against the chill of the night air. The air smelled foul out here, and it was more than just the river. It smelled like something had died and was rotting in the street below. I hoped it was a dog. I looked across the river at the city, listening to the unfamiliar rattle of traffic and trying to pick landmarks through the darkness from my unfamiliar vantage point. In the daylight, I might have been able to spot the roof of the massive Emporium, but all I could see at night were the illuminated windows of the crowded insulae across the river. The grand public buildings of Rome wallowed in the darkness. The city only showed its squalor at night.

I thought of Claudius Rufanus. Whatever the circumstances of his death, he would be cremated with all the ritual honours his noble birthright warranted. I wondered if anyone would say a prayer for Sylvia. I wondered if there was anyone in the world who would even notice her passing. I also wondered if the vigiles were still laughing at me.

I wasn't as naïve as they thought. I had been around. I knew what it was like to have moral failings that were best kept secret and never entertained under one's own roof. Rufanus could have kept a pretty pleasure slave at home, either a boy or a girl, and it would hardly have been a scandal. Even a pretty boy who dressed as a girl wouldn't have ended his career, but Rufanus had built his reputation on old-fashioned Republican decency. Under Nero the artist, Rome was more liberal than men like Rufanus approved of. Perhaps the mere possibility of being mocked by the graffiti in the Forum for his hypocrisy had frightened him.

I certainly wouldn't have been ashamed to keep someone like Sylvia in my household, had my tastes led me in her direction, but there were certain defects of moral character that even newly liberal Rome drew the line at.

What was it Maro had said to me after Octavia's divorce?

"Act well, Quintus. Another scandal might haunt us."

Act well.

I took a deep breath, copped a lungful of Tiber stench, and regretted it instantly.

Behind me in the room, Atreus was still examining things, carrying the oil lamp with him as he went to inspect every little inconsequential detail like it might make a difference. I stuck my head around the door again to see that he was crouched over the body of Rufanus, having a closer look at the wound underneath his heart. I was no expert, but I could tell it was similar to the wound that had killed Marcellus Albanus. Unfortunately, it didn't mean anything. Anyone with a basic knowledge of anatomy and a strong right arm could have inflicted such a death blow.

Atreus's hands snaked around Rufanus's throat, his fingers burrowing into the folds of flesh and meeting together at the base of the dead man's skull. He cradled the head for a moment, a gesture that would have looked tender under different circumstances, before letting it drop back onto the thin mattress with a thump.

"There's nothing here," he told me. "Not in the room, not on him."

I'm not sure if that was the exact moment that the arse fell out of the Christian theory, but it certainly got shaky. It worried me enough to say, "Check again."

Atreus did. "Nothing, sir."

I debated taking another deep breath but decided against it. Instead, I waited for Atreus to think of something. As it turns out, it wasn't just the Christian theory that was imploding.

Junius Atreus straightened up and rubbed his temples. "I don't suppose that Claudius Rufanus recently made Florian his heir as well?" he asked in a rueful tone.

"I very much doubt it."

Tonight's events were good news, at least for young Florian, who, although he might have had all the motives under the sun to kill his cousin Albanus (but not the heart), probably didn't have any reason at all to do in Claudius Rufanus (of *the* Claudians). The murder of a second patrician who'd reclined at the main table at Marcellus Albanus's sumptuous party pointed to something more than a dispute between cousins over a girl.

"We're missing something," Atreus muttered. "There *must* be a connection."

It was probably my sleep deprivation and the Falernian talking, but I said glibly, "There's always Nasica."

"Who's Nasica?" Atreus asked.

It was my turn to look at him strangely. "Jupiter, Atreus, you *are* joking?"

"No," he replied. "Who's Nasica?"

"Nasica? *Decius* Nasica?" I sighed at his blank look. "I'll tell you, but not here."

"I know a place," said Atreus.

And I thought Fish Alley was dodgy.

The wineshop that Atreus had in mind must have been his local. The three of us walked back across the bridge to the Aventine—the narrow, twisted streets, the chaotic insulae looming over us at impossible angles, and people milling about in the streets. There were children playing in the filthy gutters despite the late hour and the sounds of bitter fighting and screams of laughter spilling out from unshuttered windows. It wasn't quite the Transtiberina bolthole I'd initially thought Atreus lived in—we'd just been there—but we were still close enough to the Tiber to smell it in all its filthy glory.

"Do you live around here?" I asked Atreus.

Atreus nodded. "A couple of blocks that way. Slightly nicer."

The wineshop was small and, at that hour, almost empty. A pale, skinny waiter was leaning up against the doorway, looking depressed, but he brightened when he saw us.

"Hello, Atreus," he said pleasantly to the vigile, and then took in the better cut of my tunic and the gold ring on my hand. "Sir," he mumbled in a tone of voice that suggested he was unused to anyone of rank appearing in his shop. Hardly surprising.

The waiter ushered us inside and led us through to a back room. If it saved us from joining in the game of dice taking place in the main room, I was all for it. The players looked like roughheads.

The waiter drew back a thin curtain and led us into the tiny back room.

We sat at a rickety table, and I nodded at Juba to join us.

"Why do you drink here, Atreus?"

Atreus nodded at the waiter, who had brought us some cheap wine and was now tugging the curtain back into place to give us some privacy. "I helped him out once, and I know I can trust him to keep his mouth shut."

"Runaway slave, am I right?" I asked. The waiter had that furtive, pinched look about him.

Atreus was too smart to answer that. "You were going to tell me about Nasica."

"Marcus Decius Nasica, my brother-in-law," I said, wondering where to begin picking at that particular scab. "It would be four years ago now that my father arranged things. He had already planned to get me out of his hair by shipping me off to the Tenth, and it was about the same time that he met Nasica. I got sent away before the wedding, but I met him a few times beforehand, and I liked him."

Atreus was listening intently.

"He threw me a brilliant going away party at his place on the river," I said. "Dancing girls, plenty of wine, musicians, the sort of acrobats who'll do just about anything, you know." I smiled at the memory. "I was young enough to be impressed by all of that. Even then, though, I was more impressed by the whole speech he gave about how he'd take care of Octavia and treat her like a goddess, all that nonsense, but he sounded sincere."

Atreus frowned slightly.

I leaned my elbows on the table. "When I got back to Rome, it seemed like they were still happy. I got married, my father passed away. Nasica gave another sincere speech at his funeral. I—I *relied* on him." I wasn't sure how to explain it to Atreus. How, in those first weeks after my father's death, I had felt so uncertain, so like a lost and frightened child, but Nasica, barely an acquaintance when I'd left for the Tenth, stood at my side like a brother. Perhaps he could see it in my face. "Then, about four months ago, it all changed. Nasica came to see me and told me he wanted a divorce. I was...put out."

Juba shot me a sideways look and raised his eyebrows. The whole household had heard my reaction that day: *"What? You must be* fucking *kidding me, Marcus!"*

I acknowledged Juba's look with a nod. "Well, that's actually an understatement. It was the abrupt end of our friendship. I asked for a reason, and he didn't give one." I took a drink of wine. I hated discussing Nasica. "I expected him to get remarried straight away. I'd assumed he had somebody else lined up. He didn't. As soon as it was done, Octavia moved back in with me."

"Then what happened?"

I looked Atreus in the eye. "You must have heard."

He held my gaze. "The name is vaguely familiar, but I want to hear it from you."

I drank some more of the cheap wine. Watering it down liberally had not made it lose its sting. "And then, two months ago, Nasica fell on his sword."

"Why?"

"Nobody knows. It was the biggest scandal until Albanus, but so far, I haven't met a single person who can come up with a plausible reason apart from the obvious. He was in trouble."

Atreus frowned. "What do you think?"

"I don't know what to think. We'd been friends. I thought he was decent once."

We drank in silence for a while, and then Atreus said, "What does Octavia Junilla think?"

I shook my head. "My sister shares her opinions of everything with everyone, but on the subject of Nasica, she is silent."

"And was Decius Nasica friends with Marcellus Albanus?"

I shrugged. "I don't know. Nasica was probably richer even than Albanus, and Albanus seemed the type who was attracted to money. Nasica was also at the beginning of what could have been a great political career. He would have known dozens of influential people. The old man, his patron and great-uncle, was once a consul."

"Probus Macrinus?"

"The very same," I replied. "Macrinus retired from his public career years ago, but he still has influence. He'd pinned all his hopes on Nasica, I think, and expects Octavia and me to commiserate with him. His visits only upset her."

Atreus nodded slowly. He reached out—for a breathless moment, I thought he was going to put his hand over mine—and touched the little oil lamp, his fingertips brushing over the shapes pressed into the pottery sides. "I can see why they might."

We sank into quiet reverie. I sipped my wine and watched the play of light and shadow on Atreus's forearm as he fiddled with the lamp.

"You said that Nasica is connected to everyone?" he asked at last, leaning back against the wall.

I remembered the night of Albanus's dinner party. "It was how Claudius Rufanus placed me, for starters, and he told Albanus I was Nasica's brother-in-law. Not Aemilius Valerius, son of Postumus, but brother-in-law of Nasica."

"Is that unusual?"

"What's unusual is that Paulinus did exactly the same thing," I said. "It was twice in the space of moments. Of course, they were all..."

Atreus was sharp. "Was Nasica in the Third Gallica?"

"Yes," I said, wondering if at last we were looking at the big picture and how we were meant to tell if we were. I was tired, and it was more than just the late hour. I took another mouthful of the bitter wine. "Weren't they all?"

* * *

Atreus offered to walk Juba and me back home, but since we were already in his neighbourhood it seemed unfair to keep him from his bed just for the sake of his company. He looked grateful when I declined.

"I've got Juba," I said. "We'll be fine."

"Goodnight then, sir," Atreus said and loped away on his long legs.

Juba and I headed straight home, avoiding most major trouble. I'd heard rumours about gangs of vicious plebeian thugs who roamed the streets

190

robbing their betters, but we saw none. I'd heard rumours of gangs of spoiled rich kids who roamed the streets assaulting their peers, but it was obviously past their bedtime. Juba and I made it home with only one obscene proposition from a prostitute, one plea for money from some lowlife hanging around the Porta Capena, one death threat from the same lowlife who took my refusal badly, and only one near miss with a cart filled with bricks and a carter who didn't believe in giving way to pedestrians. I could allow him that—it was the way he whipped up the oxen into a brisk trot when he saw us stepping out onto the road that really annoyed me.

Fulvia was waiting up for me when I got home.

"You know, Quintus," she said as she rose from her chair to meet me, "this is getting to be a bad habit."

"What's that?" I asked.

"The dinner party followed by the dead body and the late night," Fulvia said, unpinning my cloak and folding it over her arm.

"You don't have to wait up."

"Don't be silly. Of course, I do," she said.

"I knew there was a reason I married you."

She smiled. "No, you married me because you had to. This is the reason we stay married."

I reached out and took her hand, and we stood there together for a long moment in silence until I could finally move again.

Chapter Eleven

I did not sleep well. I was haunted that night by images of Claudius Rufanus lying dead in that dingy little Transtiberina apartment, his sightless eyes staring at the ceiling. I was haunted as well by Sylvia and her bright yellow robe and mass of dark curls. And I thought of Albanus, lying where his killers had found him, on the cold tiles of his small triclinium, his blood pooling out underneath him. I felt their deaths acutely in the darkness.

I thought about The Third Gallica as well.

In the hazy light of the dawn, the military connection didn't seem so sinister. By the time the brightening sunlight bathed my bedroom walls, I wasn't even sure it was plausible. Just because the Third Gallica was how Marcellus Albanus and Claudius Rufanus had met, it didn't necessarily follow that the Third was the reason they had been killed. A lot of men had served in the Third Gallica at one time or another. A lot of men had also attended the party at Marcellus Albanus's house that night. Those two groups had been bound to overlap at some point. It was a connection, certainly, but was it the only one? Military service was hardly an elite club.

If there was one thing that I remembered from my childhood philosophy tutor (and I wasn't sure there was) it was that silly game: *All dogs have four legs. That horse has four legs. Therefore, that horse is a dog.*

I worried that Atreus and I were chasing dogs and finding horses instead.

During the night, I had run through what I knew about the legion anyway. Julius Caesar had levied the Third Gallica for his campaign in Gaul, where he famously came, saw, and conquered. Despite the pithy catchphrase, it

192

had been a lot of years and a lot of work. My own legion, the Tenth, had starred. The Third Gallica had gone along for the ride. The Third Gallica and the Tenth both served with Mark Antony in his campaign against the Parthians and later in the civil war against Octavian. The Third Gallica surrendered at Perugia, while the Tenth held out until Actium. I had once teased Nasica about it: *My legion was tougher than your legion,* but it had been misplaced pride. The Third Gallica had backed the right horse in what had ultimately been a very murky choice between Caesar's right-hand man and his nephew. In the end, Octavian triumphed. Whoever holds the most legions wins.

After the civil war, both legions were reformed and sent east. The Third went to Syria. The Tenth ended up there as well after a brief stint in Judaea. They were now both garrisoned in Syria, where the great Corbulo commanded them, along with the Sixth Ferrata and the Twelfth Fulminata. Parthia remained the thorn in Corbulo's side.

How could serving in the same legion have condemned both Albanus and Rufanus? They were years apart in age. They could not have served together. My ex-brother-in-law had also served in the Third Gallica, and he was dead as well.

Therefore, that horse is a dog.

Perhaps we were trying too hard to look for answers; it felt as though we were attempting to draw water with a sieve. Only a day ago, I had been worrying that sinister Christians were working to destroy Rome from within and that theory no longer held water. Claudius Rufanus hadn't had an amulet placed by him after his death. He was no sacrifice to some dead-end cult.

I crawled out of bed, pulled on a tunic, yawned, scratched, and headed outside to get the shock of my life. My atrium was full of people.

If the murder of Marcellus Albanus had brought me to the edge of public recognition, then the subsequent murder of Claudius Rufanus had swept me from the periphery and dumped me right in the middle of it. My atrium was full of former acquaintances and long-lost associates who had chosen today to renew the stale bonds of friendship. When I'd tried it a few months ago as part of my job-hunting, not one of these men could spare me any time in their busy schedules, but now the tide had turned.

Nobody had seen me yet from my vantage point at the top of the stairs, and I wanted to keep it that way. I didn't like most of these men, and they certainly didn't like me. Why didn't they go and bother Severus if they wanted all the latest gossip? Although possibly they had, and this crowd was the overflow from his house. More to the point, how in Tartarus did the whole city already know?

Hursa, who should have been watching the door, popped up at the bottom of the steps and began to climb them jauntily. He was wearing his blue tunic from the night before. This morning it was greasy and stained with whatever he'd been shovelling into his face, but he still wore it proudly.

"Good morning, sir," he whispered theatrically when he reached the top of the stairs and saw me ducking for cover. He was loving it.

I drew back towards the doorway of my bedroom, beckoning at Hursa to follow.

"Hursa," I asked once I was back inside, "what is going on here?"

Hursa beamed. "Oh, sir, all these men are here to find out what happened to Claudius Rufanus last night."

"How do they even know?" I asked, picking up last night's toga off the floor and wondering if it would do.

"Apparently, sir," Hursa said enthusiastically, "your name is being mentioned in the *Acta Diurna!*"

"Excellent," I said glibly. "That way, the whole city will know who to blame when it goes to shit."

That gave Hursa pause for thought, an event as unexpected as a triumphal parade in his honour and entirely without precedent. In a moment of astonishing lucidity, he said, "I wonder if that's why Septus Severus wanted you aboard, sir."

"Severus isn't that devious," I told him, but once the thought had been planted in my head, it was difficult to get out.

Hursa only shrugged and then fetched me a fresh toga from the trunk at the end of my bed and helped wrap me in it.

194

"Where's Juba?" I asked, holding my arms out.

"He's answering the door, sir," said Hursa. He was left holding too great a length of my toga, so we had to start from scratch. "He said I was making a dog's breakfast of it."

I was sure he was right.

"Actually, sir," said Hursa, his face screwed up with excitement, "I'm not making a dog's breakfast. I'm making a *fortune!*"

He dumped the folds of my toga on the floor, dug around in the pouch at his belt, and produced a handful of bronze and silver coins that gleamed against his grubby palm.

"That's not a bad haul, Hursa." The advantage of Hursa having such low expectations was that he was always pleasantly surprised when Fortuna smiled at him at all. "Of course, I'm not going to see any of those men privately."

"Aren't you, sir?" Hursa asked worriedly.

"No."

Hursa looked at the coins in his hand and painstakingly calculated the worth of his little fortune against the worth of his own hide. He obviously liked the answer, because he looked up and showed me a sneaky smile. "I can handle them, sir."

Our second attempt with the toga was much more successful than the first, and I sighed as I thought of the modest crowd below. It would have given me great pleasure to stride through the atrium, trailing my toga and ignoring the lot of them, but with celebrity came responsibility, apparently. I drew a deep breath.

I headed down the steps, trying to look dignified and sombre. I felt like one of the great dictators of times past. When I reached the bottom of the stairs, space opened up for me, and when I began to speak, everyone else fell silent. I thanked these men for coming to see me (hypocrites, all of us!) and promised that between Septus Severus and myself, the murderer of Claudius Rufanus would not go unpunished. It was a dark day for all Romans, I added pompously, when the best of patrician nobility was so cruelly cut down.

I caught a glimpse of Atreus, half hidden by one of Uncle Maro's borrowed statues, listening to my speech with one eyebrow raised slightly.

I was no orator, but I felt like Mark Antony must have in that fateful hour when he stood upon the Rostra and delivered his eulogy for Julius Caesar. I held the modest crowd in the palm of my hand. They nodded and murmured in agreement whenever a platitude dropped from my lips, and I knew my speech would be repeated throughout the city. I hoped it would be embellished by men who knew longer words.

Octavia was standing with Atreus. I caught her eye briefly and expected a mocking smile at my hypocrisy, but her face was serious.

I listed all of Rufanus's virtues: his service to Rome, his dignity, his pedigree, and his gravity. (His vices would go up in smoke with him on the pyre.) I reminded my crowd that Rome had lost a great son and that all of us, in our own fashion, mourned him. And we should honour him as well, by continuing his legacy of exemplary public duty. I finished with the old cliché about those whom the gods love best dying soonest. It was clumsy, given Claudius Rufanus must have been nearing fifty, but the crowd, sombre and serious, seemed to swallow it. In any case, I could hardly have said that those of whom the gods were moderately fond died in their late forties. The logical extension was that the gods really hated old people, and who could blame them?

I was no orator. I'd had the usual training in my adolescence, but I could never remember what specific posture to adopt or what to do with my hands. It was a more complex art than it looked, but despite my ineptitude, I had always been fascinated by the power of oratory. Mark Antony was again the best example. If there was one thing that he knew, and Brutus and the others should have, it was to make sure you always got the last word in.

I solemnly took my leave, holding up my hand to fend off their questions, and then I put on a burst of speed that would have made Felix jealous. I managed to escape into the ladies' sitting room, where I hoped to find sanctuary. My household slaves closed ranks as I made it inside.

"Sweet Juno!" I exclaimed. "It is *mad* out there!"

Fulvia looked up from her reading couch. She was untroubled by the fact that our home had turned into a halfway house for a fair chunk of patrician society. Both of her former husbands had been more important men than me, so this was nothing new to her.

"Good morning, Quintus," she said, rolling up the scroll she was reading. "Did you sleep well?"

Mouse was sitting on the floor playing with his toy legionaries. Perella was playing with him, her broom discarded by the doorway.

"Did you hear my speech?" I asked Fulvia, who sat up to leave me room on her couch.

"I did. It was very good."

"Really?" I asked proudly. I would have fished for more compliments except at that moment Atreus entered.

"I suppose we should go and see Severus," I said.

Atreus looked like he hadn't slept again, and I wondered if it was Rufanus's death that had kept him up, or if the gangster Bano was still leading the cohort on a wild goose chase throughout the district.

"Yes, sir."

I had no idea what we were going to tell Severus. I hoped that Atreus would offer me some suggestions on the way, because I had nothing. Only last night, over good wine and good company, I had been singing a very optimistic tune. Fortuna brevis, indeed.

As it happened, we didn't need to visit Severus's house. Atreus and I were preparing to run the gauntlet back through the atrium when a small, scrawny boy arrived bearing a message from my favourite mad relation.

"Aemilius Valerius," the boy recited, "my master Aemilius Lucullus Maro asks that you attend him at his home. The magistrate Septus Severus is there."

He was new. For a start, he was still scrawny, something that mad Aunt Marcia would soon remedy. Her slaves were the fattest in the street, but contrary to popular advice, it had never bred laziness or disrespect. The boy was also way too formal. Maro's last messenger had been much more relaxed: *'scuse me, sir, your uncle wants you over.* He had also been notoriously forgetful, got lost a lot, and was often dazed and confused. It explained why Maro had sold him. It didn't explain why I'd bought him, though. In my defence I thought I'd been buying a hitherto unknown slave of German descent. I'd got Hursa instead.

The man in question poked his scruffy head around the door. "Oh!" he said and made a face while he tried to remember. "Sir, Cornelius Paulinus wants to know if you'll see him."

"I have to see Severus first," I said. "He can wait, if he likes."

"Yes, sir," said Hursa, and wandered off again.

I exchanged an uneasy look with Atreus. "I wonder what Severus will have to say," I said.

Atreus looked weary. "Whatever he has to say, sir, I doubt I will enjoy hearing it."

He was dead right.

* * *

Severus wasn't happy, and for once, he was paying attention to a lowly vigile. It wasn't the sort of attention that he wanted, but Atreus did his best to keep his face impassive while Severus vented his spleen. Atreus wasn't happy either, and it showed on his serious face despite all his efforts; he wore the shadow of a scowl across his forehead, his mouth was a tense line, and his jaw was set like he was doing some serious teeth-clenching.

It had taken a single night, and already the wags that wrote the graffiti were on the case. I'd seen a particularly scathing one on the way over, where Severus and I were too busy examining our own anatomy to notice the senator beside us getting stabbed to death. At least we'd been given generous genitalia, I supposed. Severus, who must have seen it as well, wasn't as forgiving as me, and he was taking it out on Atreus. The problem as I saw it (from my position reclining on a couch eating honeyed figs) was that Atreus was the only one out of all of us who had any idea what he was doing. So far, it had been the wrong idea, but it had been an idea nonetheless. Points for effort. I chewed on a fig and glanced around the room.

198

Mad Uncle Maro's informal triclinium was a mishmash of styles. Some of the columns around the walls were the traditional Doric. Some were the more ornate Ionic. Some were the elaborate Corinthian. And some were a crazy hybrid of the lot that had been dreamt up by the drunken architect Maro had been convinced was a genius. Uncle Maro thought it was eclectic. Everyone else thought it was an eyesore. The columns at least diverted attention from the frescoes: on the northern wall, an ochre-coloured Romulus grimly staked out the boundaries of his city-to-be with his plough. The gods looked down approvingly on his labour. On the wall next to that the Sabine women were being carried away by the Roman men, and all of them looked to be thoroughly enjoying the experience. The few gods not stalking Romulus watched the abduction from a nearby olive grove. Opposite Romulus, good Horatius defended the bridge single-handedly from the Etruscan horde. While some might say the gods had been watching out for him on that fateful day, Uncle Maro's artist had already used up the entire Pantheon on the other walls, leaving Horatius to be watched by a couple of wolves, an eagle, and some other ill-defined birdlife.

I turned my gaze away from the fresco and back towards where Atreus stood in front of the main couch being attacked by Severus. My attention had wandered in the last few moments, but Severus's attack had been particularly cyclical, and I joined in again, just at the point where he mentioned Burrus again.

Burrus:

"Burrus?" I'd asked the first time. "As in, *Afranius* Burrus?"

But since we'd already been here before, I knew the answer.

Afranius Burrus, despite the rumours of his worsening health, was easily the most powerful military figure within Rome. He was prefect of the Praetorians. More importantly, he was part of the triumvirate that had installed Nero as emperor. He was also the man that Severus needed to impress if he ever wanted to get that equestrian brother-in-law of his in with the Praetorians.

"Burrus!" Severus declared. "Burrus came to my house and as good as told me that we are about to lose this investigation!"

We'd been here before, several times. Uncle Maro and I exchanged weary looks. Around and around and around we go. It had been a long morning.

The Christians:

"What a monumental waste of time!" Severus exclaimed. "You come up with bullshit about secret cults and assassination attempts and how dangerous they are, and now you tell me to forget about it!"

"It was a working theory, sir," Atreus said patiently. He'd said it the last three times as well. I wondered why he was still bothering. Severus had already moved on to his next topic.

The Third Gallica:

"I've yet to see any evidence that Albanus and Rufanus were killed simply because they were in the same legion," Severus scoffed. "None at all!"

"It's a working theory, sir," said Atreus, but Severus hated the idea.

"The Third Gallica is a fine legion!" the magistrate exclaimed, as though Atreus had unjustly impugned every single man who had ever saluted the Syrian sun. I probably should have warned Atreus earlier that the general currently commanding the Third Gallica was none other than Severus's close family friend Corbulo. I had the distinct feeling that Severus would defend the Third's reputation more stridently than Corbulo himself. I'd once heard Corbulo say of the Tenth: *They're a pack of dogs. Let the Parthians thin them out.* I doubt he was any more kindly disposed towards the Third Gallica.

But of course, Severus had already changed topics again.

The Urban Cohorts:

"And now Burrus has threatened to turn the whole investigation over to the Urban Cohorts!" Severus fretted.

"Burrus is not the Prefect of the Urban Cohorts, sir," Atreus answered.

Even I rolled my eyes at that. It didn't matter if he was or he wasn't. He was *Burrus*. If he wanted the Urban Cohorts to take over from the vigiles, it was as good as done.

"We are going to lose our jurisdiction!" Severus hissed desperately.

Except this time, Atreus had an answer. "Then why haven't we, sir?"

"What?" Severus gaped. "What are you talking about?"

"If Burrus wants the investigation, why doesn't he already have it?" Atreus asked.

Severus probably thought he was being insolent, but Atreus had a good point. A good point was never going to get in the way of the magistrate's tirade, but something did. At that moment, my mad Uncle Maro sat up, stretched, and belched. The sound echoed through the triclinium and startled Severus out of his rant.

I took the opportunity to jump in. "Atreus is right, Severus. If Burrus really wanted this investigation, he'd have it by now. He's just making all the right noises in case it goes to shit."

Severus actually drew a breath, and his beet-red face faded back to pink, probably saving him from a sudden aneurysm. *"In case?"* he managed. "From where I'm standing, Valerius, it's *already* gone to shit!"

I wasn't a lowly vigile. I didn't have to take that. The problem was he was right.

Uncle Maro covered his mouth to deaden another massive belch. "Oh dear," he said. "Excuse me. Goodness, what is in those figs? Well, what a mess, hmm? Out of the smoke and into the flame!"

It was hardly the time for one of my mad relation's little homilies, but he was full of them.

Maro belched again, adjusted his tunic, and patted his belly. His sharp eyes gleamed. He nodded at Atreus. "Severus, you're teaching a dolphin how to swim!"

Severus looked at him wildly.

"You're teaching an eagle how to fly!" Maro continued. "Believe one who has experience, yes?" He was on a roll. "You're making an elephant out of a fly," he pronounced and then burped again. "Excuse me!"

I opened my mouth to interrupt, but Maro was unstoppable.

He held up his hand. "Remember, after clouds, Phoebus!"

It did the trick. Severus collapsed under the weight of Maro's stale collection of ancient adages. He sank down onto a couch, sighing, passed a hand over his face, and deflated like an old wineskin.

"Take a litter home," Maro said kindly to Severus. "And a jar of Falernian, to ease your troubles! We will talk again tomorrow, old friend."

Out of nowhere, a pair of slaves appeared, helping the magistrate to his feet and ushering him solicitously out of the triclinium. I had no doubt they would have him sitting in his litter clutching a jar before he thought to argue.

"Well," said Maro smugly, clapping his hands, "that's Severus out of your hair!"

"You're a sly old thing," I told him, impressed despite my worry.

Maro beamed and then grew serious again. "It's as far as my help extends, I'm afraid, Quintus. If Severus is right about Burrus, you're quickly running out of time to make the right sort of name for yourself here. If Atreus is correct—" He looked around. "Jupiter, Atreus, take a seat!"

"Thank you, sir," said Atreus and sat at last.

"If Atreus is right," Maro continued, "and it really does have something to do with the Third Gallica, then I have no doubt Burrus will stick his oar in. There's nothing the Praetorians like more than justifying their own existence by maligning a serving legion."

"The Third Gallica is a connection," I agreed, "but maybe not the *only* connection."

"Of course, sir," agreed Atreus immediately, robbing me of the opportunity to impress him with my logic after all. "But at the moment, it is the only connection we have."

"Well, quite," Maro said. "And you're not likely to find another. By that, I mean the family of Claudius Rufanus has already closed ranks. They're *the* Claudians, of course, and they certainly won't own up to any skeletons."

"How do you know all this?" I asked curiously.

Uncle Maro tapped the side of his nose. "When you've lived as long as I have, Quintus, you can feel it in the wind."

I waited.

"Also," my mad relation said, "I went to see Rufanus's brother as soon as I heard, and even his closest clients aren't getting in the door. I don't rate your chances at all."

I sighed. Neither did I.

* * *

After an abortive attempt to visit Claudius Rufanus's home on the Viminal, Atreus and I lunched in a small caupona in the valley between the Caelian Hill and the Aventine. It was busy, noisy, and quite sordid. The leek soup was, however, excellent and easily worth the price of listening to the men on one side of us haggle with the barman over the price of the live-in prostitute and the men on the other side coming to blows over whether or not the Greens were all pederasts.

I should have been more frustrated by our lack of progress perhaps, but for all that my feet ached, and this entire thing was giving me a headache, I was *enjoying* it. I liked having something to do again. I liked feeling as though I had a purpose. And I liked spending my days with Atreus, too, in sordid little lunch places like this one. I told myself it was the same camaraderie I'd felt for my fellow junior tribunes in the Tenth, but that was at least partially a lie. My feelings weren't all brotherly: I liked sitting so close to Atreus that our shoulders knocked together as we ate, and his thigh pressed against mine. I liked it a lot more than I should have.

I don't know how they found us there, but our lunch was interrupted by a couple of massive square-headed murderous-looking bullyboys. They muscled through the door, and the entire caupona fell silent. They were thugs, each of them as broad as two men. They were wearing non-descript brown cloaks and boots that looked like they were made for kicking heads in. They advanced on our table, and my heart almost stopped. Why had I left my gladius at home? Sure, it was prohibited to carry it here in Rome, but bloody stupid not to in a dive like this. I could argue the legality of it later with Atreus, if either of us made it out of here.

My father was right. I was going to get murdered in a slum. I pictured him waiting on the other side of the Styx, lending me a hand to get out of the boat and showing me his most disappointed look: *I told you so, Quintus.*

Then one of the bullyboys spoke:

"Boss," he said to Atreus, and my heart rediscovered its regular rhythm, "I've got a message for you."

"What is it?" Atreus asked.

"Some bloke by the name of Philosthones wants to see you," he said.

Atreus and I exchanged a hopeful look. Had our luck turned at last?

My accountant Philosthones lived in a large apartment on the third floor of an insula near the Porta Capena. Not having been born to wealth, he'd nurtured every little bit he got his hands on as carefully as a gardener tending seedlings. Now, in his declining years, Philosthones was at last reaping the rewards of his labours. He could have afforded a house but chose instead to live in the insula he owned. As the onsite landlord, he was not bothered by troublesome neighbours. He had evicted those long ago. Philosthones was a shining example to every slave who strived for manumission.

He met us at his front door himself and showed us to the sitting room. It was light and airy and opened onto a wide balcony that overlooked the Porta Capena. Diaphanous curtains fluttered in the warm breeze. The noises of the busy street drifted up on the air.

"Quintus, my boy!" Philosthones said. He had a gleam in his eye, so I guessed this would not be a wasted trip. "Good to see you!"

Atreus and I both sat, and Philosthones sat down across from us. From underneath his couch, he drew out the box I'd last seen on Atreus's desk.

"Have you found something, sir?" Atreus asked.

"Indeed I have," beamed Philosthones proudly. He looked at the pair of us from behind his beaky nose. "Tell me, which legion did Marcellus Albanus serve in?"

I felt my stomach lurch and wondered if the old man was about to confirm all our suspicions. "The Third Gallica. What of it?"

Philosthones drew out some of the incomprehensible pages Atreus, and I had mused over days earlier. "I can tell you that five years ago, Albanus was living from day to day. His wealth was tied up in property, and he had very little ready money. Then he wrote his will, and borrowed a sum of money off his uncle, that he recorded as *TM. Tribunes militium.* I presume it was to buy his equipment and passage. It is after that that these hidden accounts begin."

Atreus and I exchanged a look.

"There are only a few pages," Philosthones said, "but certainly, this is a regular income here, upwards of a hundred *aurei* every six months. What do you make of that?"

"That's a fucking *fortune*," I said. "Where does it come from?"

"I don't know that," Philosthones said. "Whatever he did in his military service made him a *very* wealthy man. But I can tell you where the money *goes*."

He paused for a long while. He had always been fond of theatrics. Atreus waited patiently, but I'd suffered it my whole life.

"Go on then, old man!"

Philosthones wasn't offended. He only gave me a knowing smile and pointed out another column of gibberish: *50 A. R. 50 A. N. 50-* the rest had been smudged out.

"These are payments," Philosthones said. "The money was divided into lots and sent to different men. The amounts change on each entry. Whatever generates this income, it fluctuates."

"That's a lot of money over five years," I said.

"Yes," said Philosthones. He sounded impressed, and it took a lot to impress the old man. "Oh, and another odd thing."

Atreus and I were hanging on every word.

"There is also a recurring payment to someone called *Eb*," said Philosthones. "Only a sestertius a month, but it's listed here on the hidden accounts, so it must relate. Their secretary, possibly."

"Eb?" I said. "Seriously?"

Philosthones sighed. "It's an abbreviation, Quintus, obviously."

"It could stand for anything," Atreus said.

Philosthones looked crafty again, so I knew the old man had another trick or two to show us. "I assume it stands for Eburnus," he said smugly and waved another page in my face. "Two months ago, Marcellus Albanus paid a private informer to track down a runaway slave called Eburnus. Again, the money comes from the hidden accounts."

I digested this news slowly.

"Find the slave Eburnus," said Philosthones, "and I bet he could tell you where the money comes from and exactly who it goes to."

I looked at Atreus. I could count on one hand the number of times he'd smiled since I'd known him. He was smiling now. I wasn't. I wasn't happy at all, because we were right back to the place I'd talked myself out of the entire night—the Third Gallica. A lot of men had served in the Third Gallica. Some of them had been at the party at Marcellus Albanus's house. Some of them were probably honourable. But others were obviously engaged with Marcellus Albanus in some dodgy scheme to line their own pockets during their military service and afterwards back in Rome. And that amount of money? Jupiter! It was *obscene*. Whatever the former tribunes of the Third Gallica were up to, it had to be bigger than the Colossus of Rhodes. This morning, I had thought the legionary connection could have been coincidental. Now, it was apparent that it would have to be a coincidence of Herculean proportions. My mind kept jumping to my ex-brother-in-law Decius Nasica. I kept making it jump away again. I did not want to think about him right now. Sometimes, a horse was a dog, after all.

"What was the name of the private informer?" Atreus asked.

Philosthones consulted his list. "*Ah, Kaeso*."

"I don't know it," said Atreus, shaking his head slightly.

"I do," I told him unhappily. "I've seen his sign chalked up in Fish Alley."

* * *

Ever since the messy death of young Marcellus Albanus, Atreus had kept half his men running around chasing down rumours of Christians. Since the bottom had fallen out of that theory when Claudius Rufanus had been killed, they'd probably thought they'd get a day off. They hadn't. Atreus had immediately reassigned them to chasing down ex-legionaries of the Third Gallica. These proved easier to find than any Christians, and as we left Philosthones's apartment, we ran into a vigile who had come to deliver

206

the news— not only had they found an ex-legionary from the Third Gallica, they'd found one who was down on his luck so badly he was willing to talk to the law. As a bonus for me, he was happy to spill his guts for the pitiful bribe that Atreus offered, and I didn't have to dip into my own funds.

We met Rubio in a dodgy bar in the Subura, and he looked like a typical ex-legionary who'd done his twenty years very hard. He was big, grizzled, and had the crooked nose and mismatched cheekbones of a man who had seen a lot of action in his time. His beefy hands, clasped around a large cup of wine, were crosshatched with scars. Like a lot of ex-legionaries, he was bitter with age and experience. He'd spent his pension within a few months of getting home. He'd lived like a king until it had all dried up, and now he was over forty years old, worn out, grey at the temples, and had never learned a trade. He spent his days drinking too much and staring at his own mortality.

"Yeah, I was in the Third Gallica," he snarled as we sat down opposite him. He spat on the floor and then looked us over. "Bastard."

Whether he was referring to the general, a junior tribune, the First Spear, his old pay clerk, or even me, it was impossible to tell. He probably didn't even know himself. It was a reflexive response from someone too drunk and too bitter to make a go at a new life.

"When did you get back?" Atreus asked.

"Eighteen months ago," Rubio snarled. That was a long time living in the gutter.

"Seems like you're doing it tough," Atreus commented.

Rubio grunted, but he was happy enough as long as Atreus kept the drinks coming.

"What can you tell me about the Third Gallica?" Atreus asked.

"Whatcha mean?" The question was too broad for an old drunk like Rubio to parse.

Atreus didn't have any military experience, so I dived in. "I was in the Tenth."

That sparked some interest, and it wasn't complimentary. Rubio turned his battered face towards me. "Is that so, tribune?" He made it sound like an insult.

I was damned if I was going to be intimidated by Rubio. I'd dealt with worse before. "That's right. Under Corbulo. You wouldn't know me, though, because while the Third was sitting on their arses in Syria, me and my men were already fighting the Parthians."

He stared at me for a moment like a mad dog, and then his lips split into an ugly grin. "Alright, tribune."

I poured him another drink from the jug. "So you'd know Marcellus Albanus?"

"Bastard," said Rubio automatically.

"So you *did* know him?"

"Yeah," Rubio said slowly. "Incompetent arsehole. Couldn't even lace his own sandals and thought he was Julius Caesar."

"What was he up to?" I asked and earned another sly look. "You know, what was the dodge in the Third?"

The dodge in the Tenth Legion, as far as I knew, was the tried but true protection racket. The legionaries took care of the local marketplace, and the junior officers ran the brothels. What the senior officers did had been anyone's guess, but they'd overlooked what the rest of us were up to in any case.

Rubio glared at his wine and then at me. "The usual, and then some."

"Apparently, they were pulling in around a hundred aurei every few months," I said. "That's more than *then some*."

Rubio growled. "There was this battle," he began.

For old drunk soldiers, it always comes down to a war story. Normally they were the brave heroes fighting against staggering odds, while their incompetent junior tribunes did everything they could to get everyone killed. I didn't mind. We had our own versions about how we could have taken Parthia by now if only the stupid fucking legionaries could hold a line together. Rubio's story, however, had a point.

"It was just a local uprising, but it was those bastards' fault they were angry anyway," said Rubio, scowling. "It was a village of about two hundred, not even on the map. Our spies told us they'd raised about fifty fighting men, so the general sent orders for a single century to sort them out." He fell silent.

"What happened?"

Rubio shook his head. "They outnumbered us."

"They had reinforcements?" I asked.

"No, tribune," said Rubio bitterly. "They outnumbered us."

I was no good at maths, but even I could see that fifty armed men did not outnumber a Roman century. Even if the century was stretched thin, there were always at least sixty fighting men in it. Ideally, there were eighty.

"How is that possible?" I asked.

"At that time, tribune, our century only had forty-two legionaries in it," said Rubio. He looked grim. "We won, but it was a near thing. Nearer than it should have been if those bastards hadn't been fiddling the books."

"How do you mean?"

"This was before Corbulo," said Rubio. "The general at that time was so stupid that the tribunes ran rings around him. The treasury was paying the wages for men that had died years ago, or men that didn't even exist except in the books."

I'd heard of the dodge before, but on a much smaller scale. Normally, it was the legionaries themselves who tried it, divvying up the wages of a dead comrade with his tentmates. I'd never heard of the tribunes trying it.

"Did Corbulo put a stop to it?" I asked, remembering how he'd sorted out the Tenth.

"His reputation preceded him," said Rubio. "The Third had mass desertions of dead men in the months before he arrived. The rest was put down to bad accounting." He raised a disconcerting smile. "Can you imagine it? Those sons of bitches actually had us out hunting for imaginary deserters, just to put on a show for the new general when he arrived."

I was astonished at the audacity of it. It was fraud on a massive scale, and every single man in the Third must have known about it. I wondered why nobody reported it. It was my next question.

Rubio looked shifty. "Decimation."

I recalled his earlier turn of phrase. "And then some?"

"It was worth our while to shut our mouths," Rubio admitted. "We got our pick of prisoners for slaves."

That was the usual and common agreement in all of the legions, but it didn't feel right. The Third Gallica had an almost identical history to the Tenth. Where were they finding all those prisoners of war?

"I didn't know the Third fought any major battles for years prior to the Parthian campaign."

Rubio gave me another unsettling smile. "Tribune, we didn't."

"You didn't?" I asked uneasily, with a hollow feeling in my guts because I thought I knew where this was going.

"But you'd know Cappadocia, tribune," said Rubio easily. "There are a lot of villages there that nobody would miss. They either paid off our tribunes, or they got crossed off the map. If anyone noticed, it was blamed on the Parthians."

"Those are Roman territories," I said.

"Yeah," agreed Rubio warily.

A man, or a like-minded group of men, could earn a fortune if they extended a protection racket to all the civilian villages and settlements they found, Roman or not. And if the villagers reneged, you sold them as slaves and wiped their houses off the face of the earth. It was a simple plan. Reprehensible, but simple.

I felt ill. "How long did this go on?"

"I saw it a couple of times," Rubio replied. "It happened in Syria, Cappadocia everywhere. The payroll scam, I have the idea that was all Marcellus Albanus's bright idea. The other, though, well, in the Third Gallica, it's as old as saluting the sun."

I was not liking this conversation.

"But that must have dried up as well when Corbulo arrived," interjected Atreus. "These payments were recent. And massive. A couple of Cappadocian villages couldn't account for all that."

Rubio nodded slowly and took another swig of wine. He wiped his mouth with the back of his hand. "Then that would probably be the silver mine."

"The *what?*"

210

"The silver mine," said Rubio matter-of-factly. "I heard it's in Syria. Some tribunes found it back in the day and kept it to themselves, you might say." He suddenly saw the implications of what he'd said and rapidly backtracked. "Well, that's the rumour, anyway. I don't know if it's true. I don't know anything about it. *I* never saw anything."

There was treason, and then there was *treason*.

A silver mine that operated without the knowledge of the imperial treasury. Could such a thing even exist? I could hardly credit it, but it explained why so much money was finding its way back to Rome to the ex-tribunes who kept the secret. It was enough to buy a legion, apparently. Was it enough to buy an empire? There was a good reason all mines were imperial property. The ex-tribunes of the Third Gallica suddenly seemed much more sinister than I'd previously thought them.

My wine tasted sourer than before. I wished we'd never found Rubio. And I wished I could've just walked away. I wanted to, but something kept me there. I hated to ask the next question, but I had to. I needed to know. "And what about Decius Nasica? Did you know him?"

"Sure," said Rubio. "The bastard. He was in it all up to his neck."

* * *

Afterwards, in the alley outside the wine shop, I punched and kicked a wall and shouted abuse at the dead.

"You fucker! You miserable treasonous *fucker!*"

Strong arms came around me from behind. Atreus's grip tightened as I tried to struggle free.

"Don't," he said, holding me close. "You'll injure yourself."

He pressed me into the wall, his lean body pushing against me, his arms keeping mine at my sides. Jupiter, but even with all the rage inside me, I wanted to lean back into him. Wanted to turn my head and press my mouth against the pulse in his throat.

Wanted to risk everything for more than this fleeting moment, like the stupid fool I was.

211

I sagged in his arms, panting for breath as my rage subsided, sweat sliding down my temples. My heart ached, and my knuckles throbbed. Angry tears stung my eyes.

I thought of all the gifts Nasica had showered on Octavia. The perfumes, and the clothes, and the jewellery, and the way Octavia always protested: *"But, Marcus, the cost!"*

The cost indeed.

Chapter Twelve

B y the time we got back to my house, it was almost nightfall and far too late to start chasing up dodgy informers in Fish Alley. I wanted an early night, and Atreus had to get back to his day job. Well, his night job. The criminal classes wouldn't beat themselves up. I invited Atreus to join me at dinner. I thought he would decline like always and lope off back down the hill into the gathering darkness, but he surprised me.

"Thank you, sir. I would be honoured."

Hursa opened the door to us and took our cloaks. Larius appeared with wine, and I gladly washed the dust out of my throat. I looked through the atrium into the house. Xanthus flitted about, lighting the lamps and braziers. There was a warm glow already coming from the third and smallest triclinium, where my womenfolk had gathered to dine.

Hursa regarded me reproachfully while he knelt down to unlace my sandals.

"What is it, Hursa?" I asked with a sigh.

"You're very late, sir," he said mournfully. "Cornelius Paulinus wanted to invite you to dinner. He waited for ages."

I'd forgotten all about Paulinus, and knowing now what I did about the Third Gallica, I wondered what that particular ex-tribune had to say for himself. I liked Paulinus and didn't want to have to re-evaluate my opinion of him. He had been my only friend that night at Albanus's party, and I had enjoyed his cheerful company. Now, I didn't trust him. I exchanged a glance with Atreus. Would a chat with Paulinus relieve our suspicions, I wondered, or confirm them? In light of ex-legionary Rubio's wine-addled testimony, I thought I knew who was to blame for the deaths of both Marcellus Albanus and Claudius Rufanus: *they* were. The treachery of the Third Gallica had resulted in their respective demises, whoever had done the deed itself. I had a theory in that direction as well. Of all the men on Atreus's famous list who had been in a position to murder Albanus on the night of his party, only one had the obvious political motive: Anicetus, ex-slave, head of the fleet at Misenum, and alleged imperial assassin. Maro had told me that if you crossed the palace, it was Anicetus you met with in a dark alley. And if Anicetus had murdered Marcellus Albanus, then he'd probably murdered Claudius Rufanus as well. It seemed a stretch to call it murder now. Summary justice, perhaps.

I heard my career give a death rattle. If I was right, and even if I could prove it, there was no way I could announce publicly what the palace was doing in secret. I was well and truly in the public eye as the determined young go-getter who was going to make his name with this investigation. I suspected that name would shortly be synonymous with failure.

"Sir?" asked Hursa curiously, bringing me back from my bleak reverie. "Sir, are you alright?"

"I'm fine, Hursa," I told him, and he beamed. Dormice were more perceptive.

"Oh, and Gavius Silanus is here for dinner as well," my useless door slave finally remembered to tell me.

"Who in Tartarus let that happen?"

"I don't know, sir. He *said* he was asked." He probably had been, but Hursa would let in a rampaging war band of the Iceni if they told him they'd been invited.

It was Larius who shed some light on the situation, cautiously. He looked at his feet while he spoke. "Master, Gavius Silanus asked Fulvia Drusa if he could dine here."

"Ah," I said, pleased. "Hopefully, the first step in having Julia moved back to his place."

Larius stared at the tiles unresponsively, but Hursa sniggered furtively.

The sound of conversation drew Atreus and me on towards the informal triclinium. We stood for a moment outside in the soft darkness of the atrium, where we could see and not be seen. We Roman men told ourselves that when we were not around, our women were quiet and modest and proper. We were fools to believe it. My womenfolk were drinking wine and laughing at something that, by the look on his face, Gavius Silanus just didn't get. As I watched, Octavia threw her head back, and the light glinted on a thin gold chain around her throat. It was modest but expensive, and it probably came from Nasica and had been paid for with his treason. Had she known her husband was a traitor? Standing in the gloom, I reminded myself that there had been three patrician deaths, not two, associated with the treason of the Third Gallica. There was also my ex-brother-in-law Nasica, who had divorced Octavia and then fallen on his sword.

"Shall we?" I said to Atreus, and we stepped into the doorway.

The womenfolk and Silanus all turned to look. Their faces were flushed red with wine and laughter and, in Silanus's case, poor circulation. His face split into a smile when he saw me there. He had revised his opinion of me since we'd last spoken. My newfound celebrity had suggested to him that I was a man to be liked and respected. It wouldn't last, not with the turn the investigation had just taken.

"Valerius!" he exclaimed with gusto, rising to his feet as he saw me and giving the couch a moment's respite. "How are you?"

"I am well, Silanus, thank you."

"It's good to see you again," he said. He clasped my arm heartily, embraced me, and I took the opportunity to make a face at Fulvia over his shoulder.

Fulvia, I hoped I communicated, *what the fuck is this?*

Silanus released me at last and lowered himself back down onto the couch. "And how is everything going, Valerius, with this business of Albanus and Rufanus?" He was as subtle as a brick. Silanus was no different than any one of the men who'd crowded into my atrium that morning, except that he'd been able to wrangle an invitation to dinner.

"Early days yet," I said. "Early days."

Silanus nodded and sat.

I sat down across from Octavia and Julia and gestured for Atreus to take the place beside me.

"So, how *is* it going, Quintus?" Octavia asked me over the eggs and salad.

"It's going much the same as yesterday."

It was at that moment that Julius Atreus's ulterior motive for accepting my dinner invitation became apparent. He regarded my sister meditatively for a moment and then spoke. "Actually, Octavia Junilla, we have made very good progress."

I shot the vigile a warning look but couldn't do much more without alerting Silanus to the fact that he was missing something gossipworthy. Octavia and Julia looked at Atreus expectantly.

"Both Marcellus Albanus and Claudius Rufanus served in the same legion," Atreus said. "The Third Gallica."

Octavia popped a piece of bread into her mouth. She shared one of those looks with Julia that women did that implied they knew everything and men were stupid. "Yes," she said. "So have several thousand men."

Atreus looked unruffled. Either he had womenfolk just as sarcastic, or he just didn't pick it up. "Of course. Your husband also served in the Third Gallica, didn't he, Octavia Junilla?"

Octavia looked him right in the eye as she corrected him. "My *ex*-husband."

"I apologise," said Atreus, and pressed on regardless. "Did you know Albanus and Rufanus?"

Octavia shrugged. "I met them. They knew Marcus." I hadn't heard her say that name in a long time, but if it was some sort of milestone, Octavia let it pass unnoticed. "Does the Third Gallica have anything to do with this?"

I'd expected Atreus to dive straight in again, but he only shook his head slightly and gave her the same reply he'd given Severus that morning: "It's a working theory."

"Considering the number of men who have served in the Third, it might need a little more work," Octavia suggested helpfully.

Julia held her hand over her mouth to stifle a giggle, and Atreus gave a good-natured smile. Julia's giggle caught Silanus's attention, and he showed

216

me a censorious frown. Not only had I brought a lowly plebeian to dinner, I'd put him right where he could make Julia giggle.

"Julia," he said, "come and sit next to your papa!"

Julia sighed and hauled herself to her feet unwillingly. She dragged herself up towards her father's couch with all the speed of Felix on the home straight, making sure everyone knew she wasn't happy about it. Octavia watched her go with a slight, sympathetic smile.

"Octavia," I said conversationally, reaching for a piece of chicken, "how was your day?"

"Apart from dodging the crowd?" she asked me with a wry smile. "Good, thank you. Julia and I went to the Emporium. Don't worry, Quintus, we spent my money, not yours."

"I'm glad to hear it," I said while I wondered what sort of wife my sister had been to Nasica. Had he trusted her enough to share his secrets?

History was full of examples of loyal wives. There was Arria, wife of Paetus, who, when the man didn't have the courage to fall on his sword, took it from him and stabbed herself with the famous last words: *It doesn't hurt, Paetus.* And there was Porcia, wife of Brutus, who killed herself by swallowing hot coals upon hearing of her husband's death. Not every man expected his wife to go to such theatrical extremes.

When we married, we hoped for an Antonia or a Calpurnia, revered in memory. We didn't get them, of course, just as they didn't get the perfect man, but most of us muddled along together anyway, well aware that we could have got something much worse. The one thing we didn't want was a Messalina. Nobody wanted a Messalina, although apparently everyone had had her.

Octavia began to tell me about the scrolls she had found: Virgil, Ovid, and Arrian. Octavia wasn't really interested in the campaigns of Alexander, so I was welcome to that. While I listened, I shook off my worry. Of course, Nasica hadn't told her anything about what went on in the Third. What man would share that particular secret with anyone? The first she'd known of any shadow in his life was when he'd fallen on his sword. That was the first any of us had known.

I remembered the morning I'd got the news. I was sleeping in, as always, and mad Uncle Maro had barged into my bedroom unannounced and shaken me awake.

"Have you heard?" he'd demanded.

It should have been patently obvious to him that I'd been unconscious for at least ten hours. "Heard what?" I'd mumbled into my mattress.

"It's Nasica!" Maro had said, flustered. "He's dead!"

"*What?*"

"Fell on his sword!"

"Jupiter!" I had exclaimed and then had the unhappy task of telling my sister.

She had been asleep as well, curled up in her bed with the blankets over her head. I had sat down beside her while Maro lingered anxiously in the doorway and woken her quietly. "Octavia? Octavia?"

"What?" she'd grumbled, as much a morning person as me.

"It's Marcus," I had said, knowing there was no good way to break it to her. "He's dead."

She'd sat up, suddenly as pale as a ghost. "What did you say?"

"Marcus is dead." I'd expected her to go into hysterics, but Octavia had always known how to surprise me.

"I suppose I should get dressed," she had said calmly.

And then she'd gone shopping, like it was any other day, although the recklessness of her spending had convinced me she'd been as much in shock as anyone. She'd returned home with a couch, a set of silk cushions, an amphora of honeyed figs, a writing desk, a tortoiseshell kitten, and the slave Larius. Her spending had trailed off over the next few weeks as her grief had lessened, and she was back to buying second-hand scrolls and the occasional pair of earrings, neither of which would put much of a dent in her bank balance.

"I told the dealer I didn't want Arrian," she said to me now as she browsed through the dish of nuts on the table, "but he said if I bought that, he'd throw in the Ovid as well, and I've always liked Ovid."

"I think I have Arrian," I told her.

"Oh, well," Octavia said with a shrug. "I'm sure it will be of use to someone."

"Mouse might be interested." I looked around the room. "Where is he, anyway?"

"You know Aulus doesn't like Silanus," said Octavia in an undertone, glancing up the length of the table towards the fellow in question.

"Neither do I, yet here I am."

Octavia raised her eyebrows. "Idiot."

If Atreus had thought I was really the stern paterfamilias of a conventional family, it was that one simple exchange that showed him otherwise. And if Atreus was perceptive enough, he would have realised that our display of such familiarity in front of him meant that Octavia had decided he was a friend. There was the old saying that friends were proved by adversity. Atreus and I had certainly had our fair share of adversity, but I wasn't sure it had translated to friendship. We were in the same boat, certainly, and making for the same shore, but to stretch the metaphor even further, we were still fucking around with the oars and getting nowhere.

And it wasn't friendship I wanted when I thought of the way he'd held me closely from behind in the alley that afternoon.

I glanced away from Atreus's profile before he caught me staring and forced my thoughts away.

Dinner was a pleasant affair, all in all. After Silanus left and the womenfolk retired, Atreus and I shared another jar of wine and made plans for the morning. We would need to speak to Anicetus, to find out if we were indeed poking into the palace's business. If we were, we would happily back away. If we weren't and we were free to proceed, we would also need to speak to the informer Kaeso, to discover if he had ever found the missing slave Eburnus. Eburnus, it was likely, knew everything there was to know about what the Third was up to. No wonder he'd made himself scarce.

Atreus rose shortly after, thanking me politely for the dinner.

"Atreus," I began and then hesitated while he looked at me questioningly. I thought of our fledgling friendship and how I liked it. How I liked *him*. "I invited you to dine with us because I consider you a friend. If you're going to interrogate my sister, I'd appreciate your asking my permission first."

"I—I'm sorry, sir," he said, and to his credit, he looked contrite. "I meant no disrespect."

Not disrespect, I wanted to say, but *trust*. Did he not trust me yet? It bothered me in ways I was afraid to articulate. And I couldn't bring myself to ask, as afraid of what the question would reveal as I was of what his answer might be.

"Thank you again for this evening, sir," he said and departed.

I lounged on the couch, sunk in my swirling thoughts, watching the flickering light from the braziers illuminate and obscure the faded frescoes in turn. Calliope cleared away the dishes, wearing the same dreamy, faraway look she usually did. She was humming to herself. Sometimes, she sang as well. She had a sweet voice. I'd almost dozed off when I heard Juba's rumbling voice: "Busy day, sir?"

I opened my eyes to find him standing above me. "Quite busy, Juba, yes."

Larius appeared on the threshold bearing a jug of wine and a glass on a tray. He kept his gaze on his feet as he moved silently across the tiles. He had the same demeanour as a whipped dog. I rolled my eyes at Juba, and Juba smiled knowingly.

Larius poured the wine and then stood back and waited until I wanted a refill.

I sat up, took my wine, and filled Juba in. "After Maro's we visited Philosthones."

"He sent here looking for you, sir," Juba nodded. "I told his man to enquire with the vigiles."

Of course, he did. Hursa wouldn't have had the nous.

"Well, it turns out," I said, sitting up, "that Marcellus Albanus and all his friends in the Third Gallica have been running more dodges than the clerks at the customs depot at Ostia."

"*All* his friends, sir?" asked Juba, raising his eyebrows.

"An ex-legionary confirmed it," I said. "Up to his neck."

Juba looked surprised.

I was conscious that Larius was lurking close by, and his ears were open to everything that was being said. Since he was only new to the household, he couldn't have known we were speaking about Nasica—he probably didn't even know who Nasica was—but I was careful not to say his name aloud in any case. The last thing I wanted was for Octavia to hear about her husband's treachery from the slaves before I had figured out how to broach the subject with her.

I held out my cup, and Larius stepped forward quickly to refill it. He stared at the floor so hard it was a small miracle he didn't splash wine all over the tiles. His cringing posture did not endear him to me. "Sons of Dis, Larius, grow a backbone!" I snapped.

He jumped like he'd been stung and dropped the bronze wine jug. It hit the tiles with an almighty crash, and wine flooded over the floor. Larius went down onto his hands and knees in a heartbeat. "Sorry, master! I'm sorry!"

I lifted up my feet before they got wet. Juba crossed to Larius and hauled him up by the neck of his tunic. He held him there for a moment, twisting like a fish on the end of a line, and then thrust him in the direction of the door. "Go and get a cloth!"

I wiped my dripping hand on my tunic. "To be fair, Juba, that was probably my fault."

"Really, sir?" Juba asked. "I doubt you would feel as charitable if he did the same at a dinner party and drenched a consul in wine."

"Like I even know any consuls."

"My point remains," Juba said. He gave me a pained look. "Talk to your sister, sir, about getting rid of him. For the sake of the rest of us, please."

I took a sip of wine. "Juba, I will add it to the very long list of things I have to talk to my sister about, none of which I shall enjoy."

* * *

That night, I was troubled by dreams. As I tossed and turned, I travelled to strange, nebulous places inhabited by shadowy legionaries. I tried to

221

look at their faces, but they kept them turned away from me. Their features were obscured by their helmets. I tried to see their standard: I *knew* it was the Third Gallica, but the standard-bearer kept disappearing, and I couldn't prove it. *I know it's you!* I told him, and then he was gone again. *I can't stop now, tribune,* he called back to me in Nasica's voice, *I have to salute the sun.*

I rose early, glad to escape my dreams, but the Third Gallica hadn't retreated far from my mind. The smallest things reminded me. The scar across my right thigh courtesy of a Parthian blade. Hursa, painstakingly counting out the four or five silver coins he'd made in his career as my door porter. Mouse, playing with his little centurion in the atrium, and Octavia, stopping to chat with him.

Atreus didn't turn up to my house that morning. I waited for a while and then decided to head down to the vigiles' station house. Juba walked with me. I bought us a stuffed vine leaf each from a stall on the street corner at the bottom of the hill and called that breakfast. I was wiping my oily fingers on my tunic as we passed under the archway in the wall of the excubitorium yard and entered the main building.

It had been a big night. There was a small crowd of people, mainly grubby and bad-tempered, each clambering for attention. The vigiles, like true public servants, had elevated ignorance to an art form. There was one sitting behind a desk looking busy, but, crucially, never looking up. It was Vibilus of the broken ribs.

"Where's my husband?" a small nut-brown woman demanded of him. "What have you done with my Ancus?"

"Had him," said Vibilus shortly. "Released him."

"Well, where is he now?" the woman demanded.

Vibilus finally raised his square head. "Dunno. I'm not his mother."

The little woman suggested some things he could do with his own mother. Vibilus had heard it all before. He looked at her with his ugly mug tilted on an angle and smiled gently as successive waves of colourful abuse rolled over him. He waited until she'd run out of breath and then nodded meditatively.

"Well, maybe we wouldn't always pick him up if he wasn't such a total shit," he suggested in a mild tone, and the nut-brown woman let fly again.

222

Vibilus ignored her and cast his eye around for a friendlier petitioner. His gaze fell on me. "Morning, sir. What can I do you for?"

"I'm here to see Atreus," I told him.

His ugly face fell. "*Atreus*, sir? Isn't he with you?"

We exchanged a look of sick anticipation.

This was not going to be a good day after all.

* * *

An empty cask was easily rolled. Atreus's days were spent with me investigating the death of Marcellus Albanus, but his nights were spent patrolling the area of the Porta Capena for signs of the criminal Bano and his fire-starting henchmen. Atreus was stretched too thin. He was exhausted. Something had to give, and something had. The vigile had forgotten to be vigilant.

"Maybe he's just slept in," I said as we climbed the steps of his Aventine insula, but I didn't believe it.

Manius, the little vigile that they'd spared to show us the way, looked worried and pale. "Maybe, sir," he said without much hope. He was a fifteen-year-old pessimist.

Atreus lived in two rooms on the fifth floor of the insula. His door was not only unlocked, it was ajar. I pushed it open cautiously. "Atreus?"

The first room was a sitting room furnished with a sturdy old couch, a woollen floor rug, a low table with a scroll box sitting on it, and two stools. There was a small alcove off the sitting room with a stove in it. There were pans and cooking utensils hanging from hooks in the alcove and a pot sitting on top of the stove. The place was cramped but well-kept. This, then, was how the other half lived.

Manius the vigile dithered in the doorway anxiously. I wasn't as polite, and neither was Juba. We'd both already seen what Manius hadn't—a trail of blood that began beside the couch and led towards what had to be the bedroom. The trail had been smeared in places by footsteps. A curtain divided the living room from the bedroom. There was a bloody mark on it that corresponded roughly with a handprint.

"Atreus?" I called again. There was a noise from the other room, but no answer.

"Oh, Jupiter!" Manius breathed at last when he'd caught up.

Juba and I were already at the curtain. Juba pulled it aside.

Atreus was lying on his bed. His face was covered in blood, and his eyes were closed. Some of the blood was already dried and flaking, but some was fresh. He was lying with one arm outstretched. The flesh was dark and bruised.

The three of us crowded around the bed. I searched his throat for a pulse, and after an agonising moment, I found one. "He's alive," I said, and Manius sagged with relief.

"I'll get a cloth," said Juba, as practical as ever, and padded off. I heard him rattling around in the kitchen while I looked over Atreus and tried to discover his more obvious injuries.

"Manius, run and fetch your physician," I said. "As quick as you can!"

"Yes, sir!" Manius was straight out the door. I heard his boots thumping down the passageway towards the stairs.

I knelt on the bed beside Atreus and wondered if it would have been more sensible to call for the undertaker instead. His face was covered in blood. Most of that seemed to have come from a cut over his eye, but I saw that one ear was bloody as well, which led my exploratory fingers to a sticky mass of matted hair at the back of his head. He'd taken a real beating. I could see where he'd bled through from under his tunic as well, but I didn't want to move him until the physician arrived.

Juba was back within moments with a bowl of water and a cloth, and we began to carefully clean up Atreus's face. He was responsive, a good sign. At the touch of the wet cloth, he flinched and inhaled sharply. One of his eyes flickered open. The other was swollen shut.

"Don't move," I told him. "The physician is on his way."

"Lucilla," he rasped. "Under the bed."

I exchanged a sideways look with Juba and wondered what woman in her right mind would still be hiding under the bed instead of ministering to her beloved. I got down on my hands and knees and found out. A little frightened face was looking back at me. Lucilla, who I'd assumed from his fleeting mention was Atreus's wife or girlfriend, was, in fact, a child no older than four or five.

"Hello, sweetie," I said in what I hoped was a friendly tone. She whimpered and shrank back. "My name's Valerius. I'm here to help your dad."

Another incorrect assumption.

"Uncle Lucius is asleep," she told me in a whisper.

My knees were starting to hurt. "He's awake now, Lucilla. Come out and see."

The little girl squirmed out from under the bed. Her tunic was covered with Atreus's blood. She must have spent the night curled up against him. She hurled herself up onto the bed beside him now and buried her face in his side. His sharp intake of breath convinced me that he had a snapped rib or two as well.

"Juba," I said, looking at the little miss, "get me a litter."

I couldn't leave Atreus in the apartment where he'd been attacked. It had been my intention to send him to the excubitorium to recover, but when I looked at little Lucilla, I realised I couldn't. A barracks was no place to house a child.

So it was that I headed home only an hour or two after having left. We made a sombre procession from the Aventine to the Caelian Hill: me, Juba, Lucilla, the hired litter and associated litter bearers, Leander, the Greek physician, and, alternately bringing up the rear or scurrying ahead, Manius, the frantic teenage vigile.

"Jupiter, sir, will he be alright?" he asked me, and, when he didn't get an answer: "*Jupiter*, Leander, will he be alright?"

"Shut up, Manius," said Leander, a man after my heart.

* * *

Fulvia, as always, was understanding. She took one look at Atreus as Leander and Manius levered him gently out of the hired litter and sent

225

a few of the slaves to prepare a spare room. Then she saw the small girl hanging around Juba's neck like a monkey and raised her eyebrows at me.

"This is Lucilla," I said. "His niece."

Juba let her down onto the tiles. Surrounded by strangers, she looked around tearfully, and her lower lip started to wobble. Fulvia knelt down beside her.

"There, there," she said in a tone not unlike the one she used with me when I recounted my many job rejections. She stuck out her hand. "Shall we go and see what's in the kitchen to eat?"

Lucilla let herself be led away. Fulvia looked at me over her shoulder. She had words to say, her look warned me, and I'd better not try and dodge her.

Our strange procession ran into Octavia and Julia on the stairs. Octavia was just as understanding as Fulvia, but unlike my wife, she didn't feel the need to postpone our words: "What in Tartarus has happened, Quintus? Is this something to do with your investigation? Are you next, Quintus? Jupiter, do you even know what you're doing?" She flung the words back at me as she led the way up the stairs.

Julia, Octavia's apparent new best friend, was joined with her at the hip today, and she nodded emphatically every time my sister flung an acerbic question in my direction and went *hmmf!* as well.

I might have said something, except I was busy concentrating on not dropping Atreus's left foot, which was the part of him that I'd been entrusted to lug. Between Leander, Manius, Juba, and myself, we managed to carry Atreus upstairs. Octavia and Julia had preceded us inside, and once we'd laid Atreus on a bed in the spare room, they went about smacking the dust out of cushions and shaking out blankets and checking the braziers and all those things that women do.

Leander's examination of Atreus at his apartment had been cursory. I think all of us had been very aware that whoever had attacked him there might return, cold light of day notwithstanding, and we had all wanted to be elsewhere.

The physician took a thin knife from his satchel and worked at the hem of Atreus's bloodied tunic. The threads gave, and Leander paused for a moment. He looked at my womenfolk and cleared his throat awkwardly.

"Julia," said Octavia, "go and tell Calliope to bring some hot water."

Julia looked miffed. "Can't I stay?"

"Certainly not," said Octavia primly. "You're an unmarried girl."

So was Octavia, technically, but given her previous marriage and her inappropriate interest in pornography, I doubted that anything under Atreus's tunic would surprise her.

Julia sighed and left us.

Octavia moved closer to the bed as Leander ripped his knife through the fabric of Atreus's tunic, from hem to neckline, in a single smooth motion.

"*Juno*," exclaimed Octavia, "What on earth is *that?*"

I was glad to realise she wasn't referring to the obvious, but instead to a strange pattern of bruised and bloody puncture marks against Atreus's left hip.

"Oh, yes," said Leander, nodding to himself and inspecting them carefully. "I've seen this before. They use a piece of wood with nails hammered through. It's nasty. Luckily, they missed the intestines."

Maybe it was the fact he could hear us talking about him, and maybe it was the sudden cool air against his nether regions, but Atreus opened his good eye again and did his best to take in his surroundings.

"What happened to you, Atreus?" Leander asked him in a chiding tone, working his fingers gently over the vigile's bruised ribcage.

"Bano did," Atreus managed. "The man himself."

"You should be flattered," Leander said with a slight smile. "Bano hardly ever does his own work."

Atreus's one good eye rolled in his skull, and he reached out and closed his bruised and bloodied fingers around my wrist. "Lucilla?"

I covered his hand with mine. "She's here. She's safe."

"Thank you," Atreus murmured, a tear sliding down his temple. "Thank you." Then he passed out again.

It was a relief to discover that Bano, scourge of the underworld, was Atreus's attacker. I had nothing to fear from some criminal thug, at least not inside my own home. Someone once said that it was a foolish man who ventured out to dinner in Rome without making his will, and certainly out on the street, your chances of getting knocked on the head, stabbed, assaulted, robbed, or otherwise violated were always high. But the days of armed gangs knocking down a patrician's doors and making off with his money, his women, and his life were thankfully behind us. Had Atreus's attack been related to our investigation, as Octavia had feared, I might have been worried. But Bano was nothing to me.

Calliope appeared soon after with a bowl of hot water, and once Atreus was properly cleaned up, Leander delivered his verdict—the vigile had suffered a black eye, numerous cuts and bruises, the nasty punctures on his hip, two broken ribs, a dislocated shoulder (Leander had put it back into place with his knee while the rest of us made faces at the sound), and the blow to the back of his head.

"It's nothing life-threatening," said the physician, washing his bloody hands. "He needs rest, certainly, and the dressing on his hip and his head should be changed each day. The strapping on his ribs should be tightened also, as soon as he can bear it."

"I will see to it," I said.

"I shall come and see him tomorrow." Leander began to pack up his instruments. "It was a warning, that's all. Bano didn't want to kill him this time."

"And next time?" I asked.

Leander shrugged. "There are three things with Bano, and Atreus has already refused the bribe. If I know him, he won't heed the warning either. Next time will be the end of it, one way or another."

I wasn't certain if I admired his fatalistic philosophy or found it unsettling.

"Thank you, sir, for your hospitality on behalf of all the Fifth."

"It's not a problem, Leander."

"We are very grateful," the physician said earnestly, looking at Atreus as he dozed. It wasn't until later in the day that I realised how far that gratitude extended.

* * *

I ate a subdued lunch with my family, feeling guiltily relieved that Atreus's injuries had distracted the womenfolk from pressing me about the investigation. It gave me the chance to look sombre and introspective and didn't encourage conversation. Fulvia had only asked once, matter-of-factly, "Are the men who did this going to come knocking at our door as well, Quintus?" There was no barb in the question, no sting in the tail. Fulvia was being her usual practical self. She just wanted to know if she should barricade the doors and arm the slaves.

"No," I said. "It's nothing to do with that. This, according to Atreus, and most of the Aventine apparently, is Bano the standover man sending a message to the vigiles."

Lucilla and Mouse were sitting together on one of the couches. Mouse, being eleven, didn't quite know what to make of Lucilla. Julia obviously did. Lucilla was sporting ringlets decorated with ivory hair combs. She was wearing a pretty silver bangle that kept dropping off her skinny arm onto her plate every time she reached for something to eat.

Lunch was interrupted by Hursa sticking his head around the door. "Oooh, sir!" he said. "Ooh!"

"What is it, Hursa?" I asked.

"Oooh, sir, oooh!" he said, jumping from foot to foot like a demented monkey on a brazier.

The reason for his excitement was the arrival of a man of importance at my door: Gaius Ophonius Tigellinus. Tigellinus was the Prefect of the Vigiles. His was a name I had heard before, but not one that caused my blood to run cold. In later years, he would be more or less a monster, but at the time I met him, he was an ambitious equite of modest descent and massive personal fortune whose biggest claim to fame had been his banishment under Caligula for sleeping with his sisters. Busy girls, Caligula's sisters. So many men had been banished under the same pretext that there was no way of telling if it was true, not that it mattered.

When I met him in the sitting room, Tigellinus was polite and gracious, a man slipping into his middle years with dignity. He was still in good shape, still handsome, with just a few wrinkles at the corners of his eyes and a touch of grey at his temples.

"Aemilius Valerius," he said as I appeared. He clasped my arm heartily. "I am told by the men of the Fifth that you have taken in Junius Atreus, their acting centurion."

"Yes," I said, motioning for him to sit. "If there's some collegium that looks after wounded vigiles, I'm happy to send him into their care, but it seemed the best solution at the time."

"It's very good of you," said Tigellinus. I was impressed at his attitude towards his injured subordinate. "You shall be recompensed for your trouble."

"That's not necessary."

"It was Bano, of course," said Tigellinus.

"He says it was."

Tigellinus inclined his head. "Yes, of course it was. He is perhaps too big a fish for my nightwatchmen to fry. Still, it's good to know it's not related to this Albanus business."

I regarded Tigellinus cautiously, knowing nothing of his politics except what the entire city knew—there was no love lost between Burrus and Tigellinus, the prefects of the Praetorian Guard and the vigiles respectively. I wondered if Tigellinus would shed any light on it.

"The magistrate Septus Severus believes that Burrus wants to take over the investigation," I said.

Tigellinus laughed. "Burrus? Of course he doesn't. He just wants the vigiles to fail. With Severus running things, he might have stood a chance. The man's a lawyer, not an investigator. On meeting you, Valerius, I'm more hopeful."

I wasn't.

"You seem well acquainted with the case."

Tigellinus smiled. "Personally, perhaps, but professionally, I'm keeping my distance, you understand."

I understood. Tigellinus would take the glory if it went well and claim he had nothing to do with it if it went to shit.

"Do you know Anicetus?" I asked him.

Tigellinus looked surprised at that. "Of course. He's a friend. Why do you ask?"

I toyed with the idea of asking Tigellinus to ask Anicetus to see me, but I held myself back. He called Anicetus his friend, but I had no way of knowing if that was true, so for once in my life, I opted for discretion.

I shrugged. "It's nothing much. I just wanted to ask him if he'd seen anything suspicious the night of Albanus's party. He's a hard man to pin down."

Tigellinus smiled. "Yes," he said. "Yes, he is."

Chapter Thirteen

O f all the festivals in the calendar, the Festival of Summanus had always been one of my favourites. The ratio of prayer to party fell favourably on the side of party, and unlike Saturnalia, I wasn't obliged to nominate anybody Lord of Misrule and give the slaves the day off. The Festival of Summanus was primarily a private affair. There were no massive parades or bacchanalias in the streets, meaning that it was perfectly acceptable for a man to sit on a couch all day and get quietly drunk while pretending to enjoy the company of his family. I'd done my duty first thing in the morning by offering the god of night thunder a couple of cakes while I performed my devotions to the household lares, and the rest of the day was dedicated less officially to Bacchus.

My houseguest Atreus was an uncomfortable invalid. While he could have been spending the day in bed, resting his bruises and his broken ribs, he had instead limped downstairs and propped himself awkwardly on a couch in the informal triclinium where he had received a steady stream of visitors. Leander, the physician, attended that morning, as did half the Fifth Cohort of Vigiles. They had started turning up soon after dawn, slinking in to see Atreus and trying not to leave dirty finger marks on the walls. There always seemed to be one or two lurking uneasily whenever I turned around.

Mad Uncle Maro, our previous falling out forgotten, seemed to get on well with the vigiles. "Yes, it's a nasty business, alright," I heard him telling a pair of them upon his arrival. He produced some tile samples from inside the folds of his toga. "Now, do you like the Greek key in the black or the red?"

Despite his friendliness towards the vigiles, Maro was worried at this latest turn of events. When the vigiles had gone to visit Atreus, my mad relation let me usher him into the tablinum, and then he told me so.

"It's like a damned barracks out there, boy!" he huffed.

"What do you want me to do, Maro?" I shrugged. "Throw Atreus out on the street?"

"Rubbish. Don't be so dramatic," Uncle Maro said. "Send him off back home, or back to his barracks, or back to one of his men's houses! Really, Quintus, I know I encouraged you to get involved, but you needn't bring it home with you!"

"Bring what home?" I asked. "Atreus?"

Maro thought I was teasing him. "Fool! You haven't just brought Atreus home. You've also brought home Albanus, and Rufanus, and who knows what else!"

"Which is why I don't mind the vigiles hanging around," I answered, putting my feet up on the desk. "Besides, I've already told you this has nothing to do with the investigation. This is Bano, the standover man."

"And that's your only motive for bringing him into your house, is it?" Maro asked, lowering his voice. "His safety?"

My guts twisted. "Yes, it is."

Mad Uncle Maro regarded me carefully for a moment, worry etched across his brow, and then let out a long sigh. "I tell you, my boy, I should never have asked Severus to take you on board. Particularly not with Anicetus involved. He's a dangerous man, and he's killed more important men than you."

I put my feet down and leaned forward. "Like who?"

"Britannicus, for one," Maro said.

Before the divine Claudius went delusional with paranoia towards the end, before Agrippina had cajoled him into making Nero his heir, Britannicus had been the bright and shining hope for all of Rome. He could have been one of the greatest of the Julio-Claudians, a standalone, but instead, he was murdered.

Maro sighed. "Well, Britannicus was friends with Titus Vespasianus, you know?"

"The general's son?"

Maro nodded. "Well, your father dragged me along to see young Titus after Britannicus died. We talked, commiserated, and then we left. Waiting for us just outside was Anicetus."

"Did he threaten you?" I asked.

"Not in so many words," Uncle Maro replied. "'That poor boy', he said, 'could never take his drink.' I'd never seen him before in my life, remember. 'Go home and play decorator, Aemilius Lucullus Maro,' he said, 'and stop poking around in imperial business. Why don't you plan a new fresco for your third dining room? Your Orpheus is starting to look faded.'"

I leaned my elbows on the desk. "And what did you do?"

Maro raised his bushy eyebrows. "I'm not stupid. I went home and planned a new fresco."

"So he's the palace's creature," I said and shrugged off my unease. "We knew that. But if he tells me to back off, Maro, I promise I'll back off." I sighed. "The thing is, though, it's more complicated than just that."

Maro's eyebrows shot together like two ferrets fighting. "How so?"

"Nasica's name keeps cropping up all over the place."

I hadn't told Maro yet what the embittered ex-legionary Rubio had said about Nasica's involvement in the corruption of the Third Gallica. I told myself I was trying to protect Nasica's reputation for Octavia's sake, but maybe it was for all our sakes. We had all liked Nasica once.

"That's not so strange," Maro told me. "He was well-liked and rich. He had a lot of friends. No, it's not unusual."

"What's unusual is the way he died." We had never talked about this. We talked around it when we spoke of Octavia's divorce, but we never talked about it. It was still too raw. I had never before asked Maro the obvious question: "Why do you think he did it?"

Maro poured himself another wine. "He had no debts. He had no enemies. I couldn't even turn up a mistress!"

"You looked into it?" I asked.

Maro looked defiantly righteous. "When Nasica came to you and said he wanted a divorce from your sister, of course, I looked into it! What sort of a man wants a divorce from a girl like our Octavia?"

I felt a sudden rush of affection for the crazy old man. "I assumed it was because they hadn't had any children."

Maro lowered his voice. "They didn't have children because they didn't want children yet."

"How can you know that?"

Maro looked uncomfortable. "Having lost your mother at an early age, your sister confided things in Marcia that normally remain between a mother and a daughter. Marcia never meant it to slip, but when I once mentioned it was taking Octavia forever to fall pregnant, she told me that Octavia and Nasica had decided they would wait."

Ah, contraceptives. Those things that good Roman wives shouldn't even know exist, but generally do.

"Wait for what?" I asked, trying very hard not to dwell on the finer points of my sister's marital relations.

"I didn't ask," Maro intoned. We had strayed into secret women's concerns, and that was a subject neither of us wanted to explore.

My father had begun arranging my marriage the moment he heard I was coming home from the Tenth. I had not been consulted and, stinging from the lack of the acclaim I had expected upon returning to Rome, I had just wanted to sink back into my old pre-army habits of late nights and too much to drink. I had managed to get in just a few weeks of bachelor freedom before the big day. I only met Fulvia once before the wedding. Chaperoned by my father, I hardly said two words to my future wife. My father did most of the talking, and I let him. I just sat there and stewed with resentment and hated parents the world over.

We had the wedding. It was a small, family affair—my family really, as Fulvia's collection of in-laws was so upset at losing her modest fortune they couldn't bring themselves to attend. Low-key festivities, well-wishers, and appropriate entertainment, and then, Jupiter, the wedding night. What a shock. I sat and waited for her in my room while she said goodnight to her son.

I waited and waited, sick to the stomach with nerves.

She came back. My hands were shaking. She unpinned her hair. My stomach was in knots. She came and sat on the bed next to me. I felt like throwing up. She said, "Now, just so you know, I have no interest in spending the next nine months with a sore back, swollen ankles, and the urge to piss like a racehorse, so if we do this, I intend to insert wax to prevent conception. I have been told that this might feel strange, texturally, but I'm game if you are." She cocked an eyebrow. "Or we can just skip the whole business and get out the latrunculi board, if you'd prefer."

How could I not fall madly in love with a woman like that?

"Hmmph." Mad Uncle Maro brought me out of my reverie.

I tried to get back to the subject at hand. "So you don't know why Nasica asked for the divorce?"

"I do not." Maro fixed me with a hard stare. "A man might choose to end his marriage for the most mundane reasons. The reasons he chooses to end his life, however, are usually a little more complex."

"Do you have any theories in that direction?" I asked, hoping he might be drawn into speculation.

"Do *you*?" Maro asked me pointedly.

I shrugged.

Maro was sinking into his own reverie now. "I met up with him by accident a week or two after he asked for the divorce, did I tell you? He asked after her, of course, but I was quite standoffish. Afterwards though, I got the impression he was just as upset as she was." He smiled slightly. "I like to tell myself that he fell on his sword because he let Octavia go, but that's just wishful thinking."

"Nobody dies for love except in Greek tragedies," I told him. "And that's generally for loving your own mother."

Maro's smile grew, but he refused to be side-tracked for long. He looked at me seriously. "But you know something, don't you, Quintus? About Nasica?"

"I wish I didn't," I said.

Maro was clever enough to put two and two together and realise that Nasica wasn't the golden boy we'd all once thought him, and smart enough not to ask for details. "Politics," he said at last, "is a funny game."

"Not from where I'm sitting."

"You're my case in point," Maro declared, sipping his wine. "Here you are, a hero of the Parthian campaign, and recommended by Corbulo himself, two things that should have ensured you a cushy position until you were old enough to stand for election as a quaestor, but then comes politics. You're a victim of your own success, my boy."

"Actually, I'm a victim of Corbulo's success."

"It's the same thing," said Maro. "In any other situation, a recommendation by a man as great and popular as Corbulo would be a boon. But here it is to your detriment."

"We've been through all of this before, Maro."

"Yes," said Maro, "but have you considered how politics is still against you?"

"How so?" I asked curiously.

"Corbulo sent you back to Rome as his golden boy," said Maro, "but, because they are suspicious of his popularity, the palace could never openly reward you. And now, having found yourself a position despite the odds, you're finding yourself up against Anicetus. Corbulo's golden boy versus Nero's."

"Is he Nero's man?" I asked keenly. "There are divisions, aren't there, in the palace?"

"I've asked around," Maro said. "He's Nero's man through and through. Which means you are between a dog and a wolf, Quintus."

"You should have thought of that before you got me the job."

"It's a bad business," Maro agreed, "and you do yourself no favours. When I became a quaestor do you know what I did?"

"Was it aqueducts?"

"It was," said Maro, "and I still don't care that water can't flow uphill. That was for the engineers to worry about, not me. You're not in the army anymore, Quintus. You can't expect to rush in and carry off a victory every time. This is politics. Don't be too disappointed if you don't win this one. It's enough for now that you have Severus as a patron."

I made a face. "The thing about the army, Maro, is that when I was a junior tribune, I actually knew what I was doing. I was *good* at it. And do you know the irony? If I'd been slightly less good at it, I'd still be there, and my career would still be progressing."

Maro clapped me on the shoulder. "I've always said there's nothing like success to ruin a man's plans."

"Sometimes I wonder if I should go back." I'd heard news of Corbulo and his victories against the Parthians. Part of me envied those tribunes winning their victories for Rome. "Corbulo would have me."

"Fool," said Maro, arching his bushy brows. "But who would look after Fulvia?"

"Fulvia doesn't need looking after."

"And Octavia?" Maro pressed me.

"She wouldn't admit it in a thousand years," I said and sighed. "But of course, I could never go back to the army now."

"Good boy," said Maro soundly. Now, listen, Severus sent a man around to my house this morning. How would you feel about the *theatre?*"

"I'm old-fashioned," I told him. "I'll consider most job opportunities, but I just feel the theatre is not appropriate for a man of my pedigree."

"Idiot," said Maro affectionately. "Severus has *invited* us to the theatre, as well you know."

I shrugged. "I don't know. This is hardly the right time to be going out in public."

"Aha!" said Maro triumphantly. "This is the perfect time. Now that all those sycophants are dropping off like disappointed leeches, the word is that you and Severus are getting nowhere with your investigation. If there's one thing politics has taught me, Quintus, it's that even as you're up to your clacker in crocodiles, you have to pretend you're enjoying the swim."

"Uncle Maro," I said. "You're a poet."

Maro winked at me. "It's tomorrow night. Bring the family."

We moved on to cheerier subjects. We discussed my uncle's latest home renovations, the rumour about the well-known senator's wife and the gladiators, the price of corn, the emperor's latest artistic endeavours, and how much Maro was prepared to pay for a genuine Praxiteles. We dissected every subject under the sun except the one that troubled us both so much: my ex-brother-in-law Marcus Decius Nasica, and his connection to the murdered former tribunes of the Third Gallica.

* * *

After lunch that day I attempted to see the elusive Anicetus. I had one single question to ask the man, and there was no polite way to do it: Had he been ordered to kill Marcellus Albanus and Claudius Rufanus? If he had, I was ready to wash my hands of the entire business and keep my mouth shut for the rest of my life. Which would be a long time, fingers crossed.

"I don't recommend going alone, sir," Atreus had said when I'd announced my intentions.

"I'm going to the palace, Atreus, not the Transtiberina," I'd replied. "Also, I'll have Juba with me."

My confidence wavered as we reached the bottom of the Palatine Hill, but I was committed by then. I was uneasy. I was going to ask a man with a very dangerous reputation if he'd killed a couple of senators, and I was not looking forward to the answer. It would be bad enough if he admitted to being the killer. It would be worse if he denied it, because if Anicetus *hadn't* killed them, then I was going to have to break it to him and to his superiors, exactly what the former tribunes of the Third Gallica were up to. Either way, it was going to be an awkward interview.

The imperial palace had once been a series of private homes spread across the Palatine Hill, either owned originally by the Julio-Claudians or purchased by them once the family star began to rise. They were linked by porticos, covered walkways, terraced gardens, and private paths. A lot of it was purpose built nowadays—the emperor not only had his family and hangers-on to house, he had the whole state machine living on the hill at the tips of his fingers. Some people claimed that the Temple of Jupiter was the centre of the world. It was actually a short hop to the southeast, in the hive of vast stately buildings that made up the palace. Not knowing where to find Anicetus in that massive labyrinth of both opulence and bureaucracy, I started at the southern end of the Clivus Palatinus and headed up the hill.

I had been to the palace before, but always on invitation and always with someone to show me the way. It would have been easy to get lost in the miles of marble and tile, broken here and there by swathes of ornamental garden, but there seemed to be a steady stream of pedestrian traffic heading in a particular direction, so that was the direction I took. I hoped we weren't all just following one another and that someone at the front knew where he was going. I was afraid Juba and I would end up on an unscheduled tour of the earthworks where Nero was building himself a cryptoporticus, but we branched off before that. We were following a fellow who looked like he'd come from the furthest corners of the empire with his satchel of military missives under his arm. He seemed like he had a sense of purpose, and I was hopeful he would deliver us somewhere useful in this strange bureaucratic labyrinth.

He did, too. He took us right into the Domus Tiberiana, where an unctuous oily slave sat in a marbled reception room and sneered openly at the line of waiting petitioners. I let Juba wait in line for me while I inspected the tile work. Juba padded over to fetch me when it was my turn.

I straightened my toga and strode over to the desk. I informed the slave in my snootiest patrician tone that I wished to see Anicetus. Being a palace slave, the skinny little fellow dealt with snootier patrician tones than mine all day and was singularly unimpressed. I took a seat at his suggestion and waited.

The sun slipped from its zenith, and the shadows began to grow.

People went in, came out, and still I waited.

I waited until my backside went numb, and then I paced for a while.

My pacing brought me to the skinny slave's desk again, to the disgust of those in the queue. "Aemilius Valerius," I reminded the slave tersely. "To see Anicetus."

He looked at me through his dark little eyes, like pieces of flint set into pale dough. He had disproportionately large ears, which he had tried to disguise by letting his hair grow long. He looked like an anaemic rabbit. He was from one of the less attractive and physically unimpressive Germanic tribes. Probably the same one as Hursa.

"Yes, sir," he said mildly. "If you'll just take a seat."

I sat some more, and the day wore on. Even Juba, patient and steadfast, was starting to grumble under his breath.

I found myself at the slave's desk again.

"Yes, sir?" he asked.

"Aemilius Valerius," I said, fighting the urge to strangle him. "To see Anicetus."

"Oh, yes," he said. "I'll check."

He toddled away.

A few moments later, he was back, wearing the bland face of an unhelpful bureaucrat. "I'm sorry, sir," he said, and he obviously wasn't. "Anicetus is unavailable. If you would like to leave your name?"

"Aemilius Valerius," I said through clenched teeth.

He scratched it into his wax tablet and looked up at me expectantly. "Was there anything else, sir?"

"Yes," I said, my anger having given me some bravado. "You might ask him if he killed Marcellus Albanus and Claudius Rufanus, if it's not too much trouble."

His dark little eyes widened in shock. "If he killed..."

"You heard," I said, and turned on my heel and left.

"Jupiter, sir," said Juba as we headed back towards the public road. "That should get his attention."

The look he gave me made me wonder if it had really been such a good idea.

* * *

There was one more thing I could chase up on my own while Atreus was laid up, so Juba and I headed there straight after the palace. In the familiar

241

shabby environs of Fish Alley, feeling like a spy, I attempted to make contact with an informer. I had seen his chalked sign before but had never had any need to avail myself of the services of such a man. If my wife was adulterous, I'd rather not know. If my business partners were cheating me, best of luck to them. If I required witnesses in a court case, I'd rather have real ones. And if I ever needed some dirt to blackmail important senators into nominating me as a quaestor, well, that was a career option I might one day have to employ. But to date, I had never yet solicited the dubious services of a public informer.

Fish Alley was busy, as always. Masso, the baker, was planted on a stool outside the wineshop. He looked as though he'd passed out there. His wife was standing in front of him, showering him with abuse he couldn't hear. She was backed up by several of her friends, who took up the slack when she got tired. Lacus, the beggar, was leaning under the faded awning of the sandal maker's shop, plaiting thin strips of leather together. He had finally found some paid employment, and he looked mournful. I caught a glimpse of the infamous Pollia Marca, decked out in a fluttering orange stola, stalking proudly down the alleyway with her grubby illegitimate children toddling along behind her. I tried to do a headcount, but they disappeared into the doorway of their dodgy apartment block before I could manage it.

Juba and I wandered along until we were standing at the section of the street that my barber claimed as his workspace. There was a sign chalked up on the nearby wall, advertising the reasonable rates of Kaeso, the informer. My accountant Philosthones had told me that Marcellus Albanus had paid this man to track down a runaway slave called Eburnus. If he was the same *Eb* as listed in Albanus's hidden accounts, then he probably had a very good reason to lay low. I needed to know if Kaeso had found him.

Centhus was cleaning his razors. "Aemilius Valerius, are you here for a shave?"

"Not today," I told him. "What do you know about this Kaeso character?"

Centhus snorted. "He's an *informer*, Valerius!"

There may have been some honest informers in Rome, but they kept a low profile. Public informers once testified in prosecutions as a civic duty. Then someone came up with the bright idea of paying them to testify, and an entire industry of claims and counter-claims was born, with a paid witness for every eventuality. Now, like every other public duty from senator to temple sweeper, it was rotten to the core. My father once told me that I was too cynical for my age. He'd thought public duty was a sacred responsibility and not just the opportunity to take bribes and gratuities off a wide range of people. I was a realist. Just like the slaves who swept the temples, senators weren't paid a salary, so they took it where they could. Just because my father was one of the few men who had never walked into the Curia with his palm outstretched didn't mean the world was honest.

"What do you want an informer for anyway? Legal troubles?" Centhus asked. His curiosity was tempered with concern, so I wasn't offended.

"No, it's the Marcellus Albanus murder," I told him. "I'm investigating it, and I need to talk to him."

Centhus gave a low whistle. "Congratulations, sir! I'll have to start charging you more when you become famous."

"You already charge me more than anyone else."

"Only because you can afford it, sir," Centhus replied smoothly. "Well, Kaeso might be a rat, but he knows a lot of people, and he did track down the sandal maker's son for Pollia Marca after his father had packed him off into hiding."

"Is the wedding still on?"

"Last I heard, Pollia had already bought the sacrificial goat," Centhus said. A customer planted himself on the barber's stool. "Good luck with it all, sir."

The chalk sign in the alleyway told me that I could find the informer Kaeso in the wineshop three blocks back. The wine shop was just what I expected—a cheap, dark hovel crammed into the alley between a brothel and a stinking laundry, existing under the oppressive shadow of the Marcian Aqueduct as it cut its way through the city towards the Capitoline Hill. The Marcian Aqueduct was once known for its cool, clear water. Now, by the time it got to the Capitoline Hill, so much had been siphoned off into private houses the flow had become a lazy trickle.

Kaeso, the informer, was also just what I expected—a slimy character so entirely stereotypical he looked like he'd just wandered off the stage of a particularly convoluted comedy where he'd played the snivelling villain. He was small and wiry and oily all over. He looked like a greasy rodent who'd just crawled out of the Cloaca Maxima, much to the relief of all the other rodents, and he blinked a lot.

"Do you do much work for patricians, Kaeso?" I asked after we'd made our introductions. I'd bought him a drink, and we'd pulled up stools at the counter.

He tapped the side of his crooked nose and winked in what he thought was a conspiratorial manner. "I have even been known to work for the palace."

I flicked a silver sestertius on the bench top. "Good. Consider yourself hired."

Kaeso's eyes narrowed suddenly. "To do what?"

"To tell me why Marcellus Albanus hired you," I asked. "Something about a runaway slave, wasn't it?"

"Something like that," said Kaeso, eyeing my sestertius greedily. "But I didn't take the job."

I nodded at the sestertius. "Why not?"

Kaeso snaked out a thin arm and closed his hand over the coin. He looked at me beadily. "Because it wasn't his slave, friend, and if I'd found him and taken him to Albanus, it would have been theft."

Kaeso didn't strike me as the principled sort. I raised my eyebrows. "Really?"

Kaeso shrugged his thin shoulders. "More trouble than I need. Whatever Albanus was up to, I didn't want to get involved."

I suppose in his line of work, Kaeso had developed a keen sense of self-preservation. "So, whose slave was Eburnus?"

"I don't know," Kaeso blinked. "A *friend's*, Albanus said. When he couldn't produce proof of ownership, I was out of there. I've been caught like that before, and it wasn't nice. I'm not going to end up in the courts just because

244

two patricians are fighting over some pretty bumboy."

I thought immediately of Claudius Rufanus.

Kaeso shrugged again. "I did recommend another informer to him, more desperate for work than me."

"Who?"

Kaeso narrowed his eyes at me, so I put another coin on the counter. Kaeso ran his thumb over the coin, lingering on the embossed profile of the emperor. His gaze never left my face. "A fellow called Colchus. You'll find him near the Temple of Diana in the Aventine."

"Good," I said and then frowned slightly. "You said you've worked for the palace?"

"I have," replied Kaeso.

"Have you ever worked for Anicetus?"

Kaeso showed me his sharp teeth with a smile. "Friend, you don't have enough gold in your purse to get an answer to that."

Fair enough.

I gave Juba the nod, and we left the dank little wine shop. I couldn't wait to shake the place off. The encounter with Kaeso, the informer, had left a bad taste in my mouth. I doubted Colchus would be any more pleasant.

* * *

The Temple of Diana was at the top of the Aventine Hill. It was marble. It was shiny. It was a piece of greatness in the middle of the slum. Tourists came to be dazzled by its glory and get robbed by the locals. I wasn't as easily impressed. By the time Juba and I got there, we were hot, thirsty, and ill-tempered. I had gone there not to petition the goddess in her silver chariot, but to find an informer called Colchus. I didn't see a sign, so in the end Juba and I approached a scrawny fellow sitting in the shade of the only temple portico that wasn't currently being used by the local prostitutes. It was the middle of the day, but the girls were already hard at it. So were their clients.

The fellow was sitting in the shade with a tray of paltry little temple offerings resting across his knees. It was fruit, mainly, and some bread. There was a cage of pigeons at his feet. I supposed the one good thing about his sad little line of work was that he got to eat the leftover stock at the end of the day.

"Hey," I said, red and sweaty. "I'm looking for an informer called Colchus. Where does he work from?"

He looked me up and down and shrugged. He paddled his grimy feet in the dust. He had one of those hard little faces you saw on the people in the slums. He could have been fourteen. He could have been forty. It was impossible to tell.

"Colchus," I said firmly. "Have you heard of him?"

"No, sir," he said at last, peering up at me through his scruffy fringe. "I'm born and bred here, I'm at the temple every day, and there's nobody called Colchus in this neighbourhood. There's the oil shop owner a few blocks back from the river, Colchitus, but he's not an informer."

I exchanged an annoyed look with Juba. We'd wandered all the way up the hill to the temple for no reason.

He looked apologetic and then hopeful. He stuck out his tray of goodies. "Want to buy an offering for Diana, sir?"

I thought of how far we'd walked.

"I might as well," I said with a sigh. "What have you got?"

* * *

Coming out of the Temple of Diana, smelling like incense and singed feathers, Juba and I ran into a mob of tourists. They were as excitable as a group of children on an outing to the games. They were pointing at everything, chattering loudly in their incomprehensible language, and blocking the entire street.

"Aemilius Valerius! Hello!"

It was Caraca and his tribe, and they were all delighted to see me. Clearly, they hadn't yet put Felix through his paces. Caraca told me, via his translator, that they were on their way to visit the Temple of Diana. They wanted to see *all* of the temples, the translator told me earnestly.

"In that case, you'll be here the rest of your life," I told him. "Rome has a temple on every street corner!"

"Ah!" said the translator. "Just the big ones!"

"Then Diana will not disappoint you," I assured them.

Caraca smiled broadly, clasped my arm, and said something incomprehensible.

"Yes," said the translator. "Aemilius Valerius, please to come to dinner and entertainments with family."

"I would be delighted," I said, wondering if either the food or the entertainment would be at all recognisable to my Roman sensibilities. Then I wondered when I'd gotten so pompous. Who cared if they juggled geese? It would be fun.

"Not now," the translator clarified. "Soon, when we have better house."

That piqued my interest. "Is there something wrong with where you're staying?"

Caraca brought his thumb and forefinger together.

"Small?" I asked. "Too small?"

"Very too small," the translator agreed.

"I know of a place that might be better for you," I said, remembering that favour I had promised old Macrinus. "Do you know the Porta Flumentana? The Palatine?"

Caraca and the translator consulted for a moment, and both looked vague.

"Where are you staying now?" I asked.

"The Esquiline," said the translator, entirely mangling his pronunciation. "The house of Mettilus, by the Servian Wall."

"Alright," I said. "If you want to look at this other house, I'll send someone to fetch you. Does tomorrow morning suit you?"

"Yes," said Caraca. "Yes!" His Latin was improving daily.

"I'll see you there," I said, waving them on their way.

"Goodbye!" the translator called, and his enthusiastic call was echoed by the rest of them with varying degrees of success.

"Well," I said to Juba as we headed back down the Aventine Hill, "at least that's one less thing to worry about."

* * *

I spent the rest of the day at home, wandering the house and watching as the afternoon softened into the evening. I had a feeling I'd been ripped off. What sort of world did we live in when you couldn't trust a rodent-like oily informer whose name you got off a wall in Fish Alley? I had a good mind to bring a prosecution against Kaeso, that lying rat bastard.

I didn't dine with my family that night. Instead, I ate with Atreus in his room, with my aching feet up on a couch and a plate resting on my lap. Larius stood just out of reach with a jug of wine. He could sense my foul mood, just like a whipped pup. He looked skittish. Perversely, that only made me more annoyed. We did not complement one another, Larius and I. Sooner or later, it was going to end in tears. Not for me, though, obviously.

"I've never heard of any informer called Colchus," Atreus said. He was resting under the blankets, propped up with pillows. The bruises on his torso were starting to yellow, and his forehead was creased with its familiar frown.

"I suppose Kaeso lied," I growled.

"Maybe," said Atreus. "I don't know every informer in the Aventine."

We were disturbed at that moment by Octavia, who came bearing a jar of salve and a bundle of dressings.

"Octavia Junilla," began Atreus, "thank you, but—"

"I am going to change your dressings," she informed him. She reached for his blankets. "Please don't make a fuss."

"Octavia," I said, "you could have one of the slaves do that."

"Juno, Quintus, are you really so concerned I'll faint at the sight of blood?"

I was actually more concerned she'd be running her hands over a strange man's body, but I kept that to myself. Atreus lent himself uncomfortably to Octavia's ministrations as she replaced his dressings. He forgot his awkwardness when it came to strapping his ribs, though—he winced, and I could see it was all he could do to stop himself from swearing.

"Octavia," I said, "do you remember how Macrinus asked me to rent out the house?"

"I remember," said my sister from the vicinity of Atreus's armpit.

"Well, I ran into Caraca this afternoon," I said. "He's going to look at it tomorrow."

"I'm sure he'll like it."

"I'm sure he will, too," I said. "What do you think?"

"It's really none of my business," said Octavia. "It's not my house anymore."

"No," I agreed.

Octavia tugged on an end of the bandage, and Atreus winced again. "Leander said it's to be as tight as you can bear," Octavia told him. "How's that?"

"Just about as tight as I can bear."

"Good." Octavia smiled and tied the bandage off. She assisted him in rearranging the pillows and drew the blankets back up over him. "Goodnight."

"Goodnight," Atreus replied, looking flushed.

I listened for the sound of her footsteps receding down the stairs.

"So what?" I asked and picked at my dish of olives. "If Anicetus won't tell us, do we *assume* he knows exactly what the ex-tribunes of the Third Gallica are up to? Because that's a huge assumption. At this point, I'd be happy to know why Anicetus went to Albanus's party, when clearly he wasn't welcome."

Atreus smiled slightly. "You went, sir, and you weren't invited either."

"I wasn't invited," I said, "but neither was I unwelcome. There is a difference. Could Anicetus have been looking for proof of their treason?"

Atreus shook his head slowly. "The palace doesn't need proof, sir. It's the palace."

"That's where you're wrong," I said. "Anicetus is Nero's man, and Nero is just. He has never condemned anyone on rumour."

The young emperor was no Caligula. There was Britannicus, but he had been a political necessity, and the triumvirate's work more than Nero's. When he'd wanted to free himself from the influence of Seneca and Burrus,

Nero hadn't assassinated them; he'd had them brought before the senate on various charges. Seneca had been smart enough to win an acquittal, and both he and Burrus had been clever enough to recognise the warning to back off when they got it. Nero's closest political rivals, his cousins Felix and Plautus, were still alive and kicking. Under any other emperor, they might have been dispatched for the unlucky offence of shared ancestry. Even the divine Augustus had purged Rome of his rivals in his day, leaving him with such a shallow family pool to draw his heirs from that it was no wonder the Claudians had muscled in on the Julian action. Pretty soon, it had been a free-for-all all, with so many banishments and backstabbings that it was difficult to remember who died when, where, and how much of their own mattress they'd resorted to eating in the meantime. The palace wasn't the same beast it had been in the past. Nero had a reputation for mercy and leniency. He liked to be liked.

I shook my head. "It's pointless to speculate until we talk to Anicetus. Until then, I'm out of ideas."

Atreus only looked thoughtful. "The house you're renting out, sir," he said at last. "Was it Nasica's house?"

"Yes, although it's nothing but a mausoleum now." I sighed. "Goodnight, Atreus."

I headed down the stairs. It was late, but I was too wound up to sleep. I sat in the garden with a cup of wine and my memories. It was Nasica who haunted me. I had ignored him for months, but the thought of walking into that house tomorrow unsettled me. I had liked Nasica. He had been a brother to me. More than that, he'd been a man I admired, and one I had wanted to emulate. I had thought that we were family. I'd trusted him and trusted in our friendship. He'd betrayed me, just like he'd betrayed Octavia, and I'd hardly had time to resent him before he'd fallen on his sword. Even now, knowing what I knew of the Third Gallica, I was still conflicted. I knew that every one of them was corrupt, rotten, but I couldn't forget that at one time, Nasica had been my friend.

Hursa refilled my cup. "I've got a joke for you, sir," he offered, sensing my bleak mood.

"Go on, then," I said, not really expecting much.

Hursa puffed his chest out proudly. "A Parthian goes to see his friend and says, 'Help me! I think I've turned into a dog!' 'Great Jupiter!' says his friend. 'Sit down and tell me all about it!' 'I can't,' says the Parthian. 'I'm not allowed on the furniture!'"

I couldn't help smiling, and Hursa beamed.

I hated to drink alone, which translated into good news for Hursa. He could hardly believe his luck when I told him to grab a seat and fill himself a cup of wine. And I could hardly believe mine when he turned out to be a half-decent drinking partner, who let me prattle on as long as I liked about nothing and whose jokes got progressively better the more he drank. It was almost enough to put the entire nasty business of the murders, and of Nasica, out of my mind.

Almost, but not quite.

Chapter Fourteen

Except for the small complement of slaves who guarded the place from burglars, my ex-brother-in-law Nasica's house had been empty for months. The house was situated near the Porta Flumentana, on the western side of the Palatine Hill. From the outdoor triclinium you could look down the slope of the hill towards Tiber Island and watch the boats and barges threading down the river. I had known good times in this house, and now, standing on the threshold, I didn't want to go in. It was the door porter who forced the issue by coming forward. "Quintus Aemilius, sir? You are expected."

I didn't recognise the man.

"Is your master here?" I asked him as I stepped into the shade of the portico.

"Macrinus does not like to come here, sir," said the slave. That made two of us.

Atreus, limping carefully, followed me inside.

There were leaves blown into the corners of the vestibule that signified the house's emptiness.

"Sweep this floor!" I snapped, and the porter scuttled away. It had been such a vibrant house once, a place I liked to find myself. Now, it was full of dead leaves and ignorant, lazy slaves.

I stood in the vestibule while I waited, unwilling to walk through the place with just my memories for company. Atreus, holding one hand against his ribs, advanced as far as the atrium and cast his gaze over the mosaics.

Caraca and his tribe turned up shortly afterwards.

"It is a *big* house!" Caraca's translator announced, and the Gauls' enthusiasm gave me the chance to shake off my unease and slip into the role of agent. We walked through to the atrium, and I discovered Atreus inspecting the empty lararium. The tiny altar contained only dust—Nasica's household gods had been removed months ago. The place really was empty.

"Big house!" the translator said happily.

Caraca moved forward to inspect one of the mosaics. He pointed something out to one of his fellows, and I caught a glimpse of a bronze torque that he wore above his elbow.

"Did that come from the mine in Gaul?" I asked the translator.

"Yes!" said the translator. "It was from the ancestor of Caraca. All mines are Roman now."

"Yes, I remember you said that important men from Rome watched the slaves digging," I said.

The translator beamed. "Yes! My joke!"

"Are those men from the imperial treasury?"

The translator thought for a while. "From the treasury, yes, and also men from the governor and from the legion. Lots of men."

"What would happen, do you think, if the men from the treasury and the governor didn't come?" I asked him.

Despite his questionable language skills, the translator did have a quick mind. He laughed. "Very rich legion!"

I thought of the Third Gallica and managed a smile for the eager translator's benefit. "Yes, very rich."

"This is big house!" the translator said again. "Not big as yours!"

Nasica's house was newer than mine, and smaller, and had been built in the modern style. Each room served a specific purpose, of which Caraca and his tribe seemed to be happily ignorant. The triclinia gave themselves away as dining rooms because of the themed mosaics and frescoes, but I wouldn't have been surprised if Caraca set up a bedroom in the tablinum. He seemed quite taken with the room.

"The study," I told the translator. "Tablinum. Yes?"

No. A few of Caraca's tribesmen began pacing out measurements and arguing among themselves. Jupiter only knew what they were planning. I didn't wait to see the end of their incomprehensible debate—I led Caraca through to the peristyle.

"What is here, please?" the translator asked, pointing down the hallway that led to the posticum.

"This door is for the slaves," I told him. "Or for deliveries from the street. There is no stable door in this house, no stable. This is a *new* house."

We continued through the house. Caraca and his tribesmen were eager to look at every room. Each one, no matter how modest or utilitarian, had to be admired and discussed. Atreus walked with me, smiling a little at the Gauls' enthusiasm.

The rooms between the posticum hallway and the kitchens I had always presumed to be storerooms. I had never had any need to enter them. I did so now, opening them to the light for what was probably the first time in months. Amphorae of wine and oil reminded me of happier times, of long evenings spent in this house when it had been full of life. *In what room?* I wondered. Would I know it if I saw it? I had always supposed he'd done it in the tablinum, but I didn't know. I only knew what Uncle Maro had told me on that morning he'd woken me: *"He's dead! Fell on his sword!"* I could still feel the shock of it. First, he'd been my friend—my *brother*—and then I'd hated him, and then he'd killed himself. Nobody knew why. It was all speculation, and I had speculated just like everyone else.

I opened the doors of the storeroom closest to the posticum and discovered that it wasn't a storeroom after all.

It was empty except for a brazier. There were no amphorae stacked in here, but I knew at once that it had never served as a storeroom. There were frescoes on the wall and mosaics on the floor that depicted strange things, among them a scorpion, the sun, a goat, and date palms. They were desert things, I realised. Syrian things. They were the things that Nasica would have seen when he served with the Third Gallica, and each of them must have signified something to the men who had served in that legion.

I felt a sickening sense of inevitability as I looked up, knowing what I would see there before I did—on the ceiling, there was a painted rose. Sub rosa.

Atreus saw it when I did. "Under the rose," he said. "For secrecy. This is not a storeroom like the others."

"No," I said. I needed no confirmation, but I got it. On three of the walls, right above where the couches must have once stood, were bronze torch brackets fashioned to look like bulls. The emblem of the legion.

"This is the Third Gallica," I said, and just like with the little Christian temple, Atreus waited for me to translate the symbols. "Everything in here references the legion and references the east. This must be where they met, in secret, in the room closest to the posticum so they would not be observed entering or leaving the house."

"You never knew this room was here, sir?"

"No," I said, closing my eyes briefly. Ever since I'd heard the wine-addled testimony of the ex-legionary Rubio I'd known of Nasica's treachery, but knowing was not the same as seeing. It felt like taking a punch badly, and I hadn't expected that. "I didn't know it was here."

Atreus gazed up at the rose in silence.

"He chose his path," I said bitterly, but I wondered if he really had.

I remembered what it was like as a junior tribune on a lonely frontier: homesick, lonely, scared, and desperate not to show it. In the Tenth Legion I'd sunk my money into wine and debauchery but, if my fellow tribunes had pushed me towards something else, what then? Perhaps Nasica, at one time, had been too young and too naïve to realise what was going on until it had been too late to back out, but it may have been a fiction. Not everyone was as clueless as I had been as a teenager, or as susceptible to peer pressure.

"Jupiter, Quintus!" my father had once raged at me, "if your friend jumped off the Tarpeian Rock, would you do the same?"

"Which friend? Julianus or Velinus?" I'd asked, which had only confirmed all his worst suspicions of me. Thoughts of my father turned to thoughts of regret, and then back again to Nasica, and to where treason led—Marcellus Albanus, Claudius Rufanus, and the unfortunate Sylvia. At least Nasica had fallen on his sword, keeping his honour intact. We Romans were meant to forgive a man any crime as long as he took responsibility for it by ending

SUB ROSA

his own life. We'd respect his sense of public duty, send our condolences to his family, and silently pray that out own transgressions never caught us up. But I couldn't forgive Nasica. He'd been my friend.

"Ah!" said the chirpy little translator, poking his head around the door. "What is here, please?"

"It's nothing," I told him, forcing a smile. "Just another empty room."

* * *

I went into the first wine shop I saw, slapped some coins down on the counter, and drank my first cup of stinging vinegar as quickly as I could. There was nothing like cheap wine to take the edge off. I was joined at the counter by Atreus and Juba.

"The problem," I announced to them, even though they hadn't asked, "was that I *liked* Nasica."

My second cup went the same way as the first.

"He was my friend," I said. "Right up until the divorce, he was my friend. And I blamed her, you know? I thought it must have been her fault, that she'd done something to ruin it, and it turns out the whole time that he was a traitor."

Neither of them said anything.

"He was like a brother," I said, hating myself for having ever believed it.

The waiter set another cup of wine on the counter, but before I could reach for it a large, dark hand covered the rim. "Sir, you have the theatre tonight."

"At the moment, Juba, I don't care."

Juba didn't move his hand. "Sir, you ought to."

I sighed. "Fine. Drink it yourself."

Juba, showing more discernment than I had, lifted the cup to his nose, sniffed it and set it down on the counter again. Out of my reach.

"Sir," said Atreus quietly, "do you suppose your sister knows what that room signifies?"

"Signifies?" I snorted. "It doesn't signify anything, Atreus, except that the

256

ex-tribunes of the Third Gallica held drinking parties there. Nobody else knows what it means."

"Like the symbols in the Christian room," Atreus said.

"Exactly so," I said, looking longingly at the cup of wine on the counter. "Hidden in plain sight."

* * *

Octavia happened to be in the atrium when we returned home. "Will Caraca rent the house, do you think?" she asked me, helping me off with my cloak.

I tried for a jocular tone. "He's already measuring up for the furniture."

"I'm pleased."

"Are you?" I asked, aware that Atreus was watching her intently.

Octavia squeezed my arm. "I was happy in that house. I'm glad Macrinus isn't letting it fall into disrepair." She raised her eyebrows. "Now, Julia says I should curl my hair for tonight. What do you think?"

"I think you shouldn't take fashion advice off Julia," I said, and she laughed.

The afternoon was spent in a rush of preparation, for the women at least. While they decided what they were wearing and what jewellery would go with it, and how they should do their hair, I went upstairs to bed and tossed and turned for a while on Nasica's treason. I tried to ignore it, but it gnawed at me like a toothache, working to make its presence known.

I rose again just before dusk. Juba had laid out a fresh tunic and toga. My belt and sandals had been cleaned and oiled, and they gleamed. Fulvia's maid was waiting for me, and she was armed with a razor, a pair of bone tweezers, and a small pointy stick. Knowing she'd been sent by my wife, I sat on my couch and tried not to wince while I suffered my impromptu shave and manicure. Juba watched from my doorway, smirking a little. I asked him if he had anything else he could be doing, but of course he didn't. Juba being Juba, everything was already done. He'd even managed to sort out our transportation issues. While I'd been sleeping, Juba had been next door asking my neighbour, a retired senator who had never liked me much but knew Fulvia's family from way back, for the loan of some litters and bearers for the evening. Being a better neighbour than I was, he couldn't refuse.

I rewarded Juba with a sestertius for his initiative, and he tucked it into his tunic with a wry look. Poor Juba, and he was still only a bodyguard. He deserved more, and we both knew it.

Juba sighed a little as we set out later, because instead of running my entire household, for which he had proven time and time again that he would be eminently qualified, he got to walk in front of the litters to clear pedestrians out of the way.

* * *

We had arranged to meet Uncle Maro outside the Theatre of Marcellus, on the southern side of the massive arched portico. In the evening, the aspect across the river to Tiber Island was pleasant, although I wasn't fond of the crowd gathering in the street. It was a mass of torchlight, colour, noise, and movement. It was expensive people and well-groomed slaves as far as the eye could see. I even saw one man, whose name I should probably have known given his extravagance, who'd done his litter bearers up like Egyptian pharaohs. Fulvia and I exchanged a dubious glance at that, but those of us with a modicum of good taste were vastly outnumbered by those who thought *Ooh! Shiny!* was the epitome of class.

As much as I disliked the theatre, I was anxious to be inside. I felt nervous on the street. I was sure someone would recognise me and demand to know what I was doing going to a play instead of investigating a murder, but evidently, I wasn't as important as I thought I was. In the company of my immediate family and the vigile Atreus, nobody even looked at me twice.

Atreus had borrowed a toga. He looked as itchy and uncomfortable as I felt.

Uncle Maro and Aunt Marcia met us outside and then led the way into the interior of the theatre, down the long ornate gallery towards the auditorium. There we met Severus, his wife, and the two children they'd decided were old enough to attend. Accompanying Severus, in order to complete the illusion of a united front, was the eminent Marcellus Naso and his heir apparent Florian. Florian had the decency to look shamefaced when he renewed his acquaintance with Julia. Atreus and I watched the awkward exchange with interest. This was what Atreus had come for, I think. Nobody would have minded if he'd stayed in bed, given the tender state of him, but he had accepted the invitation.

"J-Julia Drusilla," Florian stammered.

Julia kept her dignity. She inclined her head graciously. "How nice to see you again, Avitus Florian."

There was no warmth in her voice. I was proud of her for that. Underneath the false flush of her cosmetics, though, I think she was a shade paler than usual.

With Severus and Naso leading the way, we entered the auditorium and took our seats. We were several rows back from the stage, close to the centre. Had I liked the theatre more, I would have been impressed but frankly, give me a chariot race any day. The play was either by Plautus or one of his many plagiarists, but most of the audience wasn't really interested in what was happening on stage. They'd seen it a hundred times before. It was the usual stuff—mistaken identities, lost children, hopeless love, double-dealing, and cross-dressing. It was performed by the usual characters—the beautiful maiden, the lovelorn youth, the braggart soldier, the greedy brothel keeper, the embarrassing father, the priggish mother, and the clever fast-talking slave who sorted it all out neatly in time for the audience to stand up and get the circulation back into their buttocks.

We were the show instead. By the second act, most of the people in front of us had dropped all pretence and were craning their necks to watch Severus, Naso, Maro and me, and our extended entourage. Even some of the actors were peering out past the torches to get a decent look. We made an odd group, I suppose. Marcellus Naso sat in the middle of the row, staring at the stage but not really seeing. He was here for appearances only. His newly adopted heir Florian sat beside him. Florian, the callow youth, wasn't as practised at this game as Naso. The scrutiny was making him nervous. Beside him sat my mad Uncle Maro, quaffing wine and nuts and dreaming up new frescos for his bedrooms. Aunt Marcia sat beside him, smiling benignly at the world. She had Julia Drusilla at her side and paused every now and then to adjust the girl's ringlets or the fall of her stola. I saw Florian cast several despairing glances in Julia's direction, but Julia, to her credit, continued to look straight ahead and ignore him.

Fulvia sat beside Julia, and I sat beside Fulvia. She held my hand under the cover of her stola and squeezed it when she sensed I was getting restless. Octavia sat on my other side, as calm and unruffled as always. Atreus sat beside her in his borrowed toga. He was the only one of us who was making no pretence at all of following the play. His kept turning his face—his patina of bruises was still quite vivid—to scan the audience, watching the watchers.

On the other side of Naso sat Severus, his wife, and their children. Severus, I could tell, was very conscious of the crowd's attention. He sat so stiffly that he looked like he'd just played a game of peekaboo with a gorgon.

The theatre was an appropriate venue for our little show of public unity. We wanted to demonstrate that despite our total lack of progress, Severus and I still had the respect and support of Marcellus Naso. The unity wouldn't hold in private. Naso was still sadly hopeful that we would uncover the name of his nephew's murderer. Severus, I suspected, was quietly trying to extract himself from the entire investigation. There were so many people waiting for us to fail; he was desperate for a way to abandon ship before we hit the rocks. He would have jumped days ago except there wasn't another magistrate in the city who'd touch this one.

Sitting there in that auditorium, trying to pretend I didn't feel the scrutiny of hundreds of pairs of eyes boring into my back, I cast a few black thoughts towards mad Uncle Maro for getting me mixed up in all of this. Not that I hadn't been willing, but I was an idiot who didn't know any better. Maro had been around for long enough that he should have recognised the beginnings of a total goatfuck when he saw one. I'd be lucky to get a position supervising the slaves who scrubbed the bird shit off the Auguraculum once this was over.

It wasn't until Fulvia stood up and dragged me to my feet that I realised at least something good had come of the night: the hero and heroine were reunited, the bickering parents were reconciled, the secret identities revealed, and at last, the interminable play was finished.

* * *

We went to Marcellus Naso's house after the play. It was a cool night, and I paced the terraces restlessly while Naso and Uncle Maro conferred together in Naso's well-appointed library. My womenfolk had been ushered off to a sitting room where, given that Naso had no wife or sisters, they would presumably have to entertain themselves. Juba and our small army of litter bearers had set up camp out in the street somewhere.

Severus and his family had not joined us. Not that I could blame him; we all had our careers to think of. My career might have been young, fragile, and easily crushed, but Severus had a lot further to fall.

Naso's back gardens looked down onto the Tiber. I could see the lamps of the ferrymen moving slowly up and down the river in ever-changing constellations. From Naso's terraced gardens, the river traffic appeared to glitter against the moonlit surface of the river, a pale reflection of the brilliant sky above. I strode along the terraces, looking down towards the sinuous river. Atreus didn't stride. He made it halfway along the first terrace, spotted a handy bench between a pair of laurels, and sat there and watched me stride instead. It was too dark to see his face, but I just knew he was looking at me with that same thoughtful little frown he always wore. After a while, I got sick of pacing and came and sat next to him.

From inside the house, I heard the delicate strains of a lyre, and a girl with the voice of a nightingale began to sing. It was a lament, naturally, which suited the cool night as well as her master's temperament of late, and it drifted faintly down the terraces towards us. It was pleasant.

After a moment, a graceful young thing slipped out of the house, forsaking the light of the braziers and lamps for the mellow darkness of the garden. It was Julia, with a cup in one hand and a dish of olives in the other, and she picked her way into the gloom uncertainly. For a moment, I worried she was on her way to a secret assignation with Florian. I wondered if her chilly greeting earlier at the Theatre of Marcellus had only been a ruse. My stepdaughter soon disabused me of it, though, when she made her way cautiously down the steps onto the first terrace, turning her head from left to right and making her ringlets dance wildly. "Valerius? Valerius, where are you?"

I stood up so she'd see me. "Over here, Julia."

Julia headed towards us. She handed me her cup of wine and her dish of olives to hold, wrapped her palla around herself to keep the wind at bay, and then sat on the ground by my feet. She was the picture of demure Roman girlhood.

I passed her the cup when she was settled but kept the dish of olives for a moment. "To what do I owe the pleasure, Julia?"

My stepdaughter snorted, sounding exactly like her mother. "I didn't want to stay in there. I can't *bear* the lyre."

I looked back towards the house just in time to see Florian appear leaning against a column, looking soulfully out towards the garden. As I watched, he trailed back inside again. Ah, unrequited love. Was there anything more cloying? I'd just been subjected to two hours of it inside the Theatre of Marcellus, and I was in no mood for any more of it. Julia sounded as though she was sick of it as well.

"Time to go home, I think," I said at last, stretching.

"Yes," said Julia in her customarily proud manner, but I noticed that her shoulders slumped slightly as she relaxed.

Julia walked with Atreus at his snail's pace, and I went ahead of them to fetch my womenfolk from the sitting room, frown at Florian, and thank Marcellus Naso for his hospitality. I found Naso and Uncle Maro still in the library. Naso had a scroll unrolled on the table and was reading out a certain passage to Maro when I entered. Maro was nodding thoughtfully. The passage was from Cicero's *Laelius de Amicitia*. I was glad Naso had remembered it. As much as I found Cicero a bore when he started rambling about law or duty, his great discourse on grief and friendship was like poetry when he considered the death of his friend: *I believe that no ill has befallen Scipio; it has befallen me, if it has befallen anyone.*

Marcellus Naso thanked me for my visit, embraced me, and reminded me that I was always welcome in his house. I couldn't even raise the ghost of a smile at the irony of that statement.

Maro and Marcia decided to stay on longer, so when Atreus, the womenfolk, and myself were finally loaded into our litters again, we made only a small procession. Juba led the way through the streets, a torch in one hand and a cudgel in the other—the city was dangerous once the sun was down.

I sat in my litter and was jostled gently as we headed for home. The litter was one that had been borrowed off my neighbour. It smelled slightly musty but was comfortable enough. I think I even dozed off. Suddenly, there was torchlight in my face. Juba was walking beside me.

"Sir," he said in a low voice, "we're being followed."

"What?" I asked, sitting up so quickly that I almost cracked my head on the roof of the litter.

"We're being followed."

"Jupiter! Are you sure?" I asked, and he only raised his eyebrows at me. "Alright. How many?"

"Just the one."

"One?" I asked in relief, and my heart rediscovered its regular rhythm. One person I could handle.

Overhead, I heard the low rumble of thunder: Summanus was still making his presence felt.

"Alright," I said. "Give me your cudgel. Where are we, by the way?"

From inside the litter, I could only see an expanse of plastered wall. It might have been any one of a thousand different residential streets in the city—the first few feet of the wall were painted red, and the rest was grimy white. It was too dark to make out any of the graffiti that might have served as a signpost. The street was wide and quiet. It might have even been my own.

"Sir," said Juba sternly, "you're not thinking of leaping out of the litter when we reach a corner, getting behind whoever is following us, and smacking them over the head with my cudgel, are you?"

"I am, as it happens," I said. I began to struggle out of the bulky folds of my toga, a difficult job in the narrow confines of the litter. "Is there a problem with that?"

"Yes, sir," said Juba frankly.

"Just give me your cudgel, Juba."

"I can't, sir."

"Why not?"

Juba shrugged his massive shoulders. "Because I already gave it to Junius Atreus, sir, and he got out of his litter about two blocks back."

* * *

I leapt out of my litter on the sheltered side of the street, hoping the jolt as my litter bearers adjusted to the sudden change in weight didn't alert whoever was following us, and lurked behind a laurel tree. Juba was at my side. When our procession passed, we hurried back down the Caelian Hill.

A pair of drunken youths in company with a pair of cheap prostitutes saw us coming and veered off into a narrow side street that led to someone's backyard. Either that was where they were intending to take care of business, or we were intimidating after all. A carter led a docile ox up the road. There was a boy balanced on top of the cart, holding the load of amphorae steady. Both the carter and the boy looked at us suspiciously as we passed them.

My street was quiet, but from below us in the city, I heard the sound of distant traffic—wheels, whips, and raised voices. I recalled the number of barges I'd seen from Marcellus Naso's terraces and remembered that tomorrow was a market day. All night a multitude of people would be labouring to bring their produce into the city, pouring in through the gates in the Servian Walls while the rest of the city slept, and at dawn, Rome's greatest spectacle would begin: the ninth-day markets.

The road turned to the northeast on its way down the incline of the hill.

As we rounded the curve, I saw a body lying on the road. For a moment, my heart caught in my throat, but it was only a drunk. He abused us for waking him and pulled his cloak back up over his head as we passed.

We met Atreus halfway down the hill. Illuminated very faintly in the light of the moon, there was no mistaking his careful gait and that elbow that stuck out as he held a hand against his ribcage. I shook my head when I saw him. Jupiter only knows what he'd been thinking when he'd jumped out of that litter.

"Atreus!"

If he was as relieved to see me as I was to see him, there was nothing in his manner to suggest it. He quickened his steps slightly but was still moving no faster than an arthritic ant when we caught up with him.

"Atreus! What happened?"

Atreus leaned against a wall for a breather and shielded his eyes from every one of the torches that got shoved in his face. Juba waved the litter bearers away.

"I lost him," Atreus said, disgusted with himself.

"Did you get a look at him?"

"Not a good look," he replied, wincing. "It wasn't anyone I recognised."

We turned back up the hill.

Octavia and Fulvia were waiting for us back at home, anxious and solicitous. They were relieved to see Atreus restored safely to the fold and surprised me by keeping their opinions of his foolhardiness to themselves. Perhaps they felt they didn't know him well enough to go straight for the jugular. I envied him that.

Atreus slowly climbed the stairs up to his room while I did the rounds of the house with Juba to make sure the place was secure. The front door was barred, and Hursa had dozed off with his back against it. The wide doors to the stable yard were closed and barred as well. They would hold back the hordes, those doors.

I was unsettled, but I knew I could trust Juba to look after the place.

I crawled into bed in the hope of uninterrupted sleep. I should have known better.

Sometime before dawn, I was torn from sleep by the sounds of shouting and feet slapping on the tiles of the atrium. I flew out of bed, my heart racing. Please, Janus, let it be a burglar. I didn't believe it, though. Trouble in the night, and I knew exactly what it was about. I just prayed it was not the palace. Who could forget the stories of Messalina, screaming at her mother to help her while the Praetorians were breaking down the door?

I wasted precious seconds rooting around in my military trunk for my sword and then slamming the lid on my fingers. Clenching my fist to try to get the blood flowing into my fingers again and holding my sword in the other hand, I hurried out onto the landing and tried to get my bearings. The Praetorians? Of course not. It was probably just the murderer, who had followed me home from Marcellus Naso's place, come to kill me in my bed.

I heard the rattle of a curtain being pulled open, and a figure in a diaphanous dressing gown peered outside into the moonlight. "What's going on?"

"Go back inside, Fulvia."

I leaned over the railing. All of the torches in the atrium had burned down, but the house was bathed in moonlight. There was no movement in the atrium except for the silver moonlight dancing in the waters of the impluvium. It all seemed quiet now. My fantasies of Praetorians, murderers, and burglars began to fade, and then all of a sudden, I heard another shout coming from the direction of the gardens.

I took the steps two at a time, almost running headlong into two burly figures that came rushing out of the interior of the house into the moonlight.

"Jupiter, sir!" one of them shouted, catching the flash of light as I drew my arm back. "It's me, Ledo!"

"And Casso!" Casso added quickly, stepping back in case I didn't believe him.

The three of us crossed the atrium at a jog. We headed through the peristyle and out into the garden. Another outraged yell led us in the right direction. In the moonlight, it took me a little while to see what was going on.

"Got him! I've got him!" Juba shouted.

At the back of the garden, closest to the wall, was a tree my grandfather had planted after bringing it home as a sapling from his travels in Baetica, or Raetia, or Moesia, or somewhere. His attachment to the place, or the tree, escaped me. I only know that the thing had grown tall and broad in the years since he'd planted it, with wide branches that touched the garden wall. I should have had it cut back years ago.

There was a man hanging in the tree, his arms and legs wrapped around one of the lower branches. Juba had him by the midsection and was trying to haul him out of the tree, like he was wrestling with a monkey. The intruder was fighting a losing battle. Juba had him on the ground in moments, first knocking the air out of him and then kneeling on his windpipe for good measure.

Hursa appeared, bearing a torch. He stayed well away until the danger was over and then approached the scene wide-eyed. Light from the torch fell on Juba and the intruder, and Juba immediately released his grip.

"Jupiter, sir!" he exclaimed.

I glared at the intruder. He was a scrawny, skinny little shit who had no place in my house. He made strange choking noises and massaged his throat.

"Ledo," I said, "go and fetch Junius Atreus. Juba and Casso, take him somewhere secure."

Juba and Casso hauled the fellow to his feet.

Hursa was almost jumping from foot to foot. "Oh, and me, sir? What about me?"

Now the excitement had worn off, I realised I was cold. I looked down at myself and saw a lot more skin than was usual for a walk in the garden. "Hursa, why don't you go and get me a tunic?"

At that moment, the scrawny fellow, like a cornered animal, turned. Juba and Casso, probably both thinking that the other one still had a decent grip, managed to let the little weasel squirm out of their grasp. In seconds, he was up the tree, over the wall, and back into the night.

"Sons of Dis!" I exclaimed.

Casso leapt into the tree, and it swayed alarmingly under his weight. He made one abortive attempt to reach for the top of the wall and ended up flat on his back on the ground, winded. Juba let go with a stream of words in his native tongue. I didn't understand any of it, but I hoped it was a particularly nasty curse and that the gods of Aethiopia were a spiteful bunch.

"Don't worry about it, Juba," I said to make him feel better.

"Sir," Juba rumbled, "didn't you recognise him?"

"No," I said.

"It's the fellow from the Temple of Diana," Juba told me. "You bought an offering from him." He growled. "He *said* he didn't know Colchus, the informer."

It fell into place for me. Kaeso the rat hadn't lied to me after all. Colchus, the informer, had been exactly where he'd told me he would be. He'd been outside the Temple of Diana with a tray of offerings resting across his skinny legs.

"Jupiter," I said. *"Jupiter!"*

Atreus arrived too late and missed all of the action.

"Colchus," he said thoughtfully once the household had settled back down into an uneasy silence, I'd gotten dressed, and we had gone into the informal triclinium for a drink. "Why would Colchus be following you?"

"It did cross my mind," I said, waiting for Atreus to offer up a theory. He didn't.

"Colchus," he repeated meditatively.

Hursa was hanging around under the pretence of serving us. Instead, he was hoping for some juicy gossip.

"Ooh, sir!" he said suddenly. "I bet I know where you can find him!"

This was unexpected.

"And where might that be, Hursa?"

"That's the man that's been selling pies."

"Pies?"

Hursa nodded eagerly. "Yes, sir. I only just remembered now where I'd seen him before. That's the man who sells pies outside in the street."

"He's not a pie seller, Hursa," I said wearily. "He's an informer. He works from the Temple of Diana in the Aventine."

"Oh, no, sir," Hursa said blithely. "He sells pies. I *bought* one."

I was about to berate him for his stupidity, but Atreus cut me off.

"How long has he been selling pies in the street, Hursa?"

Hursa frowned in thought. "Oh, on and off for weeks now, sir."

"Are you *sure*, Hursa?" I asked.

"Oh, yes, sir."

Atreus frowned slightly. "Long before we were looking for him."

"But why would he follow me?" I asked. "In fact, why would anyone follow me? Everyone knows where I live."

"Talking of following," said Atreus, "we must follow where reason leads."

Spoken like a true Stoic.

"Meaning what?" I asked. It was too late to play philosophers.

Atreus inclined his head. "Meaning, sir, that he wasn't following you at all. He was watching you."

"Semantics," I muttered.

"And when I find the little bastard," continued Atreus in that same thoughtful manner, "first, I'll break every bone in his body, and then I'll string him up by the balls."

Maybe he wasn't a Stoic after all.

* * *

I wasn't able to sleep for the rest of the night. Instead, I paced around in the garden, short-tempered and on edge, supervising my slaves as they hacked wearily away at every single tree whose branches threatened to reach the top of the wall.

Chapter Fifteen

The next day was market day and a good reminder of why I hated shopping. Every ninth day, the streets of the city were noisier and filthier than usual and packed with people on the lookout for slightly bruised vegetables at knockdown prices, a nice fat piglet for dinner, milk that hadn't sat too long in the sun, and a dozen dormice cheap at half the price.

It was just before dawn when Atreus and I left the house. There was no sign of a pie cart outside the house, not that we expected Colchus to drop into our laps quite so easily. We headed down the hill into the melee of market day. It was already crowded despite the early hour, because anyone could tell you that the freshest produce was gone by midmorning. Juba was with us, forcing a path through the growing throng like a forward scout slashing his way through a forest. He was deaf to the abuse that followed after him.

Before we hit the bottom of the hill, just as the luxurious townhouses began to give way to apartment blocks and shopfronts, Atreus took us on a shortcut. It wasn't one I normally would have tried, preferring the main streets, but it took us away from the worst of the crowd. It was still congested in the dense little labyrinth of alleys and stairs and crumbling paths, but it was nothing compared to the melee of market day back on the main thoroughfares. If the first rosy rays of dawn were beginning to filter down from the heavens and bathe the world in soft light, here it was still dark, and our way was lit by the guttering glow of torch and lamplight that spilled out of open doors and unshuttered windows. In the darkness, we dodged beggars instead of bargain hunters, pickpockets instead of pastry makers, and fortune tellers instead of fish sellers. Most of them kept their distance. On my own, I would have attracted them like flies to honey, and I doubted even Juba would have put them off for long, but they must have recognised Atreus as one of their local vigiles so we were given as wide a berth as practicable, in the narrow, twisting alleyways. Even so, I smacked shoulders a few times with the filthy, the toothless, and the mad, and sometimes a heady combination of all three.

Curious gazes, wary and predatory, looked at Atreus and took in his awkward gait and the one hand that he held against his ribs as he walked. Whispers followed us, rising and falling in a cadence until it sounded almost like the hypnotic chant of a cult: *Bano. Bano. Bano.* Atreus turned his head sharply to catch the whispers, and each time he did people looked away. The vigile was a marked man, and they all knew it. As he led us through the gloomy alleyways, women pulled their children out of his path as though they feared he was cursed.

Juba and I were watchful and on edge. We were only four blocks from the main road, but it might as well have been the Transtiberina. When my father had warned me about that notorious slum, he'd probably had no idea that there were neighbourhoods closer to home he could have invoked to scare me onto the straight and narrow. And then, as abruptly as the close alleyways had appeared, they ended, and the streets widened. I saw dawn again and was relieved.

Atreus's shortcut had brought us out at the bottom of the hill, right beside the excubitorium of the first century of the Fifth Cohort of Vigiles. Atreus led us to a side entrance that opened onto the dusty little parade ground I remembered from my first visit. We'd arrived early for a reason. The vigiles, night watchmen of the city, would be dragging themselves back to their barracks around now, and Atreus was about to break it to them that they weren't going to bed after all.

We headed inside the main building. It was quiet. I could hear the murmuring of voices from somewhere near the front entrance, and a moment later, the young pessimist Manius appeared in front of us.

"Morning, sir!" he said, looking surprised to see Atreus up and about again. "Hey! The boss is back!"

Two more vigiles appeared from one of the rooms off to the side, looking suddenly busy in that suspicious way that subordinates did when you knew they'd been skiving up until the moment you arrived.

"Are the patrols back?" Atreus asked Manius.

"Not yet, sir," Manius said.

"Anything overnight?"

"Not much," said Manius. "Couple of fights. No fires."

Atreus nodded. "Is Leander in?"

"Yes, sir."

"Good," said Atreus. "Let me know as soon as the patrols are back in."

Juba and I followed him back down the passage to the room I remembered as the one where Leander, the Greek physician, plied his unappealing trade. The door was open.

Leander smiled slightly when he saw Atreus, and then he raised his eyebrows. "If you're out of bed, it's not *good* news, is it?"

"I feel fine," Atreus said. It was an obvious lie. "I've got a full day ahead, though, and I need you to strap my ribs as tightly as you can."

Leander gave him a disapproving look.

In the light of the lamps burning inside the windowless little cell, I saw a corpse lying on the stained table. There was a length of sacking covering most of it, and a pair of blotched, bloated bare feet protruding from underneath the ragged edges. When we entered, Leander did us the courtesy of flinging some incense powder into a small brazier, which only had the effect of making the smell of decay seem strangely cloying. My nose twitched.

"Who's this?" Atreus asked, nodding his head at the pair of discoloured feet.

"A floater," said the physician. "He'd probably been in the river a few days before the boatmen pulled him out. I can show you if you like." He crossed to the table and reached for the sacking.

"I'll take you at your word," said Atreus quickly.

I was relieved, but behind me, I heard Juba give a little disappointed sigh. The vulture! Leander shrugged with the smugness of someone who knew he could handle the sight of a corpse better than a trained vigile. "Well, climb up on the table, and I'll strap your ribs."

Atreus shared the tabletop with a corpse that was definitely on the turn, and I took the opportunity to inspect the shelves in the room. These were full of the tools of Leander's trade, some as innocuous as small clay pots of unguents and ointments and others as hair-raising as sharp-toothed saws and vice-like forceps. For every eventuality, from physician to mortician, Leander had it all covered. I inspected a serried row of bronze instruments while out of the corner of my eye I watched Atreus, Leander, and a length of bandage coming to grips. The bandage looked to be winning. The grimace on Atreus's face told me that the struggle was just as painful as it appeared.

There was a tramp of boots in the passageway outside, and a moment later, Manius came to announce, unnecessarily: "Boss, the patrols are back."

"I'll see them on parade," said Atreus, readjusting his tunic and belt. "Thanks, Leander."

Juba and I followed Atreus back outside to the parade ground and leaned against the wall of the station house to watch.

Atreus, acting centurion of the first century of the Fifth Cohort of Vigiles, was the sort of commander who knew his job backwards. Of the seventy-eight men serving in his under-strength century, he knew that five were currently medically unfit, that nine were on leave, and twenty-two were on secondment to Ostia, which left him with a very paltry forty-two men. It wasn't much of a century. They were tired and grubby to a man, but seeing Atreus back on the parade ground revived them. It was obvious that he was a popular commander. He was so popular that they only grumbled at him when he told them they weren't finished yet and didn't beat him to death with their cudgels. Atreus was very young to be an acting centurion. He outranked men who had lived twice as long as he had. He carried his authority easily as well. It was no stretch to imagine him rallying troops on a hostile frontier, if only he hadn't been born plebeian.

Atreus was all business. By the time the sunlight was creeping across the dusty parade ground, he was issuing orders, dividing the Aventine up into neighbourhoods that were familiar to his men—the Plasterers' Collegium, the Janus door, Lucasta's wine shop, the warehouses, Calf Street, Laundry Street, Bridge Street, Lupa's brothel, the Medusa Fountain, the dog pit, Victorinax's shop, the leaning Mercury, the gully, and an entire colourful street index of local landmarks that meant nothing to me.

"You are looking for an informer called Colchus," Atreus told them. "Does anyone know him?"

None of them did. Either Colchus was very new to the business, or he kept a very low profile.

"He's a scrawny shit who sells offerings at the Temple of Diana," said Atreus, and a few of the vigiles looked surprised as they suddenly put a face to the name. "Ask around and ferret him out. Advise the other centuries and the Urban Cohorts. Put the word out to whoever might know on the street. I want him back here by tonight."

"What'd he do?" someone from the back called out. It was never the men in the front rows that opened their mouths. The insubordinate attitude was always designated to someone his superiors couldn't quite see.

Atreus looked at me, watching before he turned to his men again. "He broke into the home of Aemilius Valerius. I'd like to know why."

That caught their interest. I heard some murmurs of outrage in their thin ranks. Many of these men had visited my house since Atreus had been staying there, and many of them had been offered refreshments from my kitchens. It was more hospitality than they had any right to expect in a patrician household, and apparently, it had endeared me to them.

Manius, the littlest vigile, put up his hand. "What about Bano, sir?"

"Forget about Bano," said Atreus. "Today is his lucky day."

He couldn't have guessed how right he was.

* * *

Three hours later, I felt like I'd seen everything the Aventine had to offer and met more dubious characters in those close-packed streets than I ever had in my life. In the hope that Colchus hadn't twigged that he'd been recognised, we'd gone to the Temple of Diana first. There was no sign of Colchus, but the girls were still there, still touting for clients, and still hurling abuse at anyone who refused them.

Atreus, Juba, and I had visited the Medusa fountain. I had expected, literally, a fountain with a Medusa in it, or on it, or around it in some way. Instead, I discovered that it was a plain, dull fountain, and actually got its name from the group of women who worked the looms in the weaver's shop behind it and decorated their hair by twisting dyed wool through their tight little plaits. The shadows they cast as they gossiped around the fountain were serpentine, but there was nothing stony about their smiles. The women filled us in on the comings and goings of everyone in the neighbourhood, but none of them had seen the informer Colchus.

The cook at the thermopolium didn't know the name or said he didn't.

Carus, the teacher, claimed to know nothing at all, and several of his students giggled.

Actia, the laundress, complimented me on the cut of my tunic, invited Juba to stay a while, and told Atreus to piss off.

Atreus and I had a quick discussion in the street outside and decided on a snack at the caupona next door to Lupa's brothel. While we ate, we exchanged pleasantries with Lupa's girls. They were a nicer bunch than the ones who infested the porticoes outside the Temple of Diana. They seemed a bit too nice for the Aventine, but Atreus told me that Lupa liked to circulate the girls between here and her place on the Esquiline, so they needed their better manners at least some of the time. Their concerned enquiries as to Atreus's health and little Lucilla's welfare made me wonder exactly how well Atreus knew the girls. I glanced at Juba and raised my eyebrows, and Juba ducked his head to hide a smile.

My snack was a mushroom omelette that I would sooner have forgotten, but it kept repeating on me. I was still tasting it as the three of us bid farewell to Lupa's girls and headed for our next location: the curia of the Collegium of Aventine Plasterers and Tilers. Our path took us downhill towards the river.

"The collegium used to run this neighbourhood," Atreus told me. "If anyone knows Colchus, it'll be them."

Once again, I don't know what I expected, but it wasn't what I got. A short while later, Atreus was banging on the door of a dilapidated warehouse, and a skinny boy opened the door.

"Wotchawant?"

Atreus narrowed his eyes. "I want Vetus."

The boy looked Juba up and down. "Citizens only."

Juba narrowed his eyes.

Atreus shook his head. "I know this place. We'll be fine."

Juba muttered something and positioned himself outside the door as Atreus and I were admitted. They called it a curia, but the place where the Collegium of Aventine Plasterers and Tilers met every week was a decrepit warehouse on the muddy banks of the Tiber. The warehouse had holes in the roof, the rafters were infested with pigeons, and the furnishings extended as far as a couple of trestle tables and benches and a rough effigy of a goddess so tarnished and battered I couldn't make out who she was meant to represent. The warehouse was close to the point where the wine amphorae were unloaded off the barges from Ostia, and I noticed a few of these had made their way into the collegium's curia. The intricacies of bribery and backdoor deals down in the docks remained a mystery to all outsiders, but I suspected somewhere along the line, the head of the Collegium of Aventine Wine Sellers had got his home renovations done on the cheap.

Atreus was still a mess. He looked better than he had in days, but none of the three assembled plasterers and tilers sitting around one of the tables knew that. To them it must have looked like he'd just been dragged out of the arena by his feet after a day of the games. Like everyone else in this neighbourhood they looked at his fading bruises and his awkward gait and thought the same thing: *Bano.*

Looking around at their curia, it was obvious the collegium had fallen on hard times. They probably had Bano to thank for that, as well. At one time, the vigiles and the collegium must have been adversaries, but nothing dissolved antagonism faster than a common enemy.

The boy who admitted us into the collegium didn't even go and fetch the boss. He only closed the door again, leaned against it, and shouted: "Vetus!"

The three plasterers and tilers, having had an eyeful of Atreus, lost interest and turned back to their game of knucklebones. Moments later, Vetus descended the rickety stairs from the upper level of the warehouse, a kind of mezzanine that overlooked the sad little curia. It was hard to imagine that the place, or the man, had ever been anything less than wretched. The place was falling apart—the stairs shuddered, and feathers and dust rained down from the wide cracks in the sagging floorboards. The man was short, squat, and covered in a thin layer of plaster dust. His eyes were red and bleary, and he coughed a lot. His business with Atreus was brief.

"Colchus?" he coughed into his grimy fist. He knew exactly who Atreus meant. He even knew where to find him. "The informer from the Temple of Diana?"

"That's the fellow," said Atreus.

"His brother is one of my tilers," Vetus said. He narrowed his rheumy eyes for a moment. "I know where he stays."

"And where is that?" Atreus asked.

Vetus wiped his forehead with the sleeve of his tunic. "What's in it for us?"

Atreus folded his arms over his chest. "You might consider it your public duty, Vetus."

Vetus wheezed. It might have been a laugh, or it might not have been. "The last thing I need is trouble from the vigiles, Atreus. Come back tonight. I'll have him for you then."

Atreus nodded curtly. "I'd appreciate that."

And we headed back outside into the day, pleased that Fortuna was finally smiling on us. Looking back, I think I would have preferred that the cold bitch had continued to ignore us.

* * *

We stopped in at the station house when we reached the bottom of the Caelian Hill, and Atreus advised young Manius that the work for the day was done. Most of the vigiles had already reported back anyway, tired and dispirited. We headed for home after that. Atreus needed to get off his feet for a while. He hadn't said it, but it was obvious he was hurting. Juba and I did him the favour of pretending to pick over the remains of the market stalls on the long walk home, so he didn't have to ask us to slow down. I even bought a pumpkin.

I got home to discover that we had a guest—old Macrinus, Nasica's ancient, doddering uncle. He was seated in the outdoor triclinium with the women. The dark slave with the lazy eye attended him. I joined them. I'd already eaten, but I allowed myself to be tempted by the fresh market day fare: bread, cheese, and vegetables. Fulvia, Octavia, and Julia recounted some of their morning's triumphs at the markets to Macrinus, and the old man listened to them with an indulgent smile. The busy, filthy city outside seemed a world away, and in the peaceful shade of the garden, I could even hear birdsong. It was pleasant.

"I must thank you, Valerius," Macrinus wheezed at me while we waited for the fruit, "for finding me tenants for the house."

I glanced at Octavia. "It was my pleasure, Macrinus."

He clasped my hand. "The past few months have been difficult on all of us, I think. I am glad I still have your friendship."

I hoped my smile looked sincere. "Of course."

Having found it not to her taste, Octavia picked a mint leaf out of her water and flicked it away.

"I regret that I have business elsewhere," the old man said soon after, rising with the help of his slave. "I tell you, Valerius, I call myself retired, but every day I am busier and busier! Good day, ladies."

Octavia and I accompanied the old man to the front door. We made painstaking progress. Macrinus leaned on his slave for support, and he was out of breath by the time we made it to the threshold. "Good day, Valerius, Octavia."

Octavia lent her cheek to his wrinkled old lips. "Good day, Macrinus."

Hursa closed the door behind him.

Octavia lifted her hand to tuck a strand of hair behind her ear.

"Is that a new bracelet?" I asked her.

Octavia looked at it like she'd just noticed it. It was a fancy silver piece made up of intricate fretwork. "Macrinus gave it to me," she said. "It's been in his family for ages. It was a gift from Mark Antony to Macrinus's grandmother. Apparently, she was his mistress for a time."

I forced a smile. "I would have expected the consort of Cleopatra to have more expensive tastes than that."

Octavia inspected the bracelet. "Please! If Mark Antony had given all his girlfriends expensive gifts, he'd have bankrupted Egypt in a week. I think it's pretty."

"Still," I said carefully, "I wish that Macrinus wouldn't keep giving you things. I know that it can be upsetting for you."

I knew she sometimes cried after Macrinus visited and talked about Nasica, rehashing all his remembrances and regrets. She tried to hide it, but I knew.

Octavia nodded. "Yes, it sometimes is, but Macrinus is a very old man, Quintus. It gives him pleasure to send me gifts. I don't like to refuse him."

Macrinus always claimed he was close to death, but he'd been dithering on the banks of the Styx for so long now that the ferryman had got sick of waiting for him. He'd probably live forever.

"I know." I sighed. "He's just trying to get his affairs in order."

Octavia inspected the bracelet. "I think it's sort of nice."

"Do you?"

Octavia held out her arm. "It's purely a love token, isn't it? It's almost modest. It's not the sort of thing you would imagine a braggart like Mark Antony giving a woman."

"Maybe he didn't," I suggested. "It's probably just a family myth."

Octavia wrinkled her nose. "Don't spoil it!"

"Sorry."

Octavia forgave me with a smile and then became serious. "Now, this man from last night, is he the same one who followed us home?"

"Almost certainly."

"Hursa says he's a pie seller."

"Hursa should learn to keep his mouth shut," I said, casting a glance at my useless porter. He was busy scratching his scalp.

"Quintus, I wish you weren't involved in all of this," Octavia said. "Can't you find some other position?"

I snorted. I had never been interested in roads and aqueducts, and I couldn't fake it now. I felt the same about public works, the grain and water supply, markets, and games. Even the games, I felt, would lose their attraction if I had to organise them. A priesthood, sweet Jupiter, no! It left the law. I was no jurist, but I enjoyed working with Atreus. There were aspects I didn't like—the blisters and the lack of progress—but it hadn't been all bad. I liked ferreting out secrets. I liked hanging around with the vigiles. I like my new friendship with Atreus. And most of all, I liked having a sense of purpose.

"Octavia," I teased her, "what happened to the girl who wormed her way into that first meeting with Atreus with the story about a stuck bracelet just so she could eavesdrop? She's not really telling me to quit, is she?"

"She was silly and curious," Octavia said. "You're supposed to be working with Severus, Quintus, learning about boring laws and oratory, not putting yourself in harm's way."

"Don't fuss," I told her and squeezed her hand. "I'll be fine."

Her worried gaze followed me as I went off to hunt down Atreus. I found him in his room, suffering Lucilla's affection while he tried to adjust his bandages.

"Colchus," I announced.

"Colchus is intriguing," Atreus said, trying to hold Lucilla still as she giggled.

I felt he wasn't taking it seriously enough. "He broke into my house."

"Yes, sir," Atreus agreed. "But why? Why was he following you? Everyone in the city knows that you're investigating these deaths, and everyone knows where you live. And if he was already watching you, selling pies in the street, then why follow you home?"

"Maybe it wasn't me he was following," I suggested. "Maybe it was you."

Atreus smiled slightly. "I'm just a vigile, sir. I'm not important."

"I'm looking at a face full of bruises that suggest otherwise."

Atreus set Lucilla down onto the floor, pointed her towards the door, and patted her on the backside to get her started. She trailed out past me.

"So, the collegium," I asked him. "What is it?"

"It used to run the Aventine," said Atreus. "As recently as a decade ago there wasn't any business done in the Aventine that the Plasterers and Tilers didn't know about."

"So what happened?" I asked curiously.

"Bano happened," said Atreus. "He moved in, made a few recruits, the collegium's boss turned up in the Tiber, and suddenly Bano's undercutting the price of protection. He's a small operation, to begin with. The collegium can't even find him. By the time they do, months have passed, and he's more than a match for them. He's poached half their muscle, he's bringing in enough cash to hire more, and more of their clients are defecting to him every day. He's choked them out of business, and they never even saw him coming."

I mused on that for a moment.

"They used to have a place near the Temple of Diana," Atreus said. "It burned down."

"So they hate Bano?" I asked. "As much as you do?"

"Hard to imagine, isn't it, sir?" Atreus asked wryly.

* * *

Atreus was not the sort of person to rest on his laurels, scant as they were. Instead of taking the afternoon off, relaxing, and maybe going for a bath, he decided after lunch that it would be a good thing to try to locate the rat bastard informer Kaeso and see if he could shed any more light on the job offer from Marcellus Albanus that he had refused—locating the missing slave Eburnus.

Atreus thought that he would have better luck with Kaeso than I'd had, and while I might have only been new at this investigation business, I liked to believe I wasn't a complete idiot. It rankled. So, Kaeso probably knew more than he was saying. He'd also made it clear that there were some pieces of information even I couldn't afford. If money wouldn't open his mouth, I doubted anything Atreus could bring to the table would get him talking. Nevertheless, after lunch, we found ourselves heading towards the grubby little wine shop that operated in the perpetual darkness underneath the massive arches of the Marcian Aqueduct.

Juba was with us, as per usual, and he looked so happy as we strolled along that I half expected him to launch into a jaunty whistle. He was relishing all of this, and why wouldn't he? Juba had a clever, quick mind, and he was stuck as my bodyguard. He was also the overseer of the other household slaves, but how often did that give him the chance to exercise his brain? Sorting out the petty disputes of my household slaves and standing around waiting for me whenever I went out to dinner was hardly a challenge.

Kaeso was at the same wine shop I'd found him at before. He was seated at a table with a couple of similarly dodgy characters. They were rattling some dice around in a cup.

"My name is Junius Atreus," said Atreus. He put Kaeso on the wrong foot immediately by not offering to buy him a drink.

"I know who you are, acting centurion," said Kaeso, eying his bruises.

"I've come about Marcellus Albanus."

"I already told your friend here," said Kaeso, nodding at me. "Albanus asked me to track down a runaway. I didn't take the job."

"Did Colchus take it?" Atreus asked.

Kaeso picked up the dice and inspected them. "Dunno, boss. Why don't you ask him?" His smirk told us he knew exactly how slippery Colchus had been.

"You said you didn't take the job because Eburnus wasn't Albanus's slave," said Atreus, ignoring the barb.

"That's right," said Kaeso.

Atreus raised his eyebrows. "So whose slave was he?"

Kaeso shrugged. "Dunno, boss."

282

He was lying. I was perversely pleased. Atreus was no better at extracting information from Kaeso than I was.

* * *

Several things conspired against us that afternoon. As we set off from my house, our spirits were high. We called into the excubitorium, dragged a few of the men out of the barracks, and headed into the Aventine. We had Juba with us and three vigiles whose names I forgot the moment I heard them, and felt that was enough for one slippery kid. We headed towards the river, the late afternoon sun casting our long shadows behind us. It was cool enough that I didn't look out of place wearing a cloak. The reason for the cloak was simple: after last night, I was wearing my sword in public, and the law be damned. The law was walking beside me and probably wasn't fooled.

Market day was drawing to a close. The last of the traders were packing up and waiting for nightfall when they could bring their carts inside the city walls. By morning, they would be gone again, leaving nothing behind but squashed fruit, withered lettuce leaves, eggshells, and animal dung.

The day darkened into dusk, and we walked down the hill into the gathering gloom. We met the first of the wheeled traffic as we entered the Aventine. Yawning carters half-heartedly flicked switches across the flanks of their weary oxen as they rattled their way into the city. I still had a bit of a spring in my step. Despite the fact that nothing in this investigation had yet come easily, I had somehow developed the idea that Colchus was as good as ours. From him, naturally, we would find the slave Eburnus, and from Eburnus we would find out all the details of what the Third Gallica had been up to since time immemorial. And then we would tell someone at the palace, let them worry about it, and finally, I would knock the top off a really large amphora of Falernian and not face the world again until my back teeth were floating.

I had always been a slow learner.

The first thing that happened was that Atreus spotted something interesting. We were in a narrow street passing a ramshackle insula when he saw it.

"What do you know?" Atreus said in a low tone. "It's the spider."

I saw a spry little man standing on a balcony with his back to the street. The strange name, I learned later, belonged to the man who liked to follow old women home, spy on them to see that they lived alone, and help himself to their possessions. He had earned his nickname from his ability to scale the sides of insulae. It didn't matter if the old dears remembered to latch their doors because he just came in over their balconies. As poisonous as the real thing, the spider wasn't morally conflicted about smacking his victims around, either. We had caught him in the act, lurking on a shadowed first-floor balcony, and he was so intent on his work that he didn't even see us. He was pressed close to the outer wall, staring inside the apartment.

I don't know who was more surprised when two of our vigiles headed around the corner and up the stairs to the apartment—the spider himself or the old dear who was sitting with her feet up when the vigiles smashed her door open. The spider was back over the balcony before the vigiles had reached it, but he hadn't been reckoning on the third vigile, Juba, Atreus, and me waiting underneath for him.

"I wasn't doing nothing!" he wailed.

"Take him back and hand him over to Vibilus," said Atreus. "His mother was robbed last market day."

"How do you know it's the same man?" I asked curiously.

Atreus drew his brows together in a slight frown while he considered that for a moment. Then he only shrugged and said in a pragmatic tone, "Does it matter?"

He had a point.

The little man whimpered as he was hauled away, and we were one vigile down.

We continued on towards the river.

The second thing was, in hindsight, at least, too much of a coincidence to ring entirely true. We were a block away from the dingy little collegium down by the river when a fight spilled out of a wine shop right in front of us. We might have ignored it, except one of the combatants was armed with a knife and seemed to have the upper hand.

"That's Erastus, boss," said one of our remaining vigiles. "Bano's cousin!"

It was too tempting for Atreus to resist. It was meant to be.

"Get the bastard," said Atreus grimly.

The combatants fled, the vigiles followed, and then we were three.

We continued on to the collegium, and the third thing that happened was that Vetus sold us out.

The streets beside the curia of the Collegium of Aventine Plasterers and Tilers were gloomy and treacherous in the thickening night. There was mud underfoot and loose rubble, and we picked our way down the slope carefully. There was a chill wind blowing in off the river. Let the omen be absent, the old saying goes, but it didn't even occur to me to say it under my breath as I slipped in a slick puddle of stinking mud and almost lost my footing.

We hastened towards the entrance of the dilapidated warehouse.

"Citizens only," the boy on the door of the curia reminded us, and Juba waited outside.

Atreus and I entered and found the place much the same as we had earlier in the day, except dark. There was a single oil lamp placed underneath their patron goddess and a faint glow at the top of the stairs, but nothing else. There were a lot of dark corners in that old warehouse, and they were big enough and black enough to hide a couple of legions.

"Where's Vetus?" Atreus asked the boy.

"He's up in his office," said the boy, and nodded towards the rickety scaffolding that passed as stairs. Like idiots, we thanked him.

The stairs swayed and creaked underneath us as we climbed them. Vetus had an office on the mezzanine level. It wasn't much of an office, just some thin interior walls with holes in them and a curtain for a door. Lamplight shone through the moth-bitten holes in the curtain, glimmering like coins in the gloom.

Vetus was waiting for us, perched on the edge of his couch. Behind the couch was another set of stairs, even more rickety than the first, leading up to the roof.

"Junius Atreus," he said. "Evening."

Atreus wasn't in the mood for pleasantries. "Where's Colchus, Vetus?"

Vetus showed us his filthy, callused palms. "He's on his way, Atreus. Do you want a drink?"

"I want Colchus," Atreus replied.

The stairs outside creaked again.

Vetus's face lit up. "Here he is," he said and stood up.

But it wasn't Colchus who threw back the curtain and stepped into the room. It was someone I didn't recognise, and he was followed by three other men I also didn't recognise. I didn't much like the look of any of them. They were carrying cudgels and had knives stuck in their belts. I didn't have to be a genius to work it out, though. One look at Atreus's face and the grim smiles on the faces of the newcomers told me everything I needed to know. Atreus confirmed it for me.

"Bano," he said in a cold voice.

"Good evening, Junius Atreus," replied the man in question, and his henchmen chortled.

Bano wasn't a physically impressive man. He was in his middle years, of average height, with thinning lank hair. He was ugly as well. He had dark eyes set close together and a nose that had been broken so many times it looked like a lump of half-kneaded dough had been stuck to his face instead. His mouth was a thin line, and as he looked at Atreus, it twisted into a crooked smile. I remembered what Leander, the Greek physician, had told me on the day Atreus had been attacked: three things. Atreus had refused the bribe, ignored the warning, and now here we were. The air was thick with menace.

"It's nothing personal, Atreus," said Vetus, crossing the room to stand beside Bano.

"Bullshit," Atreus said, never once taking his gaze off Bano.

I could tell that Atreus was kicking himself. As for myself, I could see the irony. We'd been working on the assumption that Vetus would help the vigiles as they had a common enemy. It turns out Vetus and Bano had one as well, and it might have been useful if we'd spotted that a little earlier in the day.

The doorway was blocked now, leaving us with only one option. Atreus looked at me, and we both hoped we were thinking the same thing. Then, in a sudden flurry of movement intended to take them by surprise, Atreus and I were clambering up the stairs that led to the roof.

"Go! Go!" Atreus shouted from behind me as my muddy sandals slipped on the steps.

We emerged on the roof to find ourselves underneath a field of dim stars. The cold wind bit at us. There was no door to slam behind us, no trapdoor to bolt, and, we very quickly discovered, nowhere else to go. The curia of the Collegium of Aventine Plasterers and Tilers was a freestanding warehouse, and it was a forty-foot drop to the dark street below.

"Juba!" With the wind whipping through, it was impossible to know if my shout would even reach him.

Bano and his men were right behind us, but they were in no real hurry. They knew we were trapped.

Underneath my cloak, I was wearing my sword. Now seemed like a good time to get it out. It was nothing special, just the standard military issue gladius. We'd seen some things, this sword and I, on the distant frontiers of the empire. The first man I ever killed with this sword was a rebel bandit in Cappadocia, and the last, a Parthian spy who had infiltrated our camp and tried to kill Corbulo. And between them, more than I could remember now. My sword was nothing special, but I knew how to use it.

Bano and his men advanced, and Atreus and I waited for them.

Two of us, and four of them.

I could hear the blood pumping behind my ears. It felt strangely bracing to be waiting like this, in that long, drawn-out moment before all hell broke loose. It had been a long time. I exchanged a grim look with Atreus, and then they were on us.

Not long after that, I was pushed off the warehouse roof.

Chapter Sixteen

I had faced death before, on the cold frontiers of the empire, and lived to tell the tale. I was a hero of Corbulo's Parthian campaign. If I was fated to die at the hands of my enemies, I had always assumed it would happen out there somewhere, accompanied by the blast of the trumpets of war. I had not expected it to end so ignobly, with me hanging by my fingertips over the side of a roof while the cold wind whistled around my nether regions. It was only the darkness that protected my modesty from the crowd of interested spectators gathering below, although modesty was the last thing on my mind. The thing that was uppermost was the grim anticipation of that forty-foot drop onto the street below me. I had two options that I could see. One was to try to land well, and probably succumb in the following days to my hideous internal injuries. The other one was to land on my head and get it over with. But, Jupiter Best and Greatest, I did not want to die like this.

"Help! Anyone? Help!"

I knew there was nobody. Atreus was already dead. I'd done him the favour of taking out two of Bano's men with some acrobatic manoeuvres that would have done Achilles proud, but I'd still left him with one ugly bruiser and Bano himself. The outcome was a given. At least I'd have somebody to talk to on the ferry ride across the Styx. We'd have plenty of time on that sombre journey to go over exactly how we'd fucked up.

The first mistake: going into the Aventine Collegium without the entire cohort of vigiles at our backs.

The second: trusting them.

The third: leaving Juba outside.

I couldn't feel my fingers anymore, and my shoulders felt like they were slowly dislocating. My head. I'd definitely try to land on my head. Why prolong the inevitable? The worst part, I told myself like the proud Roman patrician I was, was that nobody would ever know of my final heroics. I replayed them to myself so they wouldn't go to waste:

The first of Bano's men, the wiry one with the beaky nose, had come at me from my left. He'd swung his cudgel too early and had been on the wrong foot when he'd dived forward with the knife. I'd sidestepped him easily, and as he'd turned around for another go, he'd propelled himself forward onto the end of my sword. His momentum had carried him through, there had been a moment of resistance, and then I'd felt the blade grating against his spine. He'd dropped to the rooftop with a surprised grunt, and that had been the end of him.

The second man had learned a lesson from the first and hadn't come at me blindly swinging. From somewhere close by, I'd heard Atreus holding his own, but I'd known that he wouldn't last long in his condition. I had to help him, and that had meant dispatching henchman number two as quickly as I could.

He had been better than the first man, cleverer and stronger. He'd come at me, I'd dodged, and he hadn't made a single misstep. He'd swung his cudgel, watching which way I jumped. Something about the calculating way he'd advanced told me he'd done his time in the army as well, and when it came to close combat, an ex-legionary could take out an ex-junior tribune any day of the week.

I'd remembered those old prayers to Mithras. So had my attacker, possibly. By that stage, we'd been quite near the edge of the roof. I'd had the idea to use that to my advantage. Again, so had my attacker.

He'd lunged, I'd dodged. I'd lunged, he'd dodged. I'd copped a cudgel across the ribs, and he'd missed a disembowelling by a hair's breadth. I'd been getting out of breath, and so had he. We'd come to grips; advantageous for him, with his knife, and not so good for me with a sword. Knowing I only had one chance at it, I'd got an elbow in his ribs and pushed him back.

He'd been off balance for only a moment, but it had been enough.

It was when I'd had him there, at arm's length, that I'd swung my sword arm. He must have seen it coming, but there had been no time for him to step back. The blade had cut across his neck, blood sprayed, and the look on his face as he grasped his throat uselessly had told me he knew he was gone. I had been standing close enough that I felt his blood hit my face like a sudden mist of hot rain. It had been my moment of glory, and I hadn't even had time to savour it. It had been followed too quickly by my moment of total disaster.

Bano's mortally wounded henchman had lunged at me with the last of his strength, granted it wasn't much, and had knocked me sideways. I'd stumbled, dropped my sword, landed awkwardly on my knees and, quite suddenly, dropped off the warehouse roof. I had no idea how I'd managed to catch myself and no idea how long I could hold on.

I hoped I would be remembered for my final act of bravery rather than my final act of clumsiness, but nobody I cared about would ever know exactly what had happened here tonight. I spared a kind thought for my wife and my sister, my mad relations, and my stepchildren. Even Julia.

My arms were killing me, and pain shot through my shoulders.

The modest crowd below me, probably all men from the collegium or the wineshop up the street who'd come bearing torches like a vengeful mob, were getting restless. I got a few ironic cheers and whistles. It was said that chance, not wisdom, governed human life, but I couldn't shake the feeling that someone a bit cleverer than me wouldn't have found himself in this position.

I hung there, making peace with the gods and, in particular, that bitch Fortuna, when suddenly somebody grabbed my wrists.

Atreus's face appeared over the edge of the roof. It was too dark for it to be true by then, but I imagined him crowned in the rays of the dying sun like a heroic Apollo. Certainly, I told myself, when I commemorated this moment with a badly written poem, golden sunlight would feature.

His fingers tightened around my wrists.

"Thank you, Jupiter!" I gasped. "Atreus! You're alive!"

290

He only grunted in return. Given his tender ribs, he must have been in agony.

Atreus was a marvel! I only hoped he had the strength left to pull me back to safety. I couldn't believe he'd actually managed to kill Bano and his remaining man. I couldn't believe it, and then I realised that he hadn't. Behind him, out of the gloom, I saw a figure looming.

"Bano!" I yelled. "Atreus, it's Bano!"

Atreus, lying on his stomach and trying to stop me from falling, could only grimace at me wryly, and I realised he'd *known* he hadn't killed Bano. He'd known, and yet he'd done something monumentally stupid like turning his back on the man just because I was falling off a roof.

His head. I'd try to land on *his* head.

Bano leaned out over the edge of the roof and looked at me. His ugly face split into an even uglier grin, as though this was the funniest thing in the world. From his point of view, of course, it was. Bano grew taller suddenly, and Atreus grimaced again. The breath squeezed out of him as though he was a pair of punctured bellows, his fingers dug into my wrists, and I realised that Bano was standing on him. I watched the straining muscles in Atreus's arms and wondered how long he could hold on.

In the street below, someone had started a slow clap that had been taken up by the rest of the spectators, like this was the arena, and they knew the gladiator was on his last legs. They were waiting for blood.

"Bano! Bano! Bano!"

Bano's awful smile grew as he heard it.

Atreus's arms started to tremble from the effort of keeping me from falling. His gaze held mine. I didn't want to give Bano the satisfaction, so I hoped my look said it all: Thanks anyway.

"You've made my life hell, vigile," Bano said at last. He stepped down from Atreus's back and drew a knife out of his belt.

Atreus couldn't see the knife, so Bano did him the favour of bending down to show it to him.

"Any last words, friend?" Bano sneered down at me. "Because when I slit this dog's throat, you're going with him."

My childhood oratory tutor had always liked to claim that properly chosen words were an arsenal more powerful than any other in the world, and certainly, there had been cases of men saving their own lives with impassioned pleas and clever chitchat. Crowds had been swayed with words alone, armies raised, and empires born. Somehow, though, I didn't think that oratory would work on a homicidal maniac like Bano. In a world where words could kill, Bano found his trusty old knife did the same with a lot less fuss. Last words?

"Go fuck yourself."

Bano wasn't bothered. He probably heard worse before breakfast.

I didn't want to see what was going to happen next, but I couldn't do Atreus the disservice of closing my eyes. I saw Bano crouch down beside Atreus and grip his hair. He pulled his head back and set the edge of his blade to Atreus's throat.

Atreus.

I imagined I saw my regret at a hundred missed opportunities reflected in his eyes.

The unearthly bellow I heard next, I thought was the sound of the underworld opening up to catch me. It was hideous, terrifying, and before I'd even made any sense of it, suddenly, the gangster Bano, scourge of the Aventine, was flying out beyond the roofline and falling past me. I caught a glimpse of the petrified look on his ugly face, heard a thin wail, and then there was a sort of revolting wet thump somewhere far below me.

Atreus and I stared at one another in astonishment.

"Jupiter, sir!" Juba's familiar face appeared over the edge of the roof. "*Jupiter!* What's going on here?"

Moments later, I was lying on the roof, luxuriating in the feel of something solid underneath me and grinning weakly while Juba fussed over me. Atreus was lying beside me, groaning and convulsing slightly as every one of his ribs jostled for a new position.

"Are you alright, Atreus?" I asked, trying to see around Juba's massive legs. He turned his face towards me, and I saw that he was actually laughing. I was alarmed. "Atreus?"

"What you said, sir," he managed. "To Bano." He groaned and then laughed again. "Oh, *Juno! Ow.*"

All I could smell was blood. I think I was lying in some. I just couldn't believe my good fortune that it wasn't mine.

I'd killed two of Bano's henchmen, thanks partially to my military training, but mainly to my disregard of the law when it came to carrying swords in public. Atreus, not at his best, had managed to break another's arm, and he'd taken off down into the curia again. It later transpired that Juba, rushing up the stairs, had met the fellow and flung him aside so roughly that he'd tripped down the rest of the stairs. He'd broken his nose, collarbone, and foot, but once the vigiles caught up with him, those were the least of his worries. And Bano himself, criminal mastermind and scourge of the Aventine, had been knocked down like a skittle.

"Juba?"

"Yes, sir?"

"Thanks, Juba," I said in a rush of breath.

Juba preened and stalked off to peer over the edge of the roof at his handiwork.

I sat up, catching my breath and charting any potential dislocations, and then shuffled my way on my arse to Atreus. I felt his chest carefully through his tunic to make sure none of his ribs were sticking into vital organs. His laughter trailed off, and his smile faded as he held my gaze.

I leaned down and pressed my mouth to his.

He let it happen for just a moment, and then he turned his head away and pushed me gently back. "No," he murmured. "No, sir."

I swallowed down my shame and my disappointment and glanced over to where Juba was pretending he hadn't noticed a thing. Finally, moving as slowly and shakily as a feverish tortoise, I climbed to my feet.

I picked up my sword. My arms were killing me still, but my fingers found their old familiar grip all the same.

"Come on," I said at last. "Let's get out of here."

* * *

Atreus, Juba, and I climbed back down the rickety stairs very slowly and very cautiously, but the collegium was empty. The street outside was suspiciously empty as well. I had a feeling that the moment Bano had flown off the roof, everyone had suddenly remembered they had very pressing business elsewhere and couldn't wait around to congratulate Atreus on his surprising survival.

There wasn't much left of Bano, really. Well, there was, but it was generally misshapen and spread around over a large area. I didn't want to inspect him too closely, but Atreus made the effort to pick his way through the blood and bits to spit on his mortal enemy's mortal remains.

We took a moment to silently ponder the capricious nature of fickle Fortuna, then limped very, very cautiously away from the collegium. News of our deeds had travelled ahead of us. Like a wave that began as a ripple, it coursed over the neighbourhood, grew in strength, washed back on itself, and flooded the Aventine. A group of six vigiles met us a few blocks away and offered us a safe escort back to the excubitorium.

Juba only snorted. "Where were they when we needed them?"

Lowly vigiles didn't get triumphs, but as far as I was concerned, that was exactly what Atreus got that night. People came out of nowhere to watch us walk through the street, like it was a parade. Some of them clapped, some of them cheered, and some of them threw flowers. Yesterday, Bano had been their hero, but self-preservation played a large part in that. Atreus had delivered the Aventine from a tyrant, and tomorrow they would be lining up to piss on Bano's ashes. Down by the river, Bano's heartland, they would hate Atreus for life, but those people who had paid their protection money and just tried to earn a living no longer had to bow and scrape to the gangster. Atreus was their hero.

Atreus was modest and uncomfortable with the attention. "Bano has left a gap," was all he told his star-struck men. "I want to know who fills it."

Then we went to the baths to let the hot water do its magic.

We attended my bathhouse on the Caelian Hill, and I tipped the door slave generously in order to get a plebeian vigile and a slave in the door. The place was empty at this late hour. Across the city, people were wining, dining, and generally socialising. Nobody bathed at this hour. My selective private bathhouse, I knew, wouldn't fill up again until the triclinia, theatres, and brothels disgorged their guests back out onto the streets.

Juba, despite the tetchiness of the door slave, joined us in the baths and the three of us floated around in there for what felt like hours. I stole glimpses of Atreus's damp skin through the steam and of the beads of water that slid down it. I wanted him, and, like a fool, I'd acted on it. What a shame the baths couldn't wash away regret.

We were interrupted once, and it was by a person so important that the door slave didn't even ask if he was a member of the place—it was Tigellinus, Prefect of the Vigiles. Tigellinus walked into the bathhouse like he owned the place, and for all I knew, he did. He was either on his way to or from dinner, because he was wearing a toga and the slave accompanying him was carrying a napkin.

"My dear fellows!" he exclaimed, raising his hand when he saw us lolling about in the water. "I hear congratulations are in order."

We climbed out of the water and wrapped ourselves in towels. The hot water had done miracles for our muscles, but no favours at all for our bruises. Atreus's ribcage was striated with them, some old and faded to yellow, and some that were red now but tomorrow would be as black as midnight. I had fared better, but there were still a few places I hesitated to touch.

Tigellinus was on his way *to* dinner, as it turned out, meaning that outside, he had a litter waiting for him. Inside that litter, like any good dinner guest, Tigellinus had been transporting a large jar of the immortal Falernian. And like any good boss, Tigellinus knew how to give credit when credit was due. He nodded his head at his slave, and the man disappeared for a few moments only to reappear, clutching the jar in a careful embrace.

"Junius Atreus," Tigellinus said, "accept this with my compliments."

His slave tottered forward with the jar and placed it gently down on the bathhouse tiles.

"Thank you, sir," said Atreus, looking at it like he wondered how the fuck he was going to carry it home. The idiot. That would be Juba's job.

I heard the jangle of coins and looked away while Atreus received his bonus. I wondered how much tonight's work was worth to his purse and thought that Tigellinus was a braver man than me if he was giving money to someone as thin-skinned as Atreus. Too little would be hugely offensive, and too much? Surely, that would only serve to remind Atreus that he worked for a living while the rest of us threw money around and had no idea of its value. What *was* the current going rate for a dead gangster anyway?

I slipped away and got dressed while Atreus no doubt received his gratuity with bad grace. When I reappeared, Tigellinus was waiting to offer me his congratulations as well. Atreus got lovely shiny money, and all I got was a firm handshake and a pat on the back. Of course, it would never do for a patrician of my standing to accept a gift of money off an equite, particularly for something as sordid as a *job*. We patricians were a proud bunch and would rather die than be mistaken for one of the working classes.

"I thought you were only investigating these senatorial murders, Valerius," Tigellinus told me with a broad smile, "but you're cleaning up the Aventine as well!"

"It would take all the strength of Hercules and a couple of diverted rivers to clean up the Aventine," I said. "I'm just doing what I can."

Tigellinus laughed heartily, but it wasn't his neighbourhood I'd just maligned. Atreus didn't look quite as amused, but he had a purse full of coins and a jar of Falernian to console him.

"I spoke to Anicetus tonight," said Tigellinus.

"Is that so?"

Tigellinus smiled. "I hear you left an interesting message for him at the Domus Tiberiana."

"I did."

Tigellinus's smile grew. "I suspect my friend Anicetus is unused to receiving such, ah, forthright messages."

"I'm sure he is."

"He did say," said Tigellinus, "that he is very interested in where the investigation might lead. He also said that he hopes you will follow it to the top."

"What does that mean?" I asked, but Tigellinus was never going to answer a question like that. He was a political animal. He wouldn't give a straight answer if his life depended on it.

Tigellinus bid us farewell and continued on to his dinner.

We left the bathhouse shortly afterwards, with Juba lugging the jar of wine. It was Atreus who suggested my bodyguard might find the burden too great to manage, and we stopped at the inviting portico of a private residence a short way up the hill and opened the jar. We sat on the step, passed the jar around, and left the empty vessel behind a potted plant for the door slave to discover in the morning. Still sore, but at least well lubricated, we continued on home.

"Juba," I said as we limped up the hill, "I intend to drink myself silly tonight, so I might need you to remind me of something tomorrow."

"Sir?" Juba asked.

"I owe you a denarius."

The relationships between masters and slaves differed from house to house. It was not uncommon for them to be friends if they were raised together from children. Juba and I hadn't been. I'd known him for less than a year. On the day I'd got back from the army, he'd opened the door to me, and that was the first time we'd met. My father had made him tag along as my bodyguard whenever I went out on a late night, and there had been a few of those when I was first back in Rome. He had always impressed me with his cleverness, his discretion, and, tonight, his homicidal loyalty. Slaves like that didn't come along every day. They deserved to be remembered, but only a few of them were. Augustus had Hyginos, Cicero had Tiro, and—not that I would dream of putting myself in their distinguished company—I had Juba. I also had Hursa, of course, but I quietly hoped he wouldn't be associated with me for all posterity.

"Thank you, sir," said Juba. It was too dark to see it, but I could hear the smile in his voice.

"Just do me a favour, and don't save up too quickly for manumission."

The smile was still there. "No, sir."

We continued on up the hill.

If the demise of Bano, the gangster, was the talk of the Aventine, in better circles nobody even knew. When Atreus, Juba, and I finally made it in the door, puffed up and unsteady on our feet, we weren't conquering heroes after all. We were loud, obnoxious, and had missed dinner. In the atrium, divesting myself of my bloodied cloak and gladius, I filled the family in on our night's exploits. My womenfolk were horrified at how close they'd come to spending their inheritance, bless them, and I basked happily in their concern while I related the entire tale. Hursa, who should have been scuttling off to fetch me fresh clothes, was rooted to the spot. He was my most appreciative audience member. As he listened to the story unfold, Hursa reacted like he was watching a lowbrow play in the street, the sort where audience involvement was actively encouraged. He gasped when the hero was put in peril, booed the evil villain, widened his eyes at the moment of awful suspense, and clapped enthusiastically when it turned out the real hero of the piece was the long-suffering slave who'd lumbered along in the background the whole time.

My womenfolk were less amused. Fulvia had a hand over her mouth, and Octavia had lost a shade or two of colour. Even Julia looked upset.

Octavia was the first to move. She reached out and put a hand on my arm, as though to reassure herself I was really there. I put my hand over hers and squeezed. "I'm alright," I told her.

I embraced Fulvia and caught Atreus's gaze. It was guarded, maybe even censorious. The mouth I'd kissed not that many hours ago was pinched into a thin line that hinted at disapproval.

"I'm fine," I promised the lot of them, forcing down my shame. "We're all fine."

Atreus looked away.

* * *

When the womenfolk had left, Atreus and I sat alone in my tablinum and enjoyed the silence they left behind. There was a jar of wine on the table, and I didn't like the odds it would survive until morning. There was only one thing to do when you'd dodged a trip to the underworld by the skin of your teeth, and that was to drink. We were but dust and shadow and might as well make a toast of it. Atreus was of the same mind. We sat in companionable silence, drinking and watching the flame of the single lamp flickering. There was nothing to say. Neither of us wanted to revisit the incident on the roof—both Bano's demise and the unwelcome kiss that had followed it—and neither of us wanted to speculate about the sorry state of the investigation. For now, it was enough to be alive.

I spotted my old latrunculi board on a shelf and brought it over to the table. Atreus was a fair player, but no real challenge. He hadn't spent all those long hours sitting on the frontiers of the empire with nothing else to do, like I had. Every junior tribune from Britannia to Bithynia became an expert through sheer boredom. The grizzled old warhorses liked to proclaim that they learned all their tricks and tactics from the chequered latrunculi board, but that was bullshit. If it were true, every junior tribune in the empire would be Julius Caesar.

Atreus was smart enough to watch for the more obvious traps I set for him, but I still captured his aquila in less than twenty moves.

The screens separating the tablinum from the atrium and the peristyle had been opened, as was the custom at night. I preferred them shut during the day. It stopped the tablinum being used as a thoroughfare and afforded me some privacy while I worked, read, or, more usually, napped. At night, when the screens were opened, the house felt larger, quieter, and older. Generations of Aemilii had been born in this house and had lived and died here. At night, when the glow of the lamps made the shadows endlessly swell and recede like the tide, I felt the weight of their presence. I wasn't the only one thinking of my ancestors that night.

From the darkness of the tablinum I saw Octavia quietly cross the atrium. Her palla was drawn up over her hair. Lamplight bathed her solemn face. She approached the alcove of the lararium and bowed her head. I watched as she made her quiet devotions to the household gods, the lares and penitates that watched over our home, our fortunes, and our family. The smell of incense filled the air and brought with it a strange melancholy.

Octavia then slipped away as silently as she had appeared, and I heard the creak of her footsteps on the stairs.

I set up the board again.

"I'm sorry, sir," Atreus said. "About earlier."

My heart skipped a beat. "You have nothing to be sorry for."

"Your wife…"

"I love my wife," I said. "I don't sleep with her."

"I don't—" Atreus sighed. "I'm not a slave, sir, or a whore."

My stomach twisted. "Yes, I know that."

"I'm a freeborn Roman citizen," Atreus said. "I am nobody's boy."

I turned a latrunculi piece over in my shaking hand and lifted my gaze to meet his. "I am aware, Atreus."

"The damage it would do to my reputation—"

"I am *aware*." I closed my fist around the piece. "Believe me, I am so *fucking* aware."

I saw the moment that realisation hit him. His eyes widened, and his mouth fell open. "It is not a boy you want."

"Of course it's not," I said, keeping my voice low. "If it was a pretty boy I wanted, I could have a house full of them, and nobody would even blink. I could even dress them like Sylvia, and it'd barely be a scandal at all."

"You want…" The thought was so shocking to a freeborn Roman citizen that, for a moment, I thought he couldn't bring himself to finish it. "You want a *man*."

"Yes." I smiled bitterly. "You think your reputation would be ruined if you bent over for another man, Atreus? Imagine what would happen to mine." My eyes stung.

Atreus regarded me silently for a very long while. His expression was unreadable. I'd ruined our fledgling friendship, I supposed. He rose and stepped forward, then reached out and put a hand on my shoulder. He squeezed it gently, then turned and left.

I sat there for a long while staring at the latrunculi board while the lamp burned slowly out.

* * *

I crawled out of bed the next morning with some difficulty; every muscle ached. I washed my face, dressed, and left my bedroom. It was an odd world. When Claudius Rufanus had met his gruesome death in a rickety insula in the Transtiberina, half the civilised world had shown up in my atrium to get the gossip. When the notorious Bano, criminal, standover man, and all-round villain, was justly dispatched to the underworld, apparently nobody cared. My atrium was empty.

Fulvia met me at the bottom of the stairs. "Are you coming to breakfast, Quintus?"

Atreus appeared in the atrium. He looked as though he'd slept as badly as I had. I wondered how much of that had been to do with our close call on the warehouse roof last night and how much of it had been to do with my uncomfortable admission.

He met my gaze steadily.

"No," I told Fulvia. "We're going out."

My leave-taking today seemed suddenly full of meaning. After last night, everything did. I shook it off, but I saw the same thought cross Fulvia's solemn face: *Is it safe?* I regrouped—it was a bright, sunny day, and Atreus and I were the heroes of the Aventine. Heroes didn't die on bright, sunny days. Except, my perverse brain reminded me, Pompey on the Egyptian shore, Cicero on the road to the beach, and Caesar himself, who was famously assassinated in the shadow of a statue of Pompey. Greater men than me had died on sunnier days.

Juba was waiting for us by the front door. So was Hursa, shifting his weight excitedly from foot to foot. Just looking at him soured my already bleak mood. I knew he was going to annoy me, and to his credit, he didn't keep me in suspense very long.

"Morning, sir," he said, trying to envelop me in a cloak.

"It's not cold," I told him, shaking him off.

He stuck to me like a scruffy German limpet. "But, sir, if you wear your cloak, you can take your sword again!"

"It's broad daylight, Hursa," I told him, trying to recall the name of that fellow who'd fed his slaves to lampreys and reflecting that perhaps he'd just been misunderstood.

"Bano had a lot of friends, sir," Hursa intoned darkly, suddenly an expert.

"It's broad daylight," I said again, holding up my hand so I could count the points off against my fingers, "it's illegal. I've got Atreus with me, I've got *Juba* with me, Bano's men will be in total disarray this morning"—I ran out of fingers, but kept going nonetheless— "and the city will be crawling with the Urban Cohorts already."

Hursa looked like he was going to argue the point.

"Hursa," I warned him carefully, "the only thing that is stopping me from choking you to death right now is the knowledge that you're only annoying me because you're concerned. Now, leave me alone, or I can no longer guarantee your personal safety."

Hursa sighed theatrically and began to fold up my cloak.

"Right," I said to Atreus, rolling my aching shoulders to try to convince myself I was up for anything, "we're still alive this morning, against all the odds. Let's make the most of it."

As inspiring speeches went, it was lousy, but Atreus nodded seriously. "Yes, sir."

Chapter Seventeen

L eaving the house, Atreus, Juba and I found ourselves awash in the brilliant sunlight of a fresh new day.

The littlest vigile in the world, young Manius, met us halfway down the street, darting between pedestrians as he hurried up the hill.

"Junius Atreus, sir!" he said and gave what might pass for a salute in strictly non-military circles. I got a deferential nod and a hesitant smile.

"What is it, Manius?" Atreus asked, stepping out of the way of a woman laden with shopping baskets.

"Boss," said young Manius, puffing his chest out proudly, "we've got Erastus!"

The Fifth Cohort of Vigiles hadn't been idle the night before. Inspired by their boss's victory on the rooftop of the Aventine Collegium of Plasterers and Tilers, they had swept through their district while the trail was still hot and even stepped on the toes of the other cohorts by descending into the Subura and by crossing the river into the Transtiberina. They had been looking for the informer Colchus, and they hadn't found him, but they had found someone who might be useful to us all the same: Erastus, Bano's cousin, the fellow from the staged knife fight at the wine shop who had outrun them at the time.

When Atreus, Juba, and I turned up at the excubitorium we were escorted straight past Leander the physician's room, down past the barracks, and to a gloomy storeroom that I hadn't seen before and didn't wish to ever see again. It was windowless, dank, it smelled putrid, and its miserable occupants were held there in the dark.

"This is your prison?" I asked Atreus as a pair of vigiles hauled the heavy door open.

"We're night watchmen, sir," Atreus reminded me. "It's not the Tullianum."

That morning, there were six men in the cell, and three of them were hopeless drunks who would be released as soon as they had sobered up and made reparation for the damage they'd done the night before. The fourth was a wretched runaway slave who hadn't even made it outside the city walls before a couple of civic-minded citizens had spotted his guilty look and handed him over to the vigiles. He waited miserably for his master to collect him. The fifth man was the burglar from the previous night, the spider. The sixth man was Erastus, Bano's cousin. He was the only one of the men who was shackled, hands and feet. When the door was opened, he squinted suspiciously into the light. I hadn't paid him much attention the night before, and I saw now that he was young.

"Get him out," said Atreus shortly.

The vigiles dragged him out of the cell and out into the passageway. He was as slippery as a fish in oil, twisting and turning as they hauled him along. Juba and I exchanged a look, wondering what we were in store for, but this was an old practice down at the excubitorium because the vigiles didn't even have to ask where they were headed. They hauled him up the steps roughly.

Outside the physician's room, there was a bracket secured to the wall, holding up a torch. There was a low bench under the torch. The vigiles lifted the struggling Erastus off his feet and hauled him up onto the bench. Then they hooked the chains linking his wrists over the bracket and hung him on the wall like the world's most awkward bas-relief sculpture.

The vigiles stepped down, leaving Erastus standing there. Then they dragged the bench away, he fell, and his toes struggled to find the floor. His full weight hung from the bracket and from his shackled wrists. Very soon, it would start to hurt. And then he and Atreus would have a little chat.

"You set me up, Erastus," said Atreus in a calm voice. He folded his arms over his chest and leaned on the wall opposite the man.

"Not me, friend," said Erastus, his voice strained with effort. "That was

304

Vetus. He came to us."

Atreus had time on his side. I remembered how my shoulders had felt the night before and still felt now, and I felt a flicker of empathy for Erastus as he grimaced in pain. His toes still scrabbled uselessly for purchase. His hands, sticking out of the wide cuffs of the shackles, were already red and beginning to swell. A thick line of blood made its way slowly down his left forearm towards his elbow.

"Maybe," said Atreus mildly.

Erastus strained. The tendons in his neck bulged. "It's the truth, vigile."

"Maybe," Atreus repeated and smiled slightly.

Erastus grimaced again, and his body shook.

As torture went, it wasn't what I'd expected from the vigiles. We were close to Leander's room, after all, and his tray of shiny, scary surgical instruments. Possibly Atreus was a little more subtle than the average vigile, and possibly more devious. Why wear himself out when he could stand back and let time, and weight, do the work for him?

Pain was a funny thing. There was no more subjective measure in the entire world. What brought one man to breaking point might have no real effect upon another. Sometimes, even the hard men didn't last as long as they thought they would, and Erastus didn't look that hard to begin with.

Erastus was still in his teens and could probably go days without shaving. He must have inherited his looks from the other side of the family; he wasn't ugly like Bano had been. He was young and, incongruously, handsome. It was a handsomeness that leaned towards the feminine. He had the sort of face that wouldn't look out of place on a statue of Ganymede, and if he hadn't been a gangster, he probably could have made a good living out of flashing his smile at wealthy widows and neglected wives or men whose tastes led that way. But Erastus was Bano's cousin; he had helped set us up the night before, and nobody standing in the gloomy little hallway made the mistake of judging him by his appearance. So we waited.

A strangled groan escaped Erastus as he hung there. "It's the *truth!*"

Atreus ignored him.

Erastus twisted for a moment, trying desperately to relieve the pain, but there was nowhere for him to go. He squeezed his eyes shut, and a tear ran down his cheek. "Atreus! Please!"

The vigiles exchanged uneasy looks, but Atreus was as implacable as only a man in his position could be: a man who last night had been lured into a murderous trap and had only barely escaped it.

"Atreus!" The blood was flowing from both his wrists now. The shackles were sharp. "It was Vetus, I swear it! He came to us!"

"And what about the informer Colchus?"

"What?" Erastus pushed himself out from the wall but couldn't hold himself there. He slumped back again, and pain shot through him like lightning. He convulsed. "I don't know! I never heard the name!"

"You're lying," said Atreus calmly.

"Bano told me to set up the fight," Erastus managed through his tears. "I don't know anything about any informer. Vetus came to *us*."

It had the ring of truth. Atreus nodded his head at the vigiles, and they pushed the bench back towards Erastus's flailing legs. The relief was instantaneous. Erastus leaned back against the wall, shaking and struggling for breath. His relief translated into gratitude:

"I don't know about any informer," he managed. "I just collect the money. I just do what Bano says. What he said."

"And who will you take your orders off now?" Atreus asked him quietly.

Erastus closed his eyes again and shook his head. "Don't know. I don't know."

"Come on, Erastus," Atreus said. "You might be pretty, but you're not stupid."

Erastus opened his eyes, and they flashed. "Fuck you."

"Ah," said Atreus with a sympathetic shrug. "Now that, my friend, was a mistake."

The vigiles pulled the bench away again, and one of them hung on Erastus's legs for a moment for good measure. It might have been my imagination, but I thought I heard something crack. Erastus screamed.

Leander, the Greek physician, stepped into the hall. He watched Erastus closely. With a caregiver's compassion or a cold scientific eye, I couldn't tell.

Erastus babbled something.

"What was that?" Atreus asked him.

"The Transtiberina!" Erastus wept. "Colchus lives in the Transtiberina!"

"That's a big area," said Atreus.

The vigile holding Erastus's legs bore down, and Erastus cried out again. The sound was more ragged than last time and weaker. Torture was a kind of art, I supposed, and it had an intricacy that was always lost on its victim. There was a line with torture, and I wondered if Atreus knew where it was. Cross it, and Erastus would be beyond any further usefulness to us.

"Atreus," Leander said in a low voice.

Atreus ignored him and watched Erastus with a keen eye.

"Near Gracho's wineshop," Erastus moaned desperately. "By the Black Athena!" His body convulsed again, and he cracked his head sharply on the wall. The vigile holding his legs grinned.

Juba growled something under his breath, and my stomach clenched.

Erastus's head fell forward, and blood washed down his neck. "Please. Please."

The hair stood up on the back of my neck to hear him; he sounded even younger than his years, but it was no time for squeamishness. If it had been up to Erastus, I'd be a dead man.

"*Please.*" The word dissolved into sobs.

"Enough," Leander said, at last, pushing forward. "Jupiter, Atreus, enough! What the fuck is wrong with you?"

"It wasn't just me who almost died last night!" Atreus snapped.

I felt myself flush as his gaze caught mine, and my heart beat faster.

"Take him down," Atreus said through clenched teeth, looking away again. "Take him down and put him back in the cell. Send a message to the Seventh and see if they can pick up Colchus. If they can, maybe this piece of shit will see daylight again."

The vigiles lifted Erastus down and dragged him into Leander's room. Leander pulled the door closed behind them. We stood for a moment in the quiet of the passage. The wall underneath the bracket was smeared darkly with Erastus's blood. The torchlight gleamed on it.

"So what now?" I asked Atreus, fighting the urge to reach out for him, to place my hand on his forearm and assure him that I was fine. That we both were. "A trip to the Transtiberina?"

Atreus seemed to shake himself awake. "No, it's not our area. Once news gets out about my boys nabbing Erastus last night, I'll have enough to explain to the tribune of the Seventh. He's gone to Tigellinus in the past."

"What, then?" I asked, and for once, Atreus came up with an answer that was just right.

To rid ourselves of the unpleasantness of torture, we set off for my bathhouse. The day seemed less bright than before, but it was a compromise with my conscience that I was happy to make. We were closing in on Colchus, the informer. We were making real progress at last.

At my bathhouse, we went straight to the massage tables. My masseuse was a big, burly girl with strength that wouldn't have been out of place on a gladiator, and she furiously assaulted the muscles in my shoulders and back as though they'd personally offended her.

"Oh, Jupiter!" I think that was her elbow in my back, and it forced all the air out of my lungs. "You're a marvel!"

She only grunted and set about rearranging my kidneys.

The girl sorted out my shoulders and back while, on the bench next to mine, Atreus took his punishment with the patience of a Stoic. Atreus's masseuse, even though she wasn't as solid as mine, still packed a punch, and she didn't spare his bruises. Afterwards Atreus and I scraped the oil off in the baths, melting in the steam, and Juba prowled back and forth above us protectively.

It was getting on to mid-morning, and the bathhouse was almost empty. We were joined by a few other members; the wealthy unemployed of the city who were waiting for their commissions in the military to come through, for their names to be noticed by the Senate, or for their fathers to drop off their perches before they came into their own. These had been my people. The fifty-one-year-old grandfather of three, who still wasn't head of his own household. The balding thirty-nine-year-old who had never managed to become more than an aedile. His thirty-six-year-old brother, who'd had a totally undistinguished military career and had hoped it would set him up for a totally undistinguished political career. A younger son of a younger son, now well into his middle years with nothing but his modest pedigree to his name. Someone had probably told him when he was a boy of his family's greatness, and he always wore a puzzled sort of expression as if he was wondering where it had gone. The rest of them were either just killing time waiting for something to come up or had given up years ago.

They were a strange sort of underclass, in that they were born and bred into the ruling class of a city of a million people that limited its senators to two hundred. Thus, the provinces thrived. Sometimes you had to go to the edges of the world just to get noticed back in Rome. Those that had managed it were currently making grand speeches in the Senate, in the law courts, and on the Palatine Hill. The rest of them were picking their way carefully across the wet tiles with handfuls of cheeses and sweet pastries. It could be a fulfilling life, in its own way, as I knew well: until the murder of Marcellus Albanus, I had been one of them.

I floated my strigil on the cloudy surface of the water, and then sank it.

"So," I said at last, "our plans for the rest of the day. We're leaving Colchus to the Seventh, which is probably the best thing."

Juba crouched down to listen.

"The Transtiberina is a worse rats' nest than the Aventine," I said and glanced at Atreus. "No offence."

"None taken, sir," he lied.

"And Colchus is a public informer," I mused aloud. "He's a low life, obviously, if he took on a job that even Kaeso didn't want. He'll be tricky to find even for the Seventh, however well they know their district. He'll be holed up tighter than Bano was."

At my mention of Bano we all took a quiet moment to savour our victory on that front at least.

"We need a fresh approach," I opined. "We need to get back to knocking on the doors of the patricians who served in the Third Gallica and try to find out why Marcellus Albanus and Claudius Rufanus were killed."

I had told Atreus when I'd first agreed to assist in the investigation that I could open patrician doors for him. Why, then, had we spent so much time in the slums of the city instead of the grand townhouses? It was time we restored the balance. It was time we asked the ex-tribunes of the Third Gallica exactly what they'd been up to in the provinces and who else knew about it.

The warmth of the water soothed me, working gently away at my muscles and loosening them. I relaxed and inhaled the steam. It was said that if you opened your veins in hot water, the procedure was fast and painless. Most men didn't. Most men, with the assistance of a trusted friend, positioned their gladius against their stomachs and fell forward onto it. Their own weight did all the work for them. That's what my ex-brother-in-law Nasica had done with the same instrument he had carried at his side as a tribune in the Third Gallica. There was a certain sense of justice in that, or at least symmetry.

I wondered which of his friends had helped him.

"The Third Gallica," I said thoughtfully. "Now, it strikes me that some of these men must be getting a little nervous, given that two of their number have already been dispatched to the underworld. I wonder if any of them are feeling a little more talkative."

Atreus looked like he was considering it, but Juba snorted.

"What?" I asked him, twisting my head.

"Nervous?" my astute bodyguard asked. "Sir, these men have been stealing silver from right under the emperor's nose. They're not nervous. They're ruthless."

Atreus nodded slowly. "No, they won't talk."

"Although," I mused, "they're dropping like flies. There's room for nervousness there, Juba."

"Mmm," said Juba thoughtfully.

"Which is why we need Eburnus," Atreus said. "We need to know exactly who was involved and exactly what's gone wrong."

"The only problem being that we haven't found Colchus yet, ergo we can't find Eburnus. We should forget him for the moment," I said.

There was one man left on Atreus's list that we hadn't managed to speak to yet: Galerius Nepos. He had been in the Third, he had been unable to account for himself after Albanus's party, and he was probably into it up to his neck. Nepos, of all of them, had the most to lose if his treason was uncovered. He was odds-on to be a consul when the elections next rolled around, which would make him one of the most powerful men in Rome. It was the highest position a man could hope for unless he was born into the imperial family. If it could be proved he was a traitor, I wondered, would he even be given time to depart? Time to depart was that particularly Roman punishment, reserved for citizens only, and based on the haughty conceit that banishment to the provinces was literally a fate worse than death. In practice, most people happily packed their bags and headed for Ostia instead of hanging around for their scheduled appointment with the public strangler. Treason, though, on the scale of that of the ex-tribunes of the Third Gallica, might not be accorded such leniency by the palace. When men were intent on making the sort of profit a silver mine could afford, you had to wonder what it was intended for. It was the sort of fortune that could buy the loyalty of the legions.

"A silver mine!" I said. "How do you hide a silver mine? There must be hundreds of people who know."

It was Juba who answered. "Probably the same as you hide anything else, sir. You pay bribes, and you make threats. If I lived somewhere there was a mine and a legion came and helped itself, I'd shut my mouth."

"We need to speak to Galerius Nepos," I said. "His is the biggest name."

"His slaves won't let us in, sir," Atreus reminded me.

"It's not like he's a housebound invalid," I said. "He goes to the Curia, and he has a social life. We just need to be in the right place at the right time."

Atreus snorted. "That has not been our strong point so far."

Juba hid a smile. "You could also revisit Probus Macrinus, sir," he suggested evilly. "He was in the Third Gallica, wasn't he?"

I curled my lip. "Maybe four hundred years ago! Your new attitude does you no credit, Juba."

"No, sir," Juba agreed, deadpan.

"Anyway," I said, leaning my back against the warm tiles of the caldarium. "Who knows? If we can get Nepos to talk, we might not even need Colchus after all!"

I meant it as a throwaway remark, but Atreus seized upon it. "No," he said thoughtfully. "Maybe not."

"What are you getting at, Atreus?" I asked.

"Colchus," mused Atreus. "It's strange, isn't it, that he's still poking around when his client Marcellus Albanus is already dead? I doubt he works for free."

"One of the others must be paying him," I said. "That makes sense."

"Yes," said Atreus meditatively. "It does make sense." He threw in one of his patented long pauses. I waited for it to end, and it didn't. Atreus just continued to look at me thoughtfully.

I scowled at the cloudy surface of the water and tried and failed to recover my sunken strigil. Atreus wasn't used to sharing his thoughts. A collaborative working relationship didn't suit him, so it was a good thing that, one way or another, we were approaching the end. It only remained to be seen if we would be triumphant or if we would crash as spectacularly as Felix's last charioteer on race day. Apparently, you could still see the marks on the wall where he'd been scraped off.

Atreus lifted his arm out of the water and wiped his hair back. His arm was covered in striated bruises of varying ages and hues. So was the rest of him, probably. And yet, he was smiling slightly. He turned his head and caught my eye. "We're getting closer," he said. "It's falling into place at last."

I almost believed him.

* * *

We tracked down Galerius Nepos easily enough. He was in the Curia, as was to be expected of a man of his station when the senate was in session. The great bronze doors of the Curia were open, but the stairs were clear of the usual gaggle of boys and their tutors who had come along to listen to proceedings. Today, there were Praetorians on the steps, at least a dozen of them, and they weren't letting anyone approach the doors. It could only mean that Nero himself was in attendance.

Like sightseers, we stationed ourselves at the bottom of the steps and waited for a break in proceedings when the senators would toddle out to warm themselves in the sunlight. Atreus was impatient, but he didn't know how to read the Curia like I did. I'd spent too many long hours sitting on these steps as a boy while my tutors tried to interest me in the legal debates being held in the Forum, in the news of the *Acta Diurna*, or in the speakers at the Rostra. I'd been more interested in the touts, the swindlers, and the thieves who came to prey on the slack-jawed tourists. But I could still read the place. The litter bearers were stretching, the hawkers were encroaching, and the bodyguards were watching the steps: a break in proceedings was imminent.

A small crowd had gathered to cheer the emperor as he left. As the doors were swung open, they surged forward hopefully, but it was a few nondescript senators who descended the steps first. Nero was clever enough to let the crowd grow a bit. The senators frowned at the crowd and squeezed down the side of the steps, disappearing under the nearby arches of the Basilica Aemilia. Within moments, the trickle of senators had become a flood. I saw a familiar face from Marcellus Albanus's dinner party and forged up the steps of the Curia to intercept him. I stepped on noble toes and elbowed important ribs. "Galerius Nepos! *Salve!*"

We eyed one another suspiciously.

"Aemilius Valerius, isn't it?" he said as we were jostled by Rome's finest.

"That's right," I said. "I'm investigating the murders of Marcellus Albanus and Claudius Rufanus."

"And?" Nepos asked me with an arched brow, as though I'd announced something as tedious as an interest in Doric architecture.

"And I was wondering if you can tell me why you were still at Albanus's party when the commissatio started, when your age precluded you," I said.

He jutted out his square chin and gazed at me imperiously. "I was not aware that I was answerable to *you*, Valerius, in any circumstances."

Translation: *Don't you know who I am?*

313

"Quite so, Galerius Nepos," I intoned, "However—"

At that moment, a massive cheer broke out in the Forum: Nero had appeared above us on the steps of the Curia. We couldn't see him from where we were, packed in like sardines somewhere towards the bottom of the steps, but the sound was unmistakable. It hit us like a wave. So did the Praetorians, who began to forge their way down the steps. Someone was jostled into me, and I almost lost my footing.

"Galerius Nepos," I attempted again and had to stop because of the deafening noise that echoed around the entire Forum. It subsided a little, and I made another attempt. "Galerius—"

The crowd cheered again, and silver shone in the sun like rain above our heads. Nero was doing his favourite trick of tossing coins into the crowd and watching to see if anyone was proud enough to resist. The slaves and the plebs and the equites loved it, and the old patricians watched them scramble for the silver with jealous eyes. If there was one thing the sour old senators didn't approve of in our emperors it was a sense of mischievous humour, most often because we patricians were the target.

Galerius Nepos's mouth tightened into a tight line. "The slaves are mistaken. I left immediately after the commissatio was announced. I left with several other men, so perhaps the slaves did not notice me."

I doubted that. Galerius Nepos was always noticed. It was his job. Next to Claudius Rufanus, he would have been the most noble of the assembled patricians at the party that night. The slaves, mistaken? In accordance with the law, those slaves had been tortured for their testimony, and it wasn't the sort of mild torture I'd seen earlier that morning at the vigiles' excubitorium.

I doubted it, but I couldn't stake the investigation on it. Because the slaves had also been drunk.

"You served in the Third Gallica, sir, is that right?" Atreus asked suddenly.

Nepos frowned slightly as though the question had no more relevance to him than the last one. "You will excuse me now."

He waded back through the sea of white-clad senators before I could think of anything to say to stop him. I exchanged a frustrated look with

Atreus.

The shifting attention of the crowd pointed to some activity in the direction of the Temple of Venus. I looked out over the sea of people and saw a litter being carried along. Word was moving ahead of it, rippling through the crowd. People were turning from Nero's shower of coins to the next distraction. The Praetorians, sensing the shift of the crowd, circled protectively around the young emperor as he stood on the Curia steps.

"What is it now?" someone behind me asked in the peevish tone of a man who just wanted to get home for lunch.

A litter forced its way through the crowd towards the immovable wall of Praetorians. Their centurion was speaking to Nero, gesturing towards the oncoming litter. The litter was set down, the curtains drawn back, and a woman emerged. Everyone knew her face. She was the most famous woman in the world: Agrippina the Younger, mother of the emperor, Nero.

The crowd cheered her.

She was still a beautiful woman. She had retained her figure. She had an oval face, high cheekbones, and wide, intelligent eyes. She looked serene, but she'd spent her entire life keeping her thoughts from showing on her face. She was the product of generations of Julio-Claudian intrigue. She was the daughter of the celebrated hero Germanicus, assassinated by his uncle Tiberus. She had been married at thirteen to her first husband, Nero's father. That same year, Tiberius had her mother and two of her brothers exiled and starved to death. It was a lesson in politics and in survival that Agrippina the Younger would not forget. Her brother Caligula survived the purge and became Emperor and had elevated his sisters to greatness. Agrippina was married twice more to wealthy, influential men, and their deaths increased both her own wealth and influence. She became truly powerful. She got rid of her rivals and her enemies and then made her most audacious move: she married her own uncle, the easily manipulated Claudius, and had him adopt Nero as his heir. She was ambitious, ruthless, and single-minded, but everything she had done was for one specific purpose: to make her son the Emperor of Rome. She had triumphed, and then he had rejected her. It must have stung, but she gave no sign of it today. She looked wise and gentle, and she entered the Forum as a supplicant, and maybe she really was a spent force, but no one who knew her history would bet on it.

We were watching a play that had been staged as carefully as anything the Theatre of Marcellus had ever produced. Nero appeared caught off guard, but he knew as well as his mother how to manipulate an audience. Because she might have been ruthless and ambitious, and everyone might have known it, but that day she was a poor mother, unjustly wronged by rumour, seeking a reconciliation with her beloved son. The entire production was being played out directly below the steps of the Curia. That couldn't have been an accident either. Agrippina wanted the senators to bear witness.

Nero's Praetorians spread out, holding the crowd back. Agrippina, accompanied by her maidservants, moved through the corridor of their shields. She was dressed modestly, almost austerely, in shades of green and grey. Her palla was drawn up over her hair, but not enough that it hid her hairstyle. She wore her hair pulled back into a single bun encircled by braids. She had eschewed fashion for tradition, every inch the Roman matron today.

She fell to her knees and held out her hands to her son. The sunlight gleamed on a simple silver bracelet around her wrist. And Nero, because he couldn't do anything else, took her hands, drew her to her feet, and embraced her. It was a happy ending, and the crowd loved it.

"There!" someone exclaimed from a step or two behind me. "I told you so!"

I twisted my head to find the source of the familiar voice and found myself staring at the jovial, bearded face of Paulinus, my erstwhile dining companion from the night of Albanus's party. And Nepos was standing right beside him. Nepos saw me looking, scowled, and dragged Paulinus back up the steps.

"Did you hear that?" I asked Atreus.

"What does it mean?"

"I have no idea."

The show was over at last. The crowd was thinning, and the senators were moving down the steps. I wanted to get out of the sun.

"It's lunchtime, Atreus," I told him. "Let's go."

* * *

We lunched in a caupona close to the Forum. It was busy, but the service was prompt, and the food was good. After doing a quick survey of what the regulars were eating, I settled at last on a ham omelette, and discovered when it arrived that it was almost as big as my head. It was tasty as well, which accounted for the line-up at the counter. Atreus munched slowly on a stuffed vine leaf. He was quieter than I had known him, and he'd always been taciturn. He seemed abstracted as he ate, abstracted enough to throw a few coins down on the table without realising that I'd already paid.

"Atreus," I said and had to repeat myself. "Atreus!"

"Sir?" he asked.

I gestured to his coins, scattered unevenly next to mine.

Atreus shook his head, smiled ruefully, and scooped his coins back up again. "Thank you."

"Are you alright?" I asked him. Maybe he'd got a knock on the head last night that was coming back to haunt him.

"Yes, sir," he said.

"Ready?" I asked him.

Atreus secreted his coins. "Yes, sir," he said. "I think it's time we talked to a friendlier face."

"Paulinus?" I asked.

Atreus nodded. "Are you a fan of pankration, sir?"

It seemed like a question that came out of nowhere, but it wasn't. I knew what Atreus was getting at, and it had nothing to do with whether or not I was a fan of that particularly ferocious form of wrestling.

"No holds barred."

"Quite so," said Atreus, and we rose and left the caupona.

It was with some trepidation that I approached the house of Cornelius Paulinus on the Viminal Hill. The last time I had been here, the circumstances were happier: I'd been trying to get the name of that Gaul from

317

dinner so I could sell a useless racehorse at an obscene profit, and Paulinus, always so friendly, had been happy to help. And now? I was uneasy.

The three of us stepped up to the portico. A slave admitted us and led us into the atrium. A few moments later, Paulinus emerged from somewhere in the back of the house.

"Hello again, Valerius!" exclaimed Paulinus, embracing me as though we were brothers. "That was you I saw earlier, wasn't it? How are things?"

"Good, Paulinus," I said. I *liked* Paulinus. "I'm working with Septus Severus now, did you hear?"

"I'm glad you finally got yourself a position," said Paulinus. "How are you finding things?"

"Interesting." I managed a tight smile. "This is Junius Atreus, a vigile. Do you mind if we ask you some questions?"

Paulinus tugged his beard. "Of course. Whatever I can do, Valerius. Come through, won't you?"

Paulinus had been reading in the garden and led us through into the sunlight. He cleared his bench of scrolls and smiled at the two little girls who were chasing one another around the bushes. They shrieked with laughter.

"Girls, go inside," he said, but Paulinus was no authoritative father, and they completely ignored him. "Girls!"

They trailed inside at last.

"My little terrors," said Paulinus proudly. He gestured to the opposite bench, and Atreus and I sat. Juba stood a little way off, but I knew he was attentive.

"I hope your family is well," I said.

"Thank you," said Paulinus. "And yours."

"And have you heard from Caraca?"

Beside me, Atreus was starting to fidget, but I'd always found that it was a good idea to open any conversation with a chatty recollection of favours and familiarity, just so everyone remembered the obligations of friendship later on when it counted.

"I've heard he's extended his stay in the city," said Paulinus. His friendly face split with another grin. "He's also bought a vineyard near Baiae and is hunting around for a villa. The man is desperate to spend his fortune!"

"Who are we to stand in his way?"

"Exactly," Paulinus said and laughed. "But tell me, what's the reason for your visit?"

Well, he started it.

"As you know, I'm investigating the murders of Marcellus Albanus and Claudius Rufanus," I said.

Paulinus looked grave for a moment. "Yes, of course."

"Paulinus," I asked, "you were in the Third Gallica, weren't you?"

"You know I was." Paulinus looked puzzled. "So were most of us there that night." He laughed. "Although we only remember to salute the sun when it's Bacchus we've worshipped first!"

I knew that feeling. "And how did you find the Third Gallica?"

Paulinus looked surprised. "That's a broad question, Valerius. What are you getting at?"

I had always liked that Paulinus got straight to the point.

"Is the Third Gallica corrupt?" I asked him.

For a moment, Paulinus was stunned into silence, and then he rallied, looking from me to Atreus and back again. "I'm sure I don't need to tell you, Valerius, the things that go on in the legions. None of them are squeaky clean, but I wouldn't call it corruption." He knit his brows together. "What have you heard?"

I glanced at Atreus, but there was nothing in his face that warned me to hold back. This was no-holds barred. I said, "I heard there was a silver mine in Syria."

"A *silver mine*?" Paulinus's mouth dropped open. He shook his head. "No, I never heard anything like that. And that's not corruption, that's *treason*. No, it's been twelve years since I was in the Third, and they weren't treasonous. It's rubbish. I think someone's been feeding you lies, Valerius."

"I would have thought it too," I said, "except that Marcellus Albanus made his fortune in the Third Gallica."

Paulinus shook his head. "This is nonsense. I invited you into my home

319

as a friend, Valerius. Because, because you were *his* friend!"

"Don't bring Nasica into this."

At that moment, Atreus leaned forward. "Albanus wasn't the only one who made his fortune in the Third, sir," he said. "There were others. Most of them were probably at his dinner party."

Paulinus narrowed his eyes at the implication. "Are you accusing me of something, vigile?"

"No, sir," said Atreus. "I'm not accusing anyone of anything."

"I'm pleased to hear it," said Paulinus.

There were no holds barred in pankration, but there were a couple of illegal moves, the eye gouge being one of them, and another, had the competitors been clothed, that would be considered definitely below the belt. Atreus employed the equivalent now. He said, in a quiet and authoritative tone, "I have the slave Eburnus."

Paulinus blanched, and, in that moment, I knew.

I knew he was guilty. I knew he was corrupt. I knew he was a traitor. And I regretted it. I really did. I'd liked Paulinus from the very beginning. I'd liked his easygoing attitude, his dirty jokes, his unpretentious house, his cranky brother-in-law, his drunken friends, and his connection with wealthy barbarians. We might have been friends, but he was a traitor.

He tried too late to laugh it off. "What is this man talking about, Valerius?"

"Do you know who killed Albanus and Rufanus?" I asked him.

Paulinus rallied as best he could, but it wasn't enough. "Jupiter, what's this nonsense? You're having a joke with me."

"Oh, no, Paulinus," I said regretfully. "It's not a joke."

A silence fell. I glanced at Atreus, who was watching Paulinus intently, and at Juba, who had moved closer. What either of them thought Paulinus was capable of, I didn't want to guess. I still thought I knew him better than that. This was Paulinus. He was almost my friend.

Paulinus stared off into the distance for a moment. "They teach you loyalty in the legions, Valerius. Remember that?"

"Yes."

"I didn't kill them," said Paulinus. "They were my brothers."

"They were traitors," said Atreus.

Paulinus was shaken, but he wasn't defeated. His slight regretful smile told us that he wasn't going to confirm anything for us. We were still fighting uphill. "It doesn't matter what you think you know," he said at last. "It doesn't matter who you have. We are untouchable."

I raised my eyebrows at that. "Are you really? Albanus and Rufanus might disagree with that."

"I cannot speak to that, Valerius." Paulinus passed his hand briefly in front of his eyes. "I would thank you to leave me now. I have some matters that need my attention. I await our next meeting."

I rose.

"My regards to your family," he said.

"And yours," I said.

We patricians never neglected our manners. Treason? Murder? Corruption? Certainly, but a lack of manners was inexcusable.

We left him sitting in the sunlit garden.

* * *

It was all I could do not to break into a run as soon as we were back in the street. After last night and our close call on the rooftop of the Aventine Collegium, I was wary. I was afraid of an ambush. We'd just poked a stick into the hornet's nest that was the Third Gallica, and we'd stirred it. As we walked away from the house, I looked back over my shoulder. I almost tripped over the gutter, but Juba steered me right.

"I can't believe Paulinus fell for that!" I exclaimed. "I can't believe he thinks we have Eburnus!"

"We had to know," said Atreus, giving me a sidelong look. "We had to force him to show his guilt."

"Sure," I said, "except that now he knows exactly how much we know."

"Everything is a gamble, sir."

"I'll feel better once we're home," I muttered, twisting my head again to make sure we weren't being followed. We turned down a side street.

The side street was a quiet one, narrow and shaded, and full of private homes. There was a constant trickle of pedestrian traffic, but there were no temples, public gardens, or shopfronts in the immediate vicinity to bring in the unwashed masses. We saw slaves lugging shopping, schoolboys accompanied by their tutors, the sedan chairs and litters of residents being manoeuvred into the back doors of wealthy homes, and messengers trotting up and down the incline of the street.

"But if they're untouchable," Atreus said, "why were they trying so hard to get Eburnus back?"

Something clicked in the back of my mind suddenly. "*Jupiter!* Because they couldn't be sure, not lately. Not until today!"

"Sir?" Atreus asked.

"The Forum," I said before I couldn't make myself heard anymore.

Our footsteps had brought us to a raucous gaggle of slave women who had stopped in the street to gossip and cackle. There must have been at least a dozen of them, each of them competing to be heard, and they were blocking the narrow street with their baskets and their expansive backsides. We slowed to pass them. As we did, a posticum door onto the street opened, and a youth stepped out right into the middle of the women. He tried to squeeze between a very rotund pair of them.

"Oh!" one of them exclaimed. "Come back here and give me another feel, you naughty boy! You don't get away that easily!"

She reached out and slapped him on the backside. All of the women shrieked with laughter, and the boy cast them an embarrassed smile. He was young, dark-haired, and dusky-skinned, and he had a lazy eye. I knew him.

Follow it all the way to the top, Anicetus had told Tigellinus to tell us, and here was a new thread to tug. Because the slave with the lazy eye didn't belong to Paulinus, and I no longer believed in coincidences.

I *knew* that slave, and my blood ran cold.

He didn't notice us. Flushed with shame, the boy picked up his pace. He didn't look back as he hurried away towards the main street.

"Excuse me, ladies," I said, just to be sure of what I thought I already knew.

322

"Whose back door is this?"

One of them glanced at the posticum door the youth had just left. "This is Cornelius Paulinus's house, sir."

And then, just as we were digesting what the slave boy's presence meant, four other men stepped out of Paulinus's posticum door with cudgels in their hands and murder in their eyes.

Great.

Chapter Eighteen

N ot for the first time in my life—Hades, not even for the first time this week—I cursed that law that forbade me to carry my sword in public. I cursed myself even more for not disregarding it. And then, since there was nowhere to run in this narrow street except straight into the gaggle of cacking slave women, that's exactly what I did.

"Ladies," I said, "I have a purse full of coins and a delicate skull that I'd prefer remain intact. And those men back there definitely mean to crack it open."

The women were as raucous and sharp-eyed as hens, and in moments Juba and Atreus, and I were being bustled down the alley, hemmed in on all sides. I didn't look back to see if we were being followed—of course we were. Even if Paulinus's slaves hadn't seen us get subsumed into the flock like lost little chicks, given that we didn't have wings, there was nowhere else we could have gone.

Still, I appreciated the way the women were so eager to involve themselves. I didn't appreciate the pinch to the arse I got from at least two of them— or perhaps just one who liked it so much she did it a second time—but I definitely preferred that kind of mistreatment to the sort Paulinus's slaves were obviously looking to dish out.

We were carried along with the women to the end of the narrow street and deposited onto a wider one. This one, down the slope of the hill, was a busy intersection full of shopfronts. I emptied my purse into the hands of one of the women, and then Juba, Atreus, and I darted into the nearest doorway.

The stench of it gave it away as an olive oil shop even before my eyes had adjusted to the comparative darkness inside.

Atreus and I stood, backs against the wall on one side of the doorway. Juba stood on the other. I could still hear the cackling women outside, their voices growing fainter as they moved away, and I hoped they were drawing our pursuers with them.

And then, suddenly, I hoped that they weren't, because if the men failed to find us in the street, where would they go next? To my house on the Caelian Hill? To my *family*?

I jolted forward, and Atreus pulled me back. "No," he said. "No." And then, to the woman behind the counter who looked as though she was about to call for help: "A moment, please. We mean you no trouble."

I grabbed Atreus's tunic, pulling him around to face me. "My *family*."

"Shut up," he said, pushing me back against the wall and crowding me in. He pressed his forearm across my collarbones to hold me there. "Just *shut up*."

I still had a fistful of his tunic, and my grip on it tightened as I heard a shout from outside and a man's voice call, "This way!"

Our pursuers? Possibly. Knowing our luck, fucking *inevitably*.

Atreus's stubble scraped my jaw as he leaned in. "Quiet," he whispered in my ear.

I stared over his shoulder at the woman behind the counter. She stared back at me, suspicious and afraid. Astute enough to know we'd brought some bullshit to her doorstep and clearly unsure if we were the threat or the men outside were.

I nodded and squeezed my eyes shut.

Jupiter Best and Greatest, I hadn't been this afraid even on the rooftop of the warehouse with Bano. Because blind fool that I was, for the first time, it had occurred to me that there was more at stake here than my life. These were not honourable men. If they went to my house looking for me and found my family instead, would anything stop them?

I thought of my house, sunlight filtering into the atrium, and the sounds of my wife and sister laughing. I thought of Mouse and his little toy centurion.

I thought of Julia, who deserved the chance to prove me wrong by growing into a woman as clever and discreet as her mother. I thought of the slaves, many of whom I'd known since childhood. I even thought of Hursa, who was an idiot, but loved my terrible jokes.

I opened my eyes and met Atreus's sombre gaze and thought of little Lucilla too.

Outside, a man called: "Here! Over here!"

The woman stepped around the counter and closed the distance between us. "There's a back door," she whispered and pointed.

"Thank you." I forced the words out past the ache in my throat.

Atreus pulled me toward the counter. Juba was already there, tugging a greasy curtain out of the way to reveal a short, narrow passageway with sunlight at the end of it. We ducked into it, and Atreus drew the curtain just as I heard the woman say, her tone aggrieved, "There's nobody come in here! Get out if you aren't buying!"

We didn't wait to listen to see if they believed her or not.

We burst out the back door into a dusty little yard full of togas slung up on lines to dry in the late afternoon sunlight. The place stank of damp wool, mud, and stale urine. A boy trampling the latest load of laundry in a tub full of old piss stared at us.

We cut through the yard into the interior of the laundry that backed onto the oil shop. Juba checked the street was clear while Atreus and I ignored the laundress, who attempted to harangue us about trespassing.

"We need to stop this," I said.

Atreus nodded, grim-faced.

The boy from the yard had followed us inside. I beckoned him closer. "I need you to take a message to my house on the Caelian Hill. The house of Aemilius Valerius." I gave him the directions. "You must speak to—to anyone but the door porter, yes?" I didn't trust Hursa not to mess it up. "Tell them not to open the door to anyone, do you understand? Not until I am home again. And I need you to run there as fast as you can."

"Yes, sir," the boy said.

I felt at my belt for my purse, remembering too late that I'd already emptied it. I drew a breath and twisted the gold ring off my finger. I held it up, and the boy's eyes widened. Even the laundress was shocked into silence.

"As fast as you can," I said again.

The boy's eyes were as wide as dinner plates. "Yes, sir!" He scarpered out the door, ducking past Juba.

"It's clear, sir," Juba said.

"Good," I said. "Because this ends now."

Chapter Nineteen

The Palatine Hill was the most prestigious in all of Rome. We headed along the Via Sacra and then turned onto the Clivus Palatinus and began to trudge up the hill. The views from the Palatine were expansive; below us, we could see the Circus Maximus, the massive construction site where Nero was building himself a new palace, and the muddy Tiber winding its way through the city. I cast a sideways glance at Atreus. Was it reason leading us now, or was it desperation? Whichever it was, I felt duty-bound to follow.

Cool breezes chased us up the hill, toying with the leaves and the dust on the street.

Nero lived on the Palatine. So, presumably, did his spy Anicetus. The entire state machine worked away here, building an empire from inside the hive of interconnected buildings that made up the imperial estate of the Palatine. But there were other houses here, too, older, still privately owned, and I had been a guest at one of them many times before. The door slave knew me of old. He admitted us quietly and led us inside to the sitting room where our host was waiting.

His milky old eyes widened when he saw me, and he smiled. He didn't rise from his seat. He couldn't. "Hello, Valerius."

"Macrinus," I said.

"And Junius Atreus," said Macrinus in his reed-thin voice.

"Sir," said Atreus.

I glanced at Juba. Juba glanced at me. The three of us approached the couch where the old man sat still, picking fussily over the remains of a meal. The attendant with the lazy eye was already back from his errand to Paulinus's house, waiting on his master.

"Hello again," I said, and the youth looked startled.

Atreus didn't waste time with preliminaries: "Probus Macrinus," he said, "you are a murderer."

The accusation was not as dramatic as Atreus may have hoped. The old man cupped a hand behind his ear. "Eh?"

Atreus repeated loudly and clearly: "You are a murderer."

"But I am an old man," said Macrinus in a wheedling tone. He gazed at us through rheumy eyes and rested his trembling hands in his lap.

Atreus folded his arms across his chest. "Exactly, sir. You are a man who needs help to stand up from his chair, and you told us that you saw yourself out at Albanus's party. All the guests were drunk. All the slaves were drunk. Who else but an old man would have needed two litter bearers to enter the house when the party was over?"

Only the old invalid Macrinus. I looked over at him. "Is it true?"

The sound of the breath escaping his body was like the rattle of dry leaves. "Yes."

I was shocked. Not only because Macrinus had admitted his guilt, but because, finally, Atreus was right.

"Why?" I asked him. "What did Albanus and Rufanus do to you?"

The old man closed his eyes and didn't answer.

Atreus narrowed his. "Macrinus was in the Third Gallica. Do you remember what the legionary Rubio said? In the Third Gallica, the corruption was as old as saluting the sun. His glory days might be long behind him, but Macrinus was one of them."

Macrinus managed a slight smile.

Atreus was Aventine born and bred. He could pick a gangster, even if he was swaddled in the folds of an off-white toga hemmed with the broad purple stripe of a senator and sitting in a majestic old house on the Palatine Hill. Atreus looked at the old man with his head on an angle. "No, not just one of them. One of the first. Is that right, sir?"

Macrinus waved the question away with a trembling hand. He wasn't going to answer that. He didn't have to.

"We saw your slave leaving Paulinus's house," I said. "You're pulling all their strings, aren't you? You have been for years. What happened with the Third?"

"They were too greedy," Macrinus said at last. He wheezed. "A silver mine! It was too much, and I warned them against it. You can't keep a silver mine a secret forever."

"Maybe you can," I said, "if you have the right friends."

Macrinus smiled at my understanding. "Oh yes, the right friends are crucial, and there was a time we had one."

I looked up at the rose on the ceiling. I knew why the ex-tribunes of the Third Gallica had thought they were untouchable. They had made a deal with a viper. Follow it to the top, Anicetus had said, and it went higher than I ever would have guessed at the beginning.

"And did your friend betray you, Macrinus?"

"Oh, no," said Macrinus. "Oh, no. She was betrayed."

"Of course, she was," I said, recalling the production we'd witnessed in the Forum. "She was betrayed by her son. Nero tried to free himself from his mother's influence before she was ready to let him go. She might have been able to protect the Third in the past, from Caligula and from Claudius, but not from Nero. I saw how relieved Paulinus looked today in the Forum, but it wasn't a true reconciliation. It was only a charade. Agrippina is no longer in charge."

Macrinus blinked his watery eyes. "Yes. She can no longer protect them from that vile palace spy Anicetus, slinking around the city like a feral dog! She can no longer even protect herself." He trailed off for a moment, and inspected his frail, wrinkled hands. Maybe he was contemplating the passage of time and his own lost youth. Or maybe the lost youth of somebody else. His voice became plaintive. "Oh, we made her rich. We channelled so much her way that there was no question her son would one day become emperor."

"And the tribunes of the Third?" I asked him.

"They became cowards," grizzled Macrinus. "They were afraid that she could no longer protect us. They were despicable. This, all of this, this *excess* was necessary. I am old, Valerius."

I anticipated the refrain: "You're putting your affairs in order."

It was the same thing he said whenever he sent a gift to Octavia.

Macrinus nodded. "Yes, I am putting my affairs in order. It is the proper thing to do, for Marcus."

I was at a loss. "For Nasica? I don't understand."

"Marcus is dead! They deserved to die as well!" The spite in his voice gave it sudden strength.

"Nasica made a choice," I said. "He made a choice, and he accepted the consequences."

"They still spit on his memory!" Macrinus wheezed. His eyes watered. "They spit on *my* legacy! He was a good boy!"

He looked at me then, waiting for me to agree, and I couldn't bring myself to do it. They were traitors, every one of them. "What went wrong?" I asked him.

Macrinus hunched forward into shadow. The skin stretched across his skull, and I saw a death's-head. "Marcus was loyal to me, to the Third, but they were so frightened of their own shadows! They thought that there was a traitor in our midst. They thought it was my Marcus, and they told him to fall on his sword!"

I felt a chill. "They told him to do that?"

"I overheard them at Albanus's party," said Macrinus. He sprayed spittle as he spoke. "Albanus and Rufanus were talking about him, about what happened, about how they made my boy *go away*."

Even I felt the sting of that, and I had mixed feelings towards Nasica.

"I couldn't allow them to live. All of my ambition," said Macrinus helplessly. "All of my fortune. It was all for him."

I wished I could believe that, but I wasn't that naïve. Maybe Macrinus had convinced himself it was the truth, but it must have been what all traitors told themselves: *I'm not doing this for me. I'm doing this for you.* This old neighbourhood had heard it a hundred times before and from far better men than Probus Macrinus.

"You heard them talking," said Atreus. "Your litter bearers came inside to fetch you, and then what? You confronted Albanus?"

Macrinus straightened up again. "Yes."

His watery old eyes focussed on something behind us. I looked around and saw four large men enter the room. Their heads were shaved and tattooed with their master's abbreviated name: *Pr MACR*. The litter bearers.

Atreus ignored them. His attention was focussed entirely on Macrinus. "And Claudius Rufanus? He must have already left that night, but you knew enough about his personal habits to know exactly where to find him later, unprotected. Your men killed him and Sylvia."

"He was a coward," wheezed Macrinus. "A coward and a traitor to the Third."

I thought of how I had seen Sylvia lying on the floor, her neck snapped. I wondered which of the four men behind us had been the one. The hair on the back of my neck stood up. I wasn't afraid, though. I was calm, exactly as calm as I had been on the warehouse roof when I'd faced Bano's henchmen. I felt the same sense of inevitability. Fear was pointless now.

"But your silver mine wasn't new," Atreus said. "The legionary we spoke to said it was older than Albanus's service, at least. What changed?"

"Everything changed," Macrinus said bitterly. "When Agrippina could no longer protect us, it was time to walk away. It was too dangerous to keep it operating with Anicetus sniffing around our business. I told them so, but they refused. And Marcus died because they were too greedy to stop and too paranoid to know he would never betray us!"

"All of this," Atreus said thoughtfully, "for greed and revenge."

Macrinus pursed his thin lips.

"They had a choice," I reminded Atreus. "Everybody has a choice."

Probus Macrinus looked at me expectantly.

"You've got a choice as well, Macrinus," I said. I gave him a moment to consider that and then asked, "Do you remember where you keep your gladius?"

Macrinus's face was a mask of scorn. "Why would I kill myself, Valerius?"

"I assume you would prefer it to the Tullianum," I countered and waited for the predictable threat.

"And do you also assume I'll just let you walk out of here?" Macrinus asked me, and a cruel smile split his haggard face.

Behind me, one of the litter bearers chortled.

"The other day, you gave my sister a silver bracelet," I reminded the old man. "It was a gift from Mark Antony to your grandmother. Octavia is wearing it again today. She likes it. It pleases her to think that even ruthless men like Mark Antony have secret hearts."

Macrinus didn't say anything.

I shifted my weight to my other foot. "What is your legacy, Macrinus? A legacy of corruption and treason, and Nasica inherited it right from you. It killed him. If it was to kill me as well, I think it would ruin Octavia."

He regarded me cautiously, but I wasn't afraid of him. I knew I was right. Nasica's death had broken Octavia's heart, and the old man had always loved her. Macrinus wouldn't do it to her again.

"Octavia," the old man murmured and then sighed.

"You can still have your revenge," Atreus told him.

He coughed dryly. "How's that?"

"Write it all down," Atreus said. "A list of the Third Gallica's income. A list of their names and that of their patrons. Betray them all to the palace for what they made Nasica do."

"There is still time to set your affairs in order," I told him. "It is the right thing to do."

It still could have gone either way, but Macrinus, like he always said, was too old and too tired. It was a grave ritual. The slave was sent for paper and ink, and Macrinus began to write, scratching away with a palsied hand. Ink flicked up onto his wrinkled flesh and the sleeve of his tunic. It was interminable. It might have been for as long as half an hour that we stood in silence and waited.

When Macrinus was finished, Atreus stepped forward to collect the list. He leaned down close to the old man's head and said something into his ear. I wasn't near enough to hear it, but something almost like a gentle smile settled for a moment on the old man's face and then vanished again.

333

"Fetch my gladius," Macrinus wheezed to his attendant, and the fearful slave obeyed. Again, we waited, listening for the sounds of the youth's feet on the tiles. At last, he reappeared, holding the weapon at arm's length. Macrinus reached out a thin, sinewy arm to take it. He seemed to have trouble lifting its weight. His swollen fingers closed around the hilt at long last. And we weren't in the clear yet.

"Well then," said Macrinus at last. "Hail and farewell."

"Hail and farewell," I said woodenly, wondering how I was going to explain this to Octavia.

Macrinus waved a spindly hand at the litter bearers. "Let them pass."

They might have been litter bearers, but they weren't entirely stupid. They didn't move.

"Let them pass, I said," Macrinus grumbled.

The four of them looked at the three of us.

"I don't think your dogs are on as tight a leash as you thought, Macrinus," I told him.

"Let them pass!" Macrinus wheezed, and they ignored him.

Their master had ordered the litter bearers to kill, but that didn't make them any less culpable. They were fodder for the arena, and they knew it.

Juba was as big as them, but he was one against four. Atreus appeared to be unarmed, the idiot. I definitely was. Who walked into a confrontation with a murderer without a weapon? We were hopeless. I caught Atreus's eye as we had exactly the same thought—the gladius. I reached for it first, and Macrinus opened up his trembling fist to let me take it. Atreus's gaze fell on the remains of Macrinus's lunch and the small cheese knife that was resting on the platter. It was better than nothing, if only by a slim margin.

"Leave them!" Macrinus cried out weakly to his litter bearers. "I said to let them pass!"

Juba looked around the room for a weapon. There wasn't much that I could see, but Juba was nothing if not creative. There was a brazier beside Macrinus's couch, unlit on this warm day. Juba picked it up as though it weighed nothing and held it ready to swing, like a man in a wine shop brawl armed with a barstool. Jupiter, he scared me. I was glad he was on our side.

The lazy-eyed slave squealed and retreated to a corner as the four litter bearers approached us menacingly. Well, as the saying went, either to conquer or to die.

The litter bearers, unarmed except for their muscles—muscles that had snapped Sylvia's neck without much effort—weren't too threatened by us. They thought they had us on the back foot. What these boys didn't know was that between the three of us, we'd defeated Bano and his henchmen and dispatched them to the underworld. And the litter bearers were big and they were muscular, but they weren't street fighters like Bano and his men. They weren't really fighters at all. They moved together like pack animals while Atreus, Juba, and I separated to give ourselves some room to manoeuvre.

One of the litter bearers advanced too far in front of his fellows. Juba swung and took him out with the brazier. It clanged against his thick skull, and he crumpled to the floor with a howl.

I took out the one advancing on me with my patented reach-and-spin manoeuvre, perfected that night on the warehouse roof, slicing neatly across the litter bearer's throat even as he stepped towards me. It was good luck for me and bad luck for him that Macrinus kept his gladius sharp. The youth cowering in the corner screamed.

I wasn't sure what Atreus did with the cheese knife, but the important thing was he tried.

Juba, swinging the brazier threateningly, moved in front of us like a particularly nasty siege engine. The sort of thing that could take down fortified walls. He had a murderous look in his eye.

With one of the litter bearers lying on the floor clutching at his bloody throat uselessly and another lying on the floor still howling and trying to hold back the stream of blood issuing from his head, the other two lost heart. They turned tail and fled the room. They were probably trying to climb the back wall to freedom by the time we'd caught our breath again.

Juba dropped the brazier to the floor with a crash. The echoes took a long time to die away.

In the corner, the slave had his eyes squeezed shut. He was rocking back and forth, hugging his knees. The poor thing probably thought he was next.

I wiped the gladius on the tunic of the dead litter bearer and presented it back to Macrinus. The old man was pale and trembling and wide-eyed. Under his own roof, the bloodshed frightened him. After all of that, he was a hypocrite as well.

"Hail and farewell," I said again, contemptuously this time, and Macrinus couldn't bring himself to look me in the eye.

After that, we left, and nobody stopped us from going.

* * *

"What did you say to Macrinus?" I asked Atreus as we stepped outside, leaving bloody footprints in the shade of the portico. "When you whispered to him?"

"'I stand in front, and I stand fast.'"

I raised my eyebrows.

Atreus smiled slightly. "It's the unofficial motto of the Third Gallica, sir."

"Now, how do you know that?" I asked as the sunlight hit my face.

"I've done my research."

A nondescript middle-aged man stood in the sunny street. He was dressed in a russet tunic and a hat and looked for all the world like a tourist meandering along waiting to get mugged. There was nothing remarkable about him, and I doubt I would have noticed him except he was waiting directly outside Macrinus's portico. Then I saw it was Anicetus, ex-slave, head of the fleet at Misenum, and imperial spy. I wondered how long he'd been following us. Since I'd gone to the palace asking for him? Since before then?

He stepped towards us. "Good day, Quintus Aemilius."

"Anicetus."

"What's that you have there?" Anicetus asked Atreus.

"His confession, sir," said Atreus, holding it out.

"Is it everything?" Anicetus asked, tucking the scroll inside the sleeve of his tunic. He looked us up and down curiously. We were sweaty, unkempt, and all three of us had been caught in the shower of blood that had burst forth from the litter bearer's carotid artery. Arterial blood seemed unnecessarily scarlet.

"Yes, sir," said Atreus.

The spy looked at us carefully. "Does it mention *her* name?"

"It does," I said, and the spy inclined his head. The power struggle between a youth and his mother that had begun the day that Nero put on the purple had ended here, outside the private home of an old man on the Palatine Hill. We'd just handed Anicetus everything Nero needed to be rid of his mother.

Anicetus's pale gaze flicked towards the house and back to Atreus.

"He was alive," Atreus said. "When we left him."

We stood for a moment in the silence and let time pass. I believe we all felt the weight of it. How long would it take for a man as old and weak as Macrinus to bleed out?

It wasn't quite a smile, but Anicetus quirked his mouth. At last, he said, "It's a nice day for a walk. I might go around the block once more."

"Enjoy your stroll, sir," Atreus said.

"This goes no further, of course," Anicetus said.

"Of course," I said.

We were about to continue on our way when Anicetus plucked at the sleeve of my tunic. "Valerius?"

"Yes?" I asked him warily.

"Please give your sister my regards."

"My sister?" It didn't sound like a threat—not that a man like Anicetus needed to spell a threat out plainly for it to be heard and understood. And yet, it didn't sound like one.

"Octavia Junilla remains in my prayers," said Anicetus with a faint smile. He adjusted the angle of his hat, smiled politely, and walked away down the hill.

* * *

"Where is Octavia?" I asked Hursa when we arrived home and then proceeded to check every single room of the house. In my tablinum we startled Cretes. In my kitchen, we almost wore a jug of garum sauce. In the informal triclinium we discovered Mouse staging a battle on the couches while Perella egged him on. In the formal triclinium we discovered Julia snoring like a piglet on a couch. In the sitting room, we found Fulvia having her eyebrows plucked.

"Quintus!" she exclaimed, sitting up too quickly. "Ow! Quintus, is that *blood* on you?"

"It's not mine, I promise."

Atreus and I headed up the stairs to Octavia's room. We entered to discover her lying on her stomach on her bed. The slave Larius was reading to her.

Octavia rose. "Is that blood, Quintus? Are you alright?"

I blurted it out: "Macrinus is dead."

"Oh." Octavia sat on the end of her bed and toyed thoughtfully with her silver bracelet. "It's over, then."

I exchanged a look with Atreus. It was not the reaction I had expected. "Yes, Macrinus killed Albanus and Rufanus, at least his bodyguards did."

"Oh," said Octavia.

"Do you want to know why he killed them?" I asked her.

My sister folded her hands in her lap. "Is it about Marcus's involvement in the treason of the Third Gallica?"

I gaped. "You know about that?"

"Of course," said Octavia. "Marcus and I had no secrets."

I exchanged a startled look with Atreus. "Nasica *told* you what he was up to?"

"Yes," said Octavia. "He felt I had a right to know."

"How very modern of him," I managed. I glanced back at the door and saw Fulvia standing there, pale-faced. She was frozen to the spot.

"Don't be so indignant, Quintus," said Octavia. She twisted the bracelet around her wrist again. "Marcus wasn't a traitor. He was a spy. He was recruited by Anicetus before he even left Rome for the Third Gallica."

I was stunned. I'd spent the last few months hating Marcus Decius Nasica, really hating him.

"He *was* the spy," said Atreus. "Macrinus didn't believe it."

"He wouldn't," said Octavia. "Not in a thousand years, the poor thing. But the rest of them weren't as trusting, hence our divorce. Marcus wanted to keep me *safe*." She said the word as though it was somehow contemptible.

"Macrinus said they told him to fall on his sword," I said.

Octavia looked at her hands. "He was mistaken. Marcus wasn't given a choice. They killed him."

"*What?* How can you know that?"

Atreus folded his arms over his chest. "I suspect that Eburnus can tell us, sir."

I looked at him blankly for a moment.

Then the slave Larius suddenly spoke, and, for the first time since I'd known him, he wasn't afraid to look me in the face. "I saw it. I saw Rufanus and Albanus kill my master."

"Eburnus," I said as it all fell into place. The fearful slave my sister brought home on the day her ex-husband died. *Nasica's* slave. And I had never even suspected it, not when Paulinus had quizzed Hursa about whether I owned a young secretary, not when Larius had avoided every occasion where he might have had to face a man who could have recognised him, and not even when that little rat Colchus—who had been paid to track down Eburnus—had broken into my house.

"Yes," said Octavia. She was holding her composure with difficulty, too proud to let it slip. Her hands lay in her lap, and she turned a ring around and around on her thumb. She was pale. "That's the name they knew him by."

"Octavia, how could you keep this to yourself?"

Octavia adjusted an earring and then turned to face me. "I couldn't tell you, Quintus. I'm sorry."

Larius reached out and touched her forearm. I bristled at the touch.

Octavia recovered herself. "I had to keep it to myself. I swore that to Anicetus."

"Yes," I said. "How long have you and Anicetus been on friendly terms?"

"I went to his house," Octavia said, "the morning after Marcus died, knowing that's where Larius would have run. I had promised Marcus I would try to keep Larius safe if anything were to happen."

"You should have *told* me, Octavia."

"I couldn't!" Octavia said. "I swore I wouldn't."

"And if Anicetus *knew*," Atreus said, "if he knew everything, then why was nothing done?"

It dawned on me. "But the palace *had* taken steps to reign in the Third. They sent Corbulo to take command of the legion."

Atreus frowned. "But what about the ex-tribunes here in Rome? Why weren't they tried as traitors?"

"That could never happen," said Octavia. She shook her head at his naivety. "Firstly, to publicly accuse a bunch of tribunes and ex-tribunes of a serving legion might cause a mutiny. And without any proof except the word of a slave? Who would believe it? His testimony would be useless, and I would never have allowed him to give it. He was Marcus's friend."

I sighed.

"I made a promise to Marcus," Octavia said. "I promised him that I would keep Larius safe. Do you know how they obtain lawful testimony from slaves, Quintus? I know that you do, Atreus."

Atreus couldn't look her in the eye.

"Anicetus owed me that much," said Octavia. "Besides, it was never the Third Gallica that Anicetus really wanted. They were only a means to an end."

"He's got what he wants now," I said. "Macrinus wrote a confession that named Agrippina."

"I hope he gets his chance to use it," said Octavia. "She is a dangerous woman, and she still has friends in the palace."

"You should have told me, Octavia," I said.

"I made a promise," my sister replied, as though that settled the matter. I had once wondered what sort of wife she had been to Nasica. I knew now.

Fulvia came forward into the room and sat beside Octavia on the bed.

340

Their fingers entwined. Octavia's deception had been laid bare, and Fulvia forgave her for it, just like that. Octavia had been lying to us for months. Everything she had said about Nasica, about the divorce and his death, had been a lie of omission. And I had believed it, because it had never even occurred to me that Octavia would try to deceive me. I envied Fulvia her generous spirit. I could hardly reconcile this guileful woman with the forthright girl I'd known her entire life.

"I think," said Octavia at last, "that it all started out differently. I think that the intentions of the tribunes must have been honourable, at least in the beginning."

Just like she thought that Mark Antony's bracelet was a love token and not a piece of metal, just shiny enough to get a woman to open her legs for a man whose greatest ambition had been to screw his way through the entire republic. After all this, Octavia still thought the best of everyone. I looked at her solemn face and wondered how that was even possible.

* * *

We had a late lunch that day, or an early dinner. I wasn't even sure that anyone felt like eating, but we did all the same. We had discovered the truth, and it wasn't as jubilant an occasion as I had fancifully imagined. There was no drunken revelry, no impromptu dancing, and not even any broad congratulatory smiles. I ate and thought of Nasica. I had hated him, and I regretted that now. I tried to remember him before the betrayal of the divorce and before I thought he was a traitor. I tried to recall his smile, and the sound of his laugh, and the way we sometimes drank too much and talked far into the night.

"Jupiter, Quintus, the things that woman does to me!" he'd exclaimed one night.

"Hey!"

He'd laughed at my outrage. *"You've got a filthy mind. I meant she drives me mad! She's the only woman I've ever known who tells me exactly what she thinks, all of the time."*

"Oh, she does that."

Nasica had smiled. *"I wouldn't change a thing about her."*

There had never been any indication of the weight Nasica must have been carrying around. He had hidden it well from the world, but not from Octavia. Not many men trusted their wives so implicitly, and not many wives would keep a secret like that from their own families.

After we ate, Octavia disappeared, and I went looking for her.

Octavia had never mourned him. How could she? Now, months after the divorce and with the ashes of his funeral pyre long cold, my little sister sat on a shaded bench in the garden and thought of Marcus Decius Nasica. Larius sat at her feet, and in companionable silence, they watched the afternoon wear on into dusk.

I leaned in the peristyle and watched the pair of them and wondered what Nasica had ever done to deserve such loyalty. My household had not protected Octavia from malicious gossip. People had wondered about the divorce, and Octavia had made the mistake of maintaining a dignified silence. Because she didn't blame Nasica in public, the public assumption was that he was blameless, and the fault must have been Octavia's. Those men who'd inquired since about her dowry had even tried to tease the truth out of me: was my sister sterile or a slut? Not knowing, I had been in no position to defend her. But she should have defended herself.

And Larius. They had been slave and master, but also friends. Who were those boys from that old story? Damon and Pythias. If I'm not back, said one, kill my friend instead. I couldn't remember which was which, and it didn't really matter. What mattered was their friendship. There was no coming back from where Nasica had gone, but Larius had remained loyal all the same. The ex-tribunes of the Third Gallica had hired an informer to track him down to prevent him from telling their secrets. He'd seen what they'd done to Nasica, what they intended to do to him, and he'd gone straight to Anicetus, a man who could have tortured him for his testimony. And I'd thought him a timid, fearful slave.

Watching Octavia and Larius sitting together in the shade, I wished I'd known Nasica better. I wished I'd seen the side of him that they both had. I wished he'd trusted me with his secrets. It was apparent now that he was a good man, and even if the truth never came out, at least some of us would remember him that way.

There was a certain sweetness of the spirit in melancholia. I saw it in Octavia and Larius. I felt it in myself. I mourned Nasica as well that afternoon, in my own way. I mourned his passing, because he had been a good man. He had not been as politically great as his great-uncle Macrinus had hoped, but he had been a resolutely good man, and there were fewer of those than triumphal demigods. They were not remembered by the masses, but they were rarer than gold.

I stood in the shade and watched Octavia and Larius sitting there in quiet remembrance of a man they had both loved.

Chapter Twenty

The death of Probus Macrinus was well remarked upon throughout the city, and rumour linked it to the deaths of Marcellus Albanus and Claudius Rufanus. Suddenly, Severus and I were popular again, if only for our uncanny ability to leave a trail of corpses wherever we went. And nobody knew, or would ever know, the exact truth behind their deaths. The palace was keeping a very tight lid on things, either because they didn't want the world to know their grip on the legions was not as tight as it ought to have been, or simply because Nero had no wish to publicly call his mother a traitor, I had no idea. During that summer, however, several very prominent patricians chose to fall on their swords. They had all received messages from the palace announcing that they no longer had the friendship of the emperor. Galerius Nepos and Cornelius Paulinus were among them; all of Nepos's ambitions of a consulship went with him up in smoke. The deaths were not limited to Rome; on the far edges of the empire, the Third Gallica lost many of its serving tribunes to the Parthians. These tribunes had chosen to lead their men into battle against all odds and would be remembered as heroes. Too bad for the legionaries they took with them.

Agrippina the Younger, Nero's mother, officially retired to the coast. I heard a lot of speculation from a lot of different people, but again, nobody knew the truth. Severus and I dined one night at the palace. We shared a couch beside the emperor's, so the gossips knew that we had not failed, even if they could not see exactly how we had succeeded. We weren't entirely sure ourselves, but it was enough that Nero knew our names and called us his friends. I renewed my acquaintance with Tigellinus. I met Burrus, head of the Praetorians, and the philosopher Seneca.

I spoke to Anicetus that night, for a short while, as we paced the tiles of a secluded gallery far away from any eavesdroppers and sycophants.

"The emperor wanted proof," Anicetus told me, "of every allegation. Not just Nasica's testimony, but *proof*."

He said it like it was a vulgar word. Maybe it always had been in his circles, or maybe it was his experience with the Third Gallica talking.

"What he didn't understand was that sometimes there is no such thing as proof. Sometimes, there is only one good man's word. It took Nasica's death for him to see that." Anicetus walked with his hands clasped behind his back. "Our emperor is young. He is not his ancestors. He would not condemn any man on rumour or hearsay. No, that is always a hard lesson to be learned. I cannot fault him for it. What man could contemplate banishing his own mother on less?"

We had reached a marble statue of Augustus, bigger than life. It was difficult to remember that he'd once been a callow youth as well. His cold, handsome face looked too clever for that.

Beside me, Anicetus sighed. "He wanted proof, and the longer Nasica stayed, the more dangerous it became. He was trying to negotiate the labyrinth, and in the end, we had both left it too late."

Anicetus sounded regretful, and I wondered if that was for Nasica or if it was for the investigation.

"Nasica was dead," Anicetus said. He reached up and brushed an imaginary speck of dust from the breastplate of the divine Augustus. "I could not use Eburnus without Nasica, so I allowed your sister to hide him. I owed her, she said, and she was right. When the guilty men started turning up murdered, at least they were reaping what they sowed. I have no doubt that it was one of my own agents, working for Agrippina, who betrayed Nasica. I will find the man."

I knew then that his regret was for Nasica's death, and I liked him for it.

"Nasica was a good man," I said. "And I have spent the last few months hating him, first for what he did to my sister and then for what I thought was his treachery."

"Most good men make for bad liars," Anicetus told me. "But not Nasica." He exhaled heavily. "I never doubted his loyalty to Rome. I never doubted that they killed him for it. You may tell your sister, if you wish, that of all those men who have since been made to fall on their swords, it was Nasica's name they heard the last. I owed her that as well."

I felt a chill and discovered that it was not unpleasant.

Anicetus regarded the statue of Augustus thoughtfully. "But the emperor wanted proof, and one does not disagree with an emperor. I think next time, he will be less circumspect. Next time, he will allow us to act quickly."

At the time, I noticed nothing sinister in his words. That only came much later, years later, with hindsight. At the time, I found the words reassuring, as I believe Anicetus intended them.

We left the gallery.

Uncovering proof of a legionary conspiracy was a real career boost. Convincing one of the main conspirators to name all the others, including the emperor's mother, before falling on his sword was the real accomplishment, and Atreus and I had managed it where even Anicetus had failed. Atreus had the satisfaction of knowing he'd done his job well, while Severus and I reaped the real reward. I was popular again, on the up and up, and determined to make the most of it. Fame was a fleeting thing, and I would not let it go to waste. I allowed myself to be courted by important men. I went to the theatre every night for a fortnight. I accepted sought-after dinner invitations. I even hosted a dinner party myself and had great pleasure in only inviting the people that I wanted there.

It was the biggest dinner party I had ever organised. We had chicken salad and stuffed gourds with lentils for the first course. This was followed by pork with wine cakes, baked mackerel, and honeyed mushrooms for the second course. We finished with patina of pears and sweet cheesecake for dessert. It was all good wholesome food, and nothing like Marcellus Albanus's ostentatious menu; this was real class, and all of my really classy guests approved.

Severus and his family were in attendance. So were the eminent Marcellus

Naso and his adopted heir Florian. Mad Uncle Maro was there, along with mad Aunt Marcia. Fulvia's ex Silanus had grudgingly accepted an invitation; he hated me, but he was too politically clever to show it now that I was a friend of the emperor. I had invited him just to annoy him, and it was a successful operation from start to finish.

There was a fair crowd of other patricians invited that night, mainly men I didn't know well but mad Uncle Maro had promised were worth knowing. These included several senators, the governor of an imperial province, a poet called Lucan, and an ex-general who had single-handedly put down a rebellion in Narbo Martius. The ex-general brought along several jars of rosemary honey for which Narbo Martius was famous. It was delicious.

I had filled up the extra spaces in the formal triclinium with a collection of prosperous freedmen and plebeians of note. Sadly, my sworn lifelong brother Caraca from Lugdunensis and his hairy tribesmen were off enjoying the seaside. Like proper Romans, however, they had replied to my invitation in ample time. I suspect the note was written by the same translator I had previously dealt with: *Caraca sorry regretting. Not come dinner friend. Salute.* In lieu of the friendly Gauls, I had invited my accountant Philosthones, the vigile Atreus, and the man that I had introduced to everyone as a family friend:

"This is Larius Decius," I had told them. "His family has a long association with mine."

Octavia had granted Larius his manumission the moment Anicetus had told her it was safe to do so. Larius, I had learned since, had known Nasica since their childhood in Arretium. Not one of my esteemed guests recognised him as the slave who had served them on previous occasions.

There were dancers, musicians, tumblers, and one particularly talented girl who could sing while performing acrobatics. She never lost a note, not even during the back flips. The adults reclined and watched the entertainment, and the children played hide and seek throughout the house.

I caught Atreus watching me more than once and couldn't read his expression.

"Are you happy, Quintus?" Fulvia asked me in a low voice during the dessert course, taking my hand in hers. She'd asked me that before, not too long ago.

"Yes," I told her, and she mirrored my smile.

Maro plonked himself down beside us and filled me in on his latest home renovations. He was having the usual problems of co-ordinating surly contractors. The plasterer had come two days late and started to cover up the wall that had only just been repainted by the painter, who was running ahead of schedule. So now Maro had to pay the painter twice and to top it all off, the plasterer refused to come back and finish the job because Maro had yelled at him. And next month, he had the plumbers in for the modest bath he was adding to the back garden.

"In the garden?" I asked, incredulous.

"Yes," said Maro. "Like a sort of woodland spring. We're decorating the wall with nymphs."

"Oh, so there will be walls, at least?"

"Of course!" Maro exclaimed and looked at me like I was the crazy one. "Have you heard about the cryptoporticus that Nero is building?"

I could see where this was going. "Maro, you don't have room for a woodland spring *and* an underground vault."

Maro's eyebrows knit together like a pair of amorous caterpillars. "But once the house is done, I'm thinking of starting on the villa."

"The house will never be done, Maro," I told him, and Maro only laughed and called for more wine.

Octavia was a vision in green, and she knew it, and she had amused herself for most of the night by politely rebuffing the attentions of important men. She caused a stir when she rose from her seat and went and sat beside Larius. Half my guests got their noses out of joint at that. They'd been waving their pedigrees at her all night, and she went and talked to a nobody. If they'd known the truth, they'd all have had conniptions.

Silanus opined at me snootily: "A woman should guard her modesty as her only fortune."

I was going to lie and say they were childhood friends, but Julia saved me.

"Oh, shut up, Papa," she told him sternly. "Don't be so pompous!" Then she flashed me a pretty smile, and Silanus *but-but-butted* to himself and wondered where he'd gone wrong as a father.

Naso and Florian were the perfect guests. It was cruel to think it, but Naso's personal tragedy had made a better man of him. His old pretentiousness was gone, and I think a lot of that was to do with Florian. Florian was dutiful and respectful, and Naso reciprocated with grateful kindness. It was not the same relationship he had known with his previous heir, but it was a more tender one. Time might even prove it a better one.

Florian and Julia renewed their acquaintance politely. There was no adolescent gushing. Like so many people in the room, the string of murders connected with the Third Gallica had changed them. They were perhaps a little more grown up and a little more tempered by experience. I caught Fulvia's glance as she watched them. It was a little bit indulgent and a little bit calculating. Things might work out for them after all.

The night went well. The talented poet Lucan granted us an impromptu recital. The Falernian seemed extra fine that night, and the night itself was sweet. For the first time in a long time, I felt content. The dinner party was a success. I was a success, even if nobody knew why. I was back on the first rung of that most slippery of ladders, the cursus honorum. I had been here before, when my military service had been curtailed by my unexpected heroism on the frontiers. It hadn't translated back here in Rome, and I'd fallen into the void between tribune and quaestor. Not this time, though. This time, I would remember to milk it. Because Nero had rewarded me, after all, in a backhanded way that only the very shrewd had noticed. He had also rewarded every other young patrician in the city. Nero had dropped the age of nomination to quaestor from thirty to twenty-five.

Two years, I told myself, and my newly fostered ambition whispered back: *And now you have friends in high places.*

I looked around the triclinium with a satisfied eye, and mad Uncle Maro winked at me. He knew exactly what I was thinking, the canny old dog. I was content, and for once, it had nothing to do with the fact I was tipsy. That was just a very happy coincidence.

* * *

I thought we were finished, so when Atreus drew Florian outside into the atrium and gestured at me to join him, I followed, intrigued. Atreus waited until I was there and suddenly fished into the pouch at his belt. He withdrew the strange little Christian talisman I'd forgotten about and let it dangle from its leather thong. It turned slowly, catching the light from the torches set around the place.

"I think, sir," Atreus said solemnly, "that this is yours."

Avitus Florian's gaze flicked from the amulet to Atreus's face and back again. He left it too late for a denial.

"Take it," said Atreus. "I don't care for it."

Florian held out his palm almost unwillingly.

Atreus dropped the amulet into his hand. "You would have saved me some trouble, Avitus Florian, had you been truthful from the start."

Florian looked at him anxiously. "Will you...?"

The question hung there for a moment, and then Atreus nodded in the direction of the triclinium. "Go back inside, sir, and don't trouble yourself. It's not my business which gods you worship."

His look said the rest: *Not this time.*

Florian looked pathetically grateful. "Thank you," he managed, looking between us anxiously, and slipped back inside.

"Of course," I said. "He was holding it."

"Yes, sir," Atreus said. "You were not the first man at that party to stumble across Albanus's body. Florian was probably passed out in the room next door when it happened and went that way when he woke up. It wasn't just an attitude of grief you found him in, sir; it was also an attitude of prayer. And, of all the men on our list, he was the only one who actually cared for Albanus."

I shook my head at him. "You'll tell me you've found Colchus the informer next!"

"I'm afraid not, sir," said Atreus. "Apparently we can't win them all."

"I think we've done alright, all things considered," I told him. "That's all the loose ends tied up, isn't it?"

Atreus held my gaze steadily. "Almost."

"Almost? What—"

He closed the distance between us in the space of a heartbeat, crowding me up against the wall. He gripped my hip with one hand and slid the other into my curls. He tilted my head back a little, a silent question on his face.

"Yes," I said and surged forward to meet his kiss.

Falling into this embrace, this kiss, was like slipping under warm water, and I wanted nothing more than to drown. His mouth tasted like Falernian. It tasted like victory—we had faced death together, and we had triumphed— but most of all, it tasted like a promise. I already knew I could trust Atreus with my life, but this was a promise I could trust him with my most secret heart as well.

I broke the kiss. "Upstairs." And then my brain finally caught up. "Shit, no. Sons of Dis, Atreus!"

He raised his eyebrows.

"First of all," I told him, clapping him on the back slightly harder than was necessary, "I have to get back in there and prevent my wife and her ex-husband from getting my stepdaughter engaged to a Christian without telling anybody why! You couldn't have brought this up before now?"

Atreus, the plebeian bastard, almost smiled. "Sir, it only occurred to me just now."

I narrowed my eyes at him. "If we're going to work together, Atreus, you need to do better than that. Understood?"

"Yes, sir," said Atreus, his mouth twitching.

"And if you're going to fuck me, you need to stop calling me 'sir.'"

And then he did smile. "Yes, s—yes, Valerius."

We went back inside to join the party.

A Note from the Author

A note on Roman names:

Roman names, generally speaking, can be divided into three categories—the praenomen (personal name), the nomen (family name), and the cognomen (additional personal name).

To keep it straightforward for modern readers, you'll get an idea of someone's relationship with Quintus Aemilus Valerius by how they address him. His close family calls him Quintus. His acquaintances call him Valerius. Anyone being respectful calls him Aemilius Valerius.

And, just to confuse things, there are a few occasions where he's called Quintus Aemilius. That's very much a formal thing.

There are so many excellent books on Ancient Roman history out there. The things I get right are thanks to all the historians out there who are so passionate and knowledgeable about their subject. Any mistakes you find, on the other hand, are entirely on me.

Acknowledgements

To Jill Smith, Elin Gregory and Sarah Drew, all of whom were kind enough to provide their invaluable feedback on earlier drafts of *Sub Rosa*. I couldn't have done it without their help. And thank you to BMR Williams for drawing the map of Rome.

About the Author

Jennifer lives in tropical North Queensland, Australia, with three cats, two dogs, and more geckos than she wants. She spends half her time as a government minion, and half her time writing. She studied History and English at university, though she likes playing with them more than she ever did studying them. Jennifer also writes mm romance under the pen name Lisa Henry.

SOCIAL MEDIA HANDLES:
  twitter: @jenburkebooks

AUTHOR WEBSITE:
  jenniferburkebooks.com

Also by Jennifer Burke

Writing as Lisa Henry:
  Not Until Noah (Star Crossed #1)
  Because of Ben (Star Crossed #2)
  Only for Ollie (Star Crossed #3)
  The Parable of the Mustard Seed
  Anhaga
  Two Man Station (Emergency Services #1)
  Lights and Sirens (Emergency Services #2)
  The California Dashwoods
  Adulting 101
  Sweetwater
  He Is Worthy
  The Island
  Tribute
  One Perfect Night
  Fallout, with M. Caspian
  Dark Space (Dark Space #1)
  Darker Space (Dark Space #2)
  Starlight (Dark Space #3)

With J.A. Rock
  Fran Cuthbert Ruins Christmas
  When All the World Sleeps
  Another Man's Treasure
  Fall on Your Knees
  The Preacher's Son
  Mark Cooper versus America (Prescott College #1)
  Brandon Mills versus the V-Card (Prescott College #2)
  The Good Boy (The Boy #1)
  The Boy Who Belonged (The Boy #2)

The Playing the Fool Series
  The Two Gentlemen of Altona
  The Merchant of Death
  Tempest

The Lords of Bucknall Club Series
  A Husband for Hartwell
  A Case for Christmas
  A Rival for Rivingdon
  A Sanctuary for Soulden
  An Affair for Aumont
  A Scandal for Stratford

With Tia Fielding
  Family Recipe
  Recipe for Two
  A Desperate Man

With Sarah Honey
  Red Heir (Adventures in Aguillon #1)
  Elf Defence (Adventures in Aguillon #2)
  Socially Orcward (Adventures in Aguillon #3)
  Cool Story, Bro
  Awfully Ambrose (Bad Boyfriends, Inc. Book 1)
  Horribly Harry (Bad Boyfriends, Inc, Book 2)
  Terribly Tristan (Bad Boyfriends, Inc, Book 2)

www.ingramcontent.com/pod-product-compliance
Lightning Source LLC
Chambersburg PA
CBHW030232120726
47903CB00005B/1455